Kate Lord Brown was a finalist in ITV's The People's Author contest and her novel *The Perfume Garden* was shortlisted for the Romantic Novel of the Year. Her books have been top ten bestsellers in the UK, Canada and several European countries. After many years living overseas, she has returned to the wild and beautiful south-west of England where she grew up.

Connect with Kate @katelordbrown

Also by Kate Lord Brown

The Beauty Chorus
The Perfume Garden
The House of Dreams
The Golden Hour

KATE LORD BROWN

The Silver Thread

SIMON & SCHUSTER

London · New York · Amsterdam/Antwerp · Sydney/Melbourne · Toronto · New Delhi

First published in Great Britain by Simon & Schuster UK Ltd, 2026

1 3 5 7 9 10 8 6 4 2

Simon & Schuster UK Ltd, 7th Floor,
199 Bishopsgate, London, EC2M 3TY

Simon & Schuster Australia, Sydney
Simon & Schuster India, New Delhi

www.simonandschuster.co.uk
www.simonandschuster.com.au
www.simonandschuster.co.in

The authorised representative in the EEA is Simon & Schuster Netherlands BV, Herculesplein 96, 3584 AA Utrecht, Netherlands. info@simonandschuster.nl

A CIP catalogue record for this book is available from the British Library

Hardback ISBN: 978-1-3985-3483-4
Paperback ISBN: 978-1-3985-3486-5
eBook ISBN:978-1-3985-3485-8
Audio ISBN: 978-1-3985-5386-6

Typeset in Bembo by M Rules
Printed and Bound in the UK using 100% Renewable Electricity at CPI Group (UK) Ltd

For LH

If you are scorched earth, I will be warm rain

— MURASAKI SHIKIBU
(c978–c1014)

PART ONE

LONDON

Lot 1

LONDON, 15 MAY 1875

My life begins today. Isobel Bright darted among the dark figures on Regent Street like a hummingbird, the emerald silk trim of her coat flashing. Men in top hats stood tall as reeds around her. Bel recognised the faces of three society ladies who had once flocked to her elegant white house to have their portraits painted by her father. She saw them whisper and turn away as she passed, their wide skirts swinging like church bells. *I can't bear their pity.* Bel winced, the bone of her patched nankeen corset poking through her chemise into her tender side. *Tonight, I'll remove these damn bones and busk and stitch a new one from the set unmade.*

She stopped in front of Farmer & Rogers' Oriental Warehouse. This was where her father had bought her Kashmir shawl for her birthday only last year. Everywhere in the city there were memories of him. Whenever there was a fresh delivery of fans or silks from Japan, the artists and designers gathered to see the staff unpack the treasures, and fight for the best pieces. Bel lingered at the window, the morning sun catching the fire in her gold hair. Suffused with light, her reflection ghosted the street where horses and carriages clipped along. *I don't belong here, not anymore,* she thought, losing her nerve. *I can't pay for a meal, let alone beautiful things—*

A flash of shame coursed hot through her. She had spotted two old friends walking in Kensington Gardens the day before, and had hurried to catch up with them. As she drew near, she overheard: *Did you see Isobel Bright at church?*

The poor girl! That shabby old coat . . .

Imagine, to lose her father and learn of his debts . . .

Bright was charming, of course. So, well, bright. Lit up any room he walked into.

So did Bel, once. Like quicksilver, that girl.

What she's endured, an orphan now.

I heard . . . no. I mustn't. I'm sure it's gossip . . .

Bel walked on, her cheeks burning at the memory. She had mended and trimmed her coat through the night with silk salvaged from a torn scarf, the needle piercing the fabric again and again, even stitches pulling tight, her silver thimble tapping as she finished it. She thought longingly of her beautiful clothes. *All gone. Probably hanging on a stall in Petticoat Lane by now.*

The invitation to the party for Mr Liberty's new shop crinkled in her pocket as she walked. *I shall find employment here today. I must. A new start . . .* Outside East India House at 218a Regent Street, Bel paused beside a flower stall, steeling her nerves. She touched the frill of a black iris with her fingertips. She longed to scoop up an armful, fill the jug in her little room, feast on their beauty for days. Bel looked up at the striped awning buffeting above her in the spring breeze. Liberty's window display was simply a drape of purple silk, but the subtle colour was perfect. Drawn by the chatter of voices and laughter, Bel stepped into the small shop. It was darkly panelled, the only decoration blue and white bowls of heady pot-pourri, vases of peacock feathers and *uchiwa* paper fans pinned to the walls.

'Bel Bright? Haven't you grown,' a young man in a green velvet jacket cried.

'Mr Wilde,' she said. 'It's my eighteenth birthday today.'

'Then we must celebrate,' he said, pressing a glass of champagne into her hand. Bel caught the eye of a young Japanese man holding a tray of glasses.

'Thank you . . .'

'Hiro. I am Hiro Kurosaki.' He was taller that her, and broad-shouldered with a strong jaw, and tanned skin. His shoulder-length black hair brushed the white collar of the undershirt beneath his indigo kimono as he lowered his head. Bel noticed the fineness of the kimono at once, an iridescent shimmer to the subtle pattern. Hiro looked down at her, clear-eyed. Bel felt a sense of recognition, drawn to his stillness.

'Thank you, Mr Kurosaki.'

He bowed, and turned away.

'Where have you been hiding, my dear?' Oscar Wilde said, taking her arm.

'I've been staying in a darling little place with friends in Kensington.' *A box room in our old coachman's mews.* Bel thought of the bare boards and ice on the windows through the winter. That morning Mrs Harris had given her a rag rug for her birthday, the only flash of colour in the room. In spite of everything, Bel was grateful for the Harrises' kindness, the comforting sound of the horses below, the robin singing in the night. *They saved me.* She could see her old house from the window of her attic room. Only a street but a lifetime away.

'Rotten shame about your papa—'

'Leave the poor girl alone,' a woman in a crimson dress said, pulling him away. 'Never trust a writer,' she said to Bel. 'The cogs are already turning for some elegant little line about grief.' She was already looking past Bel to see who else was arriving. They swept on into the party, and Bel hesitated at the edge of the crowd.

'Miss Bright? Is that you, my dear?' Arthur Lasenby Liberty, a stocky man in his early thirties with fine moustaches held out his arms to her, and strode over, taking her hand. His heavy gold watch chain gleamed against his grey velvet jacket and waistcoat, an ochre silk tie knotted fashionably at his throat.

'Mr Liberty,' Bel said. 'Congratulations. Everything looks marvellous.'

'Doesn't it!' he said. 'We live in the finest city in the greatest country in the world. Our beloved Queen Victoria rules an empire without compare. These are the best of times! So we will bring London the best of the best. Silks from

Japan, Persia, India. I can show you Nagpur silk, Honan silk, Tussore, Shantung and Pongee!' He flung his arms wide. 'Or, for you, the finest Persian silk, ten guineas for six yards.' Bel laughed as he swept a length of emerald fabric around her shoulders. The staff and customers chattered around them like birdsong. 'I have fans, screens, carpets such as London has never seen on order through our agents. What is it I always say? Beauty draws more than oxen,' he said, his enthusiasm and energy infectious. 'I have a vision. 'Tis but half a shop, but we have great plans. You'll see. Within eighteen months we'll take over the whole building – no, the whole block!' He took her arm and led her to a young woman dressed in an elegant purple gown. 'Goodness, we have missed you, haven't we, Miss Blackmore?' he said to his fiancée.

'You disappeared into thin air, my dear,' she said, embracing Bel. Emma's dark hair was drawn back from her kind face, a cluster of ringlets dancing as she moved. 'I was worried about you,' she said quietly. 'I am so sorry for all you've suffered.'

'I'm quite well, Miss Blackmore,' she said. At her kindness, Bel's eyes smarted, and she blinked quickly. 'Really, I am. Please, don't pity me for what I lost. I still have the parks to walk in, and the spring flowers to enjoy, and books from the library—'

'You are a brave girl. But it's shameful how your father's creditors treated you, simply shameful,' Emma said, lowering her voice. 'I saw all your mother's lovely silver turned up in the Burlington Arcade.' *Not all of it*, Bel thought, picturing the silver mirror Mrs Harris had managed to save from the bailiffs. 'Come, sit with me,' she said, taking her arm.

'Congratulations on your engagement.'

'Thank you, we're awfully happy. But where have you been, my dear?'

'I've been staying with friends.' *Embroidering the past*, Bel thought. *What a funny phrase.* But that is what she was going to do: wind a thread between her sunlit childhood and her future. Not a dropped stitch in sight.

'What will you do now?' Emma said. Arthur Liberty called, beckoning across the room to her. 'Excuse me, Miss Bright. Promise you will stay and have lunch with me? We are not losing you again.' Emma backed away, smiling.

'I promise.'

'Do make yourself at home – place your coat and hat in the office,' she called. 'It's Mr Liberty's first day open, and he only has two people working for him – Miss Browning and Mr Kurosaki, though William Judd has said he'll work for free: *"I'll follow your fortunes, pay or no pay."* Such loyalty! We're rushed off our feet!'

Bel hung her coat in the cramped office at the back of the store, and tidied her hair in the mirror.

'Excuse me?' Hiro pushed open the door, balancing a tray of empty glasses.

'Not at all. May I help?'

'You are very kind—'

'Isobel Bright.'

'Thank you, Miss Bright.' His steady attention held her, drew her in. Bel touched the soft hair at the nape of her neck, and impulsively reached for a bottle of champagne.

'I've never done this before—' She cried out as the cork ricocheted across the room, hitting the copper lamp. Hiro swiftly caught the foam with an empty glass, laughing, and filled the rest of the coupes. He twisted open another bottle, easing the cork with a gentle pop. 'So that's how you do it?' Bel smiled. 'Papa had a sabre, too.' She mimed striking the neck of the bottle. 'He loved parties.' She glanced up as the office door swung open, and the noise and laughter from the store lifted. 'He would have loved all this,' she said quietly.

'Thank you,' a young girl said, taking the tray. 'Miss Bright?'

'Hello, Miss Browning. How lovely to see you again. Are you enjoying working with Mr Liberty?'

'Ever so. When he said he was leaving the Oriental Warehouse to set up on his own, I was the first to go with him. He'd been the manager there for twelve years and it's their loss he's gone his own way. Then Mr Kurosaki joined us, didn't you.' The young man smiled. 'He's from Japan, he is. Customers love him. He looks the part, and blow me if he doesn't 'ave an eye for fabrics.'

'My family has made silk for four hundred years, in Kyoto.' He picked up a square of silver paper from his desk, folding it as he spoke.

'How fascinating,' Bel said.

'The kimono is a simple garment in construction, but

the finest are works of art.' He glanced at her. 'The fabric is important, not the garment.'

'How do you get such lovely effects?' Bel gestured at his kimono.

'The stencils for dyeing are marked with needles, pale colours applied first . . .'

'Keep an eye out, will you? I'm nipping out for a gasper,' Miss Browning interrupted.

'Do tell me more,' Bel said to Hiro.

'Something made by hand has energy.' He ran his thumbnail along the fold of paper. 'We put our feelings into our work.'

'I love that idea.'

'Silk is alive – it has a light in it. The workrooms have this wonderful smell I loved as a child.' He looked up, smiling. 'The best kimono have many hands at work, as many as forty people.'

'Heavens! I imagine Japan to be so beautiful.'

'Kyoto was the capital, centuries ago. There, everything old and modern lives together in harmony.' Hiro nodded, making the final crease.

'All that tradition, how marvellous.'

'We must remember what we have forgotten. Every generation learns anew.' He gazed at Bel, and she felt the heat rise in her cheeks. He handed an origami crane to her, their fingers touching briefly.

'A bird!' she said, turning it in her palm. 'It's delightful.' She offered it back to him.

'No, keep it.' Hiro smiled down at her.

'Thank you.' Bel tucked it into her pocket and followed him back into the store.

'Excuse me?' A woman in a wide blue hat tapped Bel's arm. 'Do you have this silk in a darker shade of mulberry?'

'Oh, I don't . . .' Bel hesitated. *I don't work here*, she started to say. She looked over at the display of silk, spotting the exact shade immediately. *But I'd like to.* 'Do come this way,' she said, taking the swatch of fabric from the woman. 'Is it for dressmaking, or for your home, madam . . . ?'

~

'There you are, Miss Bright,' Arthur said. 'I thought we'd lost you again.'

'Should have seen her, Mr Liberty,' William Judd said. 'Talked the client up from a drawing room to the whole house.' He tapped the order book. 'She's a natural.'

'I didn't want to disappoint her,' Bel said, laughing. 'She assumed I worked here.'

'Bravo,' Arthur said, rubbing his hands.

'Perhaps I should,' Bel said, boldly.

'My dear, you're not a shopgirl?' Arthur took her arm. 'You're a young lady—'

'So I know what women want.'

'But surely—'

'Hear me out, Mr Liberty.' Bel summoned up her courage. 'I understand these women's hopes. I wish to give them the clothes and home to support them. I wish to conjure their dreams.' When she looked at Arthur, her eyes shone. She blinked quickly. 'Yes, I have known all that, and taken it for granted. I was raised as a lady. I had a beautiful home, a wonderful life—'

'Miss Bright—' he said kindly.

'Now I have to work. And I am *good* at this.'

'But you will be serving women who were your equal. Will that not be difficult?'

'The pity?' Bel said, her chest tight. 'I have that anyway. I see it every time I meet an acquaintance.' She raised her chin. 'I see no shame in working for a living. Those who knew me as the privileged child of a society painter may come just for the sport.' Bel looked him in the eye. 'You say you want to set trends? You want to give beauty to the masses? Let me help you.' When he didn't answer, she went on. 'Please may I join you?' Her gaze fell. 'You see, I desperately need to make my own way in the world.'

'Miss Bright,' he said quietly. 'I am terribly sorry.'

'Please stop,' she said, her eyes pricking. 'Your kindness breaks my heart.'

'I would hire you in an instant—' He waved an imaginary wand. 'But I can't afford any more staff. You can see how small the shop is. I only opened with Miss Browning and Mr Kurosaki, and Judd said he'd work for free until we get on our feet—'

'Then so shall I. Pay me commission on the orders I take until you can afford to pay me a salary.'

Arthur held her gaze steadily. 'Do you mean that?'

'Yes. Yes, I do.'

'Very well, then.' Arthur shook her hand. 'You would be an asset to the store, with your artistic training. Welcome to Liberty, Miss Bright.'

Lot 2

LONDON, MAY 1875

Bel stood on tiptoe at the top of the ladder, fastening lengths of silver and apricot silk to the line in the shop window. 'When I walked home last night, the moonlight through the magnolia blossom was lovely. The pinks really shone against the deep-blue sky. I thought it was the streetlamp at first.' She tilted her head. 'The effect was just like this. You are clever. It was a marvellous idea to overlap these sheer fabrics,' she said to Hiro. He stepped back to admire the branch of cherry leaves they had fashioned, and adjusted one of the pink lanterns.

'It is like kimono,' he said. 'The harmony of sheer silk on silk makes the effect more beautiful.' He reached up and moved the branch a fraction. 'A bright lining is subdued by the other.'

'I do like the way the light shines through the leaves.'

'We call it *komorebi* in Japan.' He glanced up at her. 'When you walk in a forest and the light dances in the leaves?' A memory came to Bel, of running along a forest track as a child, happy and breathless, the voices and steps of her father and their friends nearby. 'Is it acceptable to you?' Hiro said, seeing her expression sadden.

'Yes, it's lovely,' Bel said, climbing down. 'If I raise the blinds, would you check how everything looks from the street?' She tugged on the cords and clear spring light flooded the window. Looking up, she saw a tall young man in a blue velvet jacket gazing at her through the sheer gold fabric. Bel wove through the fine silks, adjusting them, and he kept pace with her. He wore his glossy dark hair fashionably long, and his clear blue eyes sparkled with amusement. Bel stopped, stepped back a couple of paces and he turned to follow her, smiling. She glanced up as one of the pink blossoms fluttered to the ground from the highest branch, and she knelt to pick it up. When she stood, he had gone.

Bel touched the glass, staring out at the anonymous crowds of dark-suited men and women for a moment. Seeing Hiro, she gestured, her arms wide, and he nodded, pointing at the top lantern.

'Raise it up?' Bel nodded before disappearing back into the shop to climb up again.

'Liberty!' A tall, bearded man in a top hat pushed his way through the crush of customers with his cane, followed by the younger, dark-haired man. 'Congratulations, old chap. Roaring success.' He swept off his hat and shook his hand, kissing Emma's in turn.

'Thank you, Mr Schiffer.' Arthur turned to his fiancée.

'Miss Blackmore, may I introduce the Hon Orlando Schiffer, the artist, and Tom Ferris, an up-and-coming architect.'

Bel cried out, overcome with dizziness suddenly. Without Hiro to steady the ladder, it rocked perilously, and the men leapt forward to catch her.

'Are you alright, miss?' Orlando caught her round the waist. He held her firmly. *Too firmly.* Bel saw his eyes narrow. *He knows me*, she panicked. *He must not tell them . . .*

'Thank you, sir,' Bel said. 'I'm quite well.'

'Schiffer, put the poor girl down,' Tom said, steadying her. 'I apologise for my friend. He has shocking manners when he's in his cups.'

'Spoilsport,' Orlando said.

'Miss Bright, have you had lunch?' Arthur said. *I haven't had breakfast, let alone lunch*, she thought. 'You've been working for hours. No wonder you're dizzy, my dear. Run along and have some sweet tea.'

'Falling from the trees like ripe fruit?' Orlando said quietly. Bel felt his gaze travel over her like an unwanted caress. 'Bruised like a peach . . .' The fierceness of her look stopped him dead.

'It is a little early in the day for Baudelaire, sir,' she said.

'And she knows her poetry, damn it?' *Pompous ass*, she thought. 'You seem familiar.' *Please, don't.* Bel's heart paced fast with fear. 'Tell me your name, girl.'

'Isobel Bright,' she said. 'Thank you for your assistance, sir.' Something about his finely trimmed whiskers reminded her of a black cat the cook kept for mousing, the way it would rumble and hum with purring if you rubbed its notched ears, but then lash out in an instant, snagging tooth and claw. She knew his reputation – artist, man about town, bon vivant. *Isn't that always a euphemism for debauchery and dissipation.*

'Perhaps you'd be kind enough to show us the new stock, Miss Bright—' Tom's blue eyes held her gaze steadily, still with that amused smile on his lips. *The bluest eyes. Cloudless summer skies eyes. Light in a sapphire eyes.* A warmth spread through her.

'Bright?' Orlando interrupted. 'Not Alexander Bright's girl?'

'The same,' Emma said, taking her arm. Bel was grateful for the support.

'A wonderful painter,' Tom said. 'I am sorry for your loss.'

'Miss Bright is working with us,' Arthur said.

''Tis a shame you have not inherited your mother's money. Nor her prettiness,' Orlando said. Bel felt sick with embarrassment. *He thinks me plain?*

'How may we help you, gentlemen?' Arthur said smoothly.

'I've just bought a new studio, in Chelsea,' Orlando said. 'Ferris is designing it for me, aren't you?'

'We were at school together,' Tom said confidingly to Bel.

'Ferris was a scholarship boy.' Orlando smirked. 'And my fag.'

'Schiffer Minor—'

'That's enough of that,' Orlando said.

'—has been kind enough to give me my first job,' Tom said, ignoring the slight. 'Perhaps you can help us with the fabrics, for the interiors, Miss Bright?'

'You're in capable hands, Mr Ferris,' Arthur said, gesturing to the rows of silk festooning the store. As he talked to Orlando, Tom and Bel walked ahead.

'Pay no heed.' Tom smiled kindly. 'Schiffer likes to keep people unsteady.'

'I care little for his opinion.' Bel's eyes flashed.

'He's toying with you, Miss Bright. Any man alive can see you are quite lovely.' Bel looked up in surprise.

'I say, Miss Bright.' Orlando swaggered over. 'We're off to Mr Scott's oyster bar. Join us for a dozen natives and *une coupe de champagne*? Or two?'

'Thank you, Mr Schiffer,' she said, remembering how marvellous it would be – the golden light reflected in the mirrors, the palms, the Prince of Wales at his usual table, perhaps. Her stomach tightened with hunger, and she thought of the lonely room above the mews house waiting for her. The corset that still needed boning. The silver chainmail purse with only a couple of coppers left inside. *I can always pawn the purse itself.* She sensed Schiffer watching her closely. *He smells weakness.* She thought of the Harrises' hen coop, raided by a fox the last weekend, the flutter of white feathers in the wind.

'You really are awfully familiar . . .'

Her hunger turned to anger. *Does he think me fallen? Some doxy he can have his way with?*

'I have plans tonight, sir.'

'Another time, perhaps?' Tom said.

Lot 3

LONDON, MAY 1875

A few days later, as Liberty's closed for the night, Bel set off on the long walk home to Kensington. She had been on her feet all day, and the cardboard she had pasted in the bottom of her boots was giving way, every pebble, every piece of gravel a stab of pain. Kensington was half built, still, the roads churned to mud in places, scaffolding and the smoke from brick kilns marking the skyline. She went out of her way to avoid the workhouses. *As if we'd let you end up in there*, Mrs Harris had said. Bel's stomach tightened with anxiety at the thought of how close she had come. She glanced in at the golden-lighted windows of a restaurant as she passed, the scent of sage and thyme, of roasting onions winding enticingly around her. A group sat in the window, a woman in her twenties laughing, raising a glass of amber tonic wine.

'Miss Bright?' A man's voice from the road. She turned, searching along the row of carriages. 'Miss Bright? It's Mr

Ferris.' Tom waved from the hansom, and jumped down. 'Where are you heading?'

'Sussex Place,' she said from habit.

'Why, I am meeting a client near there! Allow me to drive you,' he said, ushering her to the carriage. Bel hesitated. *Better than walking, or the stench of the omnibus, but . . .*

'I swear you will be quite safe.' He smiled. 'Are you not more afraid, walking alone? They say forty per cent of women walking the street are . . . well, working.'

'Then sixty per cent of us are perfectly respectable.' Her aching feet overcame her reluctance, and she settled in beside him.

'Stop at Sussex Place,' Tom called to the driver.

'You are not with Mr Schiffer, this evening?' Bel dabbed her nose with her handkerchief.

'Later, at his studio,' Tom said, his eyes creasing. 'He can be a dreadful ass at times, but he has impeccable taste, and I must work, Miss Bright,' he said, resting his hand on the leather portfolio at his side. 'I began as an improver in the hurly-burly of Sir Ernest George's practice. Now I am making a name for myself.' *Ambitious, then.* He leant closer. 'Can you keep a secret?' Bel nodded. 'I am colour-blind. I see structures in my mind, but I have no facility for finishes or adornment.' His deep-blue gaze held hers. 'Would you be my eyes?'

Too soon, the cab clopped to a halt, and Bel tore herself away from their conversation, her heart beating high and fast.

'Thank you,' she said, jumping down. 'Do you live in Kensington, Mr Ferris?'

'No, I have a set in Albany. Perhaps we could take tea at Fortnum's one day?'

'I'd like that very much.'

'Which house is yours?' Tom said.

'Over there,' Bel said, nodding. 'Please, do not trouble yourself. My . . . my aunt is waiting for me. Thank you, Mr Ferris.'

'I bid you goodnight, Miss Bright.' She raised her hand in farewell and walked slowly away, listening to the retreating carriage. She glanced over her shoulder to make sure Tom was going in the opposite direction, and strode quickly on towards Cornwall Mews.

Bel skipped around an oily puddle, slipping on the grimy cobbles. The mews was a shambles with the sweet scent of hay and dung, and horses being groomed. A woman sitting on a doorstep nearby cleaned ten pairs of boots in decreasing sizes. Carriages clattered along the cobbles, readying themselves to take the residents of Cornwall Gardens out for the night. Bel closed the front door behind her and sighed, relieved at the thought of her narrow bed.

'Is that you, miss?' Mrs Harris called from the kitchen. She cranked the handle of a mangle, steam rising from the laundry on the range.

'Only me—' At a knock on the door, Bel turned.

'Miss Bright?' Tom stood on the doorstep, her handkerchief in his hand.

'Mr Ferris?' Her hand went to her throat.

'You dropped this, so I came after you . . .' He held up his hand. 'I promise, I wasn't prying.' He passed her the handkerchief. 'There is no aunt, is there?' he said gently.

'No aunt, no parents, just me,' she said, her voice catching.

'This is where you live?' He stooped, looking in to the low, dark hall.

'It's not so bad. I adore horses—'

'Miss Bright . . .'

'Don't,' she said, raising her chin proudly. 'I can't bear the pity in your eyes.'

'Please, won't you come for supper? Tell me your story?' Tom's gaze softened. 'Perhaps I can help?'

'This is my lot, and I am going to make the best of it,' she said, balling the soft lawn cotton in her fist. 'Once, we were equals. I led a charmed life—'

'Equals?' Tom looked down at the flagstones for a moment. 'Miss Bright, you must know how I admire you.' He raised his gaze and its intensity astonished her. 'You *are* my equal. My superior in many ways, I'm sure.'

'Indeed, I can see colours, sir.'

Tom laughed. His smile was conspiratorial, not pitying, she decided.

'Whatever misfortune has befallen you is temporary. You will prosper, I am sure.' Tom tipped his hat. 'Please, consider me a friend. Allow me to help you, however I can.'

Lot 4

PARIS, 24 JULY 1985

> People ask me 'who was Isobel Bright?' Why does she matter, after all this time? So little remains now of her work. She matters. She <u>was</u> the New Woman. Our life was a conversation that ended too soon. Our work is a conversation that goes on. My fabrics supported her art. My love, I hope, supported her life. When we were young we were always rushing, rushing towards the end. The first time I saw Bel she was eighteen years old. She emerged from the dark figures on Regent Street, small and quick and bright as a flame. I loved her from that moment. Time and life race away from us all. Every man and woman on that street is gone now, including Bel, and I am old. We will all be gone, one day. What matters is love. Love survives . . .

Mira checked the address she had scribbled down on the photocopy of Hiro Kurosaki's interview, and knocked on the unlatched door, calling out: 'Hello?' The longcase clock in the apartment on Avenue Junot chimed nine. She pushed back the headphones of her Walkman, and Madonna's voice faded. 'Hello? Is this Isobel Bright's apartment?' She clicked off the cassette and reached to knock again on the tall, blue-grey door on the first floor, but it swung open at her touch.

'... what on earth are they doing sending some wet-behind-the-ears art history graduate in here ...' A man's voice, English, drifted through to the hall. In the background, the sound of something heavy being dragged across the room cut him off. 'I'm perfectly capable of cataloguing this job myself.' *The right place, then.* A door slammed. 'I really don't need some so-called consultant slowing us down ...' A tall man with collar-length dark hair strode through to the dining room, clipboard in hand, so intent on his work he didn't notice her standing in the doorway. He loosened his sky-blue silk tie. 'It's boiling in here. Can you wedge that door open, Serge?'

'Sure. Big items out first, Monsieur Brookes?' a man with a French accent said.

'Yes, but empty each piece first. Mark this down for Tokyo.' He pointed at an elegant black sideboard.

'Japanese?' Serge said.

'Influenced by. It's a Godwin, 1867–1888. They made around ten of them. This one is similar to the one he gave his mistress, Ellen Terry.' He was followed by a muscular man in a white t-shirt and tight back brace, who grinned seeing Mira. A wolfish, easy smile. *Serge, I assume?* Something about his stance, the corseted back support, made her think of a bullfighter in his suit of lights.

Seeing a simple gilded frame spotlit in the entrance hall, Mira walked in the opposite direction. *Picasso*? she thought, leaning in to check the signature. It was an ink sketch, the paper yellowed with age, a fair young woman looking down at a dark-haired child, her face unseen. *Isobel.* The drawing was intimate, filled with love. *I can't believe I'm here, in your home.* Mira caught her reflection in a bevelled mirror nearby, rainbow edges refracting in the sun. A trace of glitter still shimmered in her hairline from the night before, and she licked her index finger, wiping it away.

'Art Nouveau, Liberty.' The man's voice drifted through to her as he handed a pewter clock to Serge.

'It is so French?' he said, shrugging. 'Like the Paris Métro.'

'I see what you mean, like the Guimard entrances. It has a Maison Liberty label, and that closed down in 1932, I think? My assistant will check the date. Mark it down for Tokyo.' He looked up, walking through, and noticed Mira at last. 'Hey – you can't just walk in—'

'Excuse me, you're blocking my view of the Picasso,' she said.

'That's rather rude.' He stepped to one side.

'You started it.' Mira glanced at him. 'What have you got against art history?'

'Ah, you must be—'

'The so-called consultant?' She studied the drawing. 'It's charming.'

'Is that your professional opinion?'

'You're quite charming, too, aren't you?'

'I try.'

'I think you'll find that's a Godwin as well.' She pointed at an ebonised chair.

'Why is it architects never design for comfort?' He stuck a blue label on it. The mirrored hall reflected several elegant Miras with her dark hair slicked back into a chignon. Her Chanel red smile was confident rather than friendly. 'Miranda Hutchinson. Mira.'

'How do you do? Edward Brookes,' he said, shaking her outstretched hand.

'What do your friends call you?'

'Ned.' She noticed he didn't apologise. *Never complain, never explain.* Wasn't that Kim's motto, too?

'Do we know one another, Edward?' she said.

'No. I would have remembered you.'

'Hmm. You're terribly familiar.'

'There's a lot of us about. I'm with Bonhams. This is Serge, from the local art movers.'

'*Enchanté, mademoiselle,*' he said, then noticed the simple gold band on the ring finger of her hand as she folded her arms. '*Madame, pardon.*'

'Is Mr Hutchinson travelling with you?' Ned said.

'I've been let out for good behaviour,' Mira said.

'I wasn't fishing. I was just curious.'

'Yes, well you know what they say about that.'

'I'm the cat in this scenario?'

'Let's start again, shall we?' She didn't wait for Ned to answer, and opened the high double doors to the salon, where she turned, slowly, allowing her gut instinct to kick in about the room.

'Surprising, isn't it?' Ned said, following her. Even in the half-light, she could see that the apartment was strikingly modern. White silk drapes hung around the shuttered windows, and a pale carpet covered the light oak boards. Low white couches sat either side of the marble fireplace, above which a circular silver mirror with a coronet hung.

'They said this hasn't been touched since the twenties?' Mira unclipped her red leather folio and pulled out the papers.

'1923, apparently,' Ned said. 'The client is selling up, including the contents.' He put one hand in his pocket and leant against the doorframe. *Confident*, Mira thought. *Knows he's attractive.* She couldn't help smiling as Serge strutted chest-first like a rooster through the apartment to the kitchen with a stack of carboard boxes, winking at her. *So does he.*

'What do we know so far?'

'Not a lot.' Ned gestured at a bunch of keys on the table. 'The lawyer has just gone. He was holding the keys for our client—'

'The Kurosakis?'

'Yes. Isobel Bright's heir, Genji Kurosaki, has just died.' Ned said. 'Why *are* you here?'

'I didn't get the grades to be a brain surgeon?'

'Oh, really,' Ned said, walking away.

'You give up rather easily,' Mira said, tilting her head.

'I have work to do. And I'm more than capable of doing it without distractions.'

'My godmother, Kim, worked with the Kurosakis' textile firm. She's a designer.'

'Nepotism, then?' Ned sighed dramatically. 'Usual story—'

'She had no idea Isobel's apartment existed until the family contacted her for advice. She suggested I might be useful. I wrote my thesis on Maison Bright. Very little is known about Isobel's designs, but she was revolutionary. She should be as big as Chanel. If you are concerned about my credentials—'

'Not at all. A First from the Courtauld, a Masters from Parsons, and you've worked with some of the top designers—'

'You've done your homework.'

'I took some persuading.'

'And?'

'I want all this assessed and packed quickly and efficiently. We have one week in Paris before everything closes down for the summer—'

'Shall I tell you a secret?'

'I *love* secrets.'

'I shouldn't be here.' Mira's index finger tapped a warning. 'I'm midway through a project in London, but Kim thought I might be able to help, so I'm doing her a favour.' Mira looked around the room, thinking. 'No one knows what happened to Isobel Bright. One minute she was producing some of the most exciting fashion and interiors in Paris, and then she just disappeared. Hopefully we'll find out why.' Mira frowned.

'Have you noticed something?' She unhooked the shutters and flung them back, daylight spilling into the room from the French windows. Standing at the balcony looking out across the tree-lined Avenue Junot below, she stared down at a young couple walking along the leafy street, lost in one another. *I wish Luke was here.*

'I have noticed it is time for a break.' Serge smiled, looking from Ned to Mira, sizing up the tension. 'The café on the corner? We can discuss everything like civilised adults.'

'Look.' Mira turned back to Ned, and ran her finger across the top of a marble table. 'No dust.' She waved her hand in the air. 'This apartment hasn't been sealed up since 1923.' She sniffed dramatically. 'Smell it. It's aired.'

'You're right.' Ned looked around with renewed interest. 'Someone's been keeping an eye on it.'

'What else?'

'All the mirrors?' The alcoves either side of the fireplace had been hung with floor-to-ceiling mirrors just like the hall.

'It doesn't make sense. It's so empty, and airy. If Isobel died, or went away in 1923, she lived through the *Belle Époque*. People's taste tends to form early on. Their houses become time capsules of their glory years. Few people keep pace with fashion.' She stood in the centre of the room, turning three hundred and sixty degrees. 'Isobel Bright was cutting edge.'

'You mean this place should be awash with stuffed ostriches and gilt canvases?'

'Exactly.' Mira leant on the fireplace. 'Where's the history? The taxidermy? The heavy velvet drapes?' She frowned. 'If someone had removed any paintings later on, you'd expect to see picture hooks, and ghosting on the walls.' The wall opposite her was panelled in immaculate white silk. *They're screens*, she realised, noticing the fine oak track at the top and bottom. An electric jolt of adrenaline coursed through her, just as it always did when she made a find. She strode over, and ran her fingers down the seam of the panels. The mechanism was stiff, but she felt it give a little.

'Now what are you doing? We can't just pull the apartment to pieces—'

'Can you help?'

Ned threw down his clipboard. She caught a breath of his heady Givenchy cologne as the screens pulled slowly apart. 'What on earth made you notice this?'

'The mirrors either side of the fireplace are raked, to reflect something on this wall.' The sliding screens juddered and stopped. Mira caught a glimpse of iridescent blue in the darkness beyond. She remembered seeing a damselfly as a child – that unearthly blue green. It had been so long since she had really *seen* colour, like that. Colour that made her feel alive. 'There's something here,' she said, her voice catching with excitement. They pulled in opposite directions. Here was the scent of dust, of sealed air she had expected from the whole apartment.

'I don't believe it,' Ned said, stepping back. A black lacquer frame stood almost to the ceiling. Hanging from it, a blue silk kimono with a pattern of waterlilies draped to the floor. 'It's exquisite. Falling water's a common enough subject, but I've never seen one this good.' Mira took a pair of white cotton gloves from her case, and touched the luxurious fabric, the still-bright colours of the silk. 'I'll be damned,' Ned said, turning. The kimono was reflected perfectly in the mirrors either side of the fireplace. 'You are good.'

'It's the waterlily kimono!' Mira grabbed the photocopy of an old letter from her file to show Ned. 'When I did my research I came across an interview with Hiro Kurosaki in the Liberty archive talking about how he met Isobel. He mentioned the kimono.' She gazed up at the gown, the silver threads sparkling in the light like sunshine on water. 'Why is it hidden away here? It's an important piece.'

'You're not kidding.'

'No, look, the sleeves,' she said, lifting them. There are *kosode, hirosode*, but this is *furisode* – a very wide, very long sleeve.'

'I thought you were European not Asian design?'

'I happened to read a book, at my godmother's place last night.'

'Did you now?'

'Couldn't sleep, and it was on the nightstand. Kim's a textile designer.' Mira unfurled the wide obi belt across the carpet. 'This is over four metres long. It's a formal *ontono* obi, a palace sash.'

'The kind of thing an Emperor's consort would wear?' Ned rubbed his chin, thinking. 'I'd say mid-Edo, eighteenth century?'

'Now I'm interested,' she said. 'What happened to Isobel, and why was that hidden there?'

Lot 5

PARIS, 24 JULY 1985

'So, Edward, are you based in Paris?' Mira said as they walked back from the café-zinc along Avenue Junot. Dappled sunlight cloaked the pavement, the white trumpets of tobacco plants nodding in the breeze.

'Tokyo,' he said.

'Is that the link, with the kimono? The pared-down feel of the apartment?'

'*Shibui*,' Ned said. 'Elegant simplicity.' He frowned, scanning his notes. 'I'd rather hoped for more. Bonhams sent me and my assistant over from Tokyo because we were told this was going to be an important sale. On first glance we have an early Picasso sketch in the hall, a nice Georgian silver mirror. There are some good first editions, and a well-chosen collection of arts and crafts, and Art Nouveau furniture, plus some Japanese pieces. Yes, the kimono is great, but Isobel Bright was a well-known designer. I was expecting a treasure trove, stuffed to the gills.'

'Where are the clothes?'

'And the homeware she designed? The kitchen looks like it's never been used.' He brushed a fleck of croissant from his tie. 'God, what I wouldn't give for a decent bacon sandwich . . .'

'There's so much ephemera in life,' Mira said. 'With clients it's always the same. Their life is in all the nonsense – the tickets marking pages in books, the letters and photographs. It's like their homes miss them, when they're gone. This one seems to have been picked clean.' Mira thought of her own mews house in London, the boxes of photos she kept meaning to put into albums, the duplicate paperbacks and records on the shelves when she and Luke merged their collections. There was so much she had meant to sort out when they moved in together, but their home had become a cosy, messy blend of their lives before they met. *Still, who wants to live in a show home*? she thought. *Isobel did.*

'Our instructions are that house clearance items go to Drouot. Anything of importance ships to Tokyo for inspection before the auction,' Ned said. 'It's really not going to take long.'

'Items from a Private Collection?' Mira said. 'Is that how you'll stage the sale?'

'Something like that. My area is twentieth-century decorative art and furniture. It will go into a mixed sale.'

'You'd get a better result if there's a story behind the collection.' Mira pulled a grainy photocopy of an art catalogue from her folder, and Ned whistled. 'This nude by Orlando Schiffer was rumoured to be of Isobel Bright.'

'You *have* done your homework,' Ned said, folding his arms.

'It disappeared after that show. Perhaps it's in the apartment somewhere—'

'Look, Mira, please don't tell me my job, and I won't tell you yours. Whatever that is.' Ned said under his breath.

'Hold on.' Mira placed her hand on Ned's arm. 'I understand that you don't like "so-called consultants".'

'It was unfortunate you overheard that.'

'I am good at my job. I have curated several collections worth millions of pounds.' She held his gaze. 'The Kurosakis have employed me to make the most of this estate sale, and that is what I'm going to do. From what I understand, with the death in the family, the younger generation aren't interested in keeping the apartment going. It's our job to get the best price for the contents. If you prefer, you do your work and I'll do mine, Ned.'

'Ned, now, is it?' She saw him relent.

'I'd prefer it if we work together.'

'Deal,' he said, shaking her outstretched hand. 'You've already proved yourself. We might have missed the kimono, if it wasn't for you.' Mira slipped on a pair of Ray-Bans. 'Late night?' he said, seeing her wince.

'I caught up with a few friends.' She glanced down Villa Léandre as they walked on. The English-styled Art Deco houses on the cobblestone lane reminded her of somewhere. 'Do you believe in *déjà vu*?'

'Crikey, I haven't felt that for years.' He glanced at her.

'Are you staying nearby?' Serge stood by the entrance to the apartment building, whistling and waving traffic past a white van that had parked up on the pavement. A team of men unloaded blankets and bubble wrap, carrying them inside.

'Kim is out of town, so I'm staying at her place on the Île Saint-Louis.'

'Wow. I love it over there.'

'It's tiny, but it has the most amazing view.' Mira jotted down the address, and tore out a page from her notebook. 'In case you need to get hold of me. Kim doesn't have a phone, but you can always drop by. Where are you?'

'Hôtel Chopin,' he said. 'Do you know it? Great old place in Passage Jouffroy. It's convenient for Drouot, and the light in those places, it's like you're underwater . . . Well, I like that old Paris feel.'

'I knew the heart of a romantic beats behind that clipboard.'

'Makes a change from Tokyo,' he said.

'The city with no memory?'

'Ha. Tokyo's constantly changing. I took a run through my old neighbourhood the other day, and they've already demolished my first apartment building.'

'How did you end up there?' Mira asked, her heels clipping across the tiled courtyard of the building. Men were loading packing materials into the narrow iron elevator, so they took the stairs.

'SOAS, Oriental department at Sotheby's, fell in love with a girl, usual story.' He looked down at her. 'The job at

Bonhams came up, and I like Japan.' They stood at the door to the apartment. 'After you,' he said.

'Hold on,' Mira said as it swung open. 'Didn't we lock this door?'

'Hello?' Ned strode into the hall. Mira heard the sound of running water in the kitchen.

'They're in there,' she said, and Ned strode ahead. A tiny old woman with soft white hair pulled back in a low bun stood at the sink rinsing out the saucer Serge had used as an ashtray.

'Bonjour,' she said. 'I would prefer it if you don't smoke in the apartment.'

'Who are you, madame?' Ned said in French.

'I am the housekeeper,' she said, gesturing with her chin. 'I live upstairs.'

'Madame,' Mira said, 'is it you who has taken care of the apartment all these years?'

'I was not born when Mademoiselle Bright left,' she snapped. 'My grandmother worked for her at first, and my mother, then when they passed away, I took care of it as I promised them I would. Now, my job is done.' She pointed to her key on the counter. 'I was born in this building. The owner pays me a pittance to keep an eye on the apartment, but it was not about the money. I love this place.'

'Perhaps we should introduce ourselves.' Ned said. 'I'm with Bonhams. We have been appointed by the owner's lawyers to assess and clear the contents.'

'Vultures,' the woman said, clicking her tongue. She

walked through to the salon, her soft leather ballet pumps making no noise on the deep carpet. She glanced at the kimono and gestured for the screens to be closed. 'It should be covered. It is very ancient, very precious. The light is not good for the silk.'

'Madame,' Mira said, 'what else is there?'

'You'll see,' she said. A black cat waiting on the first step in the hall followed her upstairs, its tail an exclamation mark against the marble steps.

Lot 6

LONDON, 1875

'Anyone in, miss?' a delivery driver asked Bel, jumping down from his coach in Kingly Street. He rubbed his hands. ''Ave a word with your boss. Howell and James have the right idea – free beer and cheese under the shop for the coachmen.'

'I'll see what I can do,' Bel said. The door opened and she swept inside. Liberty had flourished and thirteen people joined the original staff, each hand-picked by Arthur Liberty. *It's more like a family than work*, she realised as she walked through the bustling offices. She bid good morning to Mr Liberty, who sat at the cash desk with two female clerks going through the ledger.

'Morning, Miss Bright,' he said, glancing up. She could see he was in one of his stormy moods, so she walked on. 'Next time a client insists on settling his bill in gold, tell me,' he said to the clerks.

'Good morning, Mrs Judd,' Bel said as the woman swept past carrying a tea tray. She was armoured with whale bone, her brawny arms red from washing the cups ready for elevenses.

'Mr Judd's out this morning,' Miss Browning called over, checking the order book as Bel took off her coat and hat. 'He's taken some goods on appro up Princes Gate.'

'Shall we start with the new delivery, then?' Bel said, rolling up the sleeves of her white blouse and tying an apron on.

~

'How's your new boarding house?' Miss Browning said later to Bel as they unpacked the last tea chest of blue and white porcelain. 'Do you like your rooms?'

'Room,' Bel said. She pulled the packing straw from a vase, and unwrapped the print protecting it. 'But I am moving up in the world. There's a tweenie who takes care of housekeeping for us all. It's heaven,' she said, noting down a description of the Moon Vase in the stock book. 'Mr Kurosaki helped me move my trunks in.'

'Did he now?' She raised an eyebrow.

'Not like that. He's so kind. We had to sneak in. My landlady is a bit of a battleaxe . . .'

'No gentlemen callers,' Miss Browning said, putting on an accent. 'Lots of girls have an uncle who's not an uncle . . .'

'This is a proper house, for proper young ladies,' Bel said, imitating her refined tone. She sucked at the burn on her index finger.

'I know the sort.' Miss Browning gestured with her chin. 'What've you done now?'

'This? I burned myself on the goffering iron helping Mrs Harris last night.'

'You're still working for her, too?'

'I don't like to leave her short-handed with the laundry, and she said I'm the best she's ever had with the fine ruffles and ribbons.'

'With your nimble fingers, you could work for Worth or Doucet.'

'Haute couture? Don't be silly.'

'Why not? You'll wear yourself out, you will.' Miss Browning shook her head. 'You shouldn't be working all the hours God sends.'

'I'm making my way, don't you know?' Bel shot her a quick smile. She thought of the simple white room and gleaming brass bed waiting for her, and smiled. She had lain on her stomach late last night, leafing through her copy of *The Ladies' Oracle* by Cornelius Agrippa. *Shall I soon be courted?* she asked, turning the pages to find the answer: *One thinks about it and only needs a word of encouragement* . . . She wrote her journal by lamplight each night: *'Tom, Tom, TOM . . .'* There were pages describing their every meeting. *'Our conversation went something like this: Good day, Miss Bright. Good day, Mr Ferris . . .'* His dress, his hair, his countenance were dissected in minute detail. *'He is the kindest, most charming of men . . .'* She drew a lavish heart with 'TF & IB' enshrined in lace. *'We have so much in common. I could talk to him for hours about art and design – I learn so much!'* There was an entire page filled with her practice signature: *Isobel Ferris. Mrs I Ferris. Mr and Mrs Thomas Ferris . . .*

'Bel?'

'Sorry.' She came back to the present, and turned over a cloisonné vase. 'Mark this down for five guineas a pair.' She glanced up at a cry of pleasure from a group of men inspecting the new delivery of ceramics. She recognised a couple of the painters with Orlando Schiffer among them.

'There is *so much* one can learn from a teapot,' one of them declared.

'Those Pre-Raphaelites would turn up to the opening of an envelope,' Bel said.

'It was the same at the Oriental Warehouse. Soon as they heard there was a delivery from Japan, they'd be round. I always think they look like a flock of rooks picking over the bits, flapping around.' She gestured at Schiffer. 'He's a right one. Tried to get me to go to some séance with that Home fellow. I don't hold with all that spirit-rapping nonsense.'

'Me neither.' *Japan*, Bel thought, unwrapping a ginger jar. *How I'd love to see it.* 'All the artists are mad for anything exotic, have been since the International Exhibition.' Bel smoothed out the Japanese print. Hiro glanced over her shoulder on the way past to the office. 'I can't believe they use these for packing china.'

'Fuji-san,' he said, pointing at the mountain.

'They're so beautiful, they should be framed.' She tilted her head. 'Perhaps we could use some in the scheme for Mr Schiffer.'

'It would be like giving coins to a cat.' Hiro glanced at Bel. 'He does not have the subtle eye you do. This is Nagasaki,' he said, picking up a print of a geisha walking through a snowstorm. 'A floating world of pleasure.'

'Floating?' Bel said.

'*Ukiyo-e*. Only make-believe.'

'I think it's lovely.' Bel tucked it under the counter.

'It is not real Japan,' he said firmly, walking away to the offices.

'People need make-believe places . . .' She paused hearing Orlando exclaim: '*Hello* . . .'

A Japanese woman in a lavender kimono and wooden sandals entered the store. Her black hair shone, swept up in a gleaming roll, secured with gold pins that caught the spring sunlight from the street. She stood in the doorway, framed by the light, and gazed calmly around the store, looking for someone.

'Stay *right* there.' Orlando leapt up. He framed the doorway with his hands, and pulled a small sketchbook from his pocket, quickly measuring up her figure with his pencil. '*Kirei desune*,' he said. 'Very pretty.'

'*Dozo yoroshkiu. Sumimasen*. Excuse me,' the woman said. Her voice was low and softly accented.

'Don't move,' Orlando said, sketching furiously.

'May I help you, miss?' Bel said, sweeping past him.

'I am looking for my brother,' the woman said. 'Hiro-san.'

'Of course,' Bel said, gesturing to the office. *She has the same stillness to her*, she thought. *The same strength*. Bel studied her face. *But a melancholy, too*. She liked her on instinct. 'I'm Isobel Bright.'

'Ah, Miss Bright. I am Chō Kurosaki,' she said, bowing. 'My brother talks of you.'

'Does he?' she said as they walked through the store.

'He says you have excellent taste.'

'Thank you,' Bel said, pushing open the door. *Taste?* she thought, surprised to find she was disappointed. *Is that all he said of me?*

'Chō-san?' Hiro rose from his desk. 'Is that the time already?'

'Miss Kurosaki? We've been so busy all day, the time has flown,' Arthur said, pushing back his chair. 'How are you enjoying working at the new Japanese Village? I said to Emma we must visit you in Ally Pally.'

'Thank you, sir.' Chō bowed. 'It is . . .' Bel saw the woman frown. *You're too good for that place.* 'It is agreeable, sir.'

'Splendid.' He slammed shut the large ledger in front of him. 'Are those blasted artists still out there cooing over the fans? Show them out, would you, Miss Bright? Get young Mr Carty to help you if you need reinforcements.'

Bel strode back into the store, and clapped her hands. 'Gentlemen, the shop is closing now,' she said. 'Do return on Monday if you wish to purchase any of the items—'

'That girl.' Orlando sauntered over. 'Who is she?'

'Mr Kurosaki's sister.' Bel ushered him to the door.

'Giver her my card, would you?' Orlando slipped a silver case from the pocket of his purple velvet jacket. 'I should like to paint her.'

'I do not think she is an artist's model, sir.'

'Any gel would be lucky to be painted by Orlando Schiffer. And I pay a fair rate – seven shillings an afternoon.' He stared pointedly at her. 'A fair rate, isn't it?'

A man who refers to himself in the third, Bel thought, her smile holding, just.

'They're queuing up for portraits, isn't that right, Rossetti?' he said as the artists walked out. 'They say Millais has three hundred guineas a painting. Now, if you were to sit for me, Miss Bright, I should double that . . .'

'I don't think so. Good day, Mr Schiffer.' Bel closed the door behind the last of them, and turned the sign to 'closed', her heart pounding. *He knows what I did.* She remembered the cold air on her skin, the stares of the men. *He's just toying with me.* Bel bit her lip. *What if he tells Tom?*

'Blimey, my feet,' Mr Carty said as they pulled down the blinds.

'I could hardly walk home last night,' she said. *Home*, she thought, still thrilled at the novelty of it.

'You'll get used to it, miss, we all do,' Mr Carty said. 'Soak 'em in a bit of Epsom salts, and then rest with 'em up against the wall for a while.'

'Miss Bright,' Hiro said, his sister at his side. 'We would like to invite you to take tea with us tomorrow.' Chō smiled and bowed, offering her a card with both hands. 'My sister has not met many English ladies and she would like to get to know you better.' He paused, and something in the warmth of his expression quickened her. 'As would I.'

Lot 7

LONDON, 1875

'Welcome, Miss Bright,' Hiro said, bowing as he opened the door. 'Please come in.' He was dressed in a plain blue kimono, and white tabi socks with woven slippers.

'Mr Kurosaki.' She felt unmoored, seeing him out of context. Hiro looked younger, less formal. At the door, he gestured for Bel to remove her boots, and take a pair of slippers. She took his offered hand for support, and felt his lean strength.

'Did you have a good journey?'

'Yes, I haven't been out here since the old Ally Pally burned down,' she said, wriggling her feet into the slippers. 'Thank you.'

'It is an amusing place, full of visitors.' Hiro led her through to the back of the house. 'Judd sold two cases of Japanese sunshades during the exhibition over the bank holiday, a shilling a piece, he said.'

'What brought you here?'

'The Japanese Village,' Hiro said, turning to her. 'When we decided to seek our fortunes in London, people from our village near Kyoto had already settled here, working in the grounds of the Palace.'

'How interesting.' Bel offered him a waxed paper parcel tied with silver string. 'I brought you an almond cake.'

'You are too kind,' he said, bowing.

'Thank me later. I am not much of a cook.'

'Chō-san is very happy you are able to join us for tea,' he said, leading the way to the garden flat at the back of the house. '*Sadō*, the way of tea, is very important in our culture. It has the spirit of *wabi sabi*.'

'What's that?'

'It is a belief that beauty is imperfect, impermanent.' Hiro looked down at her, his dark eyes gleaming in the half-light. 'It celebrates simplicity and nature.'

'Gosh, all that from a cup of tea?' Bel smiled up at him. 'I always think it's the slight imperfections that make someone beautiful too.'

'The gap in the teeth?' Hiro gestured to her lips. Bel was aware suddenly of their closeness, the warm sandalwood incense scent of him. She could hear the sound of a family in the apartment above, the cry of a small baby, someone pacing across the wooden floor. She thought of the nightingale floors she had read about, in a castle in Kyoto, designed to squeak and chirrup with the lightest ninja's tread. This house seemed to pulse with life.

'Do come in,' he said.

Once the door to Hiro's rooms closed, she found herself in a tranquil white space, with a woven tatami rug on the bare boards, and a low wooden table fashioned from what looked like a cut-down kitchen table. The doors at the back of the flat opened out onto a small gravelled yard, with plants in low terracotta pots.

'How lovely,' she said, walking outside. 'So peaceful.'

'Thank you.'

'Have you lived here a long time?'

'My sister and I came over from Japan a couple of years ago,' Hiro said, stooping to remove a fallen leaf. In a corner of the yard, windchimes blew softly in the breeze. 'For two hundred years, Japan was cut off from the West – we say *sakoku*. Then, a few years ago, the "bamboo curtain" fell.' He swept his arms dramatically, and Bel laughed.

'You make it sound like a fairy tale. Sleeping Beauty.'

'Precisely. A floating world of dreams, like the prints you enjoy. People say in Japan we live for the pleasures of the moon, the snow, the cherry blossom. We drink, we sing . . .'

'You're teasing me,' Bel said, smiling. 'Do you miss it?'

'Always,' he said. 'But we have made a good home in London for now. There is a spirit we have – *gambatte*. You must go out and embrace life, seek good fortune.' Hiro folded his hands into the sleeves of his kimono. 'I was lucky to meet Mr Liberty at the Oriental Warehouse.'

'Luck has nothing to do with it. Mr Liberty told me he had never seen such fine fabric designs. No wonder he took you on rather than let you go to Swan & Edgar.' She nodded. 'We make our own luck, you and I.'

'Yes, we do.' Hiro held her gaze steadily.

'Since the exhibitions in Paris and London, it seems everyone loves Japanese designs. The painters cannot see enough of Hokusai and Utamaro.' Looking at him, warmth bloomed low in her stomach as she thought of an intimate print of lovers she had seen.

'You are here!' Chō said. She was wearing a violet silk kimono with iridescent chrysanthemums woven into the design, and a crimson robe beneath. Her hair hung loose, shining blue black in the dim light. She bowed before Bel. 'I am so pleased to meet you properly, Miss Bright.'

'Please, do call me Bel.' She glanced at Hiro. 'Both of you.' Bel gestured at her dress. 'Your kimono is beautiful.' Chō twirled slowly, bowing.

'It is my *furisode* kimono, for coming-of-age day.' She held out her arms. 'Please, may I take your coat and hat?' Bel wore her newly acquired, if not entirely new, white blouse and a high-waisted pale skirt, with her old blue coat.

Chō ran her hand over the silk repairs. 'It is beautiful. We say *boro*.'

'Patchwork,' Hiro explained.

'*Mottainai* is good. Make use of old.'

'Your English is excellent,' Bel said. 'I do hope you will teach me some Japanese.'

'It would be my honour,' Chō said.

'Many Japanese are learning English,' Hiro said, 'now

that the country is open to Westerners, but we do not like to speak it, still.'

'You like my trees?' Chō said, seeing Bel studying the garden. 'They are bonsai. We make them stay small.' She led Bel outside. 'My favourite. Gingko,' she said. 'Sacred tree. Very ancient. I like him very much.'

'So they are like family?' Bel said.

'Yes, yes – precisely!' Chō said, laughing.

Hiro showed Bel to the honoured seat beside the family *tokonoma* altar, a simple alcove of gold leaf by the table. In an elegant slender white vase, Chō had placed a branch beside a photograph of a young woman with two children, and a lacquer plate of incense. 'Thank you,' Bel said, relaxing on the low *zabuton* cushion, her skirt settling around her like the petals of a tea rose. 'Is this you?' she said to Hiro.

'Yes,' he said, looking at the photograph with a sad smile. 'That is our mother, the last photograph we have of her.'

'She died?' Bel glanced at Chō. 'I'm so sorry.'

'Chinese call Japan Queen Country. Our women are clever, and independent. Some of our best artists and writers are women – Lady Murasaki, Sei Shōnagon.'

'When they wrote their books, Europe was still in the Dark Ages,' Hiro said.

'Our mother was an artist, too.' Chō nodded. 'Our father was from Tokyo. He was a bad man.' Bel glanced at Hiro, who lowered his gaze. 'She ran away with us to Kamakura, to Tokeiji temple. Only place women have safety, can seek divorce. Our uncle in Kyoto take us in. She was a good mother. But we have only each other now.'

'Then you are lucky.' Bel smiled wistfully. 'I wish I had family. My mother died when I was born, and now my father . . .'

'We will be family for you,' Chō said, nodding.

'I will take care of my sister, until she marries,' Hiro said.

'Long wait,' Chō said, laughing softly. 'I am too old!' She carried over a steaming iron pot of water, and placed it on a straw mat on the table. 'Different from English tea, yes?' She showed Bel a bamboo casket of green powder.

'I must admit I was expecting Earl Grey,' Bel said. 'I'm not sure my cake goes well.'

'It is perfect,' Hiro said, unwrapping it, carefully coiling the silver thread around his fingers. Chō noticed the blush in his cheeks, and she looked slowly from him to Bel. She leant towards her, her eyes sparkling with mischief.

'You know string theory, Bel?' She shook her head. 'In Asia we say a red thread ties people together forever.'

'I always imagined it more as a silver thread,' Hiro said. 'Memories strung like jewels along it, tying us to the people and places we love.'

'Ah,' Chō said. 'It is auspicious you have given my brother this.' Bel caught Hiro's gaze, her stomach fluttering like a butterfly's wings.

'Tea – *cha-no-yu*, is an important part of life in Japan,' he said, gruffly.

'Chance to reflect. Enjoy simple pleasure.' Chō arranged the tray.

'As I said, we believe in *wabi sabi*,' Hiro added. 'The beauty in imperfection – like this broken cup.' He passed it to Bel and she saw it had been mended with a seam of gold. 'This is *kintsugi*. When something is broken it can be beautiful. So many people now want new things,' he said. 'But there is beauty in age and simplicity.'

'My life is very simple now,' Bel said quietly. 'Not through choice – I had little to do with it.' She looked down at her hands. 'My father was an artist, too, and a wonderful man, but not good with money. When he died, everything was lost.' She smiled bravely. 'All I have is my mother's mirror and some old clothes.'

'In Japan we believe the mirror is the symbol of a woman's soul,' Hiro said kindly. 'So your mother is with you.' He picked up a square of origami paper from the dresser.

'Thank you. That's comforting. I feel lucky to have had such happiness, truly I do. I know it's possible, now. What I lack in money I'll make up for in ingenuity and hard work.'

'There is an assumption that everything gets better,' he said, folding the square as he spoke. 'All we know, we grow accustomed to. We assume that life will always be this way – that we will grow happier, healthier, wealthier.' He ran his thumbnail along the seam of paper. 'But it is not always so.'

'Hiro-san always say life not like this.' Chō drew a straight line in the air. 'He say it is circle, like snail shell. We come back again and again to same thing – love, hate – until we learn lesson.'

Maybe that's true, Bel thought, looking at him. She loved the stillness of him. Hiro's tanned fingers worked the paper smoothly. *He has an artist's hands.*

'There are worse things than travelling lightly in the world,' Hiro said, glancing up. 'From loss you can regrow stronger. Japan is a country always rebuilding after natural disasters – typhoons, tsunamis, earthquakes. That is why we love the *sakura*, the cherry blossom. Life is tender, beautiful, fleeting.'

He's right, Bel thought. *All we have are moments of happiness.*

'Death always shocks,' Chō said.

'Like an earthquake?' Bel said, thinking. 'I hadn't thought about it like that.' *The aftershocks. The way grief catches you out, unseats you again and again.*

'*Ame futte ji katamaru,*' Chō said. 'After rain, earth hard. Adversity bring strength.'

'Everything passes. Grief. Happiness. Everything has its season.' Hiro creased a final fold in the paper. 'All you can do is sit with it, allow the emotions to shake through you.' Hiro handed Bel an origami crane, and placed his hands on his knees. He tilted his head, watching her delight.

'Now I have two. They can keep one another company.' Bel smiled. 'Thank you.'

'When it feels like the world is whirling around you, remember that the soul is a steady lamp burning in you.' He nodded. 'When I have experienced great sorrow, it has comforted me to return to that thought in meditation.'

'Do you believe in soulmates?' Bel said suddenly.

'Two souls, meant to find one another?'

'See! Thread of life,' Chō said, clapping her hands.

'I think,' Hiro said carefully, 'sometimes it is easy to confuse a mirror with a soulmate.'

'You are too young to be so wise,' Bel said. She felt the tension in her relaxing in the warmth of their company.

'Our uncle says Hiro-san should be a holy man, not kimono maker,' Chō said, laughing.

'But I have a responsibility to the family.' Bel saw an emotion pass over his face. *Regret?*

'My brother like *bushido.* Courage, respect, honour, loyalty.' Her eyes twinkled with mischief as she glanced at Bel. 'He's a good man . . .'

'Chō-san—' Hiro said.

She hummed to herself arranging three porcelain bowls, and whisked a green powder into a froth in each, wiping the rim and passing the first and most beautiful to Bel. '*Dozo.*'

'Thank you,' she said. 'How . . . curious.'

'I know, it looks like pea soup,' Hiro said. 'Try it.'

'It is tradition. Three sips, pass cup back to me,' Chō said. 'Make comment on what you like about cup.'

Bel took a tentative sniff of the tea. It smelt sweetly of freshly cut grass. She took three sips. 'It's delicious.'

'We say *oishi desu*,' Chō said. 'I give you more tea?'

'Thank you.' Bel studied the cup. In the distance a church bell chimed the hour.

'Pale clouds on a cup, bells chime on a summer breeze, she

sips her first tea,' Hiro said, studying Bel, a gentle smile on his lips. Chō clapped her hands in appreciation.

'Poetry as well,' Bel said. It was always so busy in the shop that she hadn't really had time to see Hiro clearly before. *How old are you? Twenty-five perhaps? Chō's a little older.* At home and relaxed, she saw how handsome he was, with a strong jaw and dark, kind eyes. *Chō is lucky to have you watching out for her.*

'Tell me about your family,' she said. 'You come from a long line of kimono makers, is that right?'

'Yes!' Chō said. 'Hiro-san will show you our family kimono. Very rare, very beautiful.'

He went through to another room and brought back a black lacquer chest. As he opened it, the evening sun caught the silver gilding inside the lid. Chō knelt before it and carefully lifted out a parcel wrapped in linen. She stood and let a fine blue kimono the colour of sea glass and summer skies fall free. She walked a few paces back, letting the length of silk spread like water, and she extended the arms.

'I've never seen anything so beautiful,' Bel said, her lips parting. Woven into the design, white lotuses and pink water lilies seemed to float in three dimensions on the shimmering surface of the silk, picked out with pure silver thread.

'Family legend has it that our ancestor made this for the Emperor's consort,' Hiro said. 'But his wife loved it so much, he gave it to her instead, and made a second, lesser, kimono. Another woman was so jealous when she saw her wearing it, she told the Empress, and our ancestor was told to commit *seppuku*.'

'Seppuku?' Bel said.

'Ritual suicide.' Hiro mimed the thrust of a sword. 'It is better to die with honour.'

'He died for beauty?' Bel said, and touched the cool, heavy silk.

'He died for love,' Hiro said, holding her gaze.

Lot 8

LONDON, 1875

'Where on earth are they?' Bel stood on the doorstep of Orlando's house in Chelsea, boxes and tea chests arranged around her. She pressed the bell again. At last she heard the sound of footsteps crossing the marble hall, and the heavy black door swung open.

'I'm sorry, miss,' the housekeeper said. 'Mr Schiffer is at Mr Rossetti's studio on Cheyne Walk.'

'He was expecting us at midday,' Bel said, annoyed. 'I shall leave my card.'

'Perhaps you would like to go and have a word? I believe Mr Ferris is with him.'

'Very well.' Bel turned to Hiro. 'Would you mind taking up the boxes? I'll go and fetch them—'

'Do you not think I should come with you?'

'They're artists, not monsters,' Bel said. 'I know how to manage them.'

~

Bel lifted the hem of her skirt out of the dirt of the macadam road, and waited as a carriage clopped by. She ran across, and knocked at the door of the Tudor House at number sixteen. Beyond the narrow road the stinking Thames slapped dark and oily at the bank. Bel gazed across Chelsea Reach as she waited, watching a flock of gulls clattering above the shore. A manservant in a brocade gown showed her up to the studio. She found a half-naked woman with tumbling golden hair curled on an armchair at the heart of the studio, lit by cool north light. Around her, men in dark suits conversed. Rossetti stood at the easel in a paint-smeared white smock, a brush clenched between his teeth like a cigarette holder.

'There's something restful in this pose,' Leighton said, sketching. 'I shall work it up with Dorothy.'

'Did ye hear of that gal, Sadler?' Orlando said, taking a swig of his drink. 'Fell asleep when she was eleven years and didn't wake for nine. A regular sleeping beauty.' He noticed Bel. 'Talking of which . . .'

'Miss Bright?' Tom said, rising from a plum velvet chaise-longue where he sat watching Rossetti at work. 'Is that the time already?'

'Mr Ferris,' she said, firmly. 'We arranged midday.'

'Of course.' He beckoned across the studio. 'Schiffer—'

'Do we shock you, Miss Bright?' Orlando said, gesturing at the model. 'But of course, you—'

'Not in the slightest.' She cut him off. 'Would you wish

me shocked? You forget I grew up among artists. There is no shame in it. No shame at all.'

~

Bel and Hiro worked late into the evening at Schiffer's studio, hanging silks, arranging the new lacquer and bamboo furniture, and grouping brush washers, ginger jars and other ornaments. Tom had installed screens to create a clever series of rooms within the high-ceilinged studio where all the clutter of easels, canvases and paints could be stored, leaving a dramatic podium for figure work, and more intimate spaces for the portraits Orlando Schiffer was so well known for. The walls had been painted a deep charcoal, and the old mahogany fireplace with its foxed and silvered mirror was painted a glossy black to complement the new lacquer tables.

'Something's missing,' Bel said, throwing her sketchbook down. 'I have an idea in mind, and I can't express it properly.'

'Have patience.' Hiro held his hands apart in the air. 'For an artist, when you begin, your vision and your work are far apart. With practice and attention we improve . . .' He drew his hands together, and pointed them forwards. 'Then we make something true and good.'

'But how?'

'We pay attention. A thousand years ago, Sei Shōnagon set down occasional thoughts and impressions—'

'A thousand years?' Bel said in surprise, as she unwrapped a gold Buddha.

'I will translate some of her *Pillow Book* for you the next time you come to see us? Still we love the same things – the spring dawn, fireflies on a summer night, silk the colour of plum blossom.' As Hiro spoke, Bel pictured each in turn.

'I'd like that.'

'All you have to do is pay attention. You do not need to be always striving, always searching. Just be still.' Hiro held her gaze. 'Everything you desire is already here, already exists.'

'I don't understand?' Bel studied the Buddha in her hands. 'It doesn't. Where is my wealth, and security? Where is my beautiful home? My business? My family? Where is someone to care for me?' Hiro watched as she climbed the stepladder, his gaze full of warmth.

'Here.' He looked down at his hands. 'All you have to do is reach out for it all to be yours.' She moved the Buddha a fraction on the top shelf of the fire surround.

'Perfect,' Tom said, leaning in the doorway. 'The loveliest view in all London.'

'You're outrageous,' Bel said, laughing.

'I can't help myself.'

'Try,' Hiro said under his breath.

'I thought this might be the finishing touch?' Bel said.

'It is. I love the way the light catches him in the darkness.'

'Are you pleased?' Bel sat back on the ladder and turned to Tom. Every bone in her body ached with exertion, but she looked around the room, satisfied. 'I do like those new desks from Monsieur Fortier.'

'The French chap?' Tom said. 'I swear the fellow's five foot tall and five foot wide. Can't understand a word he says.'

'We should tidy up,' Bel said, stretching.

'No,' Hiro said. 'Rest. You have worked too hard.'

'You both have,' Tom said, without moving to help. Hiro glared at Tom and gathered up the last of the packing boxes, carrying them downstairs.

'Do say you like it?' Bel said.

'Am I pleased?' Tom walked towards her, and offered her his hand as she climbed down. 'It's marvellous. Bel – may I call you Bel?'

'Of course . . . Tom.'

'Schiffer will be thrilled, I'm sure.'

'Where is he?' She touched her neck, felt the heat rising in her cheeks. *Tom.*

'He had an appointment.' He held her hand, still. 'You really are talented,' he said, looking down at her. Perhaps she was just tired, but the space between them seemed to shift and contract. 'I believe you have a great career ahead of you as a designer, if that is what you wish?' It was as if Tom had read her mind.

'I admire Mr Liberty so much, for bringing art and beauty to the masses.'

'Do you dream of that yourself?'

'One day,' Bel said, smiling.

'You never know.' Tom walked her out. 'Hard work and talent win out in the end.' He helped her into her coat. 'I do like that,' he said, noticing the flash of silk trim. 'Do you think you might make something similar for my sister, for Christmas?'

'Of course.' The night-scented stocks lining the path filled the air with heady perfume.

'You have a facility with sewing.'

'It's like breathing. I've sewn since I was three or four years of age. Always sewing or sketching and dreaming.' Bel looked out to where Hiro waited for her beside the carriage. 'It was an escape, I suppose. My designs . . . It's just a nicer world, in my imagination.' Bel flashed a quick smile. 'Next time you are passing, call in at the shop and we can choose a pattern and silk for the lining—' She jumped, startled, as a cry rent the air.

'Just Rossetti's peacocks,' he reassured her. 'You can hear his garden menagerie all over this part of town. Drives the neighbours quite mad.'

'Heavens.' She looked up at him. 'Good night, Tom.'

'Good night, Bel.' He bowed his head, and watched her walk away. 'I say, Bel,' he called, and she turned. The gas lamps either side of the doorway cast rivers of gold between them on the wet paving stones. 'Hold on to those dreams of yours.'

Lot 9

LONDON, 1875

'Miss Bright,' Orlando said, stepping forward from where he waited for her outside the store, smoking. 'Do say you'll join me for lunch?' He strode after her along the bustling pavement just as the clock above the striped awning struck one. The fabric billowed in the breeze, and flags along Regent Street snapped to attention. 'It's the least I can do to thank you.'

'I'm sorry, sir, I only have a short break, and I have clients arriving soon.'

'You must eat, surely?'

'I have my lunch.' She paused to let a man in a waistcoat and shirt sleeves pushing a handcart pass, and crossed the road, striding briskly down Hanover Street.

'Let me accompany you,' he said firmly. Bel looked up at him, perplexed. *Too confident for his own good*, she thought. *I know his sort—*

'I know you take me for an arrogant ass . . .' Bel turned in surprise. 'I have behaved badly, and I apologise. Forgive me.' He stood with his hands pressed together, beseeching, smiling. Bel walked on. 'Do let me sketch you. I have a feeling you would be the most wonderful model.'

'I don't know what you mean,' Bel said, a chill running through her.

'Just look at you, in your white blouse and skirt, the very essence of summer.' Orlando tipped his hat to an elderly lady in black, corseted and stiff as a lampshade. He strode after Bel. 'You misjudge me,' he said, more gently. 'I was a friend of your father's, you know.'

'I do not recall you visiting the studio?'

'At least, we were acquainted. In fact, I have something of your father's for you.' He tapped his breast pocket.

'You do?' She glanced at him warily.

'Agree to share your lunch with me and I shall show you.'

Bel sat on a bench in Hanover Square, with Orlando lolling at her side, his long legs stretched out. 'Do you eat here every day?' he said. His handmade shoes gleamed like conkers fallen early from the horse chestnut tree. She tore a piece of bread, and tossed it to the pigeons and white doves.

'Sometimes,' she said, rather afraid that the next time she came he would be lying in wait for her. She dusted off her hands and reached into her bag for her apples. Reluctantly, she passed him one.

'Thank you.' He took a bite, watching her. She smelt the apple skin, and bit down, her mouth filling with sweetness.

There was something about him that made her think of crocodiles' eyes, their teeth. *I don't trust you.* But he was a good client for Liberty & Co, and she had to keep him happy. *Within reason*, she thought.

'Miss Bright, Bel Bright . . . what an enigma you are,' he said, tilting his head. 'When first we met, I thought you just another *mousmé*.' Bel scowled. 'I do love that word, just the right combination of moue and imp.' He tossed the core to a stray dog loping along the edge of the square. 'You see, I do remember seeing you.'

'I don't know what you mean.' Bel glared at him, defiant, afraid. That was where she had seen him. The life class, at the Academy. *Only once*, she thought. *I so desperately needed the money.* She thought of the story about how Degas paid his model with meat, and the girl had been so hungry she had eaten it raw, there and then. *I have known that hunger.* Anger flared in her. *I will never know hunger like that again.*

'Oh, your secret is safe with me.' He smiled, the light glinting on his teeth. 'I completely understand, in your straightened circumstances. They pay the women twice the male models' rates, I hear.' His gaze slowly travelled to hers. 'The damage to a woman's reputation is worse, of course.'

'Please, don't tell them.' Bel felt light-headed with fear. 'I am not ashamed. I had no choice. No money.' Her throat tightened with proud tears. 'It was that or the street or the workhouse.' *No shame? How easily I lie.* She remembered the weight of the men's stares. *Thank god for Mr Harris.* He saw her just as one of the men tried to press her into his carriage, afterwards, and pulled her away to safety. She was ready to fight back, but then she saw his kind, familiar face.

'My lips are sealed.'

'What is it you want, Mr Schiffer?' she said, her voice tight.

'You *intrigue* me, Miss Bright.' When she did not answer, he looked at her. 'You know Ferris reckons you have quite the artistic career ahead of you.'

'I'm sure I'm very grateful, sir—'

'Don't play the shopgirl with me,' Orlando said, smoothly. He rested his head against his hand. 'You are a lady, at least on your mother's side, and a society figure thanks to your father's charm and talents.' He waited for her to look at him. 'You can do better than this, with your life. Working in a little shop?'

'It's not just a shop,' she said, her eyes flashing. 'It's more than that. It *is* going to be more than that, you'll see. Liberty is revolutionary. They have great plans. *I* have great plans.'

'Yes, what about you, Miss Bright?' His face softened into sympathy, but Bel saw his eyes remained focused on her intently. *No, not a crocodile.* Bel thought of a wolf she had seen at the zoo once, how hypnotic and cold its gaze was. *A wolf dressed as a man.* 'Do you not wish for marriage? Family?' Surely he wasn't proposing to her? 'Company . . . ?' He traced the back of her hand with one buffed nail. Bel thought as if from a distance that he was the only artist she had met who didn't have paint crusted beneath his fingernails. She looked up at him, and withdrew her hand. *So that's it. Just like all the other lonely men in London. How predictable. How insulting.* 'I can help you, Miss Bright. May I call you Bel? I really should like to paint you.'

'Thank you, but I am not a model, sir.' Bel stood and brushed the crumbs from her skirt. *Never again.*

'We'll see,' he said. 'I rarely take no for an answer.'

'Then you shall have to make an exception, sir.' Bel stepped away. 'Good day, Mr Schiffer. I must get back to work.'

'Oh, Bel!' he said, reaching into his breast pocket. He passed her a piece of paper folded into four. 'This is for you. I mentioned to my father what a marvellous job you had done with the studio, and he said: "Not Alexander Bright's girl?" He wanted you to have this. I think he won it playing cards with your father one night—' *That sounds about right,* Bel thought, unfolding it. The breath caught in her throat. 'It is you, isn't it? I knew in an instant.' Bel stared down at a fine pencil sketch of her profile.

'Yes. Yes it is. We were in Honfleur, with the Monets.' She remembered the glint of light on the water. 'He and my father were old friends. They met at Père Suisse's studio. Papa had all these wonderful stories about painting all day, and cooking beans and lentils with them over a coal stove at night.' Bel smiled. 'When Monet and Camille were war refugees, Papa helped find a place for them in Kensington—'

'Don't talk to me of Monet. I hear the bounder has 15,000 francs a year. Doctors earn only 9,000!'

Bel tuned out Orlando's jealous griping. She thought back,

the overcast London day infused suddenly with the glancing sunlight and sea air of a summer long ago at Widow Toutain's farm. They painted with the light, from 5am to 8pm, and dined on bowls of shrimp and cider. She remembered the high Norman houses near the port, the lush fields. She remembered running along the beach, past women with wide skirts and white parasols, feeling free, and alive, terribly alive, racing into the surf. She remembered it all. *I can't bear it – it's gone*, she thought. *But I shall have that life again. I shall.* She realised Orlando was studying her closely.

'You have the saddest eyes I have ever seen,' he murmured.

'Thank you, Mr Schiffer,' she said, placing the sketch in her pocket. 'It means a great deal to have something of my father's. I am grateful.'

'Grateful enough to have dinner with me tonight?'

'I don't—'

'I'm impressed with your work, y'see. There are several other rooms—'

'Then perhaps you'd care to come in to the shop at your convenience?' she said. 'We can discuss your schemes with Mr Ferris.' He pursed his lips, annoyed.

'You observe the world closely, don't you, Bel Bright?'

'I don't know about that, sir.'

'I see you observing Mr Ferris . . .' he mused, tugging at the fingers of his kid glove. 'Sadly I was born with the countenance of a villain in a Russian novel. Tom, now, Tom is the hero type. More Greek myth than Soviet tragedy.' Orlando watched her steadily. 'You wouldn't be carrying a torch for young Ferris by chance, would you?' He raised his gaze to hers. 'He is the kind of fellow who would have his valet break his shoes in. Too much ambition, that boy—' His lip curled. 'Talent but no fortune.'

'I don't know what you mean, sir,' Bel said. 'I must return to work.'

'Appearances can be deceptive.' He stepped closer. 'I know the rumours about me. That I consort with showgirls? That I fathered Lady Winton's illegitimate son? That I am to be found on a palette in a certain Soho establishment in an opium haze most Sundays?' Bel couldn't look him in the eye. She had heard all this and more. ''Tis true I prefer an interesting vice to a virtuous bore, and your tarnish entices rather than repels me.'

'Tarnish?' she said. 'How dare you, sir!'

'Tell me, Bel,' he said, his voice close to her ear. 'Have you not learnt how false the gossip peddled by Wilde and his lot is?' She felt his breath on her neck. ''Tis not true what the tattle-mongers say of you, artists' model, and more—'

'No, sir!'

'Nor is the gossip true of me.' This new contrition unsettled her. 'I do not trust Wilde. He likes his blue and white china too much, if you catch my meaning.' Orlando stuck his thumbs into his waistcoat and drummed his chest.

'Good day, sir,' she said, walking away.

'I am a patient man, Miss Bright,' he said, and tipped his hat to her.

And a dangerous one, she thought.

Lot 10

PARIS 1985

'Kim?' Mira said, pushing coins into the pay phone in the tabac.

'Mira? Darling!' In the background she could hear the beat of a salsa band. 'Hold on, let me close the door.' The noise of the party faded. 'There, that's better. Are you all settled in? The concierge called to let me know you are there. I warn you, nothing escapes that woman! If you are hoping to have a clandestine affair, a little *cinq a sept*—'

'I don't think so,' Mira said sharply.

'Nobody does that anymore, anyway. The traffic. How was your day? You are alright, aren't you, darling?' She heard her concern.

'I'm fine,' she said. *As always.*

'Have you met the auctioneers? I do hope this will be interesting. I thought of you immediately when the Kurosakis called; I knew you'd be perfect. I always wondered what happened—'

'About that,' Mira said, frowning as the noise of the party

swelled again in the background. She pushed in some more francs, and covered her ear. 'Kim?'

'Got to go, darling! Speak at the weekend.' Her godmother had covered the receiver, talking to someone. 'Love you!'

She hung up? Mira hooked the phone beneath her jaw, and dialled a number from memory. She listened to the answering message: *You've reached Luke Hutchinson. You know what to do after the tone.*

'Hey,' she said, smiling at the sound of his voice. 'Only me. I'm here safely.' She blinked. 'Everyone was talking about you last night.' She rubbed her eyes wearily, recalling the table of friends, the noise of the restaurant, the pounding beat of the club later, strobe lights cloaking her, dancing, lost in the music. 'The job's . . . well, I feel a bit out of my depth. I know, I know your motto – *fake it 'til you make it?*' She laughed softly. 'God, I wish I was as confident as you.' She closed her eyes. 'Wish you were here. Love you. Miss you.'

Mira paused at the carousel of postcards, and spun it round, selecting a Monet painting of his wife, Camille, in a Japanese kimono. She rummaged in her bag for a pen and wrote: *Chaque jour je vous espère, as Monet wrote. I love you, M x* and addressed it to Luke Hutchinson, 37 Kynance Mews, London SW7. She paid at the desk and added a stamp before slipping it in a postbox on the way to Kim's *pied-à-terre.*

~

The character of a home grows from the heart of the owner. Even now the scent of her godmother's favourite orange blossom scent lingered on the warm air of the tiny apartment in the eaves of the building at 36 Quai de Béthune. Mira flicked on the lamps. Kim's number-one rule was to avoid overhead lighting, and she had wired the flat in the American fashion, a single switch illuminating several shaded table lamps. *Lamplight is far more flattering for old houses and old faces, darling.* The whole flat – what there was of it – had been painted a warm yellow. *Like Monet's dining room at Giverny.* It was the opposite of the Avenue Junot apartment, a tiny jewel box of a place. A hearth with a small white stove drew the eye to a cosy turquoise sofa, strewn with one of Kim's famous silk throws. Somehow Kim had managed to cram both a tiny galley kitchen and a functional shower room either side of the entrance hall. *If you want a bath, book into the Lotti – number's on the board in the kitchen.* The bed was hidden behind a screen of lacquered cabinets which doubled as a wardrobe.

Mira shrugged off her jacket, and draped it over the bar stool in the kitchen. *I'm starving.* A bottle of Veuve Clicquot lay in the empty fridge, with a note propped up beside it: *Welcome, be happy, x.* Mira breathed a laugh. *Oh well, I can always go out.* She knew that the real beauty of the flat lay behind lavish floor-length curtains. Kim had trimmed yellow ikat fabric with turquoise velvet bands. *Always spend big on a couple of things*, she remembered her saying. *A decent sofa, and something extravagant – great drapes or a rug.* Somehow making a big statement in a tiny space tricked the eye into feeling the room was larger than it was.

Mira flung back the curtains and smiled. *I didn't buy this apartment for the square footage, honey*, Kim said. Unbolting the doors, she stepped out onto the roof terrace. The whole of Paris lay before her, a view stretching from the Pantheon, the Invalides to the Eiffel Tower. At dusk, a golden sunset lit the domes, the rooftops, the lights along the Seine illuminating. This was why Kim had chosen the place with her first husband, back in the 1960s. On Mira's tenth birthday, she had flung open the drapes to reveal a camp strung with paper lanterns, a magical tent where they spent the night watching cartoons on the little portable TV, eating ice cream from Berthillon.

Now she watched a party boat drift along the Seine, coloured lights shimmering across the black water. The sound of Charles Trenet singing 'Verlaine', laughter, the chink of tableware on china drifted up to her. At the sound of someone calling her name, Mira looked down to the pavement in surprise. 'Ned?'

'Hope it's not too late?' He raised a carrier bag. 'Thought you might be hungry.'

'Come on up,' she said, pressing the buzzer and unlatching the door. She hurriedly checked her reflection in the bathroom mirror, and spritzed *Eau d'Hadrien*. A minute later Ned appeared in the doorway, holding a fragrant bag of takeaway aloft.

'I was starving. Thought I'd take a chance you might be, too? We've been working flat out all day.'

'What a shame! I've just had a three-course meal.'

'Oh . . .' Ned's face fell.

'I'm kidding.' He laughed with relief. 'You are now officially my hero,' she said, searching the cupboards for plates and glasses. She took the champagne from the fridge. *Thank you, Kim.*

'And I wanted to apologise. We didn't set out on the right foot.' He followed her out onto the terrace, ducking through the low doorway. 'I—' Ned paused. 'My god, this view.'

'Amazing, isn't it?' Mira stood beside Ned, gazing out at Paris, the warm breeze lifting tendrils of her hair. 'Shall we?' she said, gesturing to the table.

~

As a clock in the apartment below chimed midnight, Mira settled on the bed and slipped off her simple gold wedding band, placing it safely in the embrace of her watch. She propped a leather travel frame open on the nightstand. A handsome man in his thirties, with ski poles resting against his shoulder, looked back at her, smiling. *You'd like him*, she thought, remembering the evening. Away from work, Ned had relaxed, and they had talked easily for a couple of hours. Mira thought of the meal, the champagne, the storm lantern holding them in a golden pool of light high above Paris. *He didn't try anything on, don't worry.* She flopped back on the soft white pillow, the clean scent of Savon de Marseille embracing her. *He even washed up.* Mira pictured Ned, sleeves rolled up, rinsing the plates in the tiny kitchen. 'Sweet dreams, handsome,' she murmured, and kissed her fingertip, pressing it to her husband's photo before she switched out the lights.

Lot 11

LONDON, 1878

'Your windows have been a great success over the years,' Arthur said to Bel, watching the crowds on the pavement stopping to admire Liberty's display. A green and yellow omnibus advertising Stone's Ginger Wine pulled by two chestnut horses clopped past. 'We mustn't rest on our laurels, though. We want to get people in off the street.' He looked around the shop, studying the customers.

'What if we were to appeal to all their senses,' Bel said, thinking aloud.

'Go on?'

'Well, when I travelled with my father in Europe and North Africa, what I loved most was not only the sights but the smell and the taste of a place.'

'Like the bazaars?'

'What if we were to bring the Orient to London?'

'Incense? Perfumes?' Arthur beckoned to Hiro. 'Tell me, lad. Where are the finest fragrances made in Japan?'

'In Awaji, sir,' he said. 'It is a very old place. The best incense – Borneo camphor, aloe wood, musk – all are popular to perfume fabrics.'

'Then that is what we shall import. Do you not call it the "breath of the gods" in Japan? That is what we shall sell it as.' He mimed a banner in the air. 'I shall write to my agent today.' Liberty caught the arm of the young man walking past. 'Carty, my lad. How much money has your department taken today?'

'Well, sir. I think about . . .'

'No "about". I want you to know exactly, at all times, the bottom line.'

Bel watched them stride away towards the office, and turned to the counter. 'He is inspiring, isn't he?' she said to Hiro. Bel wound a length of ribbon back on the spool and tidied the wrapping area. 'As soon as he has a good idea, he acts on it rather than prevaricating.' She mimed a bow and arrow. 'The French call it an *idée flèche.* The idea that gets ahead.'

'In Japan we say *fugen jikkō* – actions, not words, count.'

'I so enjoyed our weekend.' Bel smiled up at him. She remembered how proudly Hiro had explained Chō's work as she painted a calligraphy for Bel, standing above a scroll of silk with a long-handled brush. The calligraphy now hung in pride of place in her room. Every night before she slept Bel remembered Hiro describing how he once rowed out onto a lake to gaze at the moon in Japan, the mist on the shore, the gentle patter of rain on the water. *Kawaakari*, he called it, *moonlight on water.* As she drifts to sleep each night Bel imagines the steady glow of a lantern in the dark.

'We both enjoy seeing you,' Hiro said, unrolling a floor-plan on the counter.

'I was thinking, perhaps we could commission Chō to paint some scrolls for this scheme? Perhaps on a *rinzu* silk damask?' Bel glanced at him to see if he was cross. 'I don't know if that's appropriate to ask? She is too good to be working in the Japanese Village turning out nick-nacks for tourists.'

'She would be honoured, I think. Artists need to be paid.'

'Yes, they do.' *Talking of which*, Bel thought, striding towards the office. She swung open the door, and walked towards Arthur Liberty's desk, her heart thumping. 'Mr Liberty?'

'One moment, Miss Bright.' He signed off the letter and passed it to his secretary. 'How may I help you?'

'I've been working for you for some years now,' Bel said, summoning her courage. 'I'm grateful for all I am learning, and the extra commission I make on the projects—' Arthur leant forward, his gaze direct.

'And?'

'I do good work for you, Mr Liberty, and I have introduced many of my father's friends to the shop. I've secured several contracts already for us, like Miss Langtry's account for Norfolk Street—' Arthur held up his hand and she stopped.

'You've beaten me to it.' Arthur smiled. 'We are doing

well. Better than I ever hoped. We are expanding, and I have great plans. Of course you are part of that. Let me see what I can do about your salary and position.'

'Thank you, Mr Liberty,' Bel said, her stomach fluttering with relief and excitement. 'I won't let you down. I can apply my skills to any number of schemes – why, we could be producing our own designs for clothes and furniture.'

'We think alike, you and I, Bel.' His eyes glinted, amused. 'I admire someone who knows their own worth.' He stood and offered her his hand, as Tom walked into the office. 'And here's the latest member of the Liberty & Co family. Welcome, Mr Ferris.' Bel looked at Tom in surprise.

'Good afternoon,' he said, nodding to each of them in turn.

'I've hired Mr Ferris's considerable talents for a few hours each week,' Arthur said. 'He will be working on architectural fittings, and larger items of furniture. He also has some exciting ideas about costumes you may be able to help with?'

'We'll be working together?' Bel said, gazing up at Tom.

'Perhaps together we shall change the taste of London,' he said.

'Why just London?' Arthur led them out into the bustling shop. 'Liberty style will conquer the world.'

Lot 12

LONDON, 1885

As the years passed, sometimes Bel felt like the store had a life of its own – walls were knocked through overnight, and Liberty & Co soon commanded a swathe of Regent Street, with properties from the corner of East India House down Argyll Place, a warren of thirty-five rooms crammed with furnishings. There were departments for silks, embroideries, furniture, carpets and curios. There was a Japanese smoking room and an Arab tearoom, with a revolutionary ladies' loo – the first in London to accommodate its female clients. The basement of Chesham House was given over to an Eastern Bazaar, with electric lighting. Liberty could provide everything from a single Thebes chair inspired by the British Museum's collection to a whole house's decoration. No detail was too small.

As individual designers were not named, 'Liberty' became the name for fashionable London. In the upper studios, Bel and Tom often worked side by side in the costume department, with Godwin advising a few hours a week. Customers clamoured for dresses in the aesthetic style. The silks were soft and fine, appealing to a sophisticated clientele, and a small battalion of women worked for Bel in the pleating and embroidery departments.

'How did you enjoy the Japanese exhibit?' Tom said, leaning over his drawing board.

'Chō and I had a marvellous time,' Bel said, standing back to look at the dress she was styling on the mannequin. 'There's even a restaurant on the roof of the arcade on Exhibition Road.' She glanced at him. 'Raw fish, can you imagine? I settled for sixpence tea and biscuits.'

'I hear they have sumo wrestlers and dancing girls in the Native Village—'

'Hiro worries these amusements show his country in a bad light.' Bel frowned, studying the gown. 'It's still not quite right,' she said, adjusting the fall of the draped silk. The speaking tube whistled and one of the assistants went to answer the call. Bel had pinned several shades of silvery sheer silk at the shoulders, drawing it in at an empire line. 'Lord knows this has to be perfect for Miss Terry.'

'Godwin's another matter, but Ellen's not as demanding as the press would make her out.' Tom walked over and folded his arms as he stood beside Bel, looking at the costume. 'She must be able to move freely.'

'One of the dressmakers said to me this morning all her clients are rejecting corsets and bustles.'

'The future of clothing is hygienic and progressive,' Tom said.

'Free the waist!' Bel gestured at her own soft, ruched tea gown. She had dressed all the shop girls in similar outfits, with bandeaus of Liberty print fabric tied around their heads. She pulled a length of buttercup silk from the roll, and draped it across the neck. 'What about scarves,' she said. 'Stoles for summer evenings. If we were to finish simple lengths of silk like this—' She draped the silk across the mannequin. 'For a woman with a smaller dress budget she could buy the simplest, aesthetic dress and several scarves in different colours, tying them at the neck or the waist to great effect.'

'I can't quite imagine . . .' Tom tapped his pencil against his lower lip. The rain pattered on the studio window, and the gas lamps flickered against the darkening panes.

'Let me show you,' Bel said, taking the dress off the mannequin. In the cloakroom she changed out of her plain dress, pulling the soft silk over her head. As she did so, several strands of her golden hair came loose, touching her collarbones, her cheeks. The silk was deliciously light, and the cool air breathed over her skin. Tom was stoking the coal fire, and as he turned to her his face was lit by the flames. He stood slowly as she walked towards him. 'You don't like it?' she said.

'No, it's—' He turned her to the full-length looking glass. 'You look marvellous.'

'The neckline isn't quite right,' she said, adjusting the shoulder. 'What I want is something our ladies can buy direct from us, without the need for a dressmaker's adjustments. A design which gives them health and freedom.' Tom took the gold silk from her and draped it across her shoulders, watching their reflection in the mirror. 'If the under-dress is made of silk velvet, or Umritza cashmere, ladies can wear it even when it's chilly.'

'You think a lot about making people happy, don't you, Bel?' he said. The feel of the silk on her skin raised the fine hairs at the nape of her neck. She was aware of the closeness of him, that they were alone in the studio now. The sounds of the shop below seemed far away.

'I do,' she said, talking to fill the tension between them. 'I want our clients to feel like they are coming home. I want them to buy from us, but I want them to feel cherished, too. That we understand what they want. I believe that beautiful, useful things shouldn't only be for the wealthy.'

'Good for you.'

'Do you patronise me?' she rounded on him.

'Not at all. That's why I became an architect.' The firelight gilded his skin, his hair. Bel longed to kiss him. To be kissed. 'How alike we are. Did I not say once we are equals?'

Are we? she thought. *I work night and day in this studio, and you are paid more for it.* She bit her lip. *I know with your growing reputation your name has cachet, whereas 'Isobel Bright' is unknown. As yet.*

'Tom—' The studio door swung open, and they stepped apart as Arthur and Hiro walked in. 'Mr Liberty,' she said, glancing back. She saw expressions pass over Hiro's face like storm clouds – shock, anger. *Desire?*

'What's all this? Modelling as well as designing, Miss Bright?' Arthur said.

'No!' Bel caught herself. 'The new aesthetic dress, for Miss Terry, sir,' she said, colouring. *Has he told them? Has Schiffer told them what I did?* 'I was only demonstrating,' she said to Hiro.

'We were just saying, scarves would be a good idea,' Tom said, offering up the length of golden silk. 'Cheap to produce—'

'We?' Bel interrupted. '*I* suggested—'

'Indeed! Economical for those on a budget,' Arthur said. 'For those who can't afford to buy a whole new outfit each season, update with a silk scarf? You're on to something there!' Bel glared at Tom.

'Miss Bright inspired me—'

'She inspires us all.' He clapped him on the back and picked up a ledger. 'I shall see you in the morning.'

'That was my idea,' Bel said quietly once Arthur had gone.

'I know – I would have insisted, had I but a chance,' Tom said. Bel decided to keep her ideas to herself unless she spoke to Mr Liberty directly.

'Bel,' Hiro said, offering her a shawl. 'Do not get cold.'

'Thank you.' She looked up, sensing his concern.

'I can stay—'

'Thank you, Hiro,' she said, firmly. He bowed, and turned away.

Lot 13

LONDON, 1885

'I feel quite the cad,' Tom said as the cab clipped along Hampstead High Street.

'So you should,' Bel said, flashing him a glance. 'Isn't it always the way? The accomplishments of women go unrecognised.'

'You're awfully weary for – what, twenty-eight?'

'Twenty-seven,' she corrected, gazing out at the shop windows glowing gold in the evening gloom. The bare March trees stood out against the gas-lamp-lit road, and the chill air pinched Bel's cheeks. But it was cosy in the cab next to Tom, and she felt happy, she realised, for the first time in many months.

'I'm glad you agreed to let me make it up to you. It is good to get out of town, is it not?' Tom said. 'I've just returned from visiting friends in Wales. You can breathe there, the country is still wild and free . . .'

'But where are we going?'

'You'll see,' he glanced at her, smiling. 'I shall make sure you return safely home.'

'I haven't been up here for a long time,' she said, watching the elegant couples strolling by. 'We had friends in the village.' *We had friends everywhere.*

'I like it. The swimming pond on the Heath is marvellous. Have you been?'

'Is it not for gentlemen?'

'Women are welcomed on Thursdays, now,' he said. 'When I was up there earlier in the week I saw a woman police officer chasing some lads from the pond. She swept down on them, her long skirts like a crow's wings, and the boys ran for it starkers, clutching their boots.' Bel laughed. 'You know, the spiritualists say there are more ley lines on the Heath than in any other part of the country.'

'Ley lines?'

'Energy lines, in the earth.'

'Honestly.'

'One day, I shall build a fine house on the edge of the Heath and swim each morning before driving to my office.'

'It's good to dream.' Bel turned to him. 'Chō told me about a Japanese philosophy, *ichinichi ippo* – one day, one step at a time.'

'I think that's splendid. The first step in any plan is the hardest. One must begin.' Tom glanced out. 'Here we are. Driver, you may set us down,' he called. Tom helped Bel from the carriage. She could smell the scent of chestnuts roasting on the cold air, and heard the sound of a barrel organ playing. As they rounded the corner to the edge of the Heath, she saw a busy street fair, with coloured lanterns strung between the trees.

'A fair?' she said in surprise.

'If you won't allow me to take you to supper, I shall at least buy you a bag of chestnuts,' Tom said, giving the vendor some coins.

'Thank you,' she said. The bag warmed her cold hands through her gloves, and she peeled the first chestnut, handing it to Tom. 'How did you know this was here?' They walked on, past a crowd of men in greasy overcoats gathered round a boxing ring staring blankly as the bare-knuckle boxers fought.

'I was at a play with Schiffer last night, and spotted the fair on the way past. I thought it looked amusing.'

'Were you good friends at school?'

'More acquaintances.'

'Were you happy there?'

'Heavens, no. I remember standing at the station with ice water in my guts, hoping it was some awful prank. The first I knew I was off to boarding school was when my mother gave me a sheaf of notepaper so I could write home.'

'Mr Schiffer asks again and again for me to model for him.'

'Does he now?' Tom glanced at her. 'Will you?'

'Never.'

'Good. Orlando tends to ask young women he desires. I should not wish you to be used that way. We all know what kind of woman models . . .' Bel felt hot with shame.

'You know, he gave me a drawing by my father?'

'He told me,' Tom said. 'Do not feel you are beholden to him, because of that.' He smiled at her. 'They called your father "the English Renoir", did they not?'

'Yes.' Bel laughed. 'He hated that. Always saw himself as more of a Manet. He felt Renoir too decorative.' She smiled. 'That's how he met my mother. He came to her family house to paint her portrait, and took a bride.'

'How romantic.'

'It was, until her family cut her off without a penny.'

'Really?' Tom said, frowning. 'You have no fortune of your own?' Bel sensed the weight of the question. 'I thought, perhaps – your mother's family, when you marry . . . ?'

'I do not live in a single boarding room and work for Mr Liberty for amusement.'

'I do not wish to offend you.' They stood facing one another as people milled around them. 'I find your resourcefulness and independence admirable.' He stepped closer. 'Bel—' She noticed a group of boys poking behind a stall with sticks, and heard a pitiful cry.

'I say, stop that immediately,' Bel shouted, striding over to them. The boys scattered like starlings. Bel crouched down and pulled back the felt drape covering the stall. A tiny puppy, more grey with filth than white, cowered in the shadows. Above her, the muffled thunk of the balls and the cry of the crowds continued. 'Hello, little one,' she said, gently, coaxing the dog forward.

'Bel?' Tom stooped down beside her. 'You could have been hurt.'

'I'm fine, they're just boys.' She pointed under the table. 'Look.'

'Well I never.' He crawled forward to gather the puppy up. Bel took her from him, and tucked her into the collar of her coat.

'She's shaking,' she said.

'How do you know it's a "she"?' Tom said, his arm around her.

'I noticed,' Bel said, laughing. 'She's a little Westie, aren't you?' She felt its tail thump against her coat. 'My grandmother had one.' The puppy whimpered and tucked itself closer to Bel. 'What are we going to do with you?' It licked her chin and Bel laughed.

'I think she likes you.' They stepped back as another wooden ball whizzed towards the stall. The painted figure spun.

'I shall call her Sally,' Bel said.

'After the stall? You intend to keep her.'

'Of course. It was meant to be.' She stroked the puppy's head. 'I have a feeling we shall be good friends.'

'And what of me?' Tom tucked Bel's collar closer around the dog. 'Am I to always be a good friend, or more, perhaps?'

'We'll see,' Bel said, casting him a quick look as she walked on.

Lot 14

LONDON, 1886

'Miss Bright, do come in,' Orlando said as his manservant showed Bel into his drawing room. Hiro followed close behind. 'I see you've brought your chaperone, *again*,' he said, frowning. He wore a red gown and embroidered slippers, his white shirt open at the neck and cuffs. Orlando set down his glass of absinthe, looking at Sally. 'And a guard dog? Do you not trust me, Miss Bright?' The sash of his gown trailed across the Persian rug like the tail of a tiger through long grass.

'Mr Kurosaki and I devised the scheme for you,' she said, placing her portfolio on the table. 'We work together—'

'Very well.' Schiffer waved his hand. 'May I tempt you with a glass of *la fée verte*? I gained something of a taste for it in Paris.'

'No, thank you,' she said, moving aside a tray with an elaborate collection of opium pipes and untying the portfolio.

'A bottle of fizz, then?' Orlando clicked his fingers at his manservant. 'You can't refuse champagne, surely?' he said to Bel.

'I can try.'

'Ah, Miss Bright,' he said, cupping his chin on his hand. 'How I've missed you. See, now, if Sargent has decided to settle in London, and that silly kite Wilde had Godwin design his house, I shall do one better than them both. I believe I have the most attractive designer in London working on mine—'

'Would you mind propping up the design boards over there?' Bel said to Hiro.

As she talked Orlando through their plans for the drawing room, Bel held up swatches of fabric and paint for him to see against the walls in different lights. She held a length of burgundy silk at the window. 'We thought this shade would bring some warmth to the north window?' When Orlando didn't reply, she turned. 'Mr Schiffer?' He lay back on the sofa, running his thumb against his lower lip, watching her. 'Do you like it?'

'Yes, I do, very much.' He leapt to his feet. 'You shall have to discuss the final design with Ferris. He is overseeing the renovations here as he did with the studio, but he could not be here today.'

'I thought he was joining us later? Where is he?'

'Wales, I believe.' Orlando snatched up the board for his bedroom. 'Come, show me your plans in situ.' He ushered Bel ahead, pointing at the far door at the end of a dark corridor lit only by a single gas lamp. Hiro made to follow, but

Orlando stopped him, his palm flat on his chest. 'Tidy up in here.'

'Sir, I cannot—'

'You'll do exactly as I say. Do you understand? If you prize your job, remember Mr Liberty is a personal friend. One word—'

'Do not threaten me.' Hiro glared at him. 'Liberty knows who I am.'

Orlando gave him a shove backwards, and stalked after Bel, closing the door.

The drapes were drawn, and the bedside candles glowed dimly. Bel heard the door lock, and froze. *Don't panic*, she thought. *Don't let him see you are afraid.* 'I think we should get some light in here, don't you?' she said, reaching for the heavy velvet curtain. Orlando caught her hand, and pulled her into his arms.

'Bel, my Bel,' he murmured, pressing her into the heavy drapes, the weight of him against her. 'How I missed you.' Bel choked in shock, the bitter worm of his tongue forced in her mouth. *No, no, no . . .* He broke for air, and she turned away, shocked tears in her eyes.

'Mr Schiffer!' she said, struggling to free herself.

'Bel, the nights I have lain alone thinking of you—' He seemed to have as many hands as the Indian god she had seen once, pressing her, pulling at her, forcing her hard against the wall. *He is too strong. I can't move.* Bel felt she floated above herself, still and quiet.

Hiro thumped against the door, harder and harder.

'Bel,' he shouted. 'Bel?'

Think.

'We can't do this,' she murmured to Orlando. 'Not now, not like this.'

'Tonight, then?' Orlando breathed hard, releasing his hold. 'You will come to me?' Bel shoved him, and he reeled backwards, landing on the bed.

'Not if you were the last man on earth, sir.'

'I'll have you, Bel!' Orlando grabbed her as she swept past, clutching at her skirt. She smacked his hand away and unlocked the door.

'Bel?' Hiro's face was hard with anger. 'Come with me,' he said, putting his arm around her. Bel turned to Orlando, wiping her swollen lip on the back of her hand.

'Mr Schiffer, if you wish to go ahead with the designs, Tom—'

'Tom, is it now?'

'—must deal with Mr Liberty. I shall be unable to complete your project.'

'Don't be like that, Bel,' he said, staggering after them. Sally bared her teeth, growling, and Orlando kicked out at her.

'You're shaking. Did he hurt you?' Hiro said quietly. 'I'll kill him—'

'Please, don't make it worse,' she said. Hiro gathered up Bel's portfolio and walked her quickly to the door, Sally at their heels.

'I shall have you, Miss Bright,' Orlando called. 'I shall

paint you, whether you wish me to or not.' He lurched after them. 'I know you by heart. If I'll not have you in my bed, I shall have you on my canvas.'

'You wouldn't dare—' Bel turned, horrified.

'I have a marvellous recall for form.' His gaze roamed leisurely down her. 'What shall ye be? Venus, perhaps?'

'Enough,' Hiro said, stepping between them. 'You insult Miss Bright and you demean yourself. Honourable? You do not know the meaning of the word—'

'You cur—' He broke off as his manservant appeared to let them out. Orlando followed them, leaning against the doorframe. 'No one refuses me, Miss Bright,' he called. 'You'll see.'

Hiro helped Bel into the carriage. 'Dishonourable man,' he said under his breath. 'Are you sure he didn't hurt you?'

'Yes,' she said, though her hands shook still as she stroked Sally's fur.

'You must not be alone with him,' Hiro said.

'Oh, I've known men like him all my life. I can look after myself.' *Men who think they are entitled to take whatever they will,* she thought. *Spoiled men. Men who do not understand the word 'no'. Men who think a woman's body is a plaything.* Fury clutched her stomach. *You can see it, when women talk among themselves, the pain that passes across the face of her, and her, and her. The shame. But the shame is on the men, not the women they prey upon.* Bel frowned. *Will he lie and brag to Tom?* she thought. *What if he believes I was willing? Surely he wouldn't believe that of me?*

Lot 15

PARIS, 25 JULY 1985

Mira sat at Isobel's writing desk in the small study overlooking Avenue Junot, and rifled through the button tin she had found. She could hear Serge shouting instructions to his men from the salon, and the sound of parcel tape as they wrapped the sofas and armchairs for transporting to Drouot.

What's your story? Mira thought, sorting the buttons into groups on the desk. Jet mourning buttons, brass military, fine seed pearls caught the light. On a notepad she jotted down: *1923.* Mira gazed out of the window. *Why didn't you return to Paris? Too late for the Great War, too early for the Second.*

Drawer by drawer she went through the rest of the desk, pulling out blank sheets of paper, perfectly sharpened pencils, a dried-up Montblanc fountain pen, which she set aside.

'Anything of value, Hutch?' Ned said, pausing in the doorway.

'Hutch?' she span slowly round, and raised an eyebrow.

'We're pals now, aren't we?'

'The pen, perhaps,' she said, passing it to him. 'The desk is decorative, lacquered bamboo?' Ned checked the table over.

'Ursin Fortier,' he said. 'A Liberty piece.' He placed a jeweller's loupe in one eye, and studied the gold nib of the pen. 'Montblanc Rouge et Noir. I'd guess 1910, 1920? This can go to Tokyo.' He glanced up at Mira. 'If, as you suggested, we are building a story around the sale.'

'It's odd, you know.' Mira sat back in the chair. 'Small writing tables like this are normally stuffed with photos and keepsakes. But this one – it's like it's been picked clean. Like a hotel desk.' She gestured at the sheaf of blank notepaper.

Ned put his clipboard on the chest of drawers and walked over. 'It may have a hidden drawer, or cupboard. It's worth checking. Asian-style antiques often do, like the old puzzle boxes.' He pulled out the two side drawers first, and turned them over, running his fingers along the dovetailed corners. 'It's nicely made,' he said, weighing the drawers in his hands, and standing them on end by the door. He pulled out the central drawer. 'Funny. This one is heavier.' He turned it over and slid out a false bottom. 'And there you are . . .'

'A book!'

'Silver lacquer bound.' He ran his fingertip slowly along the spine.

'Come on, open it!' Mira said. She turned to the first page:

15th May 1875

My name is Isobel Bright. I am eighteen years of age, and my life begins today . . .

'It's hers! It's Isobel.' She flicked through the book and saw that every page was full of a sloping, flamboyant hand, written crossways on both sides of the paper, notes and sketches crammed into the margins.

'That's going to be difficult to decipher,' Ned said.

'Paper was valuable, then. Quite often letters were written like this – they just turned the page ninety degrees and wrote across the text.' Mira frowned. 'Most of it is in French, but Isobel was English, wasn't she?' The final pages were empty. 'Look at her last entry: August 1923.' Turning the final page, Mira found two gingko leaves pressed together, and a quote in a different hand: *Even though a river of tears flows through this body, the flame of love will not be quenched – Izumi Shikibu.* Mira gently touched the leaves. *Someone loved you.* Her lips parted slowly. *A river of tears? Someone loved you very much, and they lost you, didn't they?*

~

'*I am the product of my age, a New Woman – BB.*' Mira translated, sitting on the kitchen counter, the silver lacquered book on her lap. Serge's men emptied the cabinets around her. 'That's what Hiro Kurosaki said about Bel in an interview I found. She *was* the New Woman.'

'BB?' Ned said.

'Bel Bright, I guess?' Mira flicked through the pages. 'It's strange . . .'

'What is?' Ned glanced up from his clipboard.

'This book. It begins in May 1875 – look, this journal entry. Bel is eighteen years old, and working at Liberty.' Mira smiled to herself. *Eighteen. Same age as when I met Luke.* She turned the pages. 'The entries are all in date order, but there are big jumps.'

'So it's not a diary?' Ned said.

'No,' Mira said thoughtfully. 'It's more like a record of what was important to her, I think.' *Almost fifty years. A lifetime.* 'Why does it end so suddenly?'

'A mystery to solve. Be careful with the wine,' Serge said to the young man on the stepladder emptying the racks. 'There are several good cases of Bordeaux in the hall closet, too.'

Ned called out to a couple of men carrying an armchair across the hall. 'Pack for Tokyo.' He checked his notes and amended them. 'Rennie Macintosh, 1897. $2,000–2,700.'

'Listen to this,' Mira said. '*July 1891, Bastille Day – people dancing in the streets. To the Folies Bergères last night. All was light and mirrors, heavy fabric, heavy panting in the fountain garden.*' Serge snorted with laughter. '*I swear the elephants and monkeys have better manners.*' He strutted out of the kitchen whistling for his men to break for lunch.

'We should get a bite to eat, too.' Ned checked his watch. 'Do you like sushi?'

'Never tried it.' She slipped the journal into a padded envelope and placed it in her bag. 'I just want to make sure Serge's guys don't scoop this up into the Drouot lots.' In the hall she checked her reflection in the gilded mirror. She noticed the candle sconces either side, and pictured Isobel stopping here on the way out. *Where did you go, BB?* She imagined the whisper of long skirts, silk hems brushing the polished parquet.

'There's a little place I know near the Opéra.'

'Not sure about raw fish . . .' She saw Ned's disappointment. 'Okay, why not? Try anything once, right?'

On the street, she put a pair of tortoiseshell Ray-Bans on, and Ned hailed a cab. 'Do you know Paris well?' he said, swinging his linen jacket over his shoulder. He held the car door open for her, and settled in beside her, giving the driver an address on rue Molière.

'Fairly, thanks to Kim.' Mira watched a group of elegant women walking by. 'I've always wanted to have that *bon chic bon genre* thing all the women have.'

'Between you and me, French women intimidate me. I'd be terrified of getting something wrong all the time.'

'I admire them. They have style in their bones.' Mira gazed out as Garnier's Opéra swept past. She imagined Isobel, in a long velvet cloak climbing the steps, the dazzling marble and gilt, the vast chandelier glinting, her pale-gloved hand alighting on the arm of her companion. A white bird in a sea of dark figures, arriving at the red velvet auditorium.

What's your secret, Isobel?

Lot 16

LONDON, JUNE 1887

The commissionaire doffed his top hat as Mr and Mrs Liberty entered the store, holding open the heavy wood and brass door for them. Regent Street's windows shone in the summer sunlight, flags for the Golden Jubilee fluttering above the flower-decked pavements. As they passed through the shop, the 'cicerone' floor walkers, the sales assistants and porters wished them good morning, and Arthur addressed each by name.

'What a day! Ten miles of well-wishers for our Queen.' His gaze scanned the bustling store. 'How far we have come,' he said. 'But we cannot rest on our laurels.'

'You work too hard, my dear,' Emma said, stopping to smooth down his purple silk tie. 'I worry about you. Sometimes I wish we had stayed in East India House, with a handful of loyal staff.' Her gaze followed Bel, her light summer blouse and skirt shining against the dark shadows of the store as she walked a client through.

'I learnt from Ferris,' Arthur Liberty said quietly to his wife, 'that when young Bel started with us, she was boarding with her father's coachman.'

'His coachman?' Emma murmured. 'I had no idea. Do you think . . . Well, the rumours that she modelled at the Academy?'

'I neither care nor wish to know.'

'How brave that girl is. Not one word of her troubles. One always imagines there is someone, some family who will scoop an orphan up in those circumstances.'

'We are that someone,' Arthur said. 'Liberty is the closest thing to family she has now. She's done a splendid job at Cornwall Terrace for us.' Emma leant closer and lowered her voice.

'Do you think, Ferris—?'

'He's drawn to her,' Arthur said, watching Tom charming a female client. 'But he is ambitious. I think he will try for a more profitable match.'

'I hope he does not use her.' Emma broke off as Hiro stormed across the shop floor. 'What's wrong with our young Mr Kurosaki?'

'Is something amiss?' Arthur said.

'That man,' Hiro said, pale with anger. 'The dishonourable Mr Schiffer.'

'Steady, lad. He is an important client—'

'He insulted Bel, and now he has dishonoured my sister.' His fist clenched. 'I caught her, when I returned home to collect the bowl I wanted to show you.' He lifted up a box tied with string. 'Schiffer sent a carriage for her. She defied me, and went to him.'

'Surely not?' Arthur said.

'She has *posed* for him! You remember he once saw her, here? He followed her, introduced himself, the great artist—'

'Calm yourself,' Emma said.

'She saw him again recently, and this time he persuaded her.' Hiro shook his head. 'I will kill him.'

'Now, now. Girls can make a good income, modelling,' Arthur said carefully, glancing at Bel as she walked over. 'It is not *necessarily* disreputable.'

'Is there something amiss?' she said.

'Mr Ferris,' Arthur called him over. 'Can you reassure us that Schiffer is a decent man?' Tom hesitated a moment too long. 'He has hired Mr Kurosaki's sister as a model.'

'Ah . . . yes.' Tom caught on. 'He mentioned a series of Japanese portraits.' He smiled reassuringly. 'I have never known Orlando to take advantage of his models,' he said.

'Someone must chaperone Chō?' Bel said, afraid.

'Too late.' Hiro raked his hand through his hair. 'I was wrong to bring her to London. I hoped to protect her, and I have failed.'

'Calm yourself,' Tom said, placing his hand on Hiro's shoulder. 'We need to check over the progress at Schiffer's. Why don't we all go over there this evening and discuss this man to man?'

Lot 17

LONDON, 1887

'Where is she?' Hiro said, striding into Orlando's house. Bel handed her coat and hat to the manservant.

'Mr Schiffer is in the studio, sir. I believe they are still working.' He gestured to the sweeping staircase leading up from the columned hall. The dark turquoise tiles on the walls seemed aquatic in the dim light of the gas lamps, and Bel felt like she was swimming up the staircase, following the men. Tom knocked on the closed studio door, and pushed it open.

'Schiffer? It's Ferris. I'm with—'

'Silence,' Orlando commanded. Rain pattered on the raked glass ceiling above. It was so dark, Bel could hardly see. The air smelt of pungent smoke, and the coal of a pipe glowed in an ashtray on the table. A large canvas stood on the easel.

'Chō?' Bel said. 'Where are you?'

Orlando's brush moved smoothly over the canvas adding the final touches of light to her translucent skin. Bel felt like they had intruded on a couple making love. The heavy scented air spun like a web between them. 'There,' he sighed, stepping back. He threw down his brush. '*There.*'

He slumped back on a low divan, and reached for the pipe. *Opium?* Bel thought. There was incense burning in a bronze censer, so it was hard to tell. Chō lay dozing at his side, her hair loose and spilling around her like dark water. She wore a gold kimono, and Orlando stroked her hair as she slept. 'Look, then.' He gestured at the canvas with the stem of his pipe.

The three of them turned, and Bel gasped. The painting was exquisite. The canvas was full-length, the height of Chō herself. Schiffer had painted her standing before the dark fire surround, one arm resting on the mantle, the gold sleeve of her kimono hanging loose. Her hair hung below her waist, strands looping across her shoulder. It was realistic, but the pose reminded Bel of the figures she had seen in prints by Utamaro and Hiroshige. Above Chō's head, the gold Buddha she had placed years before gleamed. Looking at it now, hovering over the dark studio, it seemed benign, but Schiffer had made it menacing and cruel. Chō's face turned to look at the viewer, invitingly.

'Congratulations,' Tom said. 'Your best yet.'

'Whistler will be *livid*.' Orlando exhaled a plume of smoke. 'Sargent will wish he never settled here . . .'

'My sister,' Hiro said. His eyes shone darkly.

'Hiro-san?' Chō murmured. She pushed herself up and smiled sleepily. 'Hello, Bel. I am sorry. I am so tired. So much work.'

'Come,' Hiro said, holding out his hand to her. Chō stood and bowed to Orlando.

'Well done, Chō,' he said. 'A fine day's work. I shall call this *Autumn Gold*. For our next composition—'

'My sister will not model for you again,' Hiro said.

'That,' Orlando said, rising slowly, 'is not your decision to make.'

'She will do as I say.'

'You are not in Japan, now,' Orlando said, padding over to him. He pulled his wine velvet dressing gown around him. 'In this country we let our women make up their own minds.'

Do we? Bel thought.

'Hiro-san,' Chō said, bowing. 'I am sorry for deceiving you. I want to be painted by Mr Schiffer. He is a great artist. It is an honour.' She bowed again. 'Forgive me.'

'Chō has been well paid,' Orlando said, face to face with Hiro.

'Perhaps there is a compromise?' Tom said. 'Could your housekeeper not sit in when Chō models for you, Schiffer? As a chaperone.'

'Chō is a woman of over thirty. I think she can make up her own mind, don't you?' Orlando turned to Hiro. 'Mr Kurosaki. I assure you, I will take care of her. You have my word as an Englishman and a gentleman.' Tom and Bel exchanged a glance.

'I will not hear of it,' Hiro insisted.

'We'll see. Ferris – didn't you wish to see the progress on the renovations in the dining room? I believe the builders are almost done, and it will be time for you to weave your magic.' As Orlando walked past Bel, he leant in and whispered. 'See? Imagine what I would make of you if you say yes? I would immortalise you—'

'Are you God now, Mr Schiffer?' Bel said. 'I have no use for immortality.'

Bel let the men walk on ahead, and stayed behind with Chō. 'Are you unwell?' She thought her eyes seemed particularly large and dark. There was a softness to them, a languor she had not seen before. *Is she drugged?*

'I am in love,' she whispered. 'He only sees me as a pretty thing to paint. I can be more. I can be his wife.'

'No, Chō?' Bel's eyes widened in shock. She couldn't think of anything worse than being married to a man like Orlando, using up life, people, like a wildfire consuming all in his path. *Just like my father*, she realised.

'My aunt taught me to be a good wife. I am meticulous, hospitable, serene, empathetic—'

'But what about *you*. What does he do for you?'

'He tells me about art, and we work together.' She gestured to where several calligraphies hung drying.

'Chō, you need a husband who will take care of you. Cherish you. Men like Orlando—'

'He is an artist,' she said. 'I am an artist. He say rules not apply.'

'It's not the same for women.' Bel screwed up her courage. 'Chō, he . . . he tried to ravish me—'

'Artists have passions they cannot control.' Chō's eyes flashed defiantly.

'You're wrong. That is no excuse—'

'He is good to me.' She squeezed Bel's hand. 'You do not understand. I am older than you, and I want a life, a family. With him, I have a chance.'

Lot 18

BEXLEYHEATH, LONDON, 1888

Tom and Bel ran across the wide lawn of the Red House at dusk, with Sally gambolling at their feet. Three little girls played in the summerhouse, a tea party, wearing kimonos with silk cherry blossom in their hair, and one of their mothers photographed them with a Kodak camera. The children ran over and put daisy chains around Tom and Bel's necks, chattering and laughing.

It was a blue and gold day, bees muzzing the larkspur in the borders. The warm red brick house nestled in the garden William Morris had designed around his dream home, the flower borders spilling their fragrance into the evening air – jasmine, lavender and rose. Across the lawns a group was playing croquet, and Bel heard the mallet, the ball, the cheer go up. Tom carried a butterfly net with him, and swung leisurely at the air as they walked.

'Stay close,' Bel said to Sally, and the little dog wagged her stubby tail, trotting along at her heels. Tom's pale linen suit and Bel's white dress shone in the half-light. Her gold hair was swept up with a tortoiseshell comb, hanging loose at the back, and as she held up the lantern for Tom to light it, she glowed bright on the forest path.

'If I had Rossetti's skill, I would paint you, just like this.' Tom lifted the lantern high. 'I was quite jealous, watching him work. He is too handsome for his own good.'

'You, jealous? I was flattered to be asked,' Bel said. 'No one has drawn me since my father.' *At least . . .* They walked through the woods, ferns brushing her ankles. 'It was good of Charles to invite us,' Bel said. 'I never thought Morris would sell this place.' She pointed to where Sally ran ahead through the rippling tall grass. 'Will she not disturb the moths?'

'She will drive them out,' Tom said. 'Here's a good spot.' He set the lantern down at the edge of the grassland. As the light fell, dark shapes fluttered from the cool blue shadows, drawn by the bright light. Sally leapt at them, tail wagging, and Bel called her over, holding her on her lap as Tom swiped at the air, capturing the moths in the net, reciting their names like an incantation: *hawk moth, tiger, cinnabar.*

'Bel, does it not concern you what people might say about you being here, with me?' Tom said, placing a moth into a killing jar of crushed laurel leaves.

'Nonsense. I am here with old friends,' she said, leaning back on her elbows. 'I have known Mr Holme and Mr Rossetti for years, and their wives and children.' She smiled up at Tom as he offered her his hand. 'It is not as if we are alone.'

'We are now,' he said, stepping closer. 'Bel, I have wanted to be alone with you for so long. To kiss you would be a marvellous thing.' A warm wave of desire swept through Bel like fire in dry grass. Lights sparked behind her closed eyes as Tom cupped her face, her lips parting slow, longing for his touch. 'Oh, Bel . . .' Just as he pulled her to him, they heard voices from the path. Clara Benton led a file of children, carrying red and pink paper lanterns on sticks, and she waved.

'Hello, you two,' she called, and they stepped apart. She walked on with a knowing smile. 'Any luck?'

~

Bel looked down the long dining table at her old friends. *Here is art and life*, she thought. *Here is all I long for. Imagine a home, like this.* Tom sat at the opposite end to her, deep in conversation. She caught Rossetti watching her, and she elongated her neck, smiling. He mimed sketching her, and Tom looked over, frowning.

'Is it not romantic?' Charles Holme said, leaning back in his chair. 'I do not know how Morris could ever leave this place.'

'He left because it costs a bomb, and freezes in winter,' Rossetti said, laughing.

'But here is Old England,' Holme said. 'It's as if the Industrial era never happened.'

'Oh, I don't know,' Bel said. 'I am rather fond of modernity. I like a steam train, and an electric light or two.'

'You are teasing me.' Holme said.

'Can we not have the best of both?' she said. 'Morris looked back to cathedrals and medieval craft guilds. An idyll which never existed. Is it too much to hope to carry the best of the past with us and the comfort and convenience of modern life?'

'I'm in agreement with you,' Holme said. 'The machine is here to stay and we must make the most of it.' He pointed to the hall. 'Make sure you and Tom both sign the glass after dinner? There is a diamond cutter by the screen.' He looked from one to the other. 'I feel that soon everyone will know your names.'

~

After dinner, Tom settled at a table in the drawing room, pinning out his moths by candlelight. 'You've caught some beauties.' Bel paused with her hand on his shoulder.

'So has Rossetti, it seems,' he said, without looking up.

'I'm sure he would draw you too, if you asked.'

'Do not toy with me, Bel,' Tom said, placing his hand on hers. A fresh wind pattered rain against the dark window, and the fire in the great hearth crackled. The hum of conversation died away into the background, and to Bel it seemed they were alone in the circle of candlelight. She pulled up a chair, and sat beside him as he worked, pinning out the fine wings with slivers of paper. Bel picked up a sketchpad and pencil, and drew the delicate pattern, over and over, wings interlacing, repeating.

Charles Holme joined them, and looked down at Bel's drawings. 'You have your father's ability, Isobel.'

'One day,' she said, 'I shall have a studio of my own.' She darkened the curve of the wing with a flowing line. 'I shall employ a workshop of seamstresses and artists, and make beautiful the world, just as you all do.' She smiled up at him.

'I do not doubt it, from talking with you this afternoon. If ever you need advice, or help, you only have to ask.'

'Is that really what you wish for?' Tom said, after he had walked away. 'I did not realise you harboured such ambition.' He looked at Bel, the fire glinting in his eyes.

'Yes it is.' She nodded. 'I wish to make my own fortune, to be beholden to no man. I have known what it is to lose everything I believed was inviolable – home, status. I know how easily it can all fall away. It will never happen again.'

'What of family? Do you not still hope for marriage? Children?'

'Why can a woman not have both?' She picked up a beaten copper heart from the oak table, and turned it over in her fingers. 'Can I not be wife, mother, artist, businesswoman?'

'Well said,' Clara said, strolling past. She carried a sleeping child curled against her, a Walter Crane book of nursery rhymes open in her free hand. 'It is late, I shall retire now, but please, make yourself at home.'

'I shall come up with you,' Bel said, rising. Tom caught her hand, and pressed it to his lips. She felt the prick of his stubble on her fingers, and cupped his cheek for a moment. 'Good night, Tom.'

Lot 19

LONDON, NOVEMBER 1888

'Thank you, everyone,' Arthur said, clapping his hands as the last of the staff crowded in to the office. Bel leafed through the latest copy of *The Woman's World* as she waited. Oscar Wilde had included a feature on her aesthetic dresses, she saw.

'Few of us are going down Wilton's Music Hall tonight if you fancy it?' Miss Browning said.

'I'd love to,' Bel said.

Now there was standing room only, but the original members of the Liberty team sat at the table beside Arthur and Emma. 'Is that all of us? Good,' he said, and waited for the hubbub of conversation to die down. Bel set aside the magazine on the pile of papers, and looked up at him. 'Firstly, Emma and I would like to thank you all. Liberty's success has exceeded our dreams, and that is all thanks to your hard work.' A ripple of applause rolled across the room. 'We are expanding. More space means we need more stock, more original ideas. We are fortunate to have a team of talented designers working with us, but I have always believed that creative people need to fill the well of inspiration from which they draw their ideas.' He looked at Bel, Hiro and Tom in turn. 'Which is why Emma and I would like to invite Miss Bright, Mr Ferris and Mr Kurosaki to join us on our research trip to Japan next month.'

Bel's lips parted in surprise. 'Mr Liberty,' she said. 'I don't know what to say.' *Yes*, she thought. *Yes*.

'What an opportunity,' Tom said, rising and shaking his hand. 'Thank you, sir.'

'We shall be travelling with Mr Holme and the artist Mr East. Mr Kurosaki, you will be our cultural guide and interpreter,' Arthur said. He looked at the rest of the staff. 'Obviously we shall be away for some months. We shall depart from Tilbury and travel via Egypt, Ceylon, Hong Kong and on to Nagasaki, arriving in Kyoto in March. Thanks to the marvellous Tokaido Highway, we shall explore from Mount Fuji to Lake Biwa with ease!' An excited murmur went round the room. 'Mr East will be recording our travels in paint, and Mrs Liberty will be photographing our journey. Mr Holme has wholesale interests in Japan, and with him we will find the finest suppliers of fabrics, ceramics and metalwork for our store. We will bring treasures the like of which London has never seen!' People cheered. 'I am relying on you all to step up and manage the store. My new partner Mr Llewellyn will be in charge in our absence. Mrs Liberty and I plan to travel on from Yokohama to North America – I believe it is only some two weeks by steamship.

You youngsters will return to London ahead of us and get to work, applying all you have seen and learnt for the new season of designs. You have forty days on board on your return, plenty of time to reflect and work. Think of it as a creative sabbatical.'

'Thank you, Mr Liberty,' Bel said.

'We are proud of the work you have done for Liberty,' he said, shaking Bel's hand. 'Travel broadens the mind, and the heart. I hope this trip inspires you on to great things.' He turned to the gathered staff. 'Thank you, all.'

'I shall take care of Sally,' Miss Browning said. Hearing her name, the little white dog raised her head from her basket in the corner of the office. 'We couldn't bear it if you put her in kennels while you were away. We'd all miss her.'

'Thank you. I can't believe it – Japan!' Bel said as the staff dispersed. 'I've always longed to visit.' She touched Hiro's arm. 'You don't seem happy?'

'It will be my honour to show you my country,' he said, glancing at Bel as they walked through to the bustling store. 'There is so much I hope to share with you.'

'Then what is the matter?'

'What about Chō-san?' he said. 'I worry about leaving her.'

'Chō is a mature woman, not a child,' Bel said gently. 'You have friends and neighbours who can help her, people in your community?' Hiro nodded.

'It is not that which worries me. Chō is more than capable of running a home.'

'You mean Schiffer?' Bel said, frowning.

'I do not trust him.'

'Then perhaps you should trust your sister.'

Lot 20

LONDON, 1888

'Let's celebrate,' Tom said, hailing a carriage as they left the store at closing time.

'Japan! I can't believe it,' Bel said, settling beside him.

They clipped along Fleet Street, past the Law Courts, the great dome of St Paul's rising ahead of them. At the broad steps Tom leapt out, offering Bel his hand. 'Are we to go to church?' she said, confused. Her stomach was tight with hunger. 'I had hoped you might be taking me for supper?'

'Later,' Tom said, laughing. 'I have a surprise.' They ran up the steps hand in hand, and he pushed open the great door. Inside, a service was underway, and he pressed his finger to his lips, beckoning to Bel to follow him. Their footsteps echoed around the side aisle, and she followed him up a sweeping stone staircase. Higher and higher they climbed, the voices of the priest and congregation falling away. After a final narrow, steep climb, they emerged at the whispering gallery.

Tom sat Bel down and said: 'Place your cheek to the wall, and wait there.' Once he was on the opposite side of the dome, he pressed his face to the stone and whispered: 'Bel . . . Bel . . . can you hear me?' Bel's eyes opened wide in surprise.

'Tom?' she said, and he waved a hand. 'Is it really you?'

'Tell me a secret,' he whispered.

I adore you, she thought. *I think of you, all the time.*

'I'm scared of heights,' she said.

'Don't be. I'm here.' He strode around the dome, his gaze fixed on her. They walked on together through the hushed corridors until they were alone, and Tom ushered her through a doorway, into a narrow staircase leading up.

'Where are we going?' she said.

'To the best view in London.' He took her hand. 'Let me go first, I'll help you across.'

'Across where?' Bel said, clambering after him high into the dome, lifting her skirts clear. She cried out as he leapt across a sheer drop between staircases. 'Tom! Be careful!'

'Don't look down,' he said, holding out his hands to her.

'Too late,' Bel said, clinging to the banister. 'I can't. I can't do it.'

'Trust me.'

So she looked into his eyes, and leapt.

Lot 21

PARIS, 25 JULY 1985

'What do you feel like?' Ned said, pulling out a stool for Mira at the counter. 'Sushi, sashimi?'

'No idea. You order,' she said. A waiter appeared at his side.

'*Bonjour,*' Ned said. '*Des sushis, s'il vous plait—*'

'You would like a selection, sir?' the waiter said. 'May I recommend a carafe of the house *saké*?'

'Thank you.' Ned leant towards Mira after he swept away. 'See? Even the waiter replies in English, my French is so appalling.' She laid her white linen napkin on the counter and took out the silver journal. 'You will be careful with that?' Ned said.

'Relax, I'm an art historian, I know what I'm doing,' she said. 'The beginning is all about Liberty.' Mira smiled to herself, turning the pages. 'I just want to read you this passage. I'll translate it as best I can.'

~

What I Loved

In all the years of your life, the countless days and moments of your existence, what do you remember? What stays with you? A handful of memories to which you return again and again. A first kiss. A leap into the unknown.

Hiro told me you have no memories before the age of four. I disagree. I remember clearly things from when I was two, or younger, even. I remember watching my father and his friends painting in a field in Le Havre. I remember Monet's striped jacket. I remember the feel of the black mourning sash on my dress.

I remember.

How is it passing asides stick with us like splinters or rose thorns – surface wounds embedded deep. The thorn in my side, the snag, the catch, is this. I was never enough. I always felt I had to compensate for the loss of my mother. How can one girl make up for that? My mother died in childbirth, and no one thought I'd survive. My cry surprised them all.

That is one of the main advantages of being a woman. So little is expected of us, we always have the element of surprise on our side.

Now it is the winter of 1890, frigid and miserable. My boots are soaked with slush, and Paris is choked with the scent of damp coal fires. What will Genji remember of this? I hope he remembers the colour of sunrise on snow, the warmth of our hearth at night, the stories I read to him by lamplight of magic foxes and their secret fire.

When he sleeps, I pore over copies of Vogue sent over from America. I wish to understand what women want now, in fashion, books, art, theatre, for our clothes are influenced by all the arts.

Women have two ways to show who they are and who they want to be – in their clothes and in their home. My designs are versatile, for all the women they wish to be. I wish to give my women what they never knew they wanted. One has to dress every day so it may as well be pleasurable and amusing, practical and comfortable. Life is hard enough – I will take care of my women.

Be discriminating! Be impossible! Be demanding!

I am learning all I can. I am noticing all I can. I am paying attention.

A journal is a vessel for emotion, good and bad. Hiro read to me several times from the 'Pillow Book of Sei Shōnagon', translating the Japanese for me. I love her wit, her discerning eye. This is what I wish to record in this journal.

This is my pillow book.

A record of what I loved.

BB

~

Mira tucked the book away carefully as the waiter returned with their food.

'A pillow book,' Ned said thoughtfully. 'So that's what it is.'

'Explain?'

'It's more than a diary.' He smiled his thanks as the waiter bowed and left. 'Pillow books often collated journal pages, to show a lifetime of experience and observations.'

'So it only records important events and moments in her life?' Mira nodded. 'That's why it's so slim and the entries jump in time.'

'And there's the Japanese link again.' Ned opened a small notebook, writing quickly. 'The names . . . Hiro, Genji. Sounds like he was her son *and* heir?' He breathed a laugh. 'Books again – the *Tale of Genji*?'

'Afraid I haven't read it.'

'Only the first novel ever written, and by a woman. Everyone always says Cervantes was first, but Murasaki Shikibu beat him to it a thousand years ago.'

'If Genji was a baby in 1890, he must have been in his nineties when he died?' Mira checked her notes. 'Good genes. Hiro Kurosaki lived 'til he was over a hundred.'

'See, sushi *is* good for you.'

'How did you find this place?' Mira asked, snapping apart a pair of chopsticks.

'It's been around since the fifties,' Ned said, pouring her a cup of hot *saké*. 'My dad brought me here.' He smiled, seeing her uncertainty, chopsticks hovering over the plate of food. The tuna fish gleamed, pink and succulent. 'I wasn't sure at first, either, but trust me, you'll love it.' He mixed some wasabi paste in soy sauce, and dipped a piece of tuna in it, passing the plate to Mira. 'Allow me,' he said.

She ate, her eyes widening in surprise. The fish melted in her mouth.

'That's fantastic,' she said. Mira took a sip of the *saké* and coughed. 'Crikey that's strong.' The waiter placed two black lacquer bowls of soup before them, and bowed. Mira leant forward and inhaled the rich steam.

'Miso.' Ned lifted the bowl in his cupped hands and sipped.

'What's the green bit?'

'Seaweed. I know, trust me – it's really good for you.' Mira held her bowl up, and turned it to the light, the gold leaf in the lacquer gleaming.

'What happened to Isobel . . .' she said, thinking aloud.

'I asked the lawyers, but they're being very cagey. The Kurosakis are a prominent family. Like a lot of Japanese clients, they keep their private life entirely private.'

'We have five days to find out fifty years of secrets,' Mira said. 'If you're in agreement, while you do the initial sweep through the apartment, cataloguing the furniture with Serge, I'm going to focus on the journal to see if I can piece together her story.'

'You wrote your thesis on Maison Bright?'

'Yes. That was her big fashion house, on Place Vendôme. I came across some of her Liberty-era designs in the V&A archives.'

'What was special about her stuff?'

'Her *stuff?*' Mira said indignantly. 'She was ahead of her time. Total lifestyle. She knew what women really wanted. Beauty, comfort, practicality. I mean, she put pockets in *all* her clothes—'

'Okay.' Ned held up his hands in surrender. 'See what you can decipher in the book. Then we can focus on the paintings and smaller pieces together?'

Mira thought of Isobel's description of her childhood. *There's Isobel the child. Isobel the mother in the Picasso portrait. Isobel the wanton woman in Schiffer's erotic painting.* She frowned. *It's like piecing together a jigsaw. Who are you?*

'Thank you,' she said.

'What for?'

'Treating me as a colleague.'

'Perhaps I like working with you, Hutch.' Ned took another piece of sushi. 'C'mon, eat some more? I've been known to have a plate of sushi then order the same again.'

'I'm good,' she said, looking out across the tables. She spotted an elderly lady sitting alone, dressed in Chanel. For every bite of fish she took, she covertly fed the rest to the Shih Tzu sitting beneath the table. Mira glanced at Ned as he savoured the meal, and thought of a passage she had stopped at flicking through the journal:

> *When will I see you? This summer, or next? I want to suck the marrow from life with you, eat up the days. With luck, we have years and years to come. We have endless summers. No more goodbyes. No more tears.*

She swallowed down the knot in her throat with a sip of *saké*, the cup warm in her hand. 'Have we got time for a quick walk? I want to call into Shakespeare and Company.'

~

They strolled along the Avenue de l'Opéra, down through the crowds of tourists queuing for the Louvre. The morning's mist had burned off, and the Seine sparkled beneath the Pont des Arts. 'I haven't been here for years,' Mira said, as they walked along the Quai Saint-Michel, cutting down to the bookshop on rue de la Bûcherie.

'Were you looking for something in particular?' he asked, holding open the door.

'A copy of Sei Shōnagon.'

Ned beckoned for her to follow him. 'Sure I spotted one in the back the other evening.' They squeezed through the narrow aisles, and he searched the shelves. 'There you go,' he said, passing Mira a copy. 'You don't mind second hand?'

'No, I prefer it if anything,' she said, flicking through the pages. 'I love finding the notes people have left, or the inscriptions.' She glanced up at Ned, and tapped the page. 'Look, someone's underlined "Elegant Things".' *Shaved ice, silver bowl, rock crystal.* 'It feels like a conversation.' Mira reached for her wallet. 'Thank you for finding it.'

'Allow me,' Ned said, taking the book from Mira. 'My dad used to borrow books from Sylvia Beach here. He'd never forgive me if I let you buy your own book.'

'I can't—'

'Please, Hutch. A souvenir from Paris.' He picked up a new red notebook at the cash desk. 'Just in case you feel like writing your own pillow book.'

'Thank you,' she said as they stepped outside.

'We should get back.' Ned hailed a cab.

'Who knows what Serge has sent off to Drouot while we've been at lunch.'

'If I know Serge, he won't be back yet. His crew takes lunch *very* seriously.'

As the taxi whisked them back to Montmartre, Mira passed Ned a pen and the book. 'So I'll always remember.'

Ned took them from her, and turned to a blank page at the start of the book. *Not a flamboyant hand*, Mira imagined Kim saying, *but clear and even, a good slant to the right*. He closed the book and passed it to her.

'*To Dependable Things*?' Mira read. Below, Ned had written: *NB, Paris, 1985*

'You'll see,' he said, smiling.

Lot 22

JAPAN, 1888

They sailed from Tilbury in December 1888. These were days of sunlight on water, of fresh sea air and candlelit Christmas meals, of conversation, of laughter, of Tom. Always Tom. He was the last thought as Bel fell asleep in her bunk at night, and the first as she woke, well rested and humming with life. The weeks of clean air away from the soot and stench of London made her skin and hair shine.

I wish we could sail on forever, she thought, standing on deck watching the coast of Nagasaki draw closer. She thought of all they had seen in Egypt, the vivid green of Ceylon, the bustling streets of Hong Kong. Tom and the Libertys stood beside her, with Hiro at a distance. Noticing the grim set of his face, she went to join him.

'Hiro,' she asked, 'are you not happy to be home? You will see your family?'

'Yes, my uncle's family in Kyoto.' He glanced at Bel. 'I look forward to showing you my country.'

'Change of plan there,' Arthur said. 'There is so much to see I think it best if we divide our party. Mr Kurosaki, you will travel with Mrs Liberty and I in Kyoto and Osaka, and introduce us to everyone you know. Mr Holme and Mr East will join our party, and we shall focus on buying stock for the shop.' Hiro bowed, his expression unreadable. 'Miss Bright, Mr Ferris, you shall go on to Tokyo, and explore the area north. Buy any items you come across but concentrate on sketching and inspiration for your own designs.'

'Yes, Mr Liberty,' Bel said.

'I understand it is a comfortable journey now. You know, in 1868 the Emperor took a month to travel three hundred miles by palanquin? What a strange and beautiful procession that must have been. If only we had seen Japan before the adoption of Western dress and travel by so many.' He rubbed his hands together gleefully. 'But we shall travel faster. I so admire Japanese confidence and industriousness. I cannot wait to see their innovations. A friend from Tokyo said to me: "*We are on a tiger's back, and the tiger is charging – we must cling on.*"'

'Sounds rather alarming,' Tom said.

'I've sent ahead for a local guide to meet you both at the port—'

'We shall be travelling alone?' Bel interrupted.

'You are travelling on business together, with a local guide,' Arthur said. 'We have much to achieve and much to buy so we must divide and conquer. I trust Mr Ferris will take good care of you.'

'As you wish.' Bel looked up at Tom, thrilled and afraid.

Perhaps our journey is just beginning.

Lot 23

JAPAN, 1889

In Tokyo, Bel and Tom explored the great shrines, walking gravel paths among pilgrims in dark kimonos and wooden geta sandals. They lit incense in the sand-filled sensers around the great Bonsho bell at Senso-ji, and had their fortunes told with divining sticks. They spent hours at the craft stalls around the temple, buying samples of ceramics, masks and fans to send back to London.

'Do you think it quite right that we are exporting the culture?' Bel said to Tom as they walked.

'It's hardly as if we are looting the country,' he said, laughing. 'We are paying a fair price and our customers demand novelty.'

'What shrine is this?' she asked the guide, looking at a seated statue of an elderly man decked with raffia sandals. The kindness of his expression drew her to him.

'Binzuru,' the guide explained. 'He was saintly but broke his vow of chastity by noticing a beautiful woman.' The guide gestured at the temple's outer court. 'The Buddha showed forgiveness, and gave him the power to cure all human ills.'

'Why so many shoes?'

'The *riksha* coolies make offerings of old sandals hoping for strong feet. On a long journey they may go through two or three pairs of sandals.'

'Is that why the roadsides are littered with them?' Bel smiled. 'I wondered.'

In the evening, after visiting a Kabuki theatre, their guide took them to a bar in a side street where red lanterns glowed like fireflies in the mist. They turned off the main road, a tram clanging its way down the centre. Ragpickers worked in the shadows near a stack of empty *saké* tubs, a woman hauling laundry up on poles above the wooden houses. It made Bel think of the mews in London, the lamplighters and knocker-ups, Mrs Harris working night and day cleaning other people's dirty laundry. *A world away, but people are just the same.*

'Cha-ya, nightclub?' the guide said, pushing aside a split noren curtain, and ushering them forward. In the corner of the bar two large men sat drinking quietly. One reached into the fold of his kimono.

'Be careful,' Tom whispered, smiling. 'He could hide anything in there. A sword—'

'Honestly!' Bel glanced at the men. She noticed how beautiful the young man's skin was. He radiated health, an apricot flush to his skin from the *saké*.

'I'm not going to ask what he's searching for,' Tom murmured. 'The fellow is a wrestler, a sumo. He'd make mincemeat of me.'

A group of businessmen already sat at the table with two women. Servants in dark kimonos brought refreshments for them, kneeling at the low table.

'She is *maiko*,' the guide said, pointing to the younger girl, who bowed to Bel and Tom.

'Maiko?' Bel said.

'A trainee geisha. This is her sister, very famous.' Bel studied the women closely. The younger girl had more vivid make-up. Her skin was entirely white, except for a forked V at the nape of her neck. Her lips were startling red.

'The women wish to talk to you,' he said. 'The first thing a geisha is taught is to be charming to other women.'

After the meal had been served, and the men were contentedly smoking pipes, the women rushed to Bel's side and took her to a quiet corner, with the guide translating.

'*Konnichiwa*,' Bel said, bowing.

'You speak Japanese?' the geisha said, delighted.

'*Hai*. A little. My friend, Chō-san, taught me.' Bel smiled at her.

'I have never seen a Western woman before,' the younger girl said, taking Bel's hand in hers, turning it over in wonderment. 'Your hair is like fire. May I?' she reached out a hand, and patted Bel like a doll. The geisha chided her gently, and the girl sat back. '*Sumimasen,* excuse me,' she said.

'I am fascinated by your dress,' Bel said. 'And your cosmetics.'

'We make a cream with nightingale droppings,' the geisha said. 'And a little red, in places. Our eyes we use charcoal. A simple palette.'

'But so dramatic. Your neck?'

'We make "three legs" here,' She gestured to her nape. 'A little bare skin is attractive.'

'Tell me about your kimono,' Bel said. 'I am curious, how are yours constructed?'

'Beneath we wear a silk slip, *koshimaki*. Then underrobes and padding for structure,' she said. 'A white silk collar, and white tabi.' She extended an elegant toe. 'We have dressers to help with folding the kimono and tying the obi.' She slipped a silver fan from the belt, and offered it to Bel, bowing. 'Please accept this as a gift to our honoured guest.'

'Thank you, how beautiful,' Bel said, admiring it.

'Fans are sacred,' the guide said quietly. 'It is a great honour.'

'I shall treasure it.' Bel tilted her head, and removed one of her tortoiseshell pins, offering it to the geisha. She laughed in delight, and slipped it into her hair. 'Do tell me, why are you dressed differently?'

'I am geisha,' the woman said, kneeling back so that Bel could see her obi clearly. 'She is *maiko*, in our *okiya* – our geisha house. I am her big sister.'

'You are related?'

'No, no,' the girl said, giggling behind her hand. 'I am

introducing her now, so that we will find a *danna* to pay for her *mizuage*.'

'What is that?' Bel asked the guide.

'A man who will deflower her,' he said, clearing his throat.

'Oh?' Bel said, surprised.

'It is a great privilege to be the first man with a geisha.'

'But you are not . . .' Bel hesitated. 'In London, we have women who men pay for their bodies.'

'No, no. Geisha are artists – we are musicians, dancers, companions.' She gestured at her *shamisen* lute, and turned over her pale hand. 'When I was young, I made my hands tough with ice water, so I can play music for hours. To be geisha takes devotion, discipline.'

'I hear that melancholy in your music.'

'Sometimes we have *danna* – a sponsor. But men pay for our company, that is all. The tea houses pay the geisha office, and then our geisha house is paid. When the house takes on a young girl, the girl owes them a great debt. I was indentured to our house for ten years, for thirty yen. It can take many years to pay what you owe for board and kimonos.'

'And when you have?'

'Then you can choose. Continue, or leave the house. Some geisha marry, some begin their own business.'

'What will you do?' Bel said, as Tom walked over.

'I will have my own restaurant, be an old and wealthy Mama-san,' she whispered, covering her mouth and giggling, flashing her eyes at Tom.

'Bel, we have an early start,' Tom said, offering her his

hand. 'Sayonara, ladies.' They took their leave, bowing, and put their shoes back on before stepping out into the street. A night soil man shuffled past with his buckets on a pole, gathering fertiliser, and Bel pressed her handkerchief to her nose. In the shadows of the rainy night, the willow and pine trees dripped quietly. The guide gestured to the carriage waiting for them, and Bel clambered up.

What an extraordinary place, she thought, looking up at the night sky as they travelled to their hotel. *Even the constellations are different. I have never felt so at sea, anywhere. So unmoored.* She looked at Tom. *So free.*

Lot 24

JAPAN, 1889

North-west of Tokyo, their guide brought them to the Kusatsu hot springs. 'To understand Japan, you must experience *onsen*, the ritual of bathing,' he said. 'Few people have their own bathrooms, so they go to public bath houses.'

'Like the Turkish bath I frequent in London?' Tom asked.

'What is that smell?' Bel asked. 'Sulphur?'

'Yes, very good. Very clean. You see – people come clean too. Talk very easy in *onsen*.' The guide gestured to the attendant, who handed them each a cotton yukata and a wash cloth. 'Leave clothes here,' he said, guiding them to a locker room.

'Is there no bathing pond for women alone?' She looked around her in surprise, as an elderly man paced past in nothing but slippers, a tiny washcloth covering his modesty. Nearby, a woman squatted, scrubbing the back of an older woman while a chubby baby nestled against her in a papoose.

'I'm game if you are,' Tom said.

'When in Rome,' Bel said, raising an eyebrow.

In the changing room, she hung up her heavy coat, her hat. Layer by layer she removed her clothes, like peeling petals from a flower. *He loves me . . . he loves me not . . .* she thought, unbuttoning the tight cuffs and collar of her high-necked blouse. Her wide, heavy skirts fell away, then the petticoats, and she loosened the busk of her corset. She felt so light, suddenly, standing in just her chemise, it was dizzying, as if her limbs lifted in the air of their own accord in the misty light.

Bel bathed first with a hinoki cypress wood tub, washing away the dust of the journey with a sea sponge. When she emerged a few minutes later, she found their guide waiting for her. He wore the same cotton yukata gown as Bel.

'No, no,' he said, gesturing to Bel's yukata. 'Right lapel go under. If on top you dead. Come,' he said, bowing. Women and men walked easily around the bath house, washing before entering the hot springs. There was no shame, no ogling. *It's extraordinary. The most natural thing in the world*, she thought.

Once the women had cleaned themselves, they went out to the hot springs, following a path of stepping stones. The old woman beckoned to Bel. Here the air was fresh and strongly scented. Bel felt as though she shone, her body humming with life. 'Very hot,' the guide said, a little unnecessarily Bel thought, watching the steam billowing from the spring.

'We sit? In there?' Bel said, concerned. 'Do you boil like lobsters?'

'It's marvellous,' Tom said. The steam parted, and she saw him, submerged to his chin at the far side of the pool between an elderly Japanese couple. 'Best to get straight in and sit down before you think about it too much. Then stay perfectly still.'

Bel took a deep breath and threw off her gown, stepping down into the water without stopping. Tom laughed at the expression on her face. 'My god, my god – it's so hot,' she gasped. 'It cannot be good for you.'

'Stay still. You'll feel wonderful soon.'

The old woman settled beside Bel as if she were simply stepping into a warm bath. Bel's head reeled with the heat. *Shall I faint?*

'People have come here for centuries,' the guide said. 'In Nagano, there are springs where the monkeys come and sit when it snows.' As Bel's mind settled, she realised suddenly that she was sitting almost naked in a pool in the middle of Japan with perfect strangers. And Tom. She kept her feet very still, afraid of bumping anyone. The old man placed a towel across his forehead, and his wife gestured for Bel to do the same. She caught Tom's eye for a moment. Desire flowed between them like a sigh in the steam. Bel closed her eyes, lost in thoughts of him, imagined the other people disappearing one by one to leave them alone. *Tom.* She let her head fall back, and surrendered to the heat, to desire.

Lot 25

JAPAN, 1889

They rode out across the cobalt hills to Urami, the guide leading the way. The horses clopped past noblemen and their retainers, past priests and farmers on the road. Bel saw tattooed coolies in loincloths carrying heavy loads of rice and wood, and groups of women going out to the fresh green fields with children strapped to their backs. It was too early for the chirrup of insects, only the coo of wood pigeons breaking the cool dawn air from the avenues of trees. Bel rode astride – she wore a pair of culottes she had bought from a trader beneath a linen kimono. The clear air, the scent of pine crushed beneath the horses' hooves, the drip of rain in the trees enlivened her. Around them the rising sun lit the dew-soaked rice fields like sheets of gold leaf. Bel reined in her horse, and stared at the landscape. She felt absolutely present. Bel thought of something Hiro said once to her: *If you only pay attention, you see the radiance of everyday life shimmering below the surface.* Bel felt something profound move in her, a numinous sense of some understanding so tantalisingly close she could almost grasp it. *Is this life? Is this joy?* Ahead of them a dark figure walked with a white parasol. Tom rode behind her, and as the path widened, he trotted to catch up, coming abreast. The track led to a fresh green meadow, speckled with wild flowers.

'You ride well,' he said.

'For a girl?' Bel cast him a quick smile, the glimmer of insight passing. Since the baths the tension between them coursed like electricity. She kicked in her heels. The horses gathered speed, and she lowered her head, galloping across the green meadow. Tom flicked his reins and cried out, urging his horse on. The sun and the wind and the day were theirs.

A narrow path led down the gorge, a sheer descent of one hundred feet. Bel kept her feet out of the stirrups, ready to jump if her horse slipped on the steep, rocky path. She was breathless, alert, her body quick and alive, aching for Tom's touch. Bright azaleas dotted the valley and she ducked down to miss the branches reaching out to them. At the river, Bel leapt down to let her horse rest, and the guide laid out a picnic for them on a blanket. She bit into a sweet apricot, watching a group of women washing laundry on the bank, beating the sheets clean on the rocks. A woman in an indigo kimono crossed the white bridge, balancing a basket of clothes. Thunder rumbled in the hills, but Tom sent the guide on ahead with the promise that they would catch up before nightfall, and meet at the ryokan not far up the track at Chuzenji.

Tom led the horses to the river, their hooves ringing on the silver pebbles beneath the shallow rushing water. Upstream a waterfall tumbled down from rocks into a deep green pool. 'I've sent the guide on,' he called to Bel as she wandered over.

'Have you?' she said. Her breath seemed loud to her. 'Why?' Bel's hair had come loose riding, and she brushed it back from her face. Time slowed as Tom walked over to her and cupped her face in his free hand.

'Because I wanted to be alone with you, Bel,' he said, looking down at her. *Kiss me*, she thought. *Kiss me, Tom.*

'What would they say in London?'

'We're far from home, Bel.' He gazed down at her. 'All these weeks with you, all we have shared. I can't deny my feelings for you any more—'

My feelings? Bel's heart surged with joy. *At last, he declares himself!* Not wanting to rush now the moment was here, she turned away from him and tethered her horse to a nearby low branch. Tom followed suit, and unbuckled his saddle-bag. A black swallowtail butterfly looped through the sweet air beneath the canopy of trees, and Bel followed its path, shielding her eyes.

'Damn. I wish I had my net,' he said.

'I thought chaps like you always travelled prepared. You have more bags than I do.'

'Chaps like me?' Tom laughed. 'I always travel with a necessaire of brandy, at least,' he said, taking out a hipflask. 'Would you care for a tot? It might restore you after the ride?'

Bel sipped the liquor, holding his gaze. It burned her throat, filled her with warmth. 'Better?'

Bel nodded and turned away from the group of women, licking the brandy from her lips. She walked along the river out of sight, her feelings tumbling over one another like the water rolling over the glossy black stones. A fine warm rain fell, misting her upturned face.

'Wet again,' Tom said, looking up at the sky. Her heart beat high in her chest, and she heard his footsteps close behind her. 'As we're soaked, shall we swim?'

'Tom—'

'Trust me. I have the greatest respect for you, Bel. I would never take advantage of you.' He tossed his hat onto the grass. The rain darkened his hair, his shirt clung to his shoulders. He walked on towards the waterfall, kicking off his boots and socks. He grinned back at her as he loosened his neck tie and threw it onto the grass. 'But when in Japan . . . ?'

Why not? Bel loosened her kimono jacket. Beneath it she wore a simple chemise with her culottes. *No one will know*, a small voice said. *You are here, alone, with him. With Tom.* In turn they shed their clothes. Bel raised her foot to a rock, and loosened her garter, rolling down one stocking, then another. The muslin chemise clung to her wet body, her hair, her lips misted with rain.

'I feel like Adam and Eve before the fall.' Tom stepped towards her.

'Turn aside,' she said. 'Somehow this feels different, from the bath house.'

'Because we are alone?' he said, turning. 'It's the most natural thing in the world—' Tom glanced back at the sound of a splash. Bel's clothes lay abandoned on the bank of the pool, and a fine ripple spread where she had dived in. Quickly he undressed and followed her, breaking the water cleanly.

'It's glorious.' Bel surfaced a little distance from the falls, laughing, and wiped the cool water from her face.

'Wait for me.' He swam over and gathered her in his arms.

'I've waited years,' she said, touching his face.

'I want to remember this moment forever.' Something in his voice troubled her. Bel pushed it to the back of her mind. She was here, with Tom, and everything she had dreamed of night after lonely night was hers.

'I love you, Tom,' she said. 'I think I've loved you from the first moment I saw you.'

'Bel . . .' Tom kissed her then, their bodies quick and alive in the cool water. '*Aishiteru*, is that not what they say here?'

Bel pushed away from him, and swam towards the waterfall. He climbed out, and offered her his hand, leading her to a ledge hidden behind the falls. It was cool, and quiet with the rush of the water shielding them from the world, and the moss and ferns were soft against her skin as they lay down.

Lot 26

PARIS, 26 JULY 1985

'Mahogany coiffeuse and chair by Louis Majorelle,' Ned said to his assistant, who was writing the inventory. 'Gilt detail, nice central inlay of orchids. $2,000–3,000. To Tokyo.' He nodded as Mira walked past fanning herself with a silver paper fan. 'Next item, French mahogany double bed, inlaid with various fruit woods, depicting cherry blossom. $4,000–6,000.' Ned frowned as Mira unrolled a rag rug on the kitchen counter. 'Okay? Thank you, that's it for today. Most of the big pieces are already on their way to the packers. See you bright and early on Monday.' He turned to Mira. 'Where did you find that filthy old thing?'

'In the bedside cabinet with this fan.' She tilted her neck, letting the cool air reach her throat. 'Serge was about to throw it away.'

'I don't blame him.'

'But it must have been important to Isobel.'

'We can't afford to be sentimental. It's the weekend. We

only have three days next week to finish up.' He lifted two entwined dog collars from the rug, one with a silver V, the other with an engraved S. 'Not much of a market for these. This is more like it,' he said, pointing at a silver cigarette case on the counter. 'Fabergé, cloisonné enamelled irises. Sapphire push button. $1,250–1,750.' He looked closer at the other items. 'If I'm not mistaken, that little group of animals are Fabergé, too.'

'Fabergé made frogs?'

'All sorts of amusing gifts, not just the eggs.'

'Aren't you going to ask me what else was wrapped in the rug?' Mira said, pulling out a silver and enamel picture frame from beneath it. Ned leant over her shoulder to look closer.

'Liberty & Co.' He checked the hallmark with a loupe. 'Birmingham, 1902. $200–500.'

'Not the frame, the photo,' Mira said, nudging him. A young woman looked down at a dark-haired baby on her lap, her face obscured by the shadow of her wide picture hat. 'Isobel and Genji.'

'Do you think so?'

'Has to be. The Picasso in the hall, mother and child.'

'Where's Monsieur BB in all this?'

'Maybe we'll find out on Monday.' Mira stretched wearily.

'What are your plans this evening?' Ned said as he locked up. 'I was going to catch a movie at La Pagode, if you feel like it?'

'I'm . . .' Mira thought of the empty apartment waiting for her. *What's the harm?* She remembered his inscription in *The*

Pillow Book, which she'd looked up. '*In life there are two things which are dependable,*' Sei Shōnagon wrote a thousand years ago, '*the pleasures of sex and the pleasures of literature.*' She held Ned's gaze steadily. 'Sure, I'd love to.'

Lot 27

JAPAN, MARCH 1889

'I wish we could stay forever,' Tom said to Bel. They stood side by side on the dockside in Yokohama, the lights of the ship soaring above them. The soft air shimmered, taut with longing between them. 'I wish we could stay far from the world, away from everything except love—'

Love. Bel remembered watching families sitting on tarpaulins beneath the cherry trees in Ueno Park, the *sakura* blossom falling around them. Mr Liberty's lecture at the School of Art at the end of their trip had been a triumph. But it wasn't the pomp and ceremony, the British Ambassador, the Foreign Minister that impressed her. It was the ordinary people of Tokyo, singing songs and sharing *saké* beneath the trees she found so touching. *This illusory, floating world.*

'We cannot stay,' Bel said. *I wish we could,* she thought, looking down at where her hand rested on the rail beside his, the decorous space between them charged, aching. On their journey to Tokyo what felt like a lifetime ago, they had stopped at the Jishu Shrine near Kyoto. She had walked the stones in front of the main hall. *True love will come*, their guide promised her. Eighteen paces in a straight line with her eyes closed as the guide instructed, chanting the name of her beloved under her breath: *Tom, Tom, Tom.* When she opened her eyes he was watching her. She looked up at him now.

'These weeks have been the most wonderful time of my life. I shall never forget.'

'Tom?' Bel frowned. Something in his words sounded like an ending, not the beginning she hoped for.

'There they are!' Arthur Liberty waved his hat, Emma on his arm. The steamship towered over them, coal loading on from the dockside. Porters ferried trunks and luggage chalked up for the voyage onto the ship. The air was alive with noise, the tang of fish and salt. 'Our adventurers return.' He shook Tom's hand and embraced Bel. 'I've just seen your guide. Was everything quite to your liking?'

'Thank you, Mr Liberty,' Bel said.

'Inspiring, I hope? We have had a marvellous trip, most enlightening. Mr Kurosaki did a splendid job explaining the culture to us.'

'Sir,' he said, striding over, his gaze on Bel.

'Let us embark and we can trade our tales over a bottle of champagne in the saloon before your ship leaves,' Arthur said, leading the way. 'Mrs Liberty and I depart for San Francisco tomorrow.'

'Bel,' Hiro said, bowing.

'Hiro! Oh, I've missed you!' she said, taking his hands in hers. 'We've had the most marvellous trip, haven't we, Tom.'

'Your land is remarkable.' He looked down at Bel, his face softening. 'I shall remember it forever.'

'There is so much I hoped to show you,' Hiro said, not looking from Bel.

'We saw such things,' Emma said, her face lighting up. 'The temples at Ryōan-ji, and Kinkaku-ji. The silk farms! The mulberry trees reminded me of the apple orchards when I was a girl. I joined Mr Liberty in Kyoto after travelling there by ricksha. We saw such wonders—'

'There are many places not known to tourists, Bel,' Hiro said, unable to hide his disappointment. 'Perhaps next time I shall show you.'

'We came up to Yokohama on a little steamboat yesterday,' Emma said, taking Bel's arm. 'It was rather grim. We had to leap aboard one by one, in such rough seas.'

'Did you see Mount Fuji on the way past?'

'Sadly, no, too foggy. I must say I am rather glad to be booked into the Grand Hotel until our ship departs.' She clutched Bel's hand. 'Did you feel the small earthquake this morning? My chandelier was swinging!'

As Emma bustled onto the gangplank, porters wheeled Bel and Tom's cases onto the ship behind. Hiro stepped back, a simple gladstone bag in his hand. Bel was aware of him, watching her. She looked from Tom to Hiro. One so charming and amusing, the other a steady constant. Devoted. Always. *Taken for granted?* She thought of Hiro in the way that occasionally you become aware of your own pulse, your heartbeat.

'Come,' Arthur Liberty said, beckoning the group forward. 'Let's retire to the lounge. Mr Kurosaki, I am eternally grateful. If I loved the art and crafts of your country before, I have grown to love the land itself, thanks to you.' He gestured to Bel. 'Yesterday we saw the most marvellous *kiyomizu-yaki* pottery, with *noborigama* furnaces built on a slope. Quite ingenious how many pots the fellows can get in a single firing . . .'

'I wish I had seen it,' Bel said to Hiro. 'I wish I'd seen it all through your eyes.'

'You saw the cherry blossom?' he said. But then Tom drew Bel to his side, and Hiro looked from one to the other, understanding.

'Hiro—' she said, but he walked on ahead, gathering his dark robes around him.

Lot 28

LONDON, MAY 1889

In spring, the dawn . . . Bel remembered the line when Hiro read Sei Shōnagon to her. *It is good to be back.* She strolled along Regent Street early on Monday morning, swinging her parasol, Sally trotting at her side. It felt like all of London was hers. *And Tom's.* It was a warm day, and she wore a linen wrap blouse she had designed, tucking it in a deep pink velvet waist sash, like a Japanese obi belt. *I hope he likes it.* She had stitched a new plume of ostrich feathers on her wide straw hat, a simple but striking effect. *In spring, the dawn . . .*

She felt she was seeing London for the first time. Bel had always felt a sense of disconnection returning from France or Italy, but returning home was not such a shock as this. Now everything was different. The days exploring Japan with Tom felt like a distant dream. She remembered low wooden buildings, and quiet cedar woods, gravel paths, and lamplight gleaming on dark lacquer. The ryokan. Spring rain on the eaves. She thought of Tom, the gentle slide of shoji screens, of lying with him, watching him sleep at her side. For the first time, she had known pleasure with a man. *No more shame.*

But what now? she wondered. It had felt like the dawn of something new, something wonderful. *Why have I not heard from him?* Bel knocked on the staff door and waited. *Not a letter? A postcard, even?*

Liberty was bustling, everyone cooing with excitement over the boxes from Japan like pigeons around bowls of seed. The wooden crates took up half of one room, still with their chalk marks from Yokohama.

'Miss Bright!' William Judd cried. 'Welcome back. We've started opening the crates so you can talk us all through your finds.' He held up a fine gilded screen with a painting of wild geese flying, perfect in its simplicity.

Bel remembered standing on the deck of the ship, Tom beside her, watching swallows following the passage. She remembered sailors scrubbing the boards, the scent of metal polish. *There's something wrong.* She held on to her fragile happiness. *It's funny, isn't it, you expect life to just get better. Every day an improvement. You expect good fortune to last forever, when there are moments of happiness, that is all.* She remembered how alive she felt, standing at the prow of the ship, salt spray on her skin, the wind whipping her hair. And Tom. Always, Tom. *We all think we know what we are doing, which way we are going, but it's all nonsense, isn't it?* Bel looked at the wild geese, caught for an instant, held forever on the gilded screen, like the memory of Tom, and the boat, and the sea. *Something's wrong, I know it. Where is he?*

'The screen is perfect for the project I have coming up in Belgravia. The client will love it,' Bel said. She glanced around the shop. 'Is Mr Ferris not here?'

'Went to collect a friend who wants to see the treasures,' Judd said, taking an Imari plate from the packing crate. 'Look at them artists. Everyone's here to get the best pickings.'

'It's like Christmas,' Miss Browning said, holding a fine blue bowl up to the light.

'Are these the new silks?' Bel said to her, going over to a display. 'They are too harsh. Either that cerise has to go, or I shall.'

'There's Mr Ferris! Welcome home, sir!' Miss Browning cried, as Tom and Orlando walked in. Bel smiled seeing him. Her gaze fell to the petite blonde woman who walked between them. She was dressed expensively with several ropes of pearls at her throat. The rings glittering on her small, pale fingers were definitely not paste. *Orlando's latest conquest?* she thought. *What of Chō?* She resisted the urge to go to Tom. *No one knows. Only us.* She held their love like a secret gift, tucked in a pocket. Bel smiled and walked slowly across the room towards them.

'Miss Bright,' Orlando said. 'I hear you had a *splendid* time in Japan?' Something in his tone snagged like a thorn. 'I hope you have something for me?'

'We always take care of our best clients, Mr Schiffer,' she said. Bel turned to the young woman. 'Welcome to Liberty.'

'Miss Bright,' Tom said, 'may I introduce my fiancée, Miss Victoria Fraser.'

Lot 29

LONDON, 1889

'Fiancée?' Miss Browning cried. 'Congratulations! You kept that quiet, Mr Ferris.'

'I proposed some months ago, but we waited for Victoria to come of age.' He could not look at Bel. *Fiancée?* She was light-headed with shock.

'We are just betrothed,' Victoria said with a soft Welsh accent, glancing shyly at Tom. 'We don't even have a ring yet, but Tom went straight to my father on his return from his voyage.'

'*Such* romance,' Orlando said, staring at Bel.

'Papa was so delighted he's made over the investment he bought on Launceston Place to us,' Victoria said, bubbling over with excitement. 'We've just been to look at the house with Mr Schiffer, haven't we?'

'Mmm.' Orlando was being unusually quiet. Bel thought of tigers watching in the long grass. She flashed him a quick look. She saw from his expression there was no need for him to pounce. He was just sitting back, waiting.

My old street. My home. My life.

Bel fought to retain her composure. Orlando was still watching her, an amused smile on his face. *He knows*, she thought, her heart shimmering and beating like the wings of a trapped bird against glass. *Tom told him? Boasted to him?* She had to say something. *I can't just stand here.*

'Congratulations, Miss Fraser,' Bel said, steadily.

'Soon to be Mrs Fraser,' she said, beaming.

'Victoria's father asked I take the family name,' Tom said, clearing this throat. *What on earth?* Bel thought.

'Terribly modern of you, old chap.' Orlando sniffed, toying with his kid glove.

'Victoria is an only child, and he wishes that the name continue, with our children,' Tom said, colouring.

Bel stared at him, not believing what she was hearing. The girl was undeniably pretty, with a china doll fineness to her features. *But so young, eighteen at most*, Bel thought, looking from her to Tom, who had gone terribly red.

'Victoria, Miss Bright is the designer I told you about,' he said.

The designer. Bel wondered how it was possible to feel such pain and remain standing.

'I'm thrilled to meet you,' Victoria said. 'Tom says you have the most wonderful taste.'

'You must excuse me,' Bel said. 'I have work to catch up on.'

'Tom has told me all about your adventures in Japan,' Victoria said, touching her arm lightly as she made to leave. *Really?* Bel thought. 'I should so like to hear a woman's perspective of the country. Perhaps you'd care to join me for tea one afternoon?'

'I'm sure Miss Bright is too busy,' Tom said.

'Of course, I'm so sorry.' Victoria looked at Bel with such genuine kindness, she wanted to scream. 'Tom's told me of your circumstances. You are awfully brave, making your own way in life. I do admire it.' She squeezed her hand. 'I am motherless, myself, so we are in quite the same boat.' Her eyes opened wide. 'Though of course, I have my father, still . . .' She smiled up at Tom. 'And now I have you.'

'Excuse me,' Bel said, walking away. Orlando strode quickly after her, weaving through the crowds in the store.

'Miss Bright?' He sped up, as she ignored him, lengthening her pace. 'Oh, Miss Bright,' he said, catching at her arm. She snatched it away. Nearby, an elderly lady was talking to herself in one of the full-length mirrors they had recently installed:

'After you,' she said, peering at the glass through *pince-nez*. 'I say?' She tapped it with the ferrule of her parasol. 'Oh, goodness!'

'May I assist you, madam?' Orlando said.

'Young man, I'm looking for the haberdashery counter,' she said, peering at him. He called over one of the assistants, and set her on her way.

'*Young man* – ha, that's made my day. I do love these old buildings,' he said to Bel, 'but it is a rabbit warren, and your customers are confused by the mirrors daily.'

'Mr Schiffer,' she said, composing herself. 'How may I help you?'

'What do you make of our young Miss Fraser?' He leant against the tall mirror, and Bel had the sweeping sensation that two of him were bearing down on her. 'You know why he's taking her name? Money, of course. Dear Papa is some mill-owning patriarch.'

'I wish Mr Ferris and Miss Fraser every happiness in the world,' she said, her face set firm, although her throat was tight with tears.

'Mr Ferris, is it now?' Orlando leant closer. 'I hear you were rather more intimate in Japan?' She recoiled, smelling the brandy on his breath.

'I don't know what you are suggesting,' she said.

'What does Mr Ferris – Mr Fraser to be – have that I don't, eh?'

'I don't know what you mean.'

'Why are you pining for that boy when you could have me?' He pressed closer.

'What about Chō, sir?' Bel saw something in his expression, a wariness.

'What of her.' Orlando was close enough she felt the heat of him through her thin blouse. 'I want *you*, Bel, I always have, damn it . . .'

'I would not have you if you were the last man on earth,' she said, pushing past.

'You think yourself too good for me?' He breathed a cruel laugh. 'Too good to model for me? Too good for my bed? I'll show you . . .' he called after her.

That girl calls me brave? Bel raged inwardly. *Brave? What choice have I?* In the studio she stemmed an angry tear with the heel of her hand, and gathered up her things. 'Tell Mr Wyburn I am unwell,' she said to the studio manager.

'You do look rather peaky—'

'Women's troubles.' *That will shut him up.* 'I shall work on these drawings at home today.' She grabbed her hat from the coat-stand, running down the back staircase and out into the alleyway, with Sally at her heels. Bel leant against the rough brick wall, shaking with shock and anger. *How could he? Did it mean nothing to Tom? Did I?*

'Bel? Are you alright?' Hiro said on his way in from seeing a client.

'I'm fine, thank you,' she said, her breath shallow and tight.

'No, you're not. How can I help?'

'Imagine!' Bel's lip trembled. 'Tom is getting married.'

'Oh, Bel . . .' Hiro set down his portfolio and took her in his arms, holding her as she sobbed on his shoulder.

'I am such a fool—'

'No. No you are not. He is the fool.' Hiro pressed his lips to the top of her head and closed his eyes. 'I am so sorry.'

Bel stepped back and nodded, unable to speak. She hurried on towards Regent Street. When she glanced back, Hiro was still watching her, his face drawn with concern. *I can't bear it.* She ran on and on, until she stumbled, and dropped her folder in an oily puddle. 'What a mess,' she said to Sally, who looked up at her, tilting her head in concern. 'What am I to do?' she said, kneeling to gather her drawings. The legs of the passers-by and the wheels of the carriages whirled on around them. 'Oh, Sally?' she said, her face contorting in misery. 'I don't know how to do this.' The little dog nudged her hand, and wagged her tail, uncertainly. Bel stroked her soft head. *I love him*, she thought wretchedly. *I love him, and I meant nothing to him?* Seeing the dog's concern, Bel composed herself. 'Of course, you're right.' She stood and dusted herself off, drying her eyes. 'We've survived worse than this, you and I,' she said, glancing down at Sally. 'Deep breath, head high,' she said, and they walked on together through the uncaring streets.

Lot 30

PARIS, 28 JULY 1985

On Sunday morning, Mira freewheeled along the rue des Rosiers at the edge of the Saint-Ouen flea market on the red bicycle she had found in Kim's basement store. As a thunderstorm rolled across Paris, she had stayed up late reading Sei Shōnagon's *Pillow Book* with its lists of wonderful things. Now, as she rode along in the sunshine, Mira gathered fragments of beauty like a child picking blackberries from a summer hedge:

> *Splendid things: Scent of coffee, roasting. Lovers kissing, oblivious. Happy dog in a red coat. Sunlight on sequins. Ned Brookes . . .*

She saw him waiting ahead for her, leaning against a lamp post, and waved her hand. His white shirt gleamed against the dark graffiti-covered shutters behind him, and his hair was damp from the shower still.

'You're late,' he said, tapping his watch.

'No, you're early,' she said, her brakes squealing as she pulled up. 'Kim's concierge passed your message on.'

'Thanks for calling back.' He glanced at her. 'Do anything fun yesterday?'

'I caught up with some friends for lunch, and went to the new Musée Picasso. How about you?'

'All work, no play,' Ned said, pulling a face. 'Though I did bunk off for an hour to check out this place.'

'What was it you wanted to show me?' They walked side by side, and she paused to chain the bike to a railing.

'It's over here,' he said. 'Hopefully they haven't sold them.' Ned gestured to a stall selling vintage fashion. Military greatcoats and twenties flapper dresses with bugle beads glinting in the sunlight swung from the awning of the stall. A couple of Japanese students dressed in tutus and platform heels knelt on the ground rummaging through the baskets of lace and ribbons. Ned leant over the counter and spoke to the stallholder. 'You had a card of buttons, like this,' he said, pointing at the selection of cards on the counter. 'Coloured glass buttons, like bonbons.' She nodded, and searched through the bags behind the desk.

'Et voila,' she said, laying them out on the table. 'I put them aside as you asked.'

'Maison BB? Do you think . . .' Mira said, looking at the butterfly-stamped card. 'I don't believe it.' She held them up to the sunlight. Something changed in that moment. For the first time in months, the colours sang true to her, bright and clear. The buttons were heavy and smooth as marbles, each one a deep jewel colour, engraved with a fine butterfly motif. 'How on earth did you spot them?'

'Are they right, do you think?' Ned said. 'Is it our BB?'

'No, seriously. How did you find them?' Mira smiled at him. 'I can't imagine fashion is your thing?'

'Are you saying I don't make an effort?' He looked down at his well-worn suede loafers and chinos, his crumpled white linen shirt. 'Sheer luck. I was looking for a present for my sister and the colours just jumped out at me.'

'I love them,' Mira said, reaching for her wallet. 'Madame,' she said to the stallholder. 'This brand?'

'1920s,' she said. 'Maison BB.'

'Is that Isobel Bright?'

'Yes. After Maison Bright. Her work is very rare, very collectable now. Once she stood alongside Worth, Vionnet, Poiret.'

'So why doesn't everyone know about her?'

'The brand didn't carry on without her, not like Chanel or Schiaparelli.' She shrugged. 'Fashion became about the ego, the person. And reputations fade. I mean, look at Lelong – hardly anyone outside fashion knows his name now, but he was a great couturier.'

She handed some change to Mira, and they strolled away. The buttons made her think of wonderful things – jars of boiled sweets, Christmas lights. 'Thank you for finding them.' She tilted her head. 'They just make you happy, don't they?'

'They're hand-blown,' Ned said. 'Each one is a mini work of art. She knew what she was doing, our BB.' He gestured towards the Métro. 'Talking of which, I should be getting back to the hotel. We have a lot to catalogue tomorrow – I have a long night ahead.'

Mira patted her satchel. 'Me too. I'm hoping there are more clues in Isobel's book.' She unlocked the bicycle. 'There's something I don't get. It covers nearly fifty years, but it's so slim. You'd expect volumes, wouldn't you?'

'Not everyone is Pepys.' Ned shrugged. 'Maybe this Bel Bright wasn't much of a diarist, or she only wrote about the juicy bits? Most people only record the big events for posterity, good and bad, and she said this was a pillow book.'

'Perhaps.'

'You really care about her work, don't you?'

'It just feels like everyone should know about her.' Mira looked up at Ned. 'How can someone like that just disappear? I'm determined we're going to do her story justice.'

'Sure we will, Hutch.'

'Thank you.' Mira stood on tiptoe and kissed his cheek. 'See you tomorrow?'

Lot 31

LONDON, MAY 1889

Bel found Chō sitting alone in the café of Fortnum & Mason, a steaming cup of tea in front of her. At the next table, a portly Italian man with a scatter of paper and musical scores around him, sat lost in thought as his hand raced across the page, a copy of Pierre Loti's *Madame Chrysanthème* at his side.

'Chō,' Bel said, kissing her on the cheek and sitting opposite her. 'How are you? I've missed you! Did Hiro give you my gifts?' Sally settled at her feet as she ordered tea. 'He said it was urgent. I thought we were all meeting at the theatre tonight?'

'Urgent?' She smiled, and ran her palm over the swell of her stomach. 'No, we have – oh, a while until it is urgent.'

'You are with child?' Bel said, shocked. She noticed the man at the next table stopped writing, and she leant closer to Chō, lowering her voice. 'Schiffer's?'

'*Hai*. Of course.' Bel thought her usually pale skin

seemed paper thin, blue circles smudging her eyes. 'I wanted to talk to you in private. I told Hiro-san last night. He is so angry.'

'But did you not take precautions, my dear?' Bel whispered. 'Could you not bathe with vinegar, or soak a sponge with alum?'

'I *have* been careful for years. But I told you, Bel. I want this child.' *No gin and hot bath, then?* 'I am happy.'

'Are you well?'

'*Mah mah.*' Chō pulled a face.

'Have you told him?' she whispered.

'Orlando? Yes, I told him when you were away.' Chō raised her chin proudly. 'You do not understand him.' *I do*, Bel thought. *I know him all too well.* 'Hiro-san say he is using me, but he is wrong. Orlando will marry me now.'

'Oh, Chō . . .'

'In Japan women are taught to obey their father, obey their husband, obey their eldest son. I do not want to obey. I am free. He is free. He love me. He tell me he love me many times. He says we go to live in France, and he will paint, and I will paint—'

'And who will take care of the child?' Bel said gently. 'It is always the woman who gives up her life for the family, Chō. How will you paint when you have a baby?'

'I strap him to my back, just like women who work in fields in Japan,' she said. 'He will learn to be artist by watching me work.'

'Chō, babies are exhausting, and demanding, and then

they grow up and you can't just put them in a basket, like Sally.' She gestured at the dog.

'I love him,' Chō said, placing her hand protectively on her stomach. 'He will take care of me, and he will come back for me.'

'Come back?' Bel's heart sank. *Mr Schiffer would sooner take the Queen's shilling. No wonder he had a hunted look when last I saw him.* She glanced over as she saw the Italian man scribble a note. 'Where has he gone?'

'To France, this morning. He says he will come back for me once he finds a house in Toulon . . .' Her voice trailed away.

'The bounder,' Bel said, sitting back. *Toulon? The whole place is riddled with two hundred opium houses. The port will suit that cad.*

'He *will* come back. He loves me.'

'Orlando Schiffer loves only himself.'

'You think I am a fool?' Chō began.

'A fool? No.' Bel squeezed her hand. 'Just another good and devoted woman used and cast aside by a feckless and faithless man.' She threw down a handful of coins and pushed back her seat. 'It is a story as old as time.'

Lot 32

LONDON, 1889

Evening light slanted through the narrow windows above the bars in Monsieur Bertrand's fencing *salle*, gas lamps illuminating the figures in white jackets and breeches. The high room reverberated with the sound of stamping feet pacing to and fro, the swish and click of steel on steel. Bel cried: *En garde*, and sank down into position, coiled, every cell vibrating ready to lunge. Again and again she attacked her opponent, her thoughts sharp with Schiffer's betrayal. *And Tom's.* The fencing master cried out in French: *Riposte! Parry . . . Begin again. En garde!* The blood ran high in her, her heart pulsing. *Allongez! Allongez!* he cried. *Eh, bien! Better.*

She took off her mask, panting, and tucked it under her arm. She shook her opponent's hand. 'Thank you, Miss Fitzroy. I shall see you next week.' Bel caught her breath, and hung her foil on the rack lining one wall. In the cloakroom she buttoned her long coat over her fencing kit. *If only life were as simple as a salle,* she thought, washing her hands with coal tar soap. *Everyone knows the steps, the correct form. You win or you lose.* She pinned down her hat over her hair, still hot and damp from her exertion. Seeing it was raining, she pulled up her collar as she stepped out into the night.

'Bel, wait,' Tom said, running to catch up with her.

'Tom? How are you here?'

'You told me you fence every Thursday in the *salle* in Cleveland Row.' He took a step towards her. 'I went to your room, but your landlady said you had moved?'

'I felt like a change,' she said. 'But then I am not the only one.' Anger overtook her and she turned on her heel, marching on.

'Bel . . .' He caught at her arm, but she pulled away. 'Wait,' he said. 'I'm not going to chase you halfway across London.' When she didn't stop, he sprinted after her. He held her against the wall in the darkness of Russell Court. Only then did he realise she was crying. 'Bel, my love, I thought you understood?'

'My love? *My love*?' she cried, thumping his chest. 'How could you?' She struggled to get away, but Tom held her. 'I thought you loved me!'

'I do, Bel.'

'I thought better of you. You would have your way with me, and cast me aside? You used me—'

'No! I love you, but I told you of my ambitions—'

'How long have you been courting that child? How many months?'

'I have known Victoria's family for many years—'

'Years!'

'We are distantly related. They are friends of my parents—'

'Wealthy friends, Mr *Fraser*.'

'Yes, wealthy friends.' She saw emotions pass fast across his face like storm clouds. Anger. Guilt. 'Victoria's father built an empire. All he lacks is a male heir, with his name. All he longs for is a grandchild.'

'*She* is a child, Tom. Do you not want an equal?'

'I want security,' he said, his voice tight. 'Her father has taken to me as a son. If I sire his grandchildren, he cares little what I do. I want a great architectural practice of my own. I do not wish to design schemes for Liberty for the rest of my life—'

'Neither do I! I have ambition, too. We could build a good life, a creative life, together—'

'I do not wish to scrape by, like my family. I want more.'

Bel struggled, but he held her firmly around the waist. Tom kissed her then, a kiss full of passion and fury. 'Stop,' she said, breaking for air. 'Stop, Tom—' She placed her palm against his heart. 'That is the last time you shall kiss me, do you understand?'

'I will not lose you.' He held her to him. 'I don't understand. I thought we were equals, is that not what you talk of? An equal freedom? Freedom to love, and create, beyond convention?'

'Not like this,' she said.

'I never meant to hurt you. You and I, we live—'

'Lived,' Bel said, her voice hard.

'We live for the moment. I thought that was what you wanted too,' he said desperately. 'Experience, emotion, sensation—'

I wanted you, she thought. *All of you*. Her dreams of a good house, and children running through pale grass, of high summer skies, and sunlight through the panes of an airy studio where they would work together flickered through her mind like a panopticon. And went dark.

'I am marrying,' he said, 'but can we not be as before?'

'You would make me your mistress?' *No. Never.*

'I will not lose you.'

'You cannot pin down happiness like one of your moths, Tom.'

'I care for Victoria, but I love you.'

'Then I pity her.' Bel felt as if her body filled with ice. 'Your love is not enough,' she said, breaking away from him. 'Your love is *not* equal to mine.' She looked up at him, feeling the bond between them tear like silk. It was a physical pain, a wrench. She clenched her gloved hand and placed it against her heart. 'I have loved you for the best years of my life, Tom. What of me now?'

'Bel, please,' he said. 'What shall I do without you—'

'You will learn to live, you will learn to love that young wife of yours, and have many beautiful children, no doubt. And you will make your great practice with her money, and design many wonderful buildings—'

'Bel, don't.' He hung his head in shame. 'I love you. I could protect you.'

'As a kept woman?' Bel walked to the street and raised her head to the sky. Once she had composed herself, she turned and looked steadily at him as the rain drove on around her. 'I deserve more than that, and I deserve better than you.'

Lot 33

LONDON, JULY 1889

Time took on an elastic quality as Chō laboured through the night. Bel sat with her, bathing her forehead with cool towels as the Japanese midwife tended to her. Hiro paced the living room, his dark figure sweeping across the golden light of the open door like the pendulum of a clock.

The midwife said something in Japanese to Chō, who squeezed Bel's hand so hard she cried out. 'What can I do?' Bel said. Chō's eyes screwed shut in pain.

'Child too big, head too big,' the midwife muttered in English, rubbing rapeseed oil onto her hands. 'No good.' Chō's head rose up, her face contorted with effort. At her scream, Hiro stopped in the doorway, his shadow falling across the old woman as she pulled the baby free, and dangled him, clearing his throat and rubbing his back until he cried out – a thin, high mewl.

'A boy!' Bel said, her eyes filling with tears of relief. 'You have a beautiful boy!' Chō fell back on the pillow, exhausted.

Hiro knelt beside the midwife, and she showed him how to cut through the umbilical cord. She wrapped the child in a fine muslin sheet and handed him to Bel. The baby gazed up at her with fathomless dark eyes. Outside, the wind buffeted the trees, rain pattering against the panes of glass, but here the pool of golden lamplight held the three friends and the child.

'Hello, little one,' Bel said, turning so that Chō could see him. She tried to pass her the child, but she shook her head as the midwife cleared away the afterbirth. Bel's stomach clenched with nausea as she saw the woman raise a needle to the lantern, threading it.

'Let me?' Hiro knelt beside Bel. He spoke to the baby gently in Japanese, and looked up at Bel, his dark eyes gleaming with tears.

'This is your uncle, Hiro-san,' she said.

'So you are the one who has made my sister eat all the *mochi*?' Hiro's hair fell forward as he looked down at the child. Chō sighed a laugh.

'Show me?' she said wearily, wincing as the midwife worked.

He passed the baby to Chō, who looked down at his face, pushing aside the wrap.

'Ah,' she said. 'He is like his father,' she murmured in wonder, 'but with our dark eyes.' Chō blinked away tears. 'He is so big. So big.'

'A beautiful, healthy boy. What will you call him?' Bel said. The midwife washed her hands, and billowed a fresh white sheet over the bed where Chō lay.

'Genji . . . Genji-san,' Chō murmured.

'From Lady Murasaki?' Hiro said. He looked at Bel. 'It was always her favourite. I have read it to Chō-san a hundred times.' He leant forward and brushed his sister's damp hair from her face. 'It is the story of a great prince who was a poet, a musician, an artist.'

'Yes, Genji-san,' Chō murmured. 'I paint . . . I painted a scroll for him. Autumn hours . . . both departing . . .' She blinked, exhausted.

'I shall read it to you, later,' Hiro said. 'The Empress asked Murasaki Shikibu to write a new romance.' Bel soaked a clean cloth in water to cool Chō's brow. 'Do you remember your favourite story of Lake Biwa? The silver lake?' he said, soothing her with the story. 'The full moon mirror?' His smile turned to concern, as Chō's eyes rolled back in her head. 'Chō-san? What is wrong?' he touched her shoulder, shaking her gently.

'Chō?' Bel said, lunging forward to catch the child as her arm slumped. 'Help her!' she cried to the midwife. The baby's arms stiffened, startled. 'Something's wrong!' The old woman ran over and raised the clean sheet covering Chō. The child let out a piercing cry, and they looked in horror as a pool of blood spread across the bed, crimson on white.

Lot 34

PARIS, 29 JULY 1985

Mira ran along the pale pathways of the Jardins des Plantes before work, her Walkman playing Prince, 'I Would Die 4 U'. Light rain misted her skin. *It just doesn't make sense*, she thought, going over the passages she had read in Isobel Bright's pillow book the night before.

Just like Sei Shōnagon's, the pages of Bel's book captured fleeting moments of beauty. The face of a lover in sleep. The birth of a child. *But where's the rest, the everyday?* Turning the pages in the lamplight, she noticed a watermark on one page. Only one page.

'When I looked closely,' she told Ned over the phone from a tabac, 'you were right, the pages of the pillow book have been compiled from other journals. They've been skilfully bound, but they've been gathered from other diaries.'

'It's an edited account of her life?'

'Precisely.' She sipped her café au lait, and fought the

urge to buy a pack of Gauloises Blondes. 'When you think it covers 1875 to 1923, it's really short.'

'God, when I think how my teenage diary rambled on,' Ned said, laughing softly.

'You kept a diary?' Mira said in surprise.

'And I wrote awful poetry.' Ned covered the receiver and spoke to someone. 'Mercifully I burned all mine, so no auctioneer is going to be poring over my life in a hundred years' time.'

'I've been thinking. All these old buildings have storage areas. How come the client hasn't told us to go through those?'

'Great minds,' Ned said. 'I've asked Serge to talk to the concierge.'

'I'm going to grab the housekeeper on the way in,' Mira said, pushing her empty cup across the counter. 'Let's see what we can find.'

She ran on through the Place Vendôme, imagining Maison Bright behind the soaring elegant façade. She glanced up as she ran past the Ritz, thinking of Chanel. *All these lives behind the façades*, she thought, running on towards the Place de la Madeleine. She slowed her pace, and jogged down the winding mosaic stairs to the public loo.

As she washed her hands, she looked up at the Art Nouveau stained glass, the mirrored columns. She half imagined if she turned quickly she would see Bel tidying her hair in the next-door mirror, hear the sweep of her long skirts as she climbed the stairs. *She's everywhere*,

Mira thought, emerging on to the street. *Everywhere and nowhere.*

~

At the Avenue Junot, Mira caught the door as an old woman and a miniature poodle with matching pink hair stepped out. In the elevator, she raised her wrist and inhaled the fresh citrus scent of *Eau d'Hadrien* on her warm skin. She had stopped at Annick Goutal on rue de Bellechasse to stock up on her perfume. *Our fragrance*, she thought. Just the smell of the scent conjured up her first night with Luke. His freshly shaved cheek, her lips on his neck, warm cypress and musk breathing through lemon. The night when everything was new, and they were still learning one another by heart. She had found a bottle of *Eau d'Hadrien* on his bathroom shelf, and couldn't resist splashing some on her wrists the next morning. All day, through her lectures, she had felt Luke's embrace, the fragrance lingering. She had arrived home to find a gift-wrapped box on her doorstep, with the bottle and a note: *I don't mind sharing, with you x*

Mira closed her eyes, daydreaming as the lift trundled upwards. *Couldn't resist opening the new bottle.* She thought of the empty one on her dressing table in London. *It's not like Luke will mind.* She lost herself in a reverie of him, the feel of him, the taste of his skin. It took her a moment to realise she had reached the housekeeper's floor.

She knocked on the door, and waited, looking around. She had expected this to be the top floor, a garret space like Kim's apartment, but she realised there was a further storey above this. A narrow staircase led up from the landing. *Attics?* she thought. Mira heard the sound of footsteps across parquet, and the high blue-grey door unbolted.

'Bonjour, Madame,' she said. A Debussy suite drifted out of the apartment, and a piquant note of cat pee.

'Madame Hutchinson? How may I help you?' She stood in the doorway, not inviting her in. Mira glimpsed high white walls beyond, the morning light catching on a chandelier reflected in an elaborate Venetian mirror. *It's as palatial as Bel's apartment*, she realised. *The footprint must be exactly like the apartment downstairs.*

'May I ask you, are there things in storage we should be looking through?'

'Storage?' She tilted her head and smiled slowly. 'Of course.'

'You could have told us? There might be something important.'

'All that your client needs is in the apartment. The basement store is full of rubbish Isobel no longer wanted. The attic has everything we cleared from the workroom, which was here.' She gestured back at her home. 'She left that to Françoise Lambert.' *That name rings a bell.* Mira thought. *Was it in the pillow book?*

'If there's more, we should see it,' Mira said. 'It might be helpful proving provenance of the art and better pieces.'

'Very well.' She closed the door slightly, and Mira heard her talking to someone. *Is she talking to her cat?* She blinked as she heard a distinctly male voice. *I'm surrounded by mysteries. What's everyone hiding?*

The housekeeper reappeared, sorting through a large hoop of keys, and beckoned for her to follow. Mira ducked as they climbed the narrow staircase to the attics. *I feel like Alice in Wonderland*, she thought, tilting her head to walk along the sloping corridor in the high Mansard roof. They passed a number of doors, but then she stopped outside one with a peeling paper label: 'BB'. She unlocked the door and turned the brass knob.

'Help yourself,' she said. Mira looked across the dusty room, faint light chinking through the slatted oval window at the end. She pulled a cord and a bare bulb half-heartedly lit the room.

'Her drawing board?' Mira said, touching it as she passed. The mannequins stood huddled in a shadowy corner of the room, like a chorus line waiting in the wings. 'I've been reading her journal.'

'She should be remembered among Dior, Chanel, Balenciaga.' Mira heard the bitterness in her voice.

'What happened to Isobel?'

'I don't know. Something bad. My grandmother Françoise could never talk about it. All I know is she wanted Maison BB to continue, and the Kurosakis didn't. There were a lot of disagreements.'

'Françoise!' Mira remembered her thesis. 'She was Bel's muse?'

'Yes,' she snapped. 'She ignited the fire in Isobel's

imagination. I told you – this is what was in our apartment. Drawing board, mannequins, trunks and trunks of patterns and designs.' She waved her hand with a dismissive pfft. 'This is ours, the Lamberts, not the Kurosakis.' She shook her head. 'But what am I to do with all this now? Send it all to Drouot, get what you can, take a commission, I don't care.'

'Do you remember her?' Mira said, turning.

'How old do you think I am?' she said, sharply. 'I said I was not born when she left. The design studio was in our apartment, above madame's. After she left, it was like everything went to sleep.'

'Did your grandmother remember someone clearing the apartment?'

'A lot of people came and went.'

'Someone must know what happened to Isobel?'

'What is this?' she snapped, her temper flaring. 'You people, poking your nose in.' She took the key off the hook and slammed it down on the dustcloth-covered worktable. 'Why cannot things stay as they were?' She turned on her heel and left Mira alone.

Lot 35

LONDON, JULY 1889

Bel and Hiro sat in silence, the cradle beside them. The fading light fell grey and sombre in the living room. No lamps were lit, no music played. Only the *tokonoma* altar glowed gold in flickering candlelight, bright coals of incense sticks hovering like fireflies. As Bel wept quietly, Hiro knelt with his eyes closed.

'My sister ...' He hung his head. 'I should have protected her.'

'Chō lived her life on her terms.'

'The air is full of ghosts tonight.' The baby stirred in the cradle, mewling. 'What is he to do with no mother?'

'We are his family, now,' Bel said. 'Chō was like a sister to me—'

'So I am like a brother?' he said. There was something in his voice that caught her off guard. 'That is all.'

'All? It's everything,' Bel said. She stood and placed the kettle on the stove to boil water for the baby. She looked down at the feeding bottle, making sure the teat was perfectly clean. *You be careful, love, them bottles can be killers*, Mrs Harris said when she picked up supplies for the child. *Make sure you use boiling water, mind, then let it cool. You want to get a bottle of Soothing Syrup, too. Nothing wrong with a spot of opiates to calm a griping child.*

'You and Genji *are* my family,' she said. 'I promised Chō I'd care for you. Both of you.' The horror of Chō's death flashed into her mind, the frantic fight to save her. *The blood.*

'Hiro, I'd like to ask you something. I want to raise Genji as my son. For Chō. I've spoken to Mrs Harris already, and her daughter will be his wet nurse.'

'What if you wish to marry?'

'I'm over thirty, an old maid,' she said, sighing. 'I feel the chance of love has passed me by.'

'Never say that—' The baby's cry cut him off.

'Hungry again?' She rubbed the child's narrow back, and took him to the mat in the kitchen. 'Or are you wet?' she said, pulling faces to amuse him as he lay staring up at her. 'I'm not sure I'll get the hang of all this.'

'Good mothers are made, not born,' Hiro said kindly.

Genji had a soft crown of Chō's ebony hair, but Schiffer's features. *I hope that is all he has of his father*, she thought, deftly changing him. She put the sodden cloth in a bucket to soak, and cleaned him with a little boiled water. 'Hiro, do you think we should tell Schiffer that he has a son?'

'No,' he said firmly. 'He did not care for my sister in life, why should he care for her child in death.' He looked at Bel, framed by a halo of fading light in the window, as she cradled the child. 'Do you mean it?' Bel nodded. 'Take him,' Hiro said. 'I hope he is a better man than his father.' He looked down at his hands for a moment, then stood and walked over to Bel. 'People come into one another's lives for a reason,' he said. 'I am glad that you came into mine. I am a better man because of you.'

'Hiro—'

'My uncle expects me to take over the family business in Japan. He has been patient, but it is time. I will go, now there is nothing here for me.'

'No, Hiro, you have me, and Genji—'

'But I don't have you, Bel,' he said, his dark eyes gleaming. 'You think of me as a brother, nothing more—'

'Hiro?' Her lips parted in surprise.

'You were the only person who really saw me.' He swept his hand from floor to ceiling. 'I have no illusions. I was hired by Liberty as set dressing, like the *uchiwa* and the Chinese porcelain.'

'Hiro, you are more than that,' Bel said, soothing the baby. 'You are a fine artist, and a fine man. You know how valued your work is.'

'I am not talking about work now,' he said, stepping towards her. 'I am talking about you. I am talking about us, Bel.'

'Hiro—'

'It's not too late. Marry me, Bel. Come with me to Japan. Let me care for you. Let us raise this child as our own.'

Lot 36

LONDON, AUGUST 1889

Bel placed a penny bunch of violets on her parents' grave at Christ Church. *No more lavish bunches of calla lilies?* she thought. *Where are they now, my father's women? Flown away to fresh roosts no doubt, like the 'croqueuse de diamants', the diamond scrunchers and grandes horizontales.* Bel lit candles for her parents and Chō in the incense-scented shadows of the church and sat gathering her strength as sunlight faded through the stained glass, the lamp of the day burning down. *Help me,* she thought. *I don't know how to do this. I wish I still believed, as a child.*

Bel thought of Hiro, looking up at the jewel colours of the glass. She had promised to think over his proposal. She remembered his kind, handsome face. *Let me care for you.* Bel's chest tightened with longing. *It's impossible*, she thought, stirring and walking out of the church. She had felt guilty, leaving the tiny baby with Mrs Harris, but she knew he would be well looked after. *I have my work, my career to think of. I can't just up and leave for Japan.* She strolled along Victoria Road watching a robin fluttering from rail to wall, keeping pace with her. *Don't they say if you see a robin the spirit of a loved one is near?* The bird puffed out its red breast, its black glass eye glinting. *There was a robin that sang every night in the trees of Cornwall Gardens. I used to lie awake, listening.* Bel sighed with longing. *Will nothing ever be that simple again?*

Bel stood waiting on Launceston Place, gazing up at the dusty trees. She remembered in spring the pink blossoms against the midnight blue sky. Nearby some children were playing, hopscotch squares chalked on the pavement. She knew the skipping rhyme the girls in white pinafores were chanting. *It could have been me, once.* Bel leant against the newly painted railings of the Fraser's home, and cooled herself with the geisha's silver fan. She regarded her old house opposite as a carriage clattered past. From here she could just glimpse the domed observatory where her father had taught her the names of all the constellations. Victoria's house was smarter, newly painted, a flight of steps leading to a columned porch, an elegant zinc-roofed balcony extending out over the basement level. *I wager even the blossom is pinker here.* Bel flicked her fan. *We might have been neighbours. Had I still lived here, perhaps I might have bumped into you and thought: what a lovely young couple.* She tested the pain as you might a sprained ankle. Can it bear the weight? She imagined passing Tom on the street. Would their gazes have intertwined like silk scarves on the breeze?

'I'm sorry.' Tom's voice broke her reverie. He was deeply

tanned, his hair tinted gold, and he had grown a moustache, she saw. It had a reddish tone, and made Bel think of a hamster she had as a child. She fought the urge to laugh, imagining it scurrying from his top lip. *Oh, Tom*, she thought. *What else has changed?* A new linen suit in the latest fashion, a primrose silk neck tie. She thought of his simple white shirts and breeches in Japan. How she had loved to lay her head against his chest, the steady beat of his heart. She walked slowly over, aware of Tom's gaze on her.

'Bel,' he said, walking towards her. 'You look . . . well, you look wonderful.'

'Thank you, Mr *Fraser*,' she said clearly. 'You seem – changed.'

'For the better, I hope?' he smiled his old smile and in spite of the ridiculous moustache, her stomach tightened with longing.

'Splendid mustachios,' she said under her breath.

'Do you like it?' he said, stroking his upper lip. Then he saw the amused smile on her face. 'It doesn't suit me, does it? Victoria suggested—'

'Tom!' she called from the carriage. A small gloved hand waved, and Tom jogged back to help her down.

'Miss Bright! May I call you Bel?' The girl swept towards her. Bel saw at once that she was wearing a pink velvet sash around her cream skirt, and a hat trimmed with a pale ostrich feather. *You copied me?*

'I am a shocker, Bel. Tom is so patient, aren't you, my dear,' she said, gazing up at him, her face illuminated with love. 'I was quite carried away choosing my new trousseau for our Grand Tour.'

'You plan to travel?' Bel said evenly. *You have just returned from honeymoon.*

'Yes!' she said, her eyes sparkling with joy. 'We will travel all of Italy from top to toe.' She gazed up at her husband. 'Tom has never had the chance, and my father said any architect worth his salt must see all the sights.'

'You must be exhausted,' Tom said. 'I'm sorry we kept you waiting in this heat.'

'Not at all. It is a beautiful night, and I always loved this street.'

'Papa says Launceston Place—'

Sussex Place as was, Bel thought.

'—is terribly up and coming now people can buy the freeholds. Of course, there's still a smattering of bohemian sorts, but it's becoming smart and respectable. He's awfully good at investments. He has a magic touch with money.' Bel glanced at Tom. 'Aren't the villas divine?' Victoria chattered on good-naturedly, rummaging in her beaded bag for the key. 'I just know we are going to be so happy here. Do you know this part of town?'

'Yes—' *I grew up here. I loved it. I lost it.* 'My father's old coachman lives just there, in the mews. I visit them, from time to time.' She looked pointedly at Tom. 'If you need a good horseman, and a laundress, I can recommend Mr and Mrs Harris.'

'Perfect,' Victoria said. 'Do tell them to call.' It was

impossible to dislike her. Victoria's happiness made Bel feel old, and wistful. *But not envious.* She glanced at Tom. *You didn't love me enough. That is your fault, not hers.*

Victoria unlocked the door, and Tom turned on the gas lamps, illuminating the hall. They walked the empty house together, Bel with a small sketchbook in hand, making notes as they planned the schemes. The similarities to her father's house jarred. It was as if she had stepped through a looking glass – the rooms were a mirror image to those she had known.

Victoria ran on ahead, flinging open door after door. 'Bel, I truly am sorry,' Tom said quietly. 'This must be very difficult for you.'

'Not at all,' she said briskly. 'Mr Liberty was most insistent I take this commission—'

'Victoria insisted. She knows you are the best in London, and she always demands the best.' Tom's face fell. 'It is cruel, but there was nothing I could do to dissuade her without raising suspicions of our relationship.'

'We have no *relationship*,' she hissed.

'Bel,' he whispered. 'I am so sorry for your troubles. The Kurosakis and the child. I think of you—'

'You have no right.'

'I try not to,' he said hoarsely. 'But the very house I live in . . . every shade, every colour will be yours. The bed I sleep in at night will have your touch—'

'You have no right,' she said. 'I will do a good job for you, and your wife, because that is what I always do.' Victoria chattered on, walking ahead, oblivious. *It's like a doll's house to her.* Bel fought back the anger catching in her throat.

A stray hair, gold and curling on Tom's dark jacket, caught Bel's eye, and she brushed it away. In that intimate moment they did not see Victoria turn to them, her face clouding from shock to anger in realisation. She strode on into the next room.

'This shall be the nursery,' they heard her call brightly from up ahead. 'Do look, it's too divine.' Bel stepped away from Tom, and joined her. The women stood side by side at the window. 'Just look at the moonglow. I can quite imagine holding our child in my arms . . .'

'Are you—'

'With child?' Victoria nodded, her eyes bright with happiness. *And something else*, Bel thought. *A fierceness, too.* ''Tis early, but I am so happy.' She took Bel's hand. 'I know Tom has had . . . dalliances. What young man has not? But he loves me. Nothing will come between us.' She looked Bel in the eye. 'Nothing.'

High above Bel's old house, the full moon shone silver in the deep-blue sky. Gazing up at it, her resolve grew strong. *I must let go of what let go of me. Have him*, she thought. *Have all of him. I wish you happiness, I do. I wish – oh, I wish it did not hurt so.* She swallowed down her pain. 'This is the perfect room for the nursery, Mrs Fraser,' she said. 'An excellent choice.'

'Do you think so?' Victoria turned, her relief clear to see. 'I'm so glad. You see, I so want this to be right, for Tom.' She pressed her hand to Bel's sleeve. 'He always talks about your marvellous taste, and how clever you are.' Victoria waved a pale-gloved hand in the air.

'Thank you, Mrs Fraser.' Bel smiled at the girl and strode out of the room, her glance like a blow as she passed Tom. 'Mr *Fraser*.'

'By the way,' Victoria called after her, 'I adored your painting. So modern.' She giggled. 'So risqué.'

'My painting?'

'Victoria—' Tom said, frowning.

'At the Academy's exhibition?' Victoria's eyes sparkled mischievously. 'Of course, his portrait of the Japanese girl is the talk of the town, but—'

'Schiffer?' Bel said, rounding on Tom. 'What has he done?'

'Bel, I'm sorry—' Tom said, but she had gone.

Lot 37

LONDON, 1889

I paid my shilling and joined the crowds at the Academy show. Too late, someone had already reserved Schiffer's portrait of me. A triptych, a small cabinet painting. Next to *Autumn Gold*, the great and celebrated painting of Chō, it is a trifle. A little dark wood box, no bigger than a book, hiding a secret. Open its panels – gilded plain gold to the left and right, and there on a bed of teal velvet to set off the fire in my hair, spilling around 'my' naked shoulders, 'I' lie. Naked. Inviting. Whose body I shall not know, but the face my own.

I shall never forget standing motionless before the painting, sick with fury and humiliation while the summer crowds eddied around me, a river of voices and perfumes. I wore a pale veil on my summer hat lest anyone recognise me, and as I gasped, trying not to cry, the fabric billowed against my lips like a drape at an open window.

The couple staring at the painting glanced from me to it. *Everyone knows*, I thought, hot with humiliation. As I stared, a familiar voice rose above the others. Schiffer rolled through the gallery, the crowd parting around him and his entourage. Seeing me, he paused. For a moment I saw uncertainty flicker across his face. He covered it quickly.

'Miss Bright,' he said. 'What think ye of your portrait?'

The conversation lulled around us as I turned to him.

Tis but a joke, Tom had said. *You know what Schiffer is like.* A joke? A spiteful violation. *I hate him, I hate him*, was all I could think. The title? *Tyger, Tyger*, after the Blake poem. *Tyger, Tyger, burning bright.* I felt myself rise above my body in my wrath, and saw myself standing there as if from a great distance. *Burning bright.* I felt my anger blaze molten, and harden around me like armour. *It is not me. He shall never have me.* As I stared at him, I replayed every meeting with him, the feel of his hands on me; I wound back time until he grew small and insignificant. *He is nothing*, I thought, walking slowly towards him. Still he sneered. In a flash, I slapped him, the sound of my gloved hand cracking around the high room like gunshot. A gasp went up from the crowd around us.

'I deserved that,' Schiffer said, testing his lip. 'But you appreciate it is a fine painting.' His cruel mouth twitched a smile and he stepped closer as he lowered his voice. 'I wager the fellow who has bought it plans to appreciate you greatly. Every single night.' His gaze travelled the length of my body. 'I saw you pose only once, as a girl, but is it not a good likeness?' As I walked past him, my mouth close to his ear, I said:

'The reality exceeds your imagination, sir.'

'You would give yourself to Ferris, not me?' he growled.

'This is your revenge?'

'You don't think much of me, do you, Miss Bright?'

'I do not think of you at all.' I turned to him. 'How do you find Toulon, sir? Have you come to fetch Miss Kurosaki's child?' He laughed, a horrible cruel laugh. 'I thought not. He is better off without you.' I pushed my way out through the crowds. I felt as if every man looked at me, undressing me, as if every woman pitied me. I seemed surrounded by laughter.

'Miss Bright?' Oscar Wilde tipped his hat to me. 'I see from your countenance you have seen your portrait.'

''Tis no portrait, sir.' I shook with anger. 'Everyone is talking about me.'

'Better that than not being talked about.'

On the steps of the Royal Academy, I threw back my veil and strode across the courtyard to Piccadilly. *I will show them. I will show them all.*

PART TWO

PARIS

Lot 38

PARIS, SEPTEMBER 1889

Paris, Bel thought. *I can't believe I'm really here.* In the half-light, she looked around the simply furnished room. Bel checked Hiro's pewter clock on the mantlepiece. *Four, again*? she thought. *I wish I could sleep.* In a few hours she would report to Maison Liberty. She lay back on the bed and recalled her conversation with Arthur the month before.

'You wish to go to Paris?' he said. 'But Stanford Griffin is opening the store for us.'

'I am more senior than him,' she protested. 'I have worked for you longer. I should head up Maison Liberty.'

'He is my cousin, and he opened Birmingham very successfully.'

'But—'

'Griffin is an experienced hand at the helm, that is what I need.'

'*I* am experienced. Let me go. I need—' *I need a fresh start. To begin again. Far away from London, from Tom, and*

Chō's loss, and Hiro. Nothing had felt the same since Hiro left. *Did I make the right decision? I miss him so.* 'I need a challenge.'

'Very well. You shall have free rein with the creative side of the store, Griffin will take care of the business. You will make a good team.' Bel nodded, seeing the sense in this. 'By the end of the century I expect to have some hundred employees working under you at Maison Liberty.'

'Shall Mr Griffin and I be paid equally?'

'My dear,' Arthur said, laughing softly. 'I know no other woman on earth who would consider that question. You are remarkable, but you know that is not possible—'

'I have a family now, a child to support,' Bel said.

'You will have a fair salary.' *A fair salary?* she thought. *Why, most of our girls' salaries barely cover their room and board. They work from eight 'til seven, with barely a break, and still scrape by.* Arthur scribbled down a figure, and held it up to her. 'That's the best I can do. Do we have a deal?' Bel nodded. 'Good. You speak French, do you not?'

'Fluently. I spent a great deal of time in France as a child.'

'Then you shall settle in easily.' He tossed the paper into the fire. 'Leave for Paris as soon as possible. I shall arrange for my secretary to book you and the child into the Family Hotel on Passage Jouffroy. A charming place, I think you shall like it. From there you can explore the city and find an apartment to your liking, I suggest near the store.'

'Where is it?'

'38 Avenue de l'Opéra,' Arthur said, writing quickly on a

piece of paper. 'We've a splendid building, four floors, with elegant Juliet balconies on the third.'

Live near the store? No. Bel decided immediately on Montmartre. She had always loved the ramshackle village on the hill above Paris. She pictured leafy green trees shading cheap taverns, the maze of alleys, the old plaster quarries, the vineyards and vegetable plots behind the Moulin de la Galette. While below in the city Haussmann's broad, elegant avenues were shaping a new future for Paris, on the Butte Montmartre the artists and writers had found a place to call home. She thought of Renoir's painting of the 'Moulin', the Sunday afternoon dances in acacia-shaded courtyards, the dappled light on boaters and striped dresses, milliners and shop girls relaxing on their day off.

Now, Bel looked down on Genji sleeping in his cradle, and picked up the simple gold ring she had bought in the Saint-Ouen flea market that morning, slipping it onto her ring finger. *Madame Isobel Kurosaki*, she thought, trying out the new name like a cloak. *Yes, my husband died, I am a widow. That's the easiest story to tell people. The simplest pretence. People will not question a widow and her child.*

Sitting at the dressing table, she unfolded a linen-wrapped parcel – just one corner, just a glimpse of iridescent blue silk in the dim light. It was like glimpsing a butterfly in the night.

Bel remembered when Hiro handed it to her at Paddington Station. The globe lamps shone softly above the platform like a constellation of gentle moons above the trains snorting steam and smoke. The clatter of metal, voices, a long whistle echoed high in the arches, and they had to stand close, raising their voices to hear one another. Porters heaved steamer trunks onto the train, but Hiro travelled with very little, a canvas duffel bag with his few clothes, and a small carpet bag with Chō's trees, the precious family cups and bowls. The rest he had given away.

'Come with me, Bel,' he said. 'It's not too late. Come with me and be my wife. We can raise the child together.'

'Hiro, I can't,' she said, her voice catching.

'I could be happy anywhere with you beside me, Bel.' He nodded. 'But it is my duty to return to Japan. I must take over the family business.'

'Hiro, I would understand if you want to take Genji with you, to be with his relations?'

'You are his family. Chō loved you as a sister. It is what she would have wanted.' As the porters slammed the luggage compartment closed, he turned to Bel and gave her a box wrapped in linen. 'This is for you, and for the child. It is the waterlily kimono.'

'Hiro, I can't take this,' Bel said.

'Keep it safe for me.' He looked down at her and smiled, the breeze blowing his glossy black hair. 'I know, in my heart . . .' He pressed his lips together, holding his emotions in. 'One day, you will be with me. I will wait for you.'

'Hiro . . .' Her eyes filled with tears. 'I love you, I do, but there is so much I need to accomplish.'

'I will wait,' he said, taking her hand. 'Love is patient, Bel. I am patient because I have foresight.' He smiled at her, trying to ease her tension. 'I trust the end result as surely as I know how a silk thread will look and feel in the finished fabric.'

'I will miss you.' Bel smiled, tears pricking her eyes. 'I will miss you so much. What am I going to do without you?'

'You will never be without me.' He took her in his arms, and held her close, pressing his cheek to the crown of her hat. She felt the reassuring strength of him, the lean muscles beneath the soft layers of his kimono. 'Though I am not at your side, I remain with you.'

'Don't go.' The boat train billowed smoke to the high glass roof, doors closing, whistle blowing. Hiro gently wiped a smut of coal from her cheek with his thumb.

'One day the stars will align. Our time will come.' Hiro leapt up onto the train as the final doors slammed, and turned to look back at her, one last time. '*Sayonara*, Bel.'

Bel took the most recent letter from Hiro from its envelope, and lay back in bed, reading by the light of the lamp:

My Bel, it began.

Your letter was like sunlight on water to me.

I feel I can say to you in a letter what I have always been afraid to in life. In London I had few prospects, and no right to declare myself, but I will build a life and a home here, and when I am a wealthy man I will ask for your hand again, Bel.

I do not know if you will grow to love me completely, as I love you, but I can hope your love of a friend will blossom like the cherry trees.

Here, the autumn trees turn gold in the orchard. I have a view of the mountains from my garden in Kyoto. The house is simple, little more than a shack at the moment, but there is a stream nearby and I am drawing plans to make a water garden. When I imagine the garden in blossom, I think of you, Bel.

I know that your heart belongs to Ferris – or Fraser, still. I saw it every time you looked at him. But I am patient.

If it is my fate to love you, while you love him, then so be it. Because my love is not requited yet, it does not make it any less.

I love you, Bel. I hope that does not make you uncomfortable. I expect nothing from you. I only hope for our continued friendship.

I offer you my love, that is all. I offer to care for you, to support you, to create a life for you.

Remain with me,

Always,

Hiro

Bel smiled, thinking of her reply on a postcard of the new Eiffel Tower.

Hiro – I remain with you – like Cherry Blossom

Lot 39

PARIS, 1900

It feels the pages of this journal turn faster and faster each year. The months fly away from me, full of work, and amusement. My days at Maison Liberty are long and busy – a new scheme for this client, or a trousseau for that bride. All is beauty and excess. Only at night while Genji sleeps do I realise I am alone.

Hiro's letters paint a picture of his life in Japan, his work, his house. He sends a netsuke or toy for Genji, or a length of fabric for me. He describes Kabuki performances – the light and shadows, the dance of a man as a woman, the flick of a gold fan. He sent me coiled paper flowers which bloomed miraculously in water. He tells me of the sunrise on snow, pink against blue mountains. He sends caddies of fine green tea still moist as cut grass in the evening rain. He tells me about deer grazing in the forest near his house in the countryside outside Kyoto. He describes the Toro Nagashi river lantern festival, with thousands of coloured lanterns floating downstream, guiding the spirits of the ancestors home. Always there is a folded orizuru *paper crane. 'When I have folded a thousand cranes for you, I can make a wish,' Hiro wrote.*

What he really sends, of course, is love. Each of his letters is a lantern, guiding me slowly home. He tells me of the smallest things – candlelight in the house at night, the iridescent dragonflies in the water garden.

Genji and I have strung each crane Hiro sends onto silver thread, and hung them from the curtain pole beside the window where I sew in the evenings. Genji runs his hand along them every time he walks past. In this way, Hiro remains a part of our daily life. Our letters are a conversation without end. Sometimes his are just a list of observations, like The Pillow Book*:*

Things I love:
Camellias
Moonlight on snow
Sunlight through bamboo
Tigers' feet
Plum blossom on wet streets
You

In return, I paint a picture of Paris for him with my words – the sunlit squares and elegant parks, the thundering racetracks. Today I recalled how Genji used to squat on his heels in the courtyard playing with a little spade and a pot of earth, the lovely nape of his neck, his intent concentration. 'Flower!' he cried, bringing the uprooted plant to me with muddy, dimpled hands, kissing the air. Now, he is nearly as tall as me.

I conjure Maison Liberty and the couture salon for Hiro, the smart branded omnibuses and delivery tricycles, the streetlights and carriages, the avenues of Haussman's elegant buildings, the department stores and cafés. I list the smells: eau de cologne, coal smoke, pissoirs, black tobacco, drains, garlic, vin rouge. I told him of our visit to my old friend Monet, the new paintings he is working on, and how he loved the waterlily kimono.

How time flies. Each day after work I collected Genji from La Pouponnière, the tiny tot centre, and I wheeled him in his pram through the park, the sun casting shadows on the sundial's hand. Each week, as he learnt to walk, my son seemed to reach a little higher, walk a little further, always clutching the dark bear with silver eyes the Libertys sent for his first birthday. Until one day he didn't. Now he races through the park chasing a ball or hoop, with his friends after school. I record all this for Hiro. My map of Paris is a map of love for him. Through our words we walk beside one another.

We have moved to an apartment in Montmartre, next to the Bateau-Lavoir studios on Place Ravignan. If I have to work late, the old concierge in our building watches over Genji as he plays with the netsuke zoo of tigers, turtles and monkeys Hiro sent him.

When Genji sleeps, I sew for private clients, or I write to Hiro, or this journal.

I took a few hours for myself today and for twenty centimes crossed all Paris by omnibus. What a marvel it is. The electric lights on the Champs-Élysées!

My favourite place is Les Puces, exploring with Sally at my side. There is inspiration everywhere. Such beauty. I saw at least a dozen things I should have liked to pile up and bring home with us. Marvellous old chandeliers with heavy crystal drops, bentwood chairs and enamelled signs, old monogramed linen so soft and expertly patched it would be like sleeping in a cloud. I satisfied myself with a tin of old buttons today.

I'd always wished I had a tin like this, with buttons from my mother's clothes, and my grandmother's for that matter. Even Mrs Harris has a tin she keeps in the basket for mending people's clothes when she does the laundry. Even she has a history.

I realised something tonight. What is to stop me inventing my own? What is to stop me creating the woman I wish to become. I have no family. Tom is gone. Chō is gone, and Hiro is in Japan. It is just me and my son, and my little dog.

I am the mistress of my future.

I decide who I am.

Me

Lot 40

PARIS, 1900

Madame Kurosaki, Bel wrote to Hiro, *spends every evening working at her Singer sewing machine, making simple, classically inspired dresses which chime with le style Mucha which has enchanted all Paris. At first I washed and ironed the fabric myself, scaling up patterns, altering them subtly. Clients at Maison Liberty had been asking where my clothes are from. I have just taken on a seamstress to help with the orders from private clients. I have rented a small room in our building. I whitewashed it myself, and found tables at Les Puces. It is a couture maison in miniature – Maison Bright. I am so grateful for the silks you have sent, Hiro. I did not have the funds for fine fabrics, but with your support I can fill my orders. I will repay you just as soon as I can.*

I do not know how long I can go on, working by day for Maison Liberty and at night making my own designs. Mr Liberty has made me promise I won't leave too soon. It is not enough to have good taste, he says, you need sound business sense and a good head for finance. You must be able to withstand the conflicts and crises which come. He says I need a backer, as he had. He built Liberty on solid ground. They have property, investments, capital and goodwill. Liberty has a thousand employees now. One day, I will do the same.

Bel set down her pen and looked out at the peach sunrise over the grey rooves with the magpie eye of an artist. She collected the colours, the beauty of the world, tucking it away like treasure. *Pay attention*. Wasn't that always what Hiro said? She picked up his latest letter:

What you notice is a choice. What thoughts you accept is a choice, he wrote. *Learn to notice the good in the small moments that pass us by. The neighbour smiling in the street. The stranger who holds open a door for you. When I meditated in the garden today, I watched the rain on the water, the ripples it made. So is our life. I saw on the water life in all its lightness. Our birth is the raindrop; our life the water rippling, radiating, merging; our passing the stillness. Water remains water.*

Red sky in the morning, shepherd's warning, Bel thought, recalling one of Mrs Harris' sayings. She stood at her bedroom window, pinning her hair up in a fashionable bouffant roll, like Gibson's drawings. The sunrise blushed the frozen silver skyline of Paris. She had taken Genji skating the night before, lanterns strung above the silver rink. For an hour she had felt free as he played with the other children, like she was flying, her black boots hissing across the ice.

'Genji?' Bel went through to his room, and shook him gently awake, turning off the nightlight. 'Come on, sleepy head,' she said. 'Time for school. Breakfast is on the table.' She flung back his curtains, and paused to look at a photograph of them on the dresser. 'You were such a pretty baby,' she said. Genji groaned. Bel's face was obscured by the shade of a large picture hat. He was dressed in frills and lace, in a pleated smock. 'It *still* takes fifteen minutes to get you dressed,' she said, arranging his stay band, vest, shirt and drawers on the bed. Bel checked the maid had set out a jug and fresh soap for him on the stand beneath a pastel-tinted Mucha poster of Sarah Bernhardt in *Gismonda*. 'Up we get, I must go to work.'

'Maman . . .' he grumbled sleepily, rolling over.

'Don't forget your arithmetic,' she called over her shoulder, pulling on her coat. 'Have a good day, darling.' Bel fixed her hat on, and picked up her bag. 'Sally,' she called, waiting for the familiar patter of paws on the parquet. 'Sally?' Bel turned at the silence. She strode through the apartment, calling. 'Genji, is Sally with you?'

'No, Maman,' he said, stumbling from his room, rubbing his eyes. At a whimper from the drawing room, Bel turned. She ran in, and dropped to her knees.

'Sally?' She crawled forward, following the whimpering. Tucked below the sofa, Sally lay on her side near the ashes of the fire. She tried to raise her head as she saw Bel, her little tail beating. 'Oh, Sally, no,' Bel cried. She placed her hand on her chest, felt the weak beat of her heart.

'Maman, what is wrong with Sally?' Genji cried, falling to his knees. 'Is she sick? Sally?' The little dog whimpered.

'She is old, my love, and tired,' Bel said gently, her eyes welling with tears. *You've been slowing down for months, haven't you?* Bel stroked her side, soothing her. *Oh god, it's time, isn't it? I can't bear it.* A sob caught in Bel's throat. She tried to steady herself, for Genji. 'She is fifteen, darling, a good age, for a dog.'

'No! You mean she is dying?' he cried, a tear rolling down his cheek. 'No. No – don't die, Sally. Don't die.'

'It's alright, darling girl. My good girl,' Bel said, soothing her. 'My best girl.' Her tears fell onto Sally's soft fur. *Oh, Sally. I can't bear it.* The little dog gazed up at her. 'Haven't we been lucky?' Bel took a shuddering breath. 'I am so grateful for you.' She lifted her into her arms. 'There we are, Sally, I promise you won't be alone,' she said cradling her close. 'I won't leave you.' Bel screwed her eyes closed, kissing her soft head, breathing in her familiar scent. 'Genji, get dressed. We will take her to the veterinarian—'

'But she *hates* it there. You *know* she hates it there,' he said, leaping up and stamping his foot. 'I won't go!'

'Please don't argue. Sally needs us. We must make sure she isn't in any pain,' Bel said firmly. She looked down into the dog's trusting eyes. *Oh, Sally,* she thought. *We have had some adventures, you and I.* She cradled her close. *You have been my constant friend. My dear little soul.* Bel pulled a blanket from the sofa, and wrapped it around her, tucking Sally in. *You have always taken care of me. Now, I will be with you to the end.*

Lot 41

PARIS, 29 JULY 1985

'You're never going to believe what I've just found,' Mira said, running into the apartment. 'There's a whole—' She broke off as she saw Serge and several of his men struggling across the empty salon with dusty boxes in their arms.

'Morning, Hutch. You wanted stuffed ostriches?' Ned said, gesturing at a stuffed peacock on a brass stand. 'Trust Isobel to do better.'

'My god, was all this in the basement? I translated a passage in the pillow book about shopping at flea markets last night. Look at this stuff . . .' Mira caught sight of the two dog collars still on the side. *Sally*, she thought.

'I don't think Isobel ever threw anything out. I knew this place was suspiciously empty. The Victorians weren't known for their minimalism. My grandmother used to reuse bits of string, folded wrapping paper. The storage room is full from floor to ceiling.' Ned handed her a stack of letters. 'What else has BB got hidden away?'

'Follow me,' Mira said, beckoning to him, and they walked upstairs, their footsteps echoing around the sweeping stone staircase.

'You know what we haven't found so far? The Schiffer portrait of her.'

'I translated the passage where she talks about seeing it at the Academy. She said someone else bought it.'

'Maybe we can track it down?' Ned ducked into the attic store room. 'Oh my god,' he groaned. 'I thought we were nearly done.' He ran his hands through his hair, shaking a cobweb from his fingers.

'What's this all about?' Mira said. 'You have this beautiful apartment, full of a carefully curated collection of art, furniture and priceless textiles. A minimal, elegant space which would be at home in any design magazine—'

'And a basement full of all the dross we all accumulate in life.'

'Plus an attic full of her work?'

'Moreau did the same thing,' Ned said, thinking aloud. 'He curated his parents' rooms, idealised a life for posterity.'

'Do you think that's what happened here? Someone made an ideal life?'

'God knows. There's nothing for it. I'll call Tokyo and tell them what we've found.' Ned turned. 'Are you happy starting up here?'

'The housekeeper says this belongs to the Lamberts?'

'Okay, make a separate list and we'll get the lawyers to confirm it. There might be something which proves the provenance of things in the apartment. We're going to bring everything up from the basement and go through it in the salon.'

'Ned, why do you think the apartment was abandoned? There has to be a reason.' Mira folded her arms. 'I mean, it's nuts. The client has been sitting on valuable real estate, and all this stuff for decades.'

'It's not about money, is it? The client owns the apartments. We see it all the time, where people have even paid the rent on leaseholds for years.' Ned picked up an iridescent glass perfume bottle. 'That's nice. Tiffany, circa 1900. I'd say $400?'

'*Ned.*'

'You know every house has a drawer in the kitchen stuffed to the gunnels with bits of string and foreign currency?' He shrugged. 'This is just a bigger version of it. There are storage containers and bank vaults and abandoned homes all over the world. For whatever reason it's too big, or too painful, a job to face.'

'You mean the apartment is like Pandora's box? Once it's unlocked, everything will come pouring out?'

'Exactly. Who knows. Maybe the Kurosakis live in some minimalist zen apartment in Tokyo and they just have no desire for all this stuff, now her son has died. Maybe there was a falling out? Serge is good at this kind of thing. He has to deal with house clearances and estate sales all the time. I spotted a few decent pieces down in the basement, like a Godwin oak gong from 1877, and a couple of Coromandel screens, but there is a lot of . . . I don't like to say rubbish.'

'This is Bel's life,' Mira said, feeling protective suddenly.

'We really don't have time to be sentimental. We'll do a first sweep through the less valuable stuff like the glass domes of butterflies and the white peacock—'

'I rather like that peacock,' Mira said.

'He's yours.' Ned rapped his knuckles on the table. 'Sold to the lady in . . . what is that? Salmon?'

'Coral,' Mira said, brushing off her blouse. 'Salmon, honestly,' she muttered under her breath, rummaging in her pocket for her Liberty handkerchief. The print always reminded her of the Cacharel blouses Kim gave her as a child. The cotton smelt of lavender. Of home. She thought of her cosy mews house with a pang of longing. She missed her own bed. She imagined luxuriating in a hot bath with a glass of wine, chatting to Luke about the day. *I miss you*, she thought.

'I'm afraid we're in for a long night,' Ned said as he walked away.

Lot 42

PARIS, NOVEMBER 1900

We want our beloved pets to be with us forever. I miss Sally so much. Bel sat on a bench in the Jardin des Tuileries, pen in hand. *Even a walk in the park seems pointless without her company.* A short distance away the bee hives were silent in the long grass beneath a slate-grey sky. She stared unseeing at the people walking past along the rain-washed pale gravel paths – nurses airing their babies; couples, arm in arm; a group of demi-mondaines in fur-trimmed dresses; a gaggle of young men in uniform swaggering, raising their caps to them. Her letter to Hiro sat unfinished in her lap.

At work, she could wear a mask, but at home her sadness made her pricklier than usual with Genji, more irritated by his flamboyant sulks. *But then he is growing. I'm sure I was dramatic, and dreadful, too . . . Was I?* On days like today, when she had a few hours to herself, sadness cornered her. *I miss that little dog more than I can say.* She had tried everything. She'd ridden for miles in the Bois de Boulogne at first light. She had sat in the reading room of the Bibliothèque Nationale all morning, looking through endless pattern books of classical robes for inspiration. She'd walked the Palais des Mirages. Normally the fantastic interiors, the mirrors, the jungle and Indian temple, the Moorish palace amused her. Genji had always loved it when he was smaller – the elephants, the lights, the sinister cross-legged divinity. Today she found it tawdry and sad. Tonight there was a concert by Debussy to attend with friends, and while away the hours.

I took Genji on the new metro yesterday, she wrote to Hiro. *You would like the entrances by Guimard. I enclose a postcard for you.*

I keep busy – Lord knows I am busy at work. All of fashionable Paris is wild for Liberty style. But I just miss Sally, she wrote at last, facing her grief. *The apartment seems awfully quiet. How can one small creature bring such life and comfort to a house? Perhaps it is easier to grieve for an animal you love, than people, because it is so simple a love. So unclouded by misunderstanding and mistakes. The love of an animal is a pure and clear thing. The more I learn of the world the more I care for them than people.*

Genji already talks of something new – a parrot, or a kitten, but I can't bear to replace her so soon. I loved Sally, and she loved me. I held her as the veterinarian administered the fatal dose, and the last face she saw was mine. It is so strange a thing to see the life go out of one you love so swiftly, a light extinguished. My father's death was long and distressing. Chō's was sudden and shocking. Sally's was peaceful and full of the love which flowed between us. She was a good girl. My best girl.

What do you make of that, Hiro-san? What do your Buddhist and Shinto beliefs tell you about the love of a creature? Write me something comforting, old friend, for my heart is breaking.

I remain, always

Your Bel xx

She put the lid on her pen, and strolled on, dabbing at her eyes. The chill winter wind pinched her wet cheeks. *No, Mr Wilde has died?* she thought, seeing the headline on a newsstand. *How sad.* Bel paid for a newspaper, and tucked down into the fur collar of her coat. It felt like a lifetime ago, much longer than twenty-five years, when she had started at Liberty and Wilde's star rose high. *His joie de vivre had quite gone when last I saw him*, she thought, remembering his destitution. Bel breathed in the cold air. *Fashion is moving on. I long for modernity, clarity . . .*

Just as she reached the rue de Rivoli, a young woman sped past on a bicycle, and Bel stepped aside in surprise. The girl barrelled along the path, her skirts billowing, her fair hair coming loose beneath her hat. Bel laughed aloud in delight. *The speed, the freedom!* Bel hurried to catch up, longing to hold on to the vision. The girl swung out of the gates, joining the swirling traffic.

Bel was still thinking of the cyclist by the time she sat

down at her drawing board in her small studio, Maison Bright.

'A tisane,' she said to her assistant, pulling off her gloves. 'Something soothing – camomile?' The image of the young woman riding free and fast through the gardens came to her. 'Of course,' she cried. The white-coated women in the workroom fell silent. A seamstress with a mouthful of pins looked up from where she sat on her heels, adjusting the hem of a gown. Nearby, a woman was taking down a client's measurements: *bust, waist, neck to waist – cross your arms, my dear.* Bel waved at them all to carry on. She picked up a pencil and began to draw.

She knew, from watching Genji oil and clean his bicycle, there were chains and gears. *It is ridiculous to have billowing fabric near these.* She drew hard and fast, her mind clear for the first time in weeks. *I know all the insults – 'rational' dress, for 'new women'. I am both rational and new. I demand healthy clothing.* She frowned, recalling a design by Alice Bygrave she had seen for a convertible pulley skirt, and others with buttons hitching up the hems. Bel shook her head. It would not do. She thought of a lawn tennis match she had watched last summer, the girl's loose bodice, her corset cut high on the hip and low on the bust. *We need to be able to move freely.*

Frustrated, Bel picked up the latest copy of *Woman's World* and turned to the article they had printed about her:

> Madame Kurosaki, famed for her work at Maison Liberty, presented a small collection of her own 'Maison

Bright' at the Pavilion de l'Elegance at the Universal Exposition this year. Her elegance rivals that of Doucet and Worth. But while haute couture is booming, she suggests few women have the budget. Her collection this season, 'Shibui', proposes a Japanese-inspired wardrobe in which a woman will always feel beautiful and confident. 'Shibui is all about muted elegance,' she says. Layers of linen, silk, cashmere, velvet according to the time of year, draped over classically inspired shift dresses. To this she adds seasonal accents – a jewelled collar, an embroidered cuff. The shape of a garment changes entirely with the addition of a wide Japanese-style fabric belt – one side black, one white.

'I want dresses that make you feel as confident as a man,' Madame Kurosaki says. 'I give my ladies pockets so that they can go out as free as men. Be done with corsets; instead, exercise. It is nonsense that it will make you flat-chested and manly. It will make you strong!

'I make dresses so that when you look in the mirror for the first time, you see yourself, a better self. You feel: oh, *there* you are . . .' In closing, she advises: never buy a garment unless it makes you feel better than your favourite piece at home.

Yes. Confident and free, Bel thought, picking up her pen again. She worked late into the darkening evening, drawing and refining her design. When she finally left her sketches on the table for her assistants to cut the pattern in the morning, she was satisfied. *Make up in my size*, she said. *I wish to road-test the design.*

~

'Maman, are you sure?' Genji said a few days later. He stood in a quiet corner of the Bois de Boulogne, two bicycles leaning against the tree next to him.

'How hard can it be?' Bel said.

'But you are old—'

'I am forty-three, thank you very much, and I have perfect balance. My dance teachers told me so.' She stretched, limbering up. 'Mrs Harris tells me in her letter that in London they charge two shillings a lesson to be held on by some perspiring youth. We shall be more elegant.' She gave Genji a twirl. 'What do you think?' Her dress nipped in at the waist by a tailored canvas jacket swung out like the bell of magnolia blossom.

'But how are you to ride in that?' Genji said.

'Step one,' she said, bending to the hem of her gown. She took hold of two tags of teal grosgrain ribbon in the deep hem of her skirt, and pulled. The skirt rose up, revealing a coordinated split culotte beneath. She tied the ribbon around her waist, settling the outer skirt as a peplum. Genji clapped his hands. 'See? Pyjama trousers like a salwar kameez.' Then from the pockets of the trouser, Bel took two flexible jewelled cuffs. 'Straight out of the *1001 Nights*,' she said, clipping them around her ankles. 'You see?' she said, extending each foot. 'No fabric near the mechanism of the bicycle.' Bel patted the elbows of her jacket. 'Elegant tailoring but reinforced cotton to protect elbows and chest, should there be a fall.' She tapped the soft-looking teal hat she wore, and Genji heard a ring. 'To protect the head,' she said. 'Pockets here and here,' she said, pointing at the jacket. 'If the garment is cut with enough skill, they do not spoil the line. A woman can be free like a man of encumbrance, and safe from accident at the same time.' She gestured for Genji to hand over the new Steel Fairy bicycle.

Again and again, Bel pedalled up and down the quiet paths, Genji running alongside her, holding on to the saddle, helping her keep her balance. Her joy in the sensation of speed, of movement, overcame her nerves. She felt light and strong, her legs moving without the usual restraint of skirts and petticoats.

'I've got it,' she said, whizzing along the path. 'I've got it! You can let go.'

'I already have,' Genji called, laughing. Bel wobbled as she realised, but she caught herself, waving to him as she cycled on alone.

Lot 43

PARIS, MARCH 1904

Bel looked up from her *plat de jour* in the Lapin Agile bistro in Montmartre at the sound of a volley of Spanish and several gunshots. *Picasso.* Evening was falling, and the gas lamps were being lit on the street by a man with a long wand. She refilled her glass from an earthenware jug of white piccolo wine, and paused, her right hand hovering over her sketchbook, where it lay open on the red gingham cloth.

'Pay him no mind,' the waitress said. 'He gets bored when people trouble him for theory about painting. Now, he has Monsieur Jarry's revolver.'

Bel tried to ignore the argument, and gestured to Genji to get on with his schoolwork. Her mind was still full of the Moulin Rouge from the night before, the can-can dancers, the glittering costumes. She wanted to conjure that raw energy, that freedom in her new designs. She thought of Loie Fuller, her daring fire dance. *Something elemental ... She is short and stout but clever lighting and those silks extend her figure to elegance*. But the disturbance had broken Bel's concentration and her thoughts vanished like smoke. A thin man in his early twenties with a shock of dark hair falling over one eye stormed into the café like a bull, his dog Frika at his heels.

'Did you hear?' he said to the man with him. 'Monet is burning canvases again!'

'What a waste,' Braque said. 'Give me the canvases! I can reuse them.'

'He has his eye on posterity already . . .'

She recognised Picasso as the artist who lived in the building next door to her, at the Bateau-Lavoir. Bel had visited his lover Fernande to bring her an order of *passementerie* from Maison Liberty, a selection of tassels and fringed tapestry. The studios perched on the Butte de Montmartre like a shipwreck, all mismatched doors and cobbled-together wooden planks. Picasso's young group of artists and writers swaggered through Montmartre like pirates, congregating here each evening, talking and drinking.

Why should women's clothing not have something of a pirate, too? Bel sketched a bolero, frogged with gold. She thought of Poiret's shocking new dresses. *Allonger, amincir! He elongates the body and liberates us from corsets but hobbles our ankles. You fall over if you try to run for a bus.* Bel shook her head. It would not do. *What of the books I loved as a girl? The elegance of Mr Darcy, the vital energy of Heathcliff . . .* She thought of the nights she had huddled under the blankets in the Harrises' box room, losing herself in the romance of *Pride and Prejudice*, and *Wuthering Heights*.

What of that? She sketched a high-waisted dress, a tall collar with an elegant black bow as Picasso and his friends caroused. Every so often, Bel looked up to find Picasso watching her, pen in hand, those intense eyes fixed on her as she worked. *Mirada fuerte* – Fernande called it. The gaze to conquer, seduce, shock.

'Would you like a crêpe?' she said to Genji, and she spoke to the waitress.

'Yes,' Genji said, pushing away his schoolwork. 'I'm bored.'

'Yes, *please*. I know, let's play a game?' Bel said, turning to a blank page. 'Do you remember the *Pillow Book* I read to you? Let's make a list of all our favourite winter things.'

'*Marrons glacés*!' Genji said. 'Hot chocolate.'

'Apart from food?' she said, laughing. 'Wood smoke. Mist in the Luxembourg Gardens. Steam from a hot pine bath . . .'

As the group of artists rose to leave, Picasso strode over and tore off a piece of paper with a flourish.

'For you, Madame Kurosaki,' he said, bowing. Bel looked down at the exquisite line drawing of a mother and child. Picasso had captured her dark dress, the high neck embroidered with bright flowers and entwined leaves.

'You know my name?' she said.

'I asked Fernande who our lovely neighbour was,' he said. 'Perhaps you would care to model for me one day?'

'I am flattered, but no,' she said. *Never. Never again.* 'I am too old to model, and I'm sure Fernande would not care for it.'

'Ah,' Picasso said, batting away her objection. 'Fernande

does not care.' He ruffled Genji's hair. 'How old are you, boy?'

'Fourteen, sir.'

'How did you get that black eye?'

'A fight, at school, sir,' he said, blushing.

'Children can be monsters.' Picasso's eyes flashed. 'Hit first, lad, hit harder—'

'Monsieur, violence is never the answer.' Bel smoothed Genji's hair out of his eyes, and he shrugged her away.

'Perhaps Monsieur Kurosaki could . . . ?'

'He is no longer with us,' Bel said briskly.

'You will find *Montmartroises* very accepting,' Picasso said. 'It is a matriarchy here on the hill. We worship our women.' He waited for her to look at him. 'We enjoy the pleasures of love freely . . .' Bel had learnt to stare back like a true Parisian woman. She had studied the way they carried themselves, the way they walked. Now she held Picasso's gaze defiantly, acknowledging her worth.

'How goes your painting?' she said.

'My violent women? The desmoiselles d'Avignon will have their way with me.' *He loves only his art*, Fernande said, last time she saw her. *First I am on a plinth, now I am a doormat. He works naked, at all hours, locked in the studio downstairs.* Bel had seen the room, the dark African figures, the chaos, the skeletons pinned to the wall. *He eats like an invalid – water, milk, rice, a little fish.* Bel liked Fernande. She had worked for Poiret as a vendeuse and the two women shared a love of antiques, of interiors. Fernande swept through the dark chaos of the rooms in a bright yellow kimono decorated with flowers, like a Barbier illustration from *Les Modes* come to life. *I shall break with him, you will see . . .*

'We are going to watch Miss Lala at the Cirque Fernando tonight,' he said, stepping closer. Bel could smell soap, the ghost of Fernande's Chypre scent on his black wool jacket. *Be careful*, Fernande said, *he likes to find women for his friends. He will set you up, or seduce you himself.* 'Perhaps you would care to join us . . . ?' She pictured Degas' painting of the famous artiste, the terracotta walls of the circus, the roaring crowd.

'Thank you, but I have work to do. Come, Genji.' Bel pushed back the rough wooden bench, and walked out onto the street, along the vineyard's old cracked wall. Workers in their Sunday best strolled past arm in arm. *Free love?* Bel thought, as a wave of loneliness swept around her like a cape. *The chance would be fine.*

'Maman, why are you sad?'

'I'm not sad, just tired,' she said, hugging him in to her side. She studied Genji's face, the soft down of black hair on his lip, the dark points of his lashes, the livid bruise. *Did I do the right thing, bringing us her*e? she wondered. Paris thrilled her, but she knew they would always be on the outside, looking in.

Lamplight glinted on the windows of the tall houses, and the bare trees were as stark and sculptural as Modigliani's figures. They walked on towards where Sacré-Cœur was being built, and Bel stopped to browse in a gallery window, with cards and flyposters pinned to the side: *Lost Grey Parrot,*

Reward Offered. Café-Concert, Sunday . . . A row of coloured vases, cobalt and cranberry glinting in the lamplight drew her eye. She imagined jewel-bright glass buttons on a dress, tactile and lovely, a parade of models showing Maison Bright designs. *One day*, she thought, and walked on.

Lot 44

PARIS, 1909

I like the anonymity of middle age, Bel wrote in her journal. *As a young woman, the hunger of men's stares alarmed me. I have met many unhappy beautiful women in my time. If you do not feel well in your skin, it is a curse to be looked at, desired, envied all the time. The gaze is hungry. It devours. It wants. Hiding behind grief for my absent 'husband' saw off most suitors, but even they have dwindled over the years.*

Only one man pays court regularly, coming up with one scheme after another to find an excuse to work with me. Pierre de la Roche is an unlikely suitor. An elegantly dressed bear of a man in his late fifties, he owns several businesses around Paris, from restaurants to hotels. There is always something that needs my eye in one of his projects. He consults me about art, buying several pieces at Drouot with my advice, and gives free rein with furnishing and fabrics from Liberty. I like him. He makes me laugh again.

As he settled his account this morning, he picked up a banana from the bowl on the accountant's desk. 'Allô? Allô?' *he said, as if it were a telephone. 'May I speak to Madame Kurosaki?'*

'You fool,' I said.

'Pardon, wrong number,' he said, pretending to hang up. After he left, the accountant told me off.

'You must not call Monsieur de la Roche a fool,' he grumbled. 'Do you not know he is one of the wealthiest men in all Paris?'

~

'Miss King's silverware brings a delicacy to the scheme, do you not think?' Bel said to Pierre, adjusting a vase above the mantel in the lobby of his new hotel. 'I prefer it to the Cymric range. You know in Italy they are calling Art Nouveau *Stile Liberty*? We're cock-a-hoop at the free publicity.' He offered her his hand as she stepped down. 'I think we are all longing for something new,' she said, stretching wearily.

'You work too hard, madame.' Pierre gestured for his assistant to fetch Bel's coat. He held it for her himself. 'Come, we should have a little fun. Isadora is dancing tonight.'

'Miss Duncan bought yet more scarves from me,' she said, pinning down her hat. 'I brought half the store to her at the Hôtel Biron. Have you been?'

'No?'

'It's an enchanted place, the garden is something from a

fairy tale. Rodin, Rilke, Cocteau, so many artists have settled there it is practically a commune. I stayed late watching one of her rehearsals in the long gallery.' Bel noticed he did not take advantage of their closeness. *I feel safe with him*, she realised, looking up at him. *Like Hiro, not once has he behaved with impropriety, though we have worked alone many times.* 'I swear Miss Duncan has a halo of joy around her.'

'You do say the funniest things,' Pierre said.

'She told me of a system of positive thinking she subscribes to, by Monsieur Coué. Do you think you can conjure things, just by wishing them so?'

'I am sure of it.' He gestured for her to walk ahead. 'Look at all you have achieved. It strikes me that all Paris loves Liberty. All Europe, indeed. I am impressed with your success.'

'I am but a small part of it.'

'You are too modest.' Pierre bowed and kissed her hand. 'May I take you for supper, as a thank you?'

'I am meeting my son, Genji.'

'You have a son?' Pierre smiled thoughtfully. 'Well,' he said, without missing a step, 'allow me to invite you and your son to lunch on Sunday.'

'You're very kind,' Bel said. 'But—'

'I won't accept "no",' he said. 'You would be doing me a favour. The kitchen here needs a dry run before we open next week. I have invited a few friends.'

'In that case, thank you.'

'Good.' Pierre looked down at her. 'You are a remarkable

woman, madame. I admire your talent, your industry with your private clients. Haussmann's *grands boulevards* are filling up with *grands magasins* – it is a new world, a world of pleasure. We should be part of that.'

~

Over lunch, Pierre charmed them both. The kitchen produced dish after dish, tasty morsels of chicken confit and *blanquette de veau*. A bottle of Châteauneuf-du-Pape was brought up from the cellar.

'Tell me, Genji,' Pierre said, holding his ruby glass up to the firelight, 'what is it you wish to do with your life?'

'I'd like to garden,' Genji said, wiping his lower lip slowly.

'I only have tiny window boxes on our balcony in Montmartre,' Bel said, 'but it is remarkable what he grows. He's had a green thumb ever since he was a child.'

'Maman . . .' Genji said, scowling.

'You live in Montmartre?' Pierre said. 'What a coincidence. I just looked at plans for a new apartment, on the Avenue de la Tempête, or Avenue Junot as it will be.'

'I love that area. It will be an elegant street, I think.'

'It's a good investment?' He looked meaningfully at Bel.

'Yes.'

'Genji, I have a good friend at the botanical gardens,' he said. 'I'd be pleased to introduce you. It would be an excellent apprenticeship for you.'

'Would you do that?'

'Thank you,' Bel said as they left. 'Genji is only really

happy when he is in nature.' Pierre took her hand and pressed it to his lips.

'Isobel – may I call you Isobel? I should like to take you for dinner next week,' he said. 'Just the two of us.'

'I'd like that, Pierre,' she said.

Lot 45

PARIS, 1909

Bel tidied up her design boards and fabric samples, ready for her next client. The luxurious halls of Maison Liberty hummed with life, elegant women with their children dressed in Kate Greenaway smocks strolling among the displays. Bel flicked through a copy of *Les Robes de Paul Poiret* on her desk, studying Iribe's illustrations. *Ingenious*, she thought. *People will adore these pictures, the Oriental costumes*. She looked up in surprise as Genji ran in to the store, beaming.

'Maman,' he said, rushing over. 'They gave me a job! I start tomorrow at the Jardin des Plantes.'

'That's marvellous news!' As Genji chattered on, full of all he would be doing at the gardens, Bel turned her back to the entrance. She did not see the tall man with collar-length gunmetal-grey hair walk in. She didn't see him stop and look from her to Genji in surprise.

'I'll be damned. Bel Bright,' Orlando Schiffer said under his breath. He watched her for a moment, brushing aside the sales assistant. His silver-topped cane tapped across the marble floor. 'By gad, Miss Bright as I live and breathe,' he said. She froze at the sound of his voice, and turned slowly, adrenalin coursing cold through her.

Bel stepped into a shaft of sunlight, protecting Genji.

'And I shall be learning about water plants, too. Maman—' Genji broke off and turned to Orlando.

'Well, well.' The men looked at one another, eye to eye. *They have the same profile*, Bel realised, panicking. She saw Orlando's dissipated face change from surprise to realisation.

'How old are you, boy?' he said.

'Twenty, sir,' Genji said, frowning.

'Mr Schiffer!' Bel said, raising her hand to stop him.

'Who's your mother, boy?'

'My name is Genji Kurosaki. This is my mother.'

'Really?' Orlando said. 'Y'see, I knew a Kurosaki . . .'

'Genji is my son,' Bel said, anger rising in her.

'But my birth mother died when I was born,' Genji said, looking at her in confusion.

'Ha! I knew it. Don't you think it's quite striking,' Orlando said, standing side by side with Genji, facing her. She could smell the drink on his stale breath, saw the yellow tinge to his eyes. 'What are you doing this evening, lad? Come with me to the Opéra – the *foyer de la danse* is quite the place to meet young ladies. What a pair we would make—'

'Is that all you can say?' Bel rounded on him, controlling her fury. 'Chō died. My friend died, and you did nothing – nothing – to see if your child was in need.'

'She is not the first beautiful girl with an ugly story. Would you have let me see him?'

'That's not the point—'

'I am an artist. I am not made for bourgeois responsibilities—'

'Artist? From what I hear you have done nothing of worth since you stole my face for your pathetic little joke.'

'Oh, Miss Bright, Miss Bright . . .' He looked around the store, and picked up a silk scarf with the silver tip of his cane. 'The world is still a doll's house to you, is it not? Do you still believe you can play dress-up and make-believe, and make the sad, bad memories disappear—'

'How dare you, sir.'

'Peddling dreams to lost souls.' Orlando waved the scarf, and Bel snatched it away.

She stepped towards him, her fists clenched so tightly her knuckles shone like seashells.

'Stay away,' she said, under her breath, glancing round at the customers staring at them, whispering behind their hands and fans. 'I will not have half of Paris talking scandal about us.'

'Ah, but is it the good half?'

'You are monstrous.'

'You were always rather wonderful when you're angry,' Orlando said, leaning unsteadily on his cane. 'Come, let us take a drive,' he said, slapping Genji on the back. 'Let us have some cards! D'you play cards, my boy?'

'Is everything alright, Madame Kurosaki?' Pierre said, striding into the store.

'Mr Schiffer was just leaving.'

'But I've only just arrived,' he said. 'I've missed you, *Madame Kurosaki*,' he said. 'We have so much to catch up on.' He nudged Genji. 'You see, your *mother* and I are old friends—'

'Enough, sir,' Pierre said, stepping between them.

'Did ye marry that Japanese fellow who mooned around after you, then?'

'He did not *moon*,' Bel said, colouring.

'Oh, we all wanted Miss Bright—' Orlando said unsteadily.

'You, sir, are drunk.' Pierre pushed him away.

'And she is a liar,' he hissed, bumping into a display of scarves. 'That boy is mine. Look at him. Look at me.'

'I see an uncouth lush, is what I see,' Pierre said, marching him to the door with the help of the *cicerone*. 'You're washed up, Schiffer, and you don't deserve to breathe the same air as a woman like her.' He shoved him out onto the street. 'Stay away, do you hear?'

'Or else?' Orlando said, lurching.

'You'll be sorry,' Pierre said. Something vicious in his look stopped Orlando.

'Fine.' He brushed off his jacket. 'I wanted nothing to do with the bastard or his mother then, and I want nothing to do with them now. As for Miss Bright, ask her about the Academy . . .' He waved his hand dismissively, and weaved off into the midday crowds.

'Maman,' Genji said, 'who was that man?'

'No one, darling.' Bel pressed her hand to her racing heart.

'Was it true? What he said?'

'Genji, darling—'

'Tell me,' he cried. 'Was that vulgar man my father?'

'Genji, that's enough,' Pierre said. 'Show your mother some respect.' The boy looked at him in surprise, and coloured.

'Madame, you're shaking,' Pierre said, bringing a chair over for Bel to sit down.

'Thank you. It was a shock, that's all.' She forced a smile. 'After all these years . . .'

'The Academy?'

'There was a scandal, in London. He painted a nude, supposedly of me.' She looked up, gauging his reaction. *How much did Schiffer say? Did he tell him I modelled, once?* All she saw was concern. 'Schiffer is Genji's father. My friend, Chō Kurosaki, died in childbirth.'

'I am sorry.'

'For a while, after we moved to Paris, I wondered what I would do if he ever turned up here, but then in time I forgot.'

'You adopted your friend's child?' Pierre said quietly, and Bel nodded.

'My client is here,' she said, seeing an elegant woman sweep through the doors. She quickly pressed her trembling fingertips to her eyes.

'Be strong. You are worth ten of him.' Bel looked up at him, grateful for his support. *I am so tired*, she realised. *So tired of doing it all alone. Always working. Always caring. How good it is to have someone care for me.* 'Isobel, I came to check we are attending the Ballets Russes tonight? I'll send a carriage.'

'A carriage? I rather thought you would have adopted the new automobiles?'

'Oh, I have, but I maintain pairs of horses, too.' He leant towards her. 'Horses are more beautiful, more romantic, don't you think? Until tonight.' He kissed her hand. 'I have a surprise for you, too.'

Lot 46

PARIS, 1909

The carriage clipped along the Boulevard Haussmann, rain-washed pavements gleaming in the evening sun. Pierre tucked a sable rug across them, and Bel's pale-gloved hand settled on the soft fur. She looked out as the carriage slowed in traffic. A poster by Alphonse Mucha for Sarah Bernhardt's *La Dame aux Camelias* caught her eye, hanging in the window of a picture framers. *Bravo, Sarah*, she thought.

'Is it true,' he said, 'that Bernhardt sleeps in a coffin among a carpet of lilies?'

'Sarah is remarkable,' Bel said. *And a canny businesswoman. She tells me she has sold four thousand of those posters.* 'I helped her with the decoration of her palace in Parc Monceau.' Bel's magpie eye quickly plundered Mucha's design – the romantic drape of the fabric, the background of silver stars on a lavender ground. *La Dame*, Bel thought, conjuring up an image of a velvet evening cloak, a constellation of beaded, glittering stars. She reached for the tiny sketchbook hanging from the silver chatelaine clipped to her skirt and jotted a note. It felt like a new spirit was growing in Paris. Something freer, more sensual. She glanced at Pierre's handsome profile, his strong hands resting firmly on his knees as the carriage rolled along. The grey pearl in his stock gleamed softly in the half-light.

'Always working, always thinking, Isobel,' he said, winking at her.

'Sorry.' She tucked the book away.

'I admire you for it.' He glanced back at the Bernhardt poster, and plucked the white camellia from his button hole. He held it up to her, swept it behind his palm like a magician. Bel laughed in surprise.

'How . . . ?' Pierre reached behind her ear and produced it with a flourish, tucking it into the lapel of her jacket.

'Misspent youth,' he said. 'I was a little street hustler.'

'You? Never!'

'Oh yes, cups, cards, I learnt all the ways to part people from their cash.'

'You are full of surprises.'

'My favourite deception I learnt from a Japanese fellow. Have you ever seen the butterfly trick?' Bel shook her head. 'With two fans you conjure their motion.'

'Are they real butterflies?'

'No, no. They are only paper, an illusion of life.' His fingers sculpted the air.

'Where are we going?' she said, holding on to the frame as the carriage lurched and swept on through the streets of Paris into the countryside.

'It's a surprise,' Pierre said. It was a bright evening, the golden sun cast long shadows from the lime trees across the razed fields, stoops of corn gathered in. Already there was a hint of autumn in the air, a crispness, the scent of bonfires on the breeze. *In autumn, the evenings* . . . Bel thought of Sei Shōnagon as she settled back and let the scene roll past. She knew that something was afoot with Pierre. Their silences had always been comfortable. *He reminds me of Hiro in that way*, she thought, looking at his grave profile, the precise trim of his beard. *Does he dye his hair?* Tonight he seemed charged, tense. He sat upright, gazing out of the window, his index finger tapping a silent code on his thigh.

Bel wore one of her own creations – a diaphanous silk skirt and blouse in shades of autumn gold which brought out the fire in her hair. Over this she wore a warm wool coat she had designed and made up by an Italian tailor. The collar was deep and luxurious, fastening with a single gold button on her collarbone. The finishing touch, a fine Cossack hat in the Russian style.

'Look,' he said, pointing. 'Deer.' The doe and fawns raised their head as the carriage swept by. Bel remembered Hiro telling her about the Kasuga shrine in Nara. A thousand deer grazing peacefully in a forest of cedar and oak, returning to their pens each evening at the blow of a horn. She wanted to show Hiro this moment. 'Maybe that is a good sign,' he said quietly. 'You know, that is what you reminded me of the first time I saw you.'

'Really?'

'Yes, I strolled into this fashionable English shop on the Avenue de l'Opéra, that all of Paris was raving about,' he said, turning to look at her. 'And there, among the bolts of silk, I saw this beautiful young woman with Titian hair rise up and look at me with these huge dark eyes.'

'My eyes are green,' she said, smiling.

'They seemed dark, to me.' They sat comfortably together, their faces close. *Will he kiss me?* she thought. Pierre blinked and looked away. Bel exhaled, surprised at her disappointment. 'We have been friends a long time, have we not, Isobel?'

'Yes,' she said. 'Time seems to be accelerating.'

'Life is like that. When young, summers are endless. Now . . .' He clicked his fingers.

'I value our friendship, Pierre,' she said. 'Life is hard, sometimes. Friendship makes the impossible, possible.'

'Ah, life is impossible. Love is impossible.' He shrugged. 'You are an artist, Isobel, you need to toughen up for business.' Pierre knocked on the roof of the carriage.

'But keep a tender, hidden heart?'

He looked directly at her, and nodded. 'You understand,' he said. 'Good.'

'Where on earth are we?' Bel said.

'Near your friend Monet, in Vernon.' He unlatched the door. 'Come, we must walk from here.' Bel looked down at her gold silk evening shoes, and took a breath. *Dressed for dinner, not hiking*, she thought.

'Your shoes,' Pierre said, noticing her walking delicately along the rutted farm track.

'It's fine,' Bel said.

'Nonsense.' Pierre swept her easily into his arms, and she laughed. 'I knew my daily sessions in the boxing gym would be worthwhile.'

'You box?' she said, her arm around his shoulder.

'I box, I row, I fence.'

'So do I,' she said. 'Or I did. I haven't had time for years.' Bel smiled. 'I even tried *kendo* when in Japan. My friend Hiro taught me the basics in London.'

'You should take it up again,' Pierre said. 'I have a marvellous fencing master who comes to the house.'

'You are full of surprises.'

'The best is yet to come.' From behind a small copse of trees, she heard a roar of air. 'Look,' he said. In the middle of the field, a striped hot-air balloon waited for them.

'How wonderful!' Pierre set her down on the soft grass, and Bel ran towards the balloon, glancing back at him. Pierre jogged to catch up. He helped her into the gondola, and she looked up at the balloon towering above them, at the jet of flame.

'Monsieur Gifford, we are ready.' Pierre nodded to the men, and the balloon lurched into the air. Bel steadied herself, but she felt Pierre's arm around her, keeping her safe. 'I feel like I'm flying,' she said, as the balloon settled into a steady ascent.

'I've wanted to go up in one of these ever since I tried

the tethered balloon in the Tuileries as a young man!' Pierre cried. 'I knew you'd love it.' Bel's head swam with vertigo, but soon they were drifting silently above the fields, with Paris, silver, ahead of them. An assistant popped open a bottle of champagne, and offered Bel a glass.

'Thank you,' she said, fixing her gaze on the horizon.

'Look at it, Isobel,' Pierre said, lowering his face to her level as they drifted over Père Lachaise at eight thousand feet. 'All Paris can be yours.'

'Mine?' She turned slightly.

'As I said. We have known one another for some time, haven't we?' Bel nodded, her heart racing. *Surely he isn't going to—* 'I have the greatest regard for you, as a designer, a businesswoman . . .' *And as a woman?* she thought. 'Isobel, I should like to make you an offer.' She turned to him. 'I am a wealthy man. I have many businesses, but I do not have a fashion house.' He took her left hand and ran his finger over the gold band. 'This – husband of yours . . . ?' Bel shook her head.

'I wear a ring to prevent unwanted advances.'

'Like this?'

'This is a considered advance, I think.' Bel looked up. 'And not unwelcome.'

'Good, I am glad.' He pressed her hand to his lips. 'Isobel, I would like to ask for your hand. I propose that we marry, that my name will give you better protection than an absent husband. I know you do not love me—' He pressed his finger to his lip when she protested. She thought of Hiro. *Still he talks of love, and hope. But he is not here, and you are.* 'It would suit me to have a wife, to have a companion to come home to.' Bel imagined cosy evenings before the fire, with Pierre and Genji. Waking in the morning with a feeling of contentment and peace, the house vibrating with order, and love. *Not waking in panic and dread at four a.m., afraid of the worst.* 'I will give you beautiful homes, security, and enough capital to found your own business.'

'And passion? What of love? I have never had the sense that you desire—'

'My private life would remain just that. Private.' *So.* 'Our marriage would be one of companionship.'

'Convenience?' she said.

'Yes.' He held her gaze. *That is the compromise?*

'I understand,' Bel said. 'I don't know what to say.'

'Say yes,' Pierre said. 'It would give me the greatest joy to see you succeed.' He drew a nameplate in the sky. 'Imagine: Maison de la Roche. No mere emporium of fancy goods. An haute couture house, Isobel.'

'Maison Bright?' she said firmly.

'If you insist.' Pierre laughed, and held her shoulders. 'Marry me?'

'Yes,' she said, smiling. 'Yes, I will marry you.'

Pierre turned Bel to the golden view of the city, his arms around her. 'All of this, Isobel. All of Paris is yours.'

~

Postcard of a hot-air balloon:

I understand.

I believe some things are beyond time: love and friendship

I still hope - H

Lot 47

PARIS, 1909

Maison Bright, Bel thought. The reception desk of the house on Place Vendôme sat waiting, a fresh pad of paper beside the telephone. Soon the clients would be calling to make appointments with their vendeuses. The Maison would welcome the press and commercial buyers at the first show, the clients at the second. Bel's stomach tightened with anticipation. She paced through the house, checking every detail of the final decoration. Upstairs she could hear the cleaners chatting. She had taken much that she loved from Liberty. She wanted a sense of luxury, yes, but also a sense of home. She thought of her Maison like a beehive. The boutique, the salon, the *cabine des mannequins* for the models, fitting rooms, and above, the *ateliers* with her workers. She had carved out intimate rooms in the grand house, which could be dressed as seasons and fashions changed.

Bel glanced into the new salon, and raised a hand in greeting to the floor polisher, who skated across the parquet with pads on his feet as if he were on ice. Seeing her, he did a pirouette and bowed. The gilt chairs were stacked in the shadows, still in their dustsheets. Everything felt magical to her. She imagined the cameras, lights, perfume, flowers. She wanted her clients close enough to the models to hear the silk rustle, to smell their fragrance. Sarah Bernhardt and Isadora Duncan had already promised to attend the first collection. Even the changing rooms were opulent and well lit. Bel wanted her clients, famous or not, to feel and look like stars. She installed working fireplaces, and an inviting country house staircase swept up through mirrored walls to the top-floor workrooms and offices, with her private apartment above. All was light and comfort. Pierre's builders had done an immaculate job – but, then, she had come to expect nothing less from him.

Everything in Pierre's life was perfect, she had discovered. In the evenings when they were not out at the opera or ballet, or hosting a dinner for his business associates, he stayed home at their mansion in Montparnasse, and liked to sit listening to the gramophone. Sometimes Genji played for them on the grand piano. Bel let the music wash over her like warm water. As she worked on her needlepoint, she watched Pierre reading. Part of her longed to mess up his perfectly brilliantined hair.

This was the compromise I made, she thought. *I have known love, and loss. I have known devotion*, she thought, Hiro's latest letter crinkling in her pocket. *And now . . . ?*

Bel walked on through the *maison*, turning on the lamps

in the empty rooms. *This is what I wished for – autonomy, a business of my own.* She remembered the only time Pierre kissed her, after they took their vows. The night of their wedding, she lay awake, alone. *What of desire?* She looked at her reflection in the full-length mirror in the workroom, and saw a woman in her prime. *Is all passion spent?*

Bel asked the builders to line one entire wall of her studio with cork for her drawings, cuttings, photographs. *If it is good enough for Monsieur Proust,* she thought, pinning the first images up. All fashionable Paris had heard about his cork-lined room, where he wrote in bed each day.

Bel sat on a high stool at the table, working late into the night. Long after her assistants had gone home, she pinned up scraps of tapestry and silk, prints of architecture, photographs of nature – a branch of gingko. She remembered the shadowy rooms of the ryokan near Tokyo, the gleam of gold leaf on lacquer in the candlelight. She took down a bolt of midnight blue velvet, and scrunched it up, testing the weight of the fabric. *It has hand.* Bel cut a piece, and pinned it on the muslin. She sketched an opera cape, a draped hood, pinned by two silver ginkgo clasps. *East, West.*

Bel sketched the outline of a daringly simple floor-length, high-necked dress on four sheets of paper. She wrote *fire, earth, water, air* at the top. Working quickly, she pinned a sample of silk onto each one, in shades of garnet, sage, teal and alabaster. The waist of each dress was embroidered and jewel-encrusted – shimmering sparks of beads, a fall of green leaves, the glitter of a waterfall, the cold beauty of stars. The light of the beads shone on the silken pile of the jewel velvets, shimmered through the sheer silks and chiffons. It would be complex, making the weight of the embroidered beads on the sheer fabrics seem effortless, but she knew her seamstresses could do it. She could imagine her mannequins walking the salon, throwing back their cloaks to reveal the dresses below.

The ginkgo tree is very ancient, a living fossil, she remembered Hiro telling her as he trimmed the roots and branches of Chō's trees, repotting them to take home to Japan. She remembered how delicately he brushed the soil from the roots with his fingertips. *It is treasured as a symbol of resilience and hope, its leaves as yin and yang.* She sat back on the stool now, and tossed down her pencil, satisfied with the mood, the feel of the new collection. *Hope.* She thought of Hiro's heartbroken face when he realised she and Tom were lovers. *If we had only stayed with the Libertys' party in Japan, Tom would have returned to England and married Victoria, and Hiro and I—*

'Isobel? Where are you?' Pierre strode into the workroom in a top hat and tails, bringing the scent of the outdoors with him. 'Still working? Come, the performance begins soon.' She felt the cold air blowing away the past, all those missed moments, all the 'if onlys' fluttering away like autumn leaves.

Lot 48

PARIS, 1910

March 1910

My dear Hiro –

The clocks have stopped! The floods since January are devastating, dark and threatening, icy water only now receding. Boulevard Haussmann is passable only on raised passerelle *walkways. The bridges are underwater. Phones are cut off and food is scarce in the city. Genji tells me the Jardin des Plantes is devastated – a giraffe died! But we will rebuild, we will begin again.*

Monet's garden in Giverny is flooded to the top of the green bridge. He fears for his plants, and they are quite cut off. Worrying when Madame Monet is so ill.

Mrs Liberty sent me a copy of her book of photographs from Japan. What memories.

I am glad you have taken a companion. I have no right to feel so, but my heart ached when I read your letter. I remember how charming the geishas were. I understand.

We must use up our days, live every moment. How many more springs do we have to look forward to, my dearest friend? How many more seasons of blossom?

I think of you, always.

I miss you,

Bel

2nd October 1910

My dear Mademoiselle Chanel –

One of my assistants brought the article in the Comœdia Illustré to my attention. Your hat is most becoming. I should like to meet you to discuss creating a line of hats for my forthcoming collection. You are welcome to call on me at the Place Vendôme at your convenience.

Please accept this expression of my respectful sentiments.

Isobel Bright

~

Bel and Pierre strolled through the Tuileries Gardens at Paris' magic hour, street lamps glowing gold against a violet sky. Couples passed by, arm in arm, some men tipping their top hats as they recognised them. Bel pulled the black fox-trimmed coat around her ruffled collar, her high Russian boots crunching on the gravel.

'I do like that hat,' Pierre said.

'Paris has gone wild for Scheherazade.' Bel thought of

Bakst's extraordinary costumes. 'I met the most marvellous young milliner today,' Bel said. 'She will go far. Oh, and Charles sent the latest copy of *The Studio*, have you seen it?' Bel said.

'The chap you visited Japan with?'

'Yes.' Her went mind went back to that time, to Tom.

'I can't say I like that fellow Beardsley's designs for the magazine. Rather sinister.' Pierre frowned.

'There was an article about peasant costumes in Novgorod that Charles thought I'd enjoy. Marvellous embroidery.' Bel touched the collar of her coat. 'You'd enjoy his company. He knows all about trade in Yokohama and London.'

'A useful contact,' Pierre said, helping her into their carriage.

At Maxim's, they made their way through the crowds gawping at the four beauties in fur coats drinking champagne in the windows. There was an explosion of flash bulbs as Sarah Bernhardt swept through. Spying Bel, she flung her arms wide, and the women embraced. Pierre gestured to the chasseur on the way to their discreet corner table.

'Bring me a copy of *Paris Soir*,' he said, dropping coins into the man's palm.

'Sarah's invited us for supper on Friday.' Bel settled on the red velvet banquette.

'Are we free?'

'I think so,' Bel said. 'I had a letter from Emma Liberty today.'

'Have they forgiven you yet for jumping ship?' Pierre frowned and wiped a pale speck of *stabilisé* dust from the Tuileries paths from his shoe.

'Of course. She describes their new home, Lee Manor, to me. They have some three thousand acres, with tenant cottages and farms. Mr Liberty has his own marble seat at Marylebone Station—'

'Quite the emperor, this Liberty fellow.'

'Are you jealous?' She smiled. 'The manor is marvellous, full of tiger skins, butterflies, birds' eggs—'

'Sounds more like a zoo,' Pierre said, glancing over the wine list. He spoke to the waiter, and settled back. 'Is that what you wish?'

'A zoo?' Bel laughed. 'Mr Liberty's study sounds stylish. A white carpet, white Persian cat, opals—'

'A snowstorm, now?'

'You tease me,' Bel said. 'I learnt a great deal from him.'

'Are you happy? With the *maison*?'

'Yes—'

'But?'

'I've always thought good design is not just about exclusive haute couture. Working with Liberty showed me it's perfectly possible to bring beautiful design to the masses.' Bel sipped her champagne, her eternity band glinting in the lamplight. 'I would give women beauty for the body and the home. I wish to create perfumes, cosmetics—' She thought of the onsen in Japan, the scent of cypress and rosemary. 'I want to make women feel truly alive.'

'Is producing quality items *en masse* possible, or financially worthwhile?'

'Let's find out. I don't want to follow fashion. I want to make new ones.'

'Move on? From the old guard?' He leant forward and lowered his voice. 'Talking of which – see there? The woman with the Count de Montesquiou.'

'Is it true he once jewelled a tortoise?'

'Quite true. Is that not the clientele we should be courting?'

'Kept women?' She shook her head. 'These women are fettered by corsets, lace, diamonds and pearls. The weight of the clothes—'

'I overheard a wag saying to seduce such a woman requires several weeks' notice to disrobe all the layers. It is like moving house.'

'I am looking forward, Pierre.' She gestured at the restaurant. 'This excess, this sense that good times will last forever, is a fairy tale.'

'I like fairy tales,' Pierre said quietly. 'I like collecting beautiful things.' He looked at Bel. 'Do you really think it is possible to change people's taste?'

'I believe it is,' Bel said firmly.

'Would you rather be courting the intellectuals at Tortonis? Dressing the absinthe drinkers?'

'People respond to good design. Most need clear direction in taste.' She gazed around the room. 'We can give them that. Just look at the rubbish being mass-produced for the newly affluent. I would no more wish to clutter my house with knickknacks and antimacassars than die.' Pierre laughed indulgently. 'I remember my friend, Hiro, telling me how they live in Japan.'

'You talk often of him,' Pierre said thoughtfully. 'Were you ever . . . ?'

'Lovers?' Bel said, laughing too lightly. *We missed our moment, that tipping point where friends naturally become more. But why does the sight of a letter from him on the morning tray fill my heart with joy? Why do I see a painting, or a fabric and think:* I must tell Hiro?

'Isobel—' Pierre wagged his finger. 'You are avoiding the question.'

'No, of course not. Hiro was a valued colleague.' *He was – he is – more. Much more.*

'And that is all?' Pierre leant closer and spoke quietly. 'Bel, our marriage—' He took her hand. 'You are happy with our arrangement, aren't you?'

'Of course, my dear.' *Am I?* she thought. *Why do I ache so?* She felt the heat rise in her cheeks. *Why do I lie awake in a bed that burns with longing?*

'Our arrangement . . .' Pierre's conversation always made Bel think of a collector picking up piece after piece – *this word? Or this?* 'I would have no objection if you sought company—'

'Company?' *I live in that mausoleum with you, surrounded by all the gadgets and conveniences you can buy – electric lights and telephones and gramophones, and I can't breathe. I can't breathe.*

You collect things and people and places like it's a game. And you collected me.

'Having you in my life has brought me great happiness. I am proud of all you are doing at Maison Bright.'

'I could not do it without you,' she said. *Where is this leading? He sounds like he is about to confess something.*

'But—' *What now?* Bel's heart beat fiercely. *Does he regret?* 'I wish you to be happy, to be fulfilled. You are a passionate woman—'

'You wish me to take a lover?'

'As you wish,' he said. '*Une petite aventure* – a little episode is nothing, in a long marriage. I would have no objections, as long as you were discreet.' *And what of you?* she thought. *The absences, the nights 'working late' when you return in the early hours.*

'Tell me, why did you not just pay some *demimondaine* to marry you?' Her voice was brittle. She gestured towards a young woman with red camellias pinned in her hair. She sat with the Baron, a notorious ether addict, who was breathing into his cobweb linen handkerchief. The tip of her small red velvet slipper poked from below the tablecloth like the nose of a mouse.

'Isobel, lower your voice.'

'The *grandes horizontales* know perfectly well how to conjure a smoke screen, to maintain a house—'

'I have angered you. That is not what I wanted.'

'What *do* you want, Pierre?' Her eyes smarted with humiliation.

'Your happiness.' Pierre drew out a leather case from his pocket, placing it on the table before Bel. 'Please, a token of my esteem, for my beautiful wife,' he said. 'Happy anniversary.'

'Our anniversary?' She opened the box to find two Lalique haircombs.

'I know how you love butterflies.'

'Pierre, they are beautiful. Thank you.' *The butterfly trick*, she thought. *Just an illusion of life. Our marriage. My life.*

'Come,' he said, squeezing her hand. 'Let us see La Belle Otero at the Folies tonight? That always amuses you. Forget what I said.'

Lot 49

PARIS, 1911

'Next,' Bel said, ushering the model forward. She adjusted the shoulder of the draped summer dress, and the girl stepped out, hand on hip, her slender form leaning back slightly, one hand holding the number of her design aloft. The previous model swept backstage and the grey-clad dressers fell on her like pigeons chasing a morsel. A Schubert melody drifted through from the salon where all of fashionable Paris sat on a horseshoe of gold chairs, Pierre among them. The room was dressed as a summer garden, a *trompe l'œil* of the South of France rising up to a blue sky, green trees framing the doorways. Bel had the air scented with jasmine and the rugs freshly washed with Savon de Marseilles, the scents which meant summer to her.

In summer, the nights . . . Bel thought, checking the collar of a blouse with full bell sleeves. *How I long for escape.* She thought of the summers of her childhood, the light, the freedom.

'Genji,' Bel said, ushering him forward. He was the perfect height and slender build to model Bel's first foray into menswear, and he would accompany the bride at the end of her show. She brushed down his forelock of glossy black hair and he shook it out, annoyed. 'I am still your mother,' she said, and stood on tiptoe to kiss him on the cheek.

Genji raised his arm for the bride as if he were bullfighting. The wedding dress was an ingenious long lace coat over a simple pale silk shift which could be worn again. *It's ludicrous,* Bel said to the press, *that a woman should spend half her dress budget for the year on a design which she can wear only once, or cut up for christening gowns. The Maison Bright bride will have an elegant evening gown, and a delightful lace jacket which can be worn in summer, or dyed for mourning.*

'And the veil can be reused for curtaining, presumably?' one of the fashion writers said, raising a laugh from the others. Bel gestured to the window of her office, where a long length of exquisite lace billowed in the breeze.

'Precisely,' she said, coolly. 'Beauty is beauty. It is wasted if it is hoarded away in boxes and attics for best. Maison Bright believes that every day is beautiful.'

That became their tagline. Every piece that Bel designed, from vases and ashtrays to bridal gowns and golfing outfits, was illustrated with *Every Day Is Beautiful* beneath the company name.

'Tell us, Madame de la Roche,' a journalist said. 'Monsieur Poiret has launched *Martine*, his cosmetics and fragrance line. Do you have ambitions to rival him?'

'If I did not, I would not be in the game.' She leant forward. 'Rival Poiret? I will exceed him.' Several people gasped. 'We live in a time of change. In the arts we have Nijinsky, Stravinsky, Kandinsky.' The edge of Bel's hand hit her palm – one, two, three. 'We have Picasso's Cubism.'

'You are an artist now?' someone said.

'Why not?' she said.

Lot 50

PARIS, 1912

'Madame,' Bel's assistant said. 'There is a young lady in reception to see you.' Bel looked up from her drawing board. A spring storm wind buffeted the high windows, sheets of rain lashing the square.

'Are we expecting anyone?'

'No.' Bel heard the annoyance in her voice. 'But she refuses to leave.'

Bel sighed and strode through the house. 'May I help you?' she said, her voice curt. She hated to be interrupted. Until she had a design pinned down, it threatened to float away or disappear entirely like a bubble on the wind.

A woman in her early twenties with silver blonde hair turned to her, the hem of her soaked coat swinging out. 'Madame Bright?'

'Yes.' Bel's low heels clicked across the marble hall. Her practiced eye took in the woman's poise, her fine bones. *Like a racehorse*, she thought. Here was a classic French beauty, confident and nonchalant, even when she looked like someone had thrown a bucket of water over her.

'I apologise for the intrusion. My name is Françoise Lambert.' Her hand rested on the swell of her stomach for a moment, and Bel realised she was pregnant. Françoise saw her notice, and blushed, letting the coat fall free.

'It *is* an intrusion,' Bel's assistant snapped. 'You must make an appointment to see Madame at a more convenient time—'

'Enough,' Bel said. Looking closer she saw the weariness in the young woman's face. She gestured towards the coral velvet sofa in the reception, and told her assistant to bring a tisane for them. 'Please, take off your coat – you'll catch a chill.' Bel signalled to the receptionist. 'Would you fetch Mademoiselle Lambert a towel?'

'Thank you,' Françoise said, exhaling as she sat. 'I have been on my feet all day.'

'When is your baby due?' Bel said, her voice kind.

'In the summer.' She dabbed at her face, and towelled her hair.

'The father?' She looked pointedly at the woman's ringless right hand. Françoise shook her head. 'You are not the first young woman to have been treated badly,' Bel said. Françoise looked directly at her, the last piece of armour laid down.

'Your time is precious, so I'll be direct. I love your designs,' she said.

'Why?'

'You cut like you draw,' she said without hesitation. 'Your

clothes are art. I am a model. I have walked for Poiret and Worth, but now of course no one can use me.'

'Then they are missing a trick,' Bel said, sitting back in her chair, resting her head against her hand. 'Turn your profile to the light,' she said. Françoise looked towards the window, the storm light illuminating her fine features, her high cheekbones and sculpted jaw. The assistant set down the tea. 'Thank you,' Bel said. From a silver caddy, she picked out a dry ball, and dropped it into the glass teapot. 'Watch,' she said to Françoise. Slowly the chrysanthemum bloomed, its leaves unfurling.

'Like magic,' Françoise said.

'Some friends made me realise the importance of making time for tea, years ago.' Bel watched the flower infusing the water. 'I'm thinking of importing these. Do you think people would buy them?'

'I think they would, as a novelty.'

'I designed this teapot myself,' Bel said, and poured a cup for Françoise. She smiled, remembering the group of artists earnestly discussing teapots in Liberty. 'I have great ambitions, not only for the clothing line, but for interiors, too. I think people with new money need guidance about how to spend it.' She passed Françoise the cup. 'Why should all of life not be beautiful, and well made?'

'I couldn't agree more.'

'How can I help you?'

'I should like to work for you. I can sew, if you need? I began as an *arpète* when I left school at twelve. I don't mind working as a *seconde main*, or junior hand.'

'What will you do when the baby is born?'

'My family is in Saint-Tropez,' she said. 'They will watch the child.'

'I have all the improvers and jobbing hands I need.'

'I understand.' Françoise's face fell.

'However, you have exactly the look I have been searching for.'

'I do?' She raised her head.

'You are a fantastic wearer of clothes, even soaking wet.' Françoise laughed, relaxing. 'There is something surprising I like about you . . .' Bel pointed at the scarlet flash of a scarf at Françoise's throat. 'Come and work for me.'

'But don't you need references?'

'Miss Lambert, I trust my gut instinct about people.' Bel leant forwards, studying her. 'You have beauty, clearly, but you have a strength too. I design for brave women, with modern lives. I should like to advertise my new collection with your face. Later, of course, you will walk for me, and perhaps become a vendeuse. A good vendeuse must know everything about her client, their hopes, their dreams.' Bel thought for a moment, blowing steam from her tea. '*No ordinary servant need apply . . .*'

'I'm sorry?'

'It was an advertisement I saw in *The Suffragette*, for a companion to two ladies.' Bel smiled wryly.

'You were looking at such work?' Françoise said incredulously.

'Once.' She studied her. 'I know what it is to need help.

I know strength can only take you so far—' She broke off, seeing Françoise colour, her proud eyes glisten. She remembered Mr Harris's kind face: *Is that you, Miss Bel?* How he stopped the man trying to push her into a carriage outside the Academy. How he took her home, and they cared for her. 'An act of kindness at the right moment can change a life. I have been lucky – good people gave me help when I needed it. And now, I shall give you the same.'

Lot 51

29 JULY 1985

Mira worked methodically through the attic, listing the antique work tables, the drawing boards and mannequins first, to get them out the way. When she looked around the room she could imagine them set out in the high, light rooms downstairs, with Bel's immaculate white-coated assistants moving around a client on a dais podium, toiles pinned to the mannequins, brown paper pattern pieces hung on pegs on the wall. She imagined bolts of ravishing silks and chiffons unrolling across the tables.

'*Allô?*' a male voice called. 'Meeraaa?'

'In here,' she shouted. Serge poked his head through the door. '*Mon dieu*, so much!'

'It's that generation,' Mira said. 'They never threw anything away. And she lost everything in life, once.'

'Ah, this makes sense. Once you have known destitution, you will always feather your nest, just in case.'

'I mean, look at this box – how many blank sketchbooks and notebooks do you need?'

'The fear of loss secretly drives many people.' He beckoned to her. 'Come, we need to eat if we are working late.'

Mira wearily followed him downstairs, and found Ned in the kitchen, pouring three tumblers of Bordeaux. A warm baguette and an open paper wrap with a square of Pont l'Evêque stood on the counter. He passed a glass to Mira, and picked a strand of cobweb from her shoulder. Night had fallen outside, and the apartment building opposite was illuminated. Golden rectangles – lives, apartments she would never know, hovered in the warm darkness, the noise of the street drifting up through the open windows.

'To BB,' Ned said, raising his glass.

'Come, eat.' Serge pushed the cheese towards Mira. 'You waste away.'

'Thank you,' Mira said, cutting off a slice.

'We've made good progress down here,' Ned said. 'The boxes on that side of the salon are all for Drouot. They're full of books, prints, run-of-the-mill clothes and domestic goods. Some of the first editions are uncut—'

'Nothing wrong with buying more books than you have time to read,' Serge said. 'I think it's optimistic.'

'Or hoarding. There are a few nice *verreries parlantes* by Gallé which will go to Tokyo. But you'll like this,' he said, gesturing for Mira to follow him. He flicked on the light in Bel's study, and she laughed with surprise.

'The cranes she wrote about!' she said. In the warm night breeze, a curtain of origami cranes spun at the open window.

The colours had faded, but it was still a joyous thing, at odds with the stark simplicity of the room.

'I thought you might like to see how it looked in Bel's time,' Ned said, leaning against the door frame. 'She was ahead of fashion, painting the apartments white.'

'And everyone thinks Syrie Maugham was the first to do a white room.'

'Bel did it here first. The mirrors, the white couches—'

'Do you think she saw the apartment?'

'It's possible,' Ned said, shrugging. 'But those storage boxes are full of colour, and life. She had a massive clear-out, or someone did.'

'But where are the clothes?' Mira said. 'Why haven't we found any jewellery? Someone like her would have had jewels, surely? Where did they all go?' She chewed her lip. 'I think that housekeeper knows more than she's letting on.'

Lot 52

APRIL 1912

'Isn't it awful news about the *Titanic*?' Genji said to Bel, turning the pages of a newspaper as they walked to work, her puppy Vero trotting at their side.

'Those poor people, and many of them our clients.' Bel's face was ashen. 'It makes you realise how fragile life is. How we must make the most of every day.' She glanced at him. 'I had a letter from Mrs Liberty this morning. The Suffragettes smashed every window from Regent Street to Oxford Street, and Liberty did not go unscathed, much to their dismay. Mr Selfridge said women have turned against the shrines at which they worship.'

'Do you think that will happen here?'

'No.' *They should be thankful women want equality and not revenge.*

'Good.' He tossed the paper in a bin, and stretched.

'Are you happy in your new post?' she said.

'Define happy?' *Always something of Orlando in that look*, she thought. *An insolence.*

'I have heard you are doing good work, a natural, Monsieur Le Blanc said. You have a gift for gardens.'

'A gift?' Genji exhaled a laugh. 'It is plants, not art.'

'I remember Chō tending her trees. She loved them, and she was quite sure that is why they thrived.'

'Nonsense,' Genji said. 'A garden is a battleground. It is a constant fight to subjugate nature, to bend it to your will.' He gestured at a large plane tree. 'You think bonsai wish to be tiny? It is no more natural than the way the Chinese bind feet. Beauty is suffering.'

'I disagree,' Bel said, turning him to face her. She picked a piece of lint from the shoulder of his dark suit.

'Maman . . .'

'Have a good day, darling,' she said, kissing his cheek. 'Home at seven, sharp.'

Bel strolled on through the streets of Paris, Vero trotting at her side. She had designed a new range of velvet and gilt chain leads and collars which were flying off the shelves of her store, and this morning Vero wore a burnt pink to complement Bel's skirt. She loved walking the city, deliberately choosing a different path each day, discovering new markets, new stores.

> *Inspiration is everywhere,* she jotted down in her diary, sitting at a café table near the Place Vendôme. *Tell me about all the lovely ruined things. The broken things. The imperfect. The used-up. The beloved. Tell me about*

the dress you wore 'til the seams fell apart, the favourite cup washed until the pattern wore away. Tell me about the blanket you reach for, its comfort and warmth. The favourite chair. (Everyday objects have the life of the man or woman who lives with them, you know – a corset yields to the body, a cane chair takes on the warmth of the seat.) This is what I will design. Things of use and beauty, as Morris said. But I want people to use them up lavishly, with love.

She sipped her first coffee of the morning, with Vero tucked at her feet. The morning sun tipped Chaudet's statue of Napoleon on the column at the heart of the vast square. The windows of the elegant buildings gleamed like sheets of gold leaf. A full day lay ahead with the launch of the new maternity collection. Bel could not have been happier.

Perhaps children's clothes, next? She thought of a letter Hiro had sent her many years ago, when Genji was a toddler:

One day you will long for this time. Your days are full of work, and caring, and you say you do not know how you can go on. But you will. And one day when you look back at this time, and remember him – his little body fitting against your hip as you walk, the sound of his chatter and laughter in the house, the filigree of handprints on the stairs where he walks – you will long for it all.

It has all gone by so fast, Bel thought, gazing ahead. She was so lost in her thoughts that she did not notice the man in a fine grey coat and Homburg strolling across the square towards her. Only when he stood a short distance from her table did she look up, as her dog barked in warning.

'Bel,' he said.

'Tom?' she gasped.

'How are you?' he said, stooping to kiss her cheek. *He still smells the same*, she thought. *Even in Paris he smells the same.* She stood and looked up at him. He was heavier set, grey flecking his moustache now, new lines lacing his eyes. Gone was the fresh-faced boy. A man in his late fifties stood before her.

'Tom,' she said again. 'What on earth—'

'I should have written ahead, but I wanted to surprise you,' he said. 'The ladies at your studio said you might be here, taking coffee.' He leant down and rubbed Vero's ears. 'And look at you, my old friend. Haven't you travelled well from a fairground in Hampstead to the finest square in Paris?'

'Tom, this is not Sally – she would be a veterinary miracle by now.'

'Of course. How silly of me.' He read the engraved tag on the pink collar. 'Vero?' He raised his blue eyes to her, the eyes which always reminded her of summer skies. 'Truth?'

'Short for Veronique.' As he looked at her, the years fell away. She was eighteen again, gazing through a veil of silk at a beautiful boy on Regent Street. 'Are you here for work?' Bel said, recovering herself. She gestured for him to sit. 'I hear your practice is going from strength to strength.' She watched him closely, not wanting to give herself away. *I hear,* she thought, recalling the box of cuttings she kept of every one of Tom's buildings she read about in *The Times*,

The Studio – the palaces in India, the fine country houses in Scotland.

'Purely pleasure,' Tom said.

'And Mrs Fraser? How are the children?' Bel laid her gloved hands flat on her stomach, one over the other, steadying herself. *Tom.*

'The twins have gone up to Oxford,' he said. 'My old college.' He smiled sheepishly. 'But they are not charity cases like their father.'

'And your daughters?'

'Two are married, the youngest away at school, in Switzerland.'

'And how is Mrs Fraser?'

'Victoria . . .' A look of sadness crossed his face. 'She passed away recently.'

'Oh, Tom, no?' Bel said, touching his arm. 'I'm so sorry,' she said, genuinely moved. 'But she was so young?'

'It was sudden,' he said. 'A complication of influenza.'

'Madame!' One of Bel's assistants ran over to them. 'Madame! *Pardon.* I am sorry to disturb you, but the press are arriving, the first clients—'

'Of course.' Bel nodded. 'I'm so sorry, Tom.' She took his hand in hers. 'Poor Victoria. My condolences to you all.'

'Thank you.' He cleared his throat. 'It is marvellous to see you, Bel.' The warm spring air wound around them as they walked, lifting the tendrils of her hair. He glanced at the assistant, hovering nearby. 'We cannot talk now. May I take you for lunch, later?'

'I should like that,' she said, stopping outside Maison Bright. 'One o'clock?' Bel turned to a young couple entering the house. 'Lucky,' she said, kissing the dark-haired man on both cheeks. 'Mrs Chase.' The women embraced. 'Congratulations. How was your honeymoon? Do come in.'

Lot 53

PARIS, 1912

Later that morning, Bel paced her office, unable to settle to work. 'No, no, no . . .' she said to her *premier main*, flinging a sample of velvet down on the desk. 'I want Diaghilev orange. Ballet Russes orange. Not a mouldy tangerine on a barrow in Brick Lane.' The woman looked at her in confusion.

'*C'est un marché, à Londres.*' Françoise glanced up from her desk, where she was flicking through a copy of *Harper's Bazaar.*

'And this,' Bel said, snatching up a length of purple silk. 'I want the richness of Suffragette purple. Queen Victoria purple. *This* is no good. Call Liberty, ask them to send over their full range.' She paused. 'No – send a telegram to Mr Kurosaki. I want all he can supply of the mauve Chō wore the day we went to Brighton. He will know what I mean.'

'Oui, madame,' the assistant said, gathering up the samples.

'You are homesick,' Françoise said, turning the page.

'I am not.'

'You are. Look at your colour references.'

'I am unsettled, that's all.'

'For heaven's sake,' Françoise said to Bel. 'Sit down, you are making me dizzy.' She picked up a jar of bath salts bearing *Maison Bright* on a chic black and white label, and sniffed. 'I like this. Clean. Elegant.'

'I was inspired . . .' *By Tom.* 'By a visit to a Japanese *onsen*, long ago. It's just Epsom salts, bicarb and oil of cypress and rosemary. The mark-up is marvellous – I'm sure they'll fly off the shelves.' Bel waved her arms expansively.

'Then what is wrong?'

'I'm at my wit's end. What am I to do with this?' Bel said, pausing again in front of the mirror to adjust her hair. She pressed her hand to her flushed cheek. 'Why am I so hot?'

'Sit down,' Françoise said, picking up a hairbrush. She unpinned Bel's golden hair and brushed it through to the lengths. 'Have you seen the latest *Vogue*? I swear a French artist is sending sketches of Paris fashion to them by the fastest boat.'

'The last dress pattern they issued was a direct homage to our spring collection.'

'Do you not mind?'

'Mind? No. I love the idea of a housewife in Texas or Missouri being able to make up a marvellous outfit from their own paper pattern.' Bel leant in to the mirror and lifted the creases at the corner of her eyes with her fingertips, pulling the skin taut. 'Haven't I always said a young woman buying our ready-to-wear collection, or making a copy of our designs from a paper pattern at her kitchen table today could be an haute couture client tomorrow? I love the thought we give a glimpse of style, of possibility to those who cannot afford our main line.'

'So what is wrong?'

'A man—'

'Always, a man,' Françoise mumbled, hairpins in her mouth.

'I adore men. I loved my father. I love my son—' Bel paused at a tut from Françoise. *I love Hiro*, she thought. *I loved Tom*. 'But they confuse me so, and I find my patience thinning. The best of life has been my women friends, women who have raised me up every step of the way.'

'Who is this man?'

'*The* man.' Bel caught her eye in the mirror. 'Does every woman not have *the* man.'

'Well, that is different. In that case, we call Cadolle to send over new lingerie.'

'I'm not going to bed with him!'

'It's not for him, it's for you. So you feel courageous. He broke your heart, yes?' Françoise piled Bel's hair up, securing it in an elegant Gibson girl bouffant. She turned Bel towards her and took out a purse of cosmetics from her bag. 'You show him what he lost.'

'Do I need rouge? I'm nearly fifty-five.'

'*Non* . . .' Françoise clicked her tongue. 'Forty-five, surely?'

'But . . . oh, I see.'

'A woman's face is her life – you look natural, but your

best natural, no?' She tilted Bel's face to the light. 'Tell me about this man of yours.'

'He's an architect. A typical English public school boy – composed, confident, ambitious. We worked together at Liberty's,' Bel paused. 'We travelled to Japan together . . .'

'Ah, a great love then?'

'My only love.'

'No, no,' Françoise said, dabbing subtle rouge onto Bel's cheeks, her lips. 'Your first love.' She smiled sadly. 'First love stays with you.' She swirled a brush in rice powder and dabbed the shine from beneath Bel's eyes, the tip of her nose. 'You were a child.'

'I hoped . . . I hoped once we would have a future together. But he chose ambition over love.' *So I did the same, didn't I?*

'Why give him the time of day?' Françoise said, clicking her tongue.

'Because I was eighteen when I fell in love with him,' Bel said, breathing a laugh. 'Only eighteen. I think I pinned all my romantic hopes and dreams on the man I thought he was.' She paused, a slow smile on her lips. 'I wanted him so badly.'

'You gave yourself to him?' Françoise wet a small brush, and darkened her eyelashes. 'Stay still!'

'I gave him . . . oh,' Bel sighed. 'I gave him too much.' *My heart. My body*, she thought, remembering the waterfall. *Too much.*

'And now he is here?'

'Yes, and I don't know why.'

Lot 54

PARIS, 1912

By midday, Maison Bright hummed discreetly with life. Not a hanger was out of place, not a mote of dust spoiled a mirror, not a raised voice charged the air, perfumed with the trademark concoction of white flowers – gardenia, jasmine, tuberose. In the salon, the housekeepers arranged gilt chairs for the afternoon show, and the dressers placed the clothes on rails ready for the models. Customers browsed the accessories and homewares in the boutique downstairs, and the design team had broken for lunch to eat at the wide table in the kitchen.

Bel swept downstairs in a simple black dress that accentuated her small waist. The strips of mirror lining the staircase reflected back several Bels, and she paused to look down on her kingdom. When there was a show she could sit on the stairs, just here, to watch the models pacing the white-carpeted salon on the first floor, hips thrust forward, ankles dishing like thoroughbreds. Here she could glimpse the heads of people in the shop below. She saw among the women a tall male figure, and as she watched, he looked up, and smiled.

'Tom,' she said, walking down. 'Shall we lunch here?'

'Thank you?' he said uncertainly. 'I had thought the Ritz?'

'I should like you to see the design studio. I think you may enjoy it?' Tom looked around the salon as they passed, at the group of models chatting, Françoise among them.

'Bel,' she called. 'I asked Fauchon to send in lunch for you, as you requested.'

'Thank you,' she said. 'Tom, this is Françoise Lambert, my muse and good friend.'

'How do you do,' Tom said.

'We have included a range of maternity clothing, as you can see,' Bel said, smoothing down the shoulder line of the rose-pink gown she wore.

'Inspired by kimono?' he said.

'Such an efficient garment. Eight pieces, no fabric wasted. Terribly cost-effective.'

'Do you hear from Mr Kurosaki?'

'Yes. Come, let us eat,' she said, walking upstairs. She did not want to think of Hiro. She imagined him standing by the tall window, arms folded, watching. *I know, I know*, she thought. *What am I doing?* Bel pushed open the door to the staff kitchen, and the voices and laughter from her team reached them. People moved to make room for them at the table, but Bel gestured that they should relax, and she picked up a wicker hamper from the counter. 'Stay,' she said to her dog as Vero tried to follow.

'I'm impressed, Bel,' Tom said, following her upstairs to her private quarters. 'I've seen women wearing your designs in London, but I had no idea you were working in so many areas.'

'We show the main haute couture collections in January and June. I've been watching the US markets, and am planning *prêt-à-porter* in March and October.'

'Really?'

'I think it's the future. For now I like to show capsule collections, like today's maternity shows. Our top clients enjoy something exclusive, and it keeps us in the press. I think of these collections like little grenades, to keep people on their toes.'

'You always knew how to do that,' Tom said, smiling. They climbed up to the top of the building, past the small bedroom where Bel slept when she was working late, and out onto the roof where a narrow terrace held an iron table and chairs. 'You're not afraid of heights anymore?'

'She watches over me,' Bel said, pointing. On the parapet, a scale model of the Winged Victory of Samothrace stood in the curve of a box hedge, shielding their privacy.

'Do you remember all the hours we spent sketching in the cast gallery of the museum in Kensington?' He reached out and touched the white wing tip. 'You were always a more accomplished artist than me.' Bel felt a warmth, a quickening deep in her stomach as she remembered. The hours working quietly at Tom's side, sketching and studying. Michelangelo's *David*, the contrapposto thrust of his hip, the long elegant thighs, the perfect anatomy. Lips, and hands, and that most private of places she had never seen in reality. And Tom, beside her.

We were so young. Bel bit her lip, and gestured towards the chairs. 'Welcome to my secret escape.'

'What a view. I feel like I'm flying,' Tom said, looking out over the vast square.

'Like the boat to Japan?' She placed a platter of olives and charcuterie on the table, and took out a bottle of champagne and two glasses.

'We had some times, didn't we, Bel?' She eased the cork from the bottle and passed him a glass.

I'd give anything to feel that alive again. 'What are we drinking to?' she said. 'Old friends?'

'Old friends and new adventures,' he said, his eyes bright.

'Tom—'

'Please let me speak before I lose my nerve.' He took her hand. 'Bel, I have loved you all my life it seems.'

'Tom, please—' He pressed her hand to his lips and she had to look away.

'I have no right to come to you, but Victoria said—'

'Your wife?' Bel looked at him in surprise.

'As she was dying—'

'Tom?'

'She said to me: *You must go to her, Tom.*' He seemed manic, desperate to talk. Bel pictured the scene, Victoria propped up in the bed she had chosen, her fine, fair hair spread around her like spun gold on the pillow. Victoria's delicate face, waxen in the candlelight. *God, how I envied her. Poor girl.*

'*Go to Bel*, she said. *I want you to be happy, Tom*.'

'Oh, Tom . . .'

'*Go to Bel*,' he said again, urgently. 'She – she was so noble. She *knew*, all this time. She knew I always loved you.' *But not enough*. 'You see, Bel, I am a man of means now. My business is thriving.' He sat forward on his chair. 'We can have it all. We can live here, in Paris, if you wish, or come home to London. We can work together again—'

'But, Tom,' she said, holding up her hand. 'You don't understand. I am married.'

'I know the pretence, the Libertys told me – Mrs Kurosaki.' Tom laughed, his eyes glistening. 'As if you would have married *him*.'

'Stop right there,' Bel said, her temper flaring. 'Hiro Kurosaki is a fine man, and a good friend.'

'Of course!' His eyes widened. 'Indeed, his nephew can live with us—'

'My son. Genji is my son.'

'Is it Schiffer? That I took his side in the business with the Japanese girl?' Tom said. 'Surely you have forgiven me? I learnt the cad made overtures to Victoria, too, if you can believe it—'

I can, thought Bel.

'I broke with him. I'll give him a thick ear if I ever cross paths with him again—'

Of course you will . . .

'Tom, stop. I'm married,' she said. 'Really married.'

'No,' he cried, his voice catching.

'Nearly three years now.' She gestured at the house. 'To Pierre de la Roche.'

'Who?'

'My business partner. He is a good man. I owe all this to him.'

'Do – do you love him?' Tom floundered.

'I . . .' Bel hesitated. 'Not as I loved you.' As she looked at Tom, Bel realised he would never be enough. He chose Victoria over her. *All, or nothing*, she thought.

Tom's head sank into his hands. 'I have missed my moment with you, again.' Bel touched his arm. 'What am I to do?' His back trembled as he held his emotions in.

'Poor Tom. You have your whole life ahead,' she said, sighing.

'I am an old man.'

'Nonsense. You have all those children to think of. You will find another wife—'

'No, never,' he said. 'I married once for progression. Never again.' On the street, a clock chimed.

'I must get back to work.'

'Please. May I see you later?'

'My husband is away. I am invited to Monsieur Poiret's masquerade.' Bel relented. 'Perhaps you would like to join me? I might wear the Pierrot gown I wore to that carnival ball – do you remember—?'

'Let him stay away.' Tom held her to him. 'Leave him, Bel. Leave de la Roche for me.'

For a moment she allowed herself to imagine returning to London. Moving into Launceston Place as mistress of the house, blending their families. Could it be the home full of love and life and colour and laughter she had always longed for? Bel had always dreamed her home would be generous and welcoming. *Not like the tomb I live in with Pierre.* She thought of the chilly, grand rooms, their heavy brocade drapes, the green marble-floored hall.

What have I become? She thought of their quiet Sunday night suppers at the Ritz, when the servants went to evensong, the genteel Friday-to-Monday house parties at their country estate, where Bel played hostess to Pierre's older, monied business contacts. She loathed the formal gardens, the dark avenues of yew and dripping ilex, the grey weather-worn statues. There they dined *á la Russe* with a battalion of glasses and cutlery and liveried servants to impress the guests. In Paris they went to the Opéra on a Monday, the Comedie-Française on a Tuesday . . . on and on. *How cold it all is*, she thought. *How passionless.*

Bel realised at that moment she had made Maison Bright her home. The people who worked with her, who relied on her, had become her family. Bel knew each of her regular clients intimately, had learnt their hopes and dreams. *I've created the family I never had.* She couldn't walk away from all she had made here. *I can't let them down.* Bel looked up at Tom. *I was so young. It was the only time I felt truly alive, with you. I wish . . . oh, god I wish I could feel like that again.*

'Until tonight,' Tom said, kissing her hand.

I would not mind, if you were discreet … she remembered Pierre saying. *I'm going to show you what you missed, Tom. I'm going to make damn sure you know what you threw away.*

Lot 55

PARIS, 1912

Bel tried costume after costume, dressing with care. At last she chose a gold Oriental hareem dress, inspired by the Russian Ballet. She layered two long coats, one red, one mauve chiffon, and pinned a length of red silk around her head as an elegant turban. At her forehead she pinned a dazzling faux amethyst with an aigret of white feathers. Finally she slid a long silver hat pin with a sparkling diamante tip into her upswept hair to secure the whole effect.

'What do you think?' she said over her shoulder. Françoise looked up from where she lay on her stomach, flicking through an American copy of *Vogue.*

'I think you make too much effort for a man who is not good enough for you.'

'I'm going to show him what he missed.'

'Good.'

'I wore this dress to Poiret's Thousand and Second Night Ball last year, but I have nothing else to wear.'

'You are a designer!' Françoise laughed.

'What a night that was, and all to launch a fragrance.'

'He is a showman. Poiret seems to launch a new scent every week.'

'Those pink ibises in the fountain, and Madame Poiret in a gold cage.' She laughed at the memory. 'I still don't know how he managed to have flames rising from the ground, and gold and silver rain.'

'You look marvellous. Diaghilev couldn't wish for better.' Françoise swung herself up and padded over in stockinged feet. She tilted her head, and arranged the neckline of Bel's dress to show more décolleté. 'You are covered everywhere else, let this Tom admire what he cannot have.'

'Is it petty?'

'No. You deserve to have a little fun.'

'I think these jewel colours will be perfect for the winter season.' She looked up as they heard the deep doorbell ring downstairs, and the sound of the maid's footsteps across the marble hall. 'He's here.' She caught Françoise's gaze in the mirror. 'Will I do?'

'Go,' she said. Françoise reached for the bottle of rosewater on the dressing table, and dabbed Bel's neck with the cool glass stopper. 'Have a marvellous night.'

Tom stood in the hall, in white tie and tails, top hat in hand. As Bel walked towards him, he raised a black mask to his eyes and smiled. Bel took a matching gold mask from her beaded purse, and held it up in her gloved hand.

'Shall we?' he said, offering her his arm.

~

The dressing room at the palace jostled with masked women in elaborate costumes, leaning in to the lamplit mirror, powdering their faces, shiny from the rain. Bel sat calmly at the heart of the chatter, the flutter of arms and powder puffs. *Imagine*, she thought, cooling herself with a gold fan. *How many times have I dreamed of this moment?*

Tom waited for her at the foot of the stairs, turning as she swept down to meet him. 'Your dance card,' he said, taking it from her and tearing it in two. 'Tonight, you dance only with me.'

'We'll see,' she said, flashing him a look as she took another card from the silver tray a waiter held.

The masked figures on the dancefloor moved as one to the waltz. The women's bare shoulders were pale among the sea of dark suits, their lips tinted like flowers, gazes whispering behind the masks. Bel spun round and around in Tom's arms, moving freely in her loose silk gown. She felt light, as if her limbs were floating. Several older women in formal corsets and heavily draped dark dresses looked at her in wonder. She caught men gazing at her with undisguised desire. The waltz reached its end, and Bel stepped back, smiling. Tom bowed to her.

'I wish the music would go on forever,' he said. 'Bel—'

'Ferris?' He turned at the sound of a male voice booming above the hum of voices. 'Or Fraser, isn't it, now?' They turned to find Orlando Schiffer bearing down on them. Bel's stomach tightened, cold with anxiety. 'And if it isn't Miss Bright, or whatever you call yourself these days. Well, well,' he said, shaking Tom's hand but staring at Bel.

'Schiffer, I'll be damned,' Tom said. *I thought you would give him a thick ear?* Bel said to herself, annoyed by Tom's friendly demeanour.

'What brings you to Paris, eh?' Orlando said. 'Business or pleasure?'

'Both,' Tom said. The band struck up a polka, and the dancers moved around them.

'May I cut in?' Orlando didn't wait for Tom to answer, but swept Bel off among the crush of bodies.

'I'll fetch some champagne,' Tom said, his voice trailing off. He frowned, and strode towards the refreshment room where tables of ornate fowl and fish sat beside teetering piles of jellies and trifles. Bel strained to look for him over the dancers.

'Are you well, Miss Bright?' Orlando said, pulling her closer. 'How's that boy of mine?' She could smell the liquor on his breath, and something else beneath his cologne – the bitter scent of a man who was not quite well.

'Madame,' Bel said, holding herself stiffly in his arms. 'Madame de la Roche. And *my* boy is a fine young man.'

'Ah, only teasing. I know you married the wealthy monsieur.'

'You keep tabs on me, sir?'

'Missed my chance with you, didn't I, Bel?' He swung her around to the edge of the crowd, towards the open window and the dark balcony beyond.

'Your chance?' she scoffed. 'You never had a chance, sir.'

'We'll see,' he said, pulling her after him into the darkness of the abandoned balcony. A fine rain fell on her skin. Orlando pushed her against the wall, and forced his mouth against hers, smothering her. Bel struggled, but he was too strong for her, and she could not push him away. *No. No – no.* She felt him tugging up the silk skirt of her dress, pressing hard against her. Bel reached for her head, and in an instant pulled out the silver hatpin, driving it into Orlando's left thigh. He cried out in surprise, releasing her.

'What in god's name—?'

Bel clenched the pin in her fist, and turned on him in fury. 'Any more and my pin shall travel further,' she said, her voice steady, the pin pointing at the erection nudging the seam of his trousers.

'She bites, she scratches,' Orlando said, wiping the back of his hand across his lips. 'You always knew how to inflame my senses—'

'You're grotesque! You disgust me,' she said.

'No, I intrigue you,' he said, following her as she flung open the French doors to the library. 'You hate that.'

'Your *arrogance*—' She strode on across the Turkish carpet, past the shelves of leather-bound books to the billiard room. Still he followed.

'Always reminded you of your father, I believe.'

'You are *nothing* like my father.' She rounded on him, the fringed green shade above the table casting a dim halo of light on her. 'I would not have you if we were Adam and Eve.'

'Is it Ferris you languish for, still?' Orlando leisurely rolled a red ball across the green baize. 'I'll wager that husband of yours never satisfies you—' He picked up a cue, and chalked it, blowing away the excess. 'I've heard *all* about him . . .'

'How dare you,' Bel said, her voice shaking with anger.

'I bet he never touches you here,' he said, placing the tip at arm's length against her breast, let alone here . . .' He drew a line of blue chalk across the bodice of her dress to her stomach.

'Schiffer?' Tom said, striding in just as Bel reached for the other cue.

'You disgust me,' she said, stepping back and pointing it at Orlando. She raised her left arm in a fencing position.

'Ha! A swordswoman, are you?' Orlando said, raising his free arm. '*En garde*!' He jabbed, thrusting the cue at her. Bel deftly parried, deflecting his blows, breaking time, setting him off pace. She circled her cue, narrowing her eyes. A crowd gathered, following the duel as she beat Orlando back into the hall.

'Schiffer! You're in your cups. Go home, man,' Tom growled, looking from Bel to him. She drove Orlando back, cues flashing, back through the party, people and dancers parting to make way.

'She fights like a man!' Orlando cried, gaining a couple of paces on her, but Bel was too quick for him. She drove him back and back, into the lobby, towards the fountain, her cue flashing with the lightness of a foil. '*En garde*!' he cried again, trying to rally, but at the last moment his patent evening shoes lost their footing on the wet marble floor and he toppled back into the water. The gathered crowd cheered, and Bel threw down her cue.

'Take me home?' she said to Tom. She glanced back as two men hauled Orlando out of the water.

'Good day, Mr Schiffer. I do not expect to see you again.'

Lot 56

PARIS, 1912

'His face,' Tom said, helping her from the carriage on the Place Vendôme. 'There are many men whose lives he made a misery at school who will enjoy this story. I shall dine out on it for months.'

'You must be hungry?' she said, opening the door to the silent *maison*. 'I'm sorry we left before the supper.' The heavy door closed softly behind them.

'I'd far rather be here, with you.' Tom stepped forward in the shadows, took her in his arms. 'Bel, my Bel. Still you surprise me, even after all these years,' Tom said, leaning forward and kissing her. She returned his kiss, her hands in his hair.

'Tom,' she said, catching her breath.

'Tell me you do not want me, Bel.' He unpinned the fabric from her hair, letting it fall to the floor.

I do, she thought. *Oh god, it has been so long since I felt alive, really alive.*

'Let down your hair,' he murmured, and Bel loosed the Lalique combs, the butterflies tumbling to the hall table.

~

The next morning, as they lay in the soft down bed, they talked of old times. Bel had fetched a tray for breakfast, and she lay in Tom's arms as he ate a peach.

'Do you remember that picnic in Japan,' he said, turning over the peach leaf. 'I told you how Kōrin wrapped food in gilded leaves?'

'I think that is why I use gold leaves for jewellery, even now.' Bel lay with her head on Tom's chest, feeling the steady thud of his heart against her cheek. He talked to her of India, of all his plans for wonderful buildings in Delhi and Bombay. He told her of his estate in Wales. He conjured a vision of a future, together. On the mantel, the pewter carriage clock chimed nine.

'I designed that,' he said.

'No, you didn't.' Bel smiled sadly and raised her head. 'Hiro did.'

'Well, I—'

'I must get ready for work.'

'Not yet,' Tom said, holding her.

'I have to,' Bel said. 'I have a full day of meetings.' She slipped on her chemise. 'I've had no sleep. I look awful—'

'You look like a woman who has made love all night,' he murmured, tracing the line of her spine. 'You haven't changed at all. You're still the girl I remember swimming in the waterfall.' He gathered her rope of pearls from the nightstand, and tucked them in the warmth of the bed.

'I *have* changed,' she said. 'I am an old married woman, and mother, and businesswoman—'

'You are still my Bel,' he said.

'I'm not yours, Tom,' she said sadly. 'And you are not mine.'

'But this,' he gestured at the bed. 'You cannot be happy with your husband if you make love with me?' He lifted up the necklace and fastened it around her neck. 'There, I have warmed your pearls for you.'

'Thank you.' Bel half turned as he kissed her shoulder. 'Pierre and I have an agreement. He told me I may take a lover, if I wish—'

'A lover?' Tom lay back with his arm behind his head. 'You would bed me, but not marry me?'

'Remember, Tom,' she said. 'You are the one who wished me your mistress.'

'I love you, Bel. I have always loved you—'

'Your love was never enough—'

'So what is this to you?' he said, throwing back the covers. 'Revenge?' He pulled on his trousers. 'Would you use me? Humiliate me?'

'No,' she said, turning him to her. 'No.' Tom crushed her to him. 'I loved you, once,' she said, her lips against his hair. 'This night has meant everything. Everything. If I never know it again, for a single night, it reminded me how it feels to be alive. But we cannot be together.'

'Why? Why not?'

'My life is here. My work is here—'

'You would place work over happiness?'

'You did.' The silence pulsed between them. 'I would never be satisfied as mistress of your house, your children, Tom.' When she raised her eyes it was as if the last of the girl in her had gone. 'You will find a young and pliant woman to wed, and when you do, don't let her go.'

'Damn you, Bel, I don't want some girl, I want you.' Tom pulled on the rest of his clothes as she washed and dressed. He pushed open the door, and stopped her. 'Would you change it for us never having met?'

'No,' she said gently, taking his face in her hands and kissing him one last time. 'Not for the world. All I have loved. All I have lost and suffered have made me the woman I am.' She led the way downstairs. Her staff were already preparing for the show, and a birdsong of chatter filled the air.

'It has been wonderful seeing you again, Mr Fraser,' Bel said, extending her hand. He pressed it to his lips, bowing low. Bel glanced over, seeing Françoise watching them.

'I'll ask once more, and only once,' he said quietly. 'Come with me, Bel, and be my wife.' She shook her head, her throat tight. 'If we were to join forces, the world would remember us. We can do anything, together . . .'

'The world won't remember me,' she said, her eyes shining. 'But people will remember my designs, I hope.'

'Very well. Goodbye, Bel. You shall not see me again.' Tom composed himself. She watched him leave, his proud figure descending the stairs. In the doorway, in silhouette, he turned a final time to look back up at her, and was gone.

'Are you alright?' Françoise said, coming to her side.

'Never better.' Bel blinked quickly.

'My mother always says: when you are unhappy, do something to make someone else happy.' Françoise fastened one of the seed pearl buttons at Bel's neck, and patted her hand on her shoulder. 'Let's show everyone your lovely new designs.' She gestured to the waiting vendeuses.

'Mesdames,' Bel said clearly, striding into the salon, clapping her hands. 'We have a marvellous day ahead of us.'

Lot 57

30 JULY 1985

Mira arrived early at Avenue Junot wearing ripped jeans, boots and a blue stripe t-shirt, cradling a woven basket. Ned was still immaculate in a tailored Paul Smith suit.

'Dress-down Tuesday?' he said, glancing up from his notes. Half-opened boxes from the basement littered the apartment.

'If I'm spending the day in that dusty attic again, I thought I'd leave the haute couture at home,' she said, putting her bag down on the counter. 'I have a surprise for you.' She waved a box of PG Tips. 'Is there a frying pan around still?'

'Bacon!' Ned's eyes opened wide. 'I could kiss you.'

'Steady on,' Mira said, lighting the stove. *I could kiss you.* She thought of Luke, wrapping his arms around her as she cooked breakfast. Sunday papers. Black coffee in bed. *Home.* 'I told Kim about your hankering for a bacon sandwich and she told me where to go. Not quite as elegant as all the *cha-ya* I've been reading about, but I thought you could all do with something to keep you going.' The bacon sizzled, and she shook the pan.

'Tea is the universal language,' Ned said, opening the box. 'Thank you.'

'*Salut*,' Serge said from behind a huge crate. 'What is that marvellous smell?' He set it down on the living-room floor with a groan, keeping his back straight. He let out a slow whistle seeing Mira cooking. 'Call out the gendarmes, she has stolen my heart . . .'

'How much more is there to come up, Serge?' Ned said briskly.

'Every box we bring up, two grow.' Serge shrugged. 'It is like a magic storage vault,' he said, taking a crumpled pack of Gitanes from his pocket.

'Downstairs,' Ned said, wagging his finger. 'You don't want that old housekeeper on your back again.' Serge shrugged and went out, and Ned filled the kettle. 'What are you thinking, Hutch?'

'Every page of the pillow book describes one outfit or another. This morning I translated a passage about going to a masquerade ball in a hareem costume. Where's her wardrobe?'

'Perhaps we'll get lucky today. The housekeeper is out, but the concierge said she'll be back this evening. We can ask her then.'

~

At sundown, Mira stepped aside to let Serge's team remove the last of the furniture. With the big pieces safely on the way to the Drouot saleroom, she had space to tackle the final plan chests. She opened the shutters on the oval window, and eased it open. Pigeons fluttered into the rosy sky in surprise as Mira poked her head out. *What a view,* she thought, gazing down at the streets of Montmartre. 'Right,' she said under her breath, turning to the first chest. Sliding the drawer open, she lifted out a little bronze. *The Kiss?* she thought. *Surely not Rodin?* She checked the signature. *Alfredo Pina, after Rodin.* She set it aside and turned to the drawings.

An hour later she was still pulling the last of the sketches out, sorting them into categories. She stood studying a fine line drawing of a grey silk dress.

'Find anything interesting?' Ned said from the doorway.

'Look at this – there are designs for dresses, glassware, furnishings.' Mira ran the end of her pencil along her lower lip. 'She really was ahead of her time. Isobel was designing an entire lifestyle.' She laughed softly. 'Sometimes my friends and I daydream about opening a shop like this. Somewhere you can have a cup of coffee, or a glass of champagne, and find unique things.' Mira held a sketch of a wineglass up, the colours so fresh, the light rendered so vividly she felt she could pick it up from the page.

'Are the drawings signed?'

'There's just a butterfly on the corner of each one.'

'Hm?' Ned studied the drawing of a grey silk dress in her hand. 'What if it's not a butterfly. What if it's a monogram? Like Chanel's entwined Cs.'

'Of course ...' Mira exhaled. 'Maison BB.' She threw the design down, and turned to Ned. 'Come on, we need answers. Why don't you try your legendary charm on the housekeeper?'

Lot 58

PARIS, JULY 1912

'Stand straight, please.' Bel knelt before the model, shaping and pinning the unbleached cotton *toile*. 'When you send this through to the *tailleur atelier*, make sure the interfacing on the collar lies well here,' she said to an assistant, marking it with red ink. She stepped back, satisfied with the neckline. 'Did they make up the matching *fourreau* yet?'

'The *premier main* in *Flou* says it will be ready for you to confirm the buttons tomorrow, madame. There was a delay with the manufacturer sending the fabric through.' Bel tilted her head, thinking, then snipped a dart with the shears hanging around her neck on a ribbon, folding a seam at the waist. An *arpètc* held out the pin cushion for her.

'There. A successful garment needs a little tension. A shock. Baste the piping here – and I want the effect of cording, on a corset, here. A shaping to it.' Around them the white-coated first and second hands tidied their tailors chalk and thimbles away, closing up their sewing baskets for the night. 'Make a note to reinforce the underarm of the kimono sleeve with bias tape over the seam.'

'Oui, madame.' The assistant scribbled down the instructions.

'And the indispensable pocket, of course,' Bel said, smoothing down the hip.

'I like that,' Françoise said, leaning in the doorway. 'It's big enough to hide a pheasant in.'

'The coat's like origami. See the folds, the waist detail?' Bel pointed. 'Everything is in technique. I always say a *toile* should be as beautiful on the reverse as the face. We shall produce it in crêpe de chine, with a frog of soutache braid to close it. I shall call it a "blouse coat". Something versatile and sporty.'

'You should call it a day,' Françoise said, checking her watch. 'You've been working for hours and this poor girl must be exhausted.'

'Is that the time?' Bel said, looking at the clock. 'I'm so sorry,' she said to the model. 'Go home, all of you, I had no idea it is so late.'

'Merci, madame,' she said, running off to change.

'Goodnight, madame,' one of the *habilleuses* called on the way past.

Bel stalked upstairs with Françoise, a plume of blue smoke waving in the darkness like a cat's tail from her Gauloises. She flicked on the light in her kitchen, and lifted the lid on the cold plate her maid had left out for her. 'I'm not hungry. Shall we go out?'

'The opera? *Madama Butterfly*?' Françoise said. Bel clicked her tongue as she unpinned her hair and shook it loose.

'I can't bear that opera – it's too sad.' Bel turned to her mother's silver mirror and frowned, shaking her hair loose.

'Cinema, then? Let's go to La Pagoda?'

'I need a change.' Bel pulled back her hair and sawed into it with the shears.

'What are you doing?' Françoise cried. 'Have you gone mad? Your beautiful hair!'

'When a woman cuts her hair she is ready for a new life.' Bel snipped away. 'I want it short. Like the dancer, Irene Castle.'

'You haven't been yourself since that Tom visited.'

'It's over.' Bel looked at Françoise in the mirror. 'After all these years . . . I'm free.'

'Then at least go on with good hair.' She clicked her fingers for the scissors. 'We cannot have you *mal coiffée*. I shall book you in with Antoine tomorrow but let's tidy this for now.'

'What is it that French women have?' Bel said.

'The sense not to cut their own hair?' she said, tutting. 'Confidence, perhaps? One must *souci de soi* – take care of oneself. It does not matter if you are mother or a *demimondaine*.' She combed Bel's hair through. 'There is no secret – water, oxygen—' She breathed deeply through her nose.

'Like plants?' Bel laughed.

'Be discriminating. Don't they always say elegance is refusal? A little hunger is no bad thing.' A smile flickered. 'Clears the mind.'

'But you have this air . . .' Bel waved her hand. 'A nonchalance?'

'Confidence comes with grooming, moderate habits, self-respect.'

'Healthy body, healthy mind?'

'Precisely. And we study, all the time. If you make yourself more interesting, your life becomes so.' Françoise raised her chin. 'Poor posture is your enemy, too.' She mimed walking with a book on her head. 'Stand tall! Imagine a string pulling you up, up. But books belong in the head, not on the head.'

'I like that.'

'It's important – keep learning. Keep current. Diet and cleanliness matter, of course, but an inner glow comes from spirit. Money has little to do with vitality, beyond the basics.'

'Money has *everything* to do with it,' Bel said, exhaling a laugh.

'*Bof.* Of course, there is love?'

'Love? No. Not for me.' Bel shook her head.

'The nerve of this *Tom*. Imagine if the situation were reversed, and a woman asked a man to give up his business, his home, for her.' Françoise glanced at her. 'Exactly. It would be ridiculous to them. Perhaps that is a French woman's strength. We learn from an early age our worth.'

'Will you teach me?' Bel said, and Françoise laughed, snipping away at her hair.

'You are one of the most extraordinary women I know. What can I teach you?'

'Everything,' Bel said, shrugging. 'One moment I was a child, and the next . . . I never had time to learn who I am.'

She looked at her reflection in the antique mirror. 'I feel I could be so much more.'

'Every woman feels like that,' Françoise said, nudging her. She rubbed her high, hard stomach, and exhaled. 'Oof, I swear this baby will be a footballer.'

'You're tired. Why don't you go home and rest? We can have dinner another time.'

'Are you sure?' Françoise dusted the cut hair from Bel's shoulders.

'Yes, go, put your feet up.'

'By the way, I checked all the bills this afternoon. Including that *maison* in London? Mrs Harris? Can we not use some White Russians here? You know we are paying them twice the rate we pay our French embroiderers? There would be a riot if they knew.'

'But they won't know.' Bel smiled. 'Maison Harris belongs to a dear old friend of mine who helped me when I needed it most. It is a cooperative, if you will, of women who work with her.' She glanced at Françoise. 'I owe her a great deal.'

'You value your friends.'

'Like you.' She hugged Françoise. 'You will write, and tell me how you are, and the baby? I can't wait to meet my goddaughter or godson.'

'Of course. I will have little else to do at my mother's but write and wait.'

'Where does she live again?'

'Saint-Tropez. It is a little fishing village. Nothing ever changes, nothing ever happens there.' Françoise smiled.

'Pierre always likes to do the season in Monte Carlo.'

'Let him. Come and visit us! The sun will restore you. Bring Genji. It would do the boy good to have some freedom, cut loose a little.'

'Genji was born middle-aged, I think. All he cares for is his garden, and the opera. He wants fine clothes, and fine food—'

'We have made a Parisian of him.' She hugged Bel. 'I am going to miss you. I will be back at work as soon as possible this autumn, once the baby is settled with the wet nurse.'

'Take all the time you need,' Bel said. She thought of Genji as a child and her face softened. 'Make the most of your time with the baby. It all goes by so fast.'

~

Advertisement: *Women's Paper* –
Friday 16 July 1912, 1d Weekly

Maison Bright, Prêt-a-Porter –
from Paris to London

Crêpe de Chine Blouse Coat, from
an exclusive Paris model

For the beach, for holiday, for sports

A healthy body, a healthy mind

9/6. Respond to: Votes for Women,
Box 118, 4–7 Red Lion Court, Fleet Street

Lot 59

PARIS, JULY 1912

Bel let herself in at the door to the de la Roche mansion in Montparnasse, and unpinned her hat. *That's strange*, she thought, aware of the stillness of the house, the silent rooms downstairs. *This lighting.* Bel grimaced. The green tiled walls of the marble hall shone bright in the harsh electric lights. Every time she came home, it made her queasy. *Where is everyone?* Normally, the moment she arrived a servant would open the door as if by magic and take her coat. Bel laid it on the bench seat, and checked her short hair in the mirror. *So unflattering, this light, but what Pierre wants . . .* She leant to unbuckle her shoes, sighing with relief. The marble was cool against her toes, and she wriggled them, padding silently through the house. The drawing room was empty, though a fire glowed in the grate. *At this time of the year?* The stifling drapes muffled the noise of the street. She felt the weight of the house on her, the masculine dark wood closing in.

Genji should be home by now, she thought. *And didn't Pierre say he would be back in time for supper with him, as I was going out?* Pausing on the landing, she saw a crack of light from Genji's room, and a sudden flash of iridescent blue pass the half-open door. She heard Genji laugh. *Something's wrong.* Her skin prickled, chill gut instinct telling her to leave, but still she stepped silently onwards.

She drew close to Genji's suite, heard the chink of a decanter on glass, soft music playing on the gramophone. Bel pushed the door open silently, and saw Genji with his back to her. He wore the waterlily kimono, his arms outstretched, swaying to the music. He was lost in the moment, his hair loose and long, brushing his collar, his slender white arms extending, caressing the air. Bel blinked. For a moment it could have been Chō, dancing to the music. But then Genji turned, and she saw he was quite naked, except for his stays, tight around his slender waist. Bel covered her mouth, and gasped in horror, stepping back. The music wound down, seemed to change key. She knocked the doorframe and Genji's eyes flew open. He cried out and swept the kimono around himself.

'Excuse me, my darling,' she said. 'I didn't think anyone was home. I—'

'Isobel?' She turned, aghast, to see Pierre scrambling up from the bed, his collar loose, braces hanging from his trousers.

'Pierre?' She looked from him to Genji. 'No, *no* . . .' Bel felt sick, faint.

'Calm yourself. This is not how it looks,' Pierre said quietly, staring at her with that unnerving blank look she glimpsed sometimes. *No?* Bel laid her hands on her stomach.

'You, and ... my son,' she said. 'What have you done? What have you done?' She rounded on Pierre. 'Was this why you married me? To get close to him?'

'Maman,' Genji sighed. 'It is better that you know.'

'That I know?' she cried. 'How long has this been going on? How long?' she yelled.

'Isobel, do not make a scene.' Pierre shrugged his braces on, and buttoned his shirt. She realised that in all the time she had known him, she had never seen Pierre without a jacket. 'You knew who I was when we married. I made clear the terms ...'

'Terms?' she yelled. 'Lovers, yes. But *not* my son! Are neither of you going to deny it? Are neither of you going to apologise?' She threw Genji's clothes at him. 'Get dressed! That kimono was made by your ancestors ...'

'I don't care about any of that,' Genji tossed his hair. 'Why keep it locked away, when it is so pretty ...'

'Give it to me,' she yelled, yanking it from him. Genji ran for his bathroom, slamming the door shut.

Bel folded the kimono with shaking hands, wiping the shocked tears from her cheeks.

'Isobel ...' Pierre said gently.

'Don't touch me!' she cried, rounding on him. 'You disgust me. He is my child—'

'He is a man, a young man of twenty-three, who I care

deeply about,' Pierre said. 'I forced nothing. I want you to know that. He came to me.'

'And that is better?' Bel thumped his chest. 'You could have said no.'

'He needed me. There is a long and noble tradition of an older man guiding a youth in a close and loving way—'

'Noble!' Bel cried. 'You would make a Greek tragedy of us?'

'Children endure things their parents are innocent of,' Pierre said coldly.

'You dare suggest this is my fault?' Bel raged. 'Had I been a better mother—'

'Isobel . . .' he said, placating.

'We are leaving,' Bel said, gathering up the lacquered box.

'We can carry on just as before . . .'

'No, we cannot.' She shook her head in disbelief.

'We have an agreement, you and I,' Pierre said, his gaze hardening. 'I have kept my end of our agreement – are you not well taken care of? Is your business not thriving?'

'More than thriving, as you know.' Bel stood up to him. 'Thanks to me.' In that moment, she decided. *I don't need you.* 'I am leaving. I will walk away from the *maison*.'

'Be reasonable . . .'

'Reasonable? *Reasonable?*' she raged. 'What life is this? A married woman has no life of her own, no rights, no property. I will divorce you—'

'No, I won't agree—'

'Our marriage is unconsummated. Our marriage is a sham!'

'I chose you—'

'You chose me as a smokescreen. Nothing more.' Bel threw her arms in the air. 'We will not live with you, do you understand?' She thought quickly. 'The new apartment on Avenue Junot, in Montmartre. The one you bought as an investment? I will take that.'

'Isobel, please – I will give you anything.'

'Genji I will send away.'

'He is old enough to make up his own mind.'

'He has his whole life ahead.'

'What if I say no?'

'Then the whole of Paris will know your filthy betrayal, that Pierre de la Roche seduced his own son.'

'But he is not my son, or yours.' Pierre rubbed his beard. 'I have no relation to him.'

'We lived as a *family*.' Her eyes smarted with furious tears. 'He *is* my child. He *is*. I could love him no more if he came from my body.' Bel felt a physical pain in her chest. *Is this it? Is this how it feels when a heart breaks?* 'How could you both do this to me?'

'In time you will forgive him. Mothers forgive all.'

'At what cost?' she said, her voice catching.

Genji's bathroom door opened, and he stepped out, an insolent look on his face. *There you are, Orlando*, Bel thought, turning to him.

'I love him,' Genji said.

'Don't be ridiculous. Pack a bag,' she said. 'Only what you cannot live without.'

'But—'

'But, nothing,' she said. 'Goodbye, Pierre. I will never see you again.'

Lot 60

PARIS, JULY 1912

'Where have you been?' Françoise looked up from the stove in Bel's studio kitchen, and strode over, embracing her. 'Thank god you called.'

'You should be packing!' Bel said, dumping her shopping bags. She gave in to Françoise's hug.

'My train's not 'til tonight.' The windows were open to the rain-washed Paris sky, and pigeons cooed on the parapet. 'Oh, Bel . . .'

'I'm alright,' she said, her voice muffled by Françoise's shoulder.

'You should be in bed, not out in the rain.' Françoise stepped back as Bel broke into a hacking cough. Frowning, she rummaged among the bottles in the cupboard. 'Here, take some laudanum.'

'Thank you,' Bel said wearily, and sneezed. 'I passed a *nuit blanche*.'

'No wonder. The bastard.' Françoise placed a steaming

bowl of chicken soup, rich with the scent of garlic and ginger, on the table. 'Eat.'

'I'm not—'

'Eat.' She sat opposite her at the small kitchen table. Françoise took her free hand and squeezed it. Bel looked up at her and nodded, her face anguished. 'Where is Genji?'

'I put him on the first train to Vernon with a letter of introduction to Claude Monet.'

'It's more than he deserves, the little shit—'

'He's my son,' Bel said, wiping at her eyes. 'I gave him money for a room at the hotel La Musardière over the road from the gardens, and the waterlily kimono. He's . . . he's so angry.' Bel thought of the letter she had just sent to Hiro. *I'm sorry*, she wrote to him. *How did I not see what was going on under my own roof? I am sorry I didn't protect our boy.*

'I sat up last night looking at old photos.' She recalled a baby photograph of Genji sitting on her lap, in the studio in Chelsea. Genji in a lace frock, his hair long. At three, when they breeched him. On holiday on the Île de Ré at thirteen. She thought of all the boys he was, the baby to the man, all the boys she had loved. *My son.*

Genji had wept as they stood on the platform at the station, repeating over and over: *I'm sorry. I'm so sorry.*

'I always knew,' Bel said, 'that you were . . . different from other boys.'

'You don't understand!' he cried. 'What I endured! The taunts, the bullying. People calling me *hafu*.'

'Hafu?'

'Half-breed. Impure. Ugly—' He dried his eyes. 'Pierre made me feel beautiful.'

'Genji, forget him.' She stepped forward, brushing the hair from his hot cheek. 'I . . . I saw you noticing both girls and boys, as you grew up. I always worried that someone would take advantage of you.'

'So?' he said, challenging her. 'Does that make me a monster?'

'No! I love you, you are my son.'

'You don't understand. I *wanted* it.' Genji's eyes gleamed darkly. 'I seduced him. If anything, he resisted—'

'Pierre did not resist hard enough,' she said. 'He was your father.'

'No, he was *your* husband. You are not even my *real* mother.' He flinched as he saw the pain on Bel's face.

~

'Enough,' Bel said now, raising her chin. 'We begin again, on our own terms.' *I will show them. I will show them all.*

'Where have you been?' Françoise said.

'Dehillerin,' she gestured at the new copper pots in the bags. 'I love that place. It reminds me of the old kitchens in London.' *It's comforting.* She thought for a moment. 'We will stage a homeware section in the new boutique.'

'The new boutique?'

'We begin again. At Avenue Junot.' Bel tapped the table. 'Maison BB.'

'The sample carrier bags you asked for arrived this morning.'

'Good. We will take them with us. Put a selection on my desk for me to check? I want something as distinctive as Lucile's striped boxes for our new enterprise. I don't know why I didn't think of it before. If the bags are attractive enough, people will shop with us and reuse them – they will do our advertising for us.'

'I like the grosgrain ribbon handles.'

'That was inspired by children's hair ribbons.' Bel finished the soup, and checked her watch. 'Thank you. You didn't need to come round—'

'Of course I did.'

'You must get going.'

'Are you sure you will be alright?' Françoise put their plates in the sink for the maid. 'I'm serious. Pack up, leave for August like the rest of Paris.'

'Pierre has run off to Monte Carlo.'

'Good riddance.' Françoise hugged her. 'We'll get through this together. You are not on your own.' Bel nodded, unable to speak. 'Promise me, you'll come and stay in Saint-Tropez?'

~

Alone, Bel sat before her mother's mirror, and looked at her pale reflection. Once, when she was young, she had taken a candle and eaten an apple in front of the glass, hoping to see the face of her future husband appear as the old trick promised. She pictured Pierre's image, and swept her arm across her dressing table, the bottles of rosewater and lavender, cold cream and oil smashing to the wastebasket.

'We begin again,' Bel said firmly.

Tidying up, she carried the rouge and mascara down to the studio and sat at her worktable. *Make-up isn't vanity*, she thought, turning the small palettes this way and that. She inhaled the scent of roses on her fingertips. *It's armour, a disguise. It's freedom.* She sketched a perfume bottle, a simple teardrop. *What is the scent of luxury?* she thought. *Not only floral, something deeper, woody, a musk . . .* Bel jotted down notes on some of her favourite natural fragrances. *I would give women the sun, the moon, the stars.* Her pencil swept across the page, designing an elegant compact engraved with the heavens on one side, and a simple BB on the other. Inspired, she leapt up and pulled out a larger sketchbook. She drew sure and fast, an evening clutch bag with a mirror, powder, lipstick bullet, comb. *Like a bento box*, she thought, *black velvet out, red lacquer in.*

BB. Not Maison Bright. Just BB. A butterfly logo.

Set up a meeting with the owners of Bourjois in September, she scribbled on a piece of paper. Bel placed it on her desk and turned out the light. *We begin again.*

Lot 61

PARIS, 30 JULY 1985

'Are you ready?' Ned said, looking in at the attic. 'The boxes have gone off. We're done. Serge is going to pack the last of the paintings before the lawyer hands over the keys to the new buyer on Friday.'

'Nearly . . .' Mira glanced up from where she sat on the floor reading Bel's book. Ned handed her a paper bag. 'An eye mask?'

'You said your eyes were tired from translating.' He cleared his throat. 'I think you put it in the fridge, or something?'

'Thank you.' She raised her hand for him to pull her up. 'That's so thoughtful. Did you find anything good?' She rummaged through the drawings at her side.

'A nice pair of wisteria glass lamps by Handel and Co, and an Art Nouveau clock by Rappé, some Gallé vases . . .' Ned's voice trailed off. 'I found a sleeping knight, too, and an enchanted—'

'I am listening. Look at this.' She gestured to some

architectural plans. 'It's Miramar, a house she talks about in her pillow book. Ned, let's go there?'

'The lawyer didn't instruct us—'

'But what if there's more? What if it's full of Bel's possessions still?'

'Let's see if the housekeeper knows anything about it.'

~

'I suppose you want to see the clothes?' the housekeeper snapped, ushering them in. *I knew it,* Mira thought. A middle-aged man opened the door of a side room, and walked past, adjusting his tie. He glanced at Mira and Ned, and stopped to kiss her hand.

'Thank you, Natasha, I miss you already,' he murmured. The heavy front door clicked closed discreetly behind him, and Mira glanced at Ned as the silence stretched.

'Natasha?' Ned said.

She pulled the ebony spike from her hair and tossed it on the console table, padding barefoot through the apartment. 'I know what you are thinking,' she said, over her shoulder. 'I am an osteopath.'

'Oh,' Mira said in surprise. 'We didn't—'

'Yes, you did.' Natasha beckoned for them to follow her. Mira could see immediately that the apartment was identical to the one downstairs. As they went along the corridor to the kitchen, she glimpsed an elegant salon with high windows, and modern Mies van der Rohe leather couches.

'I don't have long. I am cooking for a friend,' she said,

adding a splash of Veuve Cliquot to the golden pot of chicken, shallots, tarragon and thyme she had just lifted from the oven. 'A glass of champagne? I always feel it awakens the palette.' She poured one for each of them. 'Every day should be a celebration, *non*?' She shook the pan of mushrooms sautéing with lemon juice, olive oil and sage, and turned down the heat.

'Madame, do you know anything about Miramar?' Ned said.

'Miramar?' she said. 'Of course.'

'Is it still in the possession of our client?'

'Your client? No, no . . .' she said, turning on a lamp on the kitchen table. She turned to them, the light glinting on her gold Elsa Peretti cuff as she folded her arm. 'Miramar was left to my family. To my grandmother, Françoise, to be precise.'

'I'm confused,' Mira said. 'The house and contents?'

'Yes. In spite of what the Kurosakis may say.' Her temper flared. 'Bel left Miramar to Françoise. So what if the will has been lost? It was always understood.'

'I found the plans upstairs. Perhaps you would like them?'

'Thank you.'

'Do you mind me asking,' Ned said carefully. 'Why was the house left to your grandmother? I'm just trying to connect the dots.'

'Dots?' she said, gesturing for them to follow her. 'My grandmother, Françoise Lambert, was her best friend and muse. Bel built Miramar to be close to her. She spent her happiest days with *my* family.' She blinked quickly.

'But, the Kurosakis—' Mira began.

'You wrote some little essay and you think you know her?' Natasha cut her off.

'Hold on, how do you know I wrote a thesis?'

'Pff. We knew her better than anyone. Come, this is Isobel.' She turned on the light, ushering them forward. Mira inhaled in surprise. 'They would have let it all rot in the basement. Françoise rescued her wardrobe, and stored it here.'

'Oh god, just as I thought we were done,' Ned said. Double clothes rails lined the walls floor to ceiling, with a rainbow of clothes and accessories carefully preserved.

I knew it! Mira's heart raced with excitement as she picked up a pair of aqua blue suede sandals with feathers at the heels.

'Cheruit,' Natasha said. 'Bel always found shoes amusing.'

'I recognise some of these from my research, but I had no idea any pieces had survived.' Mira grinned as she ran her fingertips along the rows of Liberty and Bright gowns. 'It feels like seeing old friends.' At the end of the room a mannequin stood, dressed in an ivory silk wedding dress, a fine lace veil draped over it. Mira gently lifted the sleeves.

'1923. Like a Heian kimono,' Natasha said. 'The veil stretched tight across the forehead, caught at the temples with the fine gold gingko leaves she designed with Maison Boivin. My grandmother said Isobel felt an affinity with the gingko. It is a symbol of resilience. She planned a simple cascade of lilies as her bouquet. It would have been a beautiful wedding.'

'This was Bel's own mannequin?' She let the sleeve fall,

awestruck. *Isobel?* The figure was shorter than her, almost childlike. 'She was so petite.'

'A tiny waist, even as an older lady.' Natasha rearranged the veil. 'They sent the dress back to be with the rest of the collection. Now, we want you to sell all this.' She nodded sadly. 'It is time. Our lawyers have negotiated with the Kurosaki's today. Half the proceeds of the couture will come to my family, half to them. If it were not for Françoise, all this would have been lost to the damp and the mice in the basement. She saved Bel's life's work.' She pointed at a cedar chest. 'All her jewellery is here, too.' Mira knelt down and opened the box. On a blue velvet tray at the top, a gold clasp crafted from two gingko leaves gleamed. She picked it up by the silver silk thread. 'See? The leaves were for an opera coat. But you could wear them as jewellery, or hairclips too. She was always ingenious.' Mira had never wanted any piece so much in her life. 'Try it on.'

'I couldn't.'

Ned took it from her, and fastened it around her throat. The twin leaves lay against her collar bones, catching the light.

'Oh my god, look at these!' Mira lifted out a pair of butterfly hair combs. 'Lalique?' She looked around the room, stunned. 'Have you ever had a fleeting glimpse of a dress and fallen for it?'

'Can't say I have,' Ned said.

'Naturally,' Natasha said.

'I have. I bet all women have. That *coup de foudre*, the dress of dreams. I once spent months trying to track down a silver dress I saw in a shop window driving through Berlin.'

'Did you find it?' Natasha said.

'Of course.'

'Why doesn't that surprise me,' Ned said.

'These are all dream dresses, aren't they? This whole room. Look!' She lifted down a bias-cut red dress with glass buttons at the shoulder. 'Look, Ned – it's our buttons!'

'Try it on,' Natasha said, walking away. 'You are a sample size, no?' She took Ned's arm. 'We shall take the champagne to the salon, and you will give us one last fashion show.'

Natasha set a tray of drinks on the low lacquered table, and opened the floor-to-ceiling windows to the night. Below, the sound of the street drifted up, melding with the music drifting from the kitchen. Ned settled back on the tan leather sofa.

'What will you do now?' he said.

'The Kurosakis are kicking me out, so I will retire to Saint-Tropez—' Natasha broke off as Mira appeared in the red gown.

'Wow,' Ned said, exhaling slowly.

'*Non, non* . . .' Natasha unfurled herself from the couch. She took a tube of lipstick from her purse, and turned Mira to the mantlepiece mirror, emphasising her lips with a deep red. She swept her hair up, securing it with a couple of hairpins from a bowl, and nodded. 'Better.' She adjusted the neckline. 'See? When fabric is cut on the bias, the fibres react to body heat. The dress melts, and flows.' She nodded her head, satisfied. '*Bon*.'

'This must be very difficult for you,' Ned said. 'I hadn't realised that you are losing this apartment too.'

'When Bel and Françoise moved in, this building was brand new. Imagine. My whole life is here.' Natasha swept her arms wide. 'We have all been devoted to her memory.'

'But who was she? Who was Isobel Bright?' Ned said.

'She should be remembered,' Natasha said. 'Isobel was *la femme nouvelle*. My grandmother said she had rebellious taste, the swagger of a pirate queen.' Natasha smiled. 'Everyone forgets, but not us.'

'Madame, was there a portrait of her?' Mira said.

'The Schiffer?' Natasha narrowed her eyes. 'No. She would never have had it in the house. Who knows what happened to it.'

'I wish I could see Bel. Even the Picasso drawing – you don't see her face.'

'Here, here is Bel.' Natasha gestured at the dress. 'Now, maybe with this sale the world will sit up and pay attention.'

'We'll be back first thing to pack the clothes,' Ned said.

'And then, I think we need to go to Saint-Tropez, don't you?' Mira said.

Lot 62

AUGUST 1912

Bel dined alone in the elegant restaurant of the Gare de Lyon as she waited for the evening Calais–Paris–Med Express. She flicked through the lavish colour plates of *Les Modes*, looking for her interview among the articles on design and fashion. She paused at a striking photograph: Hat by Gabrielle Chanel. *Brava, Coco*, she thought, turning the page.

Maison Bright is known for flattering kimono coats and silk bias garments which flatter every figure, she read. *Their eau de colognes appeal to both men and women, and their homewares are sensual and beautiful, inspired by natural elements such as the ginkgo leaf.* Bel spread out the magazine. *'Fashion is all about proportion – hemlines rise, they fall,' Madame Bright says. 'A jacket skims the hip, next season the thigh. It is all in the fabric, the cut. I play with harmony, balance, rhythm like a sculptor. I handle material, scrunch it up – does it have hand? How will it feel on the body? How will it move? Clothes change the way we feel. They change how the world sees us. Always, always, I think – what do women want? For many women, life is still one of drudgery – they cook, they feed, they clean, they care for large families. Still, we are told, women are physically, intellectually and emotionally the weaker sex. It is nonsense. I say women are the stronger sex. I say women deserve beautiful clothes and beautiful homes to make their lives, their work easier and more enjoyable. Be done with restrictive, heavy clothing. Our new designs are sixteen pounds lighter than ten years ago. Why should we not be feminine* **and** *comfortable . . .'* Deliberately, Bel ripped out the article and screwed it up. *No more de la Roche, no more Maison Bright.*

To the surprise of the *maison*, Bel left early. Usually, she worked through August with a skeleton staff, never stopping, never resting. *Ideas do not rest*, she would say. Now she needed it desperately. On her final day at Maison Bright, she moved all her personal belongings into storage. Her hand shook as she gave her keys to her tearful secretary, but Bel walked out with her head high as she left the house for the last time, and her seamstresses and vendeuses lined the staircase, applauding as she strode out onto Place Vendôme.

Now, the restaurant was full of excited families. Bel pushed her plate of onion soup away, untouched, and poured a little calvados into her coffee cup. She thought of the apple orchards in Normandy she had played in as a child. *When does everything become so complicated?* She looked at the family at the next table. The young couple were clearly still in love, happiness radiating from them. Bel smiled wistfully. *Love like that makes everyone who sees it happy.* Bel gathered her overnight bag, and pushed back her chair, smiling at the young mother as she passed.

The train ride south passed in a sleepless blur to Bel. She felt hollowed out with grief. She turned Françoise's battered postcard over on her journal and looked at the photo of a clear blue coastline. On the back she had written: *A daughter. Angêle. Come and see us. August calls. Bisous, F.*

Françoise's father collected her from the station, throwing her trunk into the back of a horse and trap. He had the same elegant profile as his daughter, but a farmer's wiry strength. The Lamberts' low white farmhouse sat in the hills above Saint-Tropez, on rolling land with fields of olive trees and vines. Françoise was hanging muslin sheets and nappies on the line in the meadow as they approached, white sheets billowing like sails against the cobalt sky. She raised her hand, shielding her eyes, and waved. *Beautiful*, Bel thought. *No woman has ever lacked elegance from an excess of simplicity.* She stood with the grace of a ballet dancer, her hair undone, and she wore a loose white dress with espadrilles.

Bel jumped down from the trap, and they embraced. 'You look marvellous,' Bel said. Françoise's mother emerged from the kitchen, drying her floury hands on a cloth, chickens scattering in her wake. She came to Bel, and placed her cool hands on her cheeks, embracing her without a word.

'I told her everything,' Françoise said quietly.

'About Pierre?'

'*Everything.*'

~

Pillow Book, August 1912

On Homely Things:

Bowl of lemons
Cicadas in long grass
Rosé wine and bouillabaisse
Swifts at dusk
Podding peas
White sheets on the line
Lavendered drawers
Scent of a baby's head

BB

~

As the weeks passed, Françoise's parents treated Bel like another daughter. For the first time in her life, Bel felt part of a large, loving family. She slept easily and deeply each night after working in the fields each day, or helping Françoise's mother bottle fruit for the winter. The women did callisthenics in the morning sun – moving, stretching, growing strong. They tried exercising in Bel's new designs to make sure women could move freely. In the afternoons she gave the teenagers painting lessons, painting *en plein air* along the coast, before swimming in the warm sea.

One day Bel sat at a café table in the market square, watching the old women in black choosing vegetables – testing melons, sniffing them for ripeness. *How simple and lovely their clothes are*, she thought. *You see the woman, not the dress.* She remembered Lillie Langtry, how her unadorned black dresses became her trademark. *A black dress*, Bel thought as she sketched a quick figure. *Not mourning, not austere as a nun's habit* . . . She sketched a square neckline, a flowing form. *Pockets of course*, she thought. *No need for a handbag or chatelaine. Space for a key, a little pin money, a compact or cigarette case* . . . Bel thought of the bolt of crêpe de chine she had in storage. *Effortless. No creasing. Freedom – just pack a little suitcase, a dress you can accessorise with pearls, or a silk scarf.* She remembered working with Tom in the Liberty design room. *I shall work with Liberty again, design a range of scarves for them to print on silk.* She felt the quickening, the excitement she knew meant she was on to a good idea. *So many women cannot afford a new outfit, but they can buy a belt or scarf or trim. We shall sell a range of small accessories, as tempting as a jewel box.*

In the afternoon, she hiked into the hills above the coast, following a dusty track up through fields scented with rosemary and thyme. Bel held down her wide straw hat, and flopped back in the pale grass. Her white linen gown billowed around her, and she gazed up at the sky, untroubled by clouds, or birds. She watched two white butterflies chasing around one another nearby, heard the hum of the insects, felt the warm earth beneath her cheek.

Pay attention. Hiro's voice came to her.

I am, she thought, leaning up on her elbows to look down at the village, at the sea sparkling like beaded silk beyond. *It begins here.*

~

'I can't thank you enough,' Bel said to Françoise that evening. 'I feel reborn. No wonder Colette says Saint-Tropez is another world.' There was a cool nip to the evening air, the scent of woodsmoke and bonfires perfuming the night. The family gathered together for a final meal on the beach, making a fire of olive wood, roasting mackerel the boys had caught that day.

'You have caught up with yourself, that is all, as Colette does in her little peasant house,' Françoise said. She looked out to sea, rocking the bassinette at her side. 'You were heartbroken and exhausted, creating two collections a year, four hundred models, overseeing the staff.' She glanced at Bel. 'Haven't I always said: everything is a question of *equilibre*. Look at you, you are glowing. To be *bien dans sa peau*, that is the secret of a good life.'

Pay attention. Hiro's voice came to her again.

Bel watched the sun, shimmering on the water, the rosy light flickering across the pale blue and silver water. *Pay attention.*

She stretched out her legs, barefoot and brown from the

sun, curling her toes in the warm sand. She smelt rosemary on her fingertips from preparing the meal, and the wine was cool and good on her tongue. The soft wind lifted the tendrils of her hair.

This, she thought. *This is what I am going to bring to my work. I want whoever takes a BB piece home to feel this. Maison BB.*

'Pierre is stalling, but I'm going to demand a divorce,' she said, not looking at Françoise. 'We begin again.' *Over and over*, she thought. *We return to the themes of our lives.* 'And I am going to build a summer home, here.'

'You are?' Françoise broke into a smile. 'That's marvellous.'

'I feel alive here. Thank you.' Bel glanced at her. 'Genji is settled in Giverny. You and I have a great deal of work to do in Paris, but I can accomplish anything with the thought of spending my summers here.'

'I am so glad.' Françoise gestured at her family. 'We will all help you. My father knows everyone in the village. We will find you a piece of land.'

'I already know where I wish to build.' She thought of the field high above the sea. 'I shall call the house Miramar.'

Lot 63

SEPTEMBER 1912

That autumn Bel moved to the apartment on Avenue Junot. The first thing she did was place a photograph of the view down to Saint-Tropez from her land on the windowsill where her desk would go in the little study. *My dream, only mine. Everything I do will be for this. Everything I design now will be to make people feel how I feel when I am there.*

Pierre arranged a generous divorce, gifting her the apartment, and a settlement to secure her future. In return, Bel walked away from her interests in Maison Bright, leaving one of her assistants to take over the helm.

'Several of the *deuxième mains* wish to come with you,' Françoise said as they walked through the empty apartment, Vero sniffing every corner. 'They see a chance to become *premiers.*'

'Good. Many of them started with me as *arpètes* when I had one room.'

With Françoise she planned what was needed, setting out

sheets of paper on the floor for the furniture, conjuring a new life. Autumn sun streamed through the high windows, gilding the top of the newly planted trees in the avenue below.

'Isn't it glorious?' Bel said. The apartment was entirely empty, freshly painted white, with pale carpeting on the parquet floors. 'It's a relief – it feels so light after the house in Montparnasse. All that grandeur is of the last century.' Her eyes twinkled. 'I remember seeing a gardener's house in Shiba. Such simplicity and order. I shall keep the rooms minimal—' Françoise snorted with laughter. 'I will!'

'You? Minimal?' she said. 'That will last two seconds. Your rooms above Place Vendôme were like Aladdin's cave. You are a little squirrel, stealing away beauty in case of winter.' She nudged her. 'Admit it. When have you ever been to Les Puces or Drouot without bringing home treasures?' Bel laughed.

'You know me too well. I admit the stuffed peacock is coming as a good-luck charm.'

'Are they lucky?'

'Oh yes. In myth, peacock flesh never rots – they symbolise immortality and renewal.' She gestured at the apartment. 'This is what we are doing. A new beginning.'

'But how will people find us, without window displays?'

'Monsieur Poiret's *maison* on Rue Pasquier had no signs or displays, and yet he prospered. Our clients will follow us, you'll see. Let them know discreetly that I have left Maison Bright.' Bel turned her hands over, thoughtfully. 'Someone I worked with in Liberty said the metier is all in the hands.

Mine are still supple and fast. All we need are a couple of hundred haute couture clients and our house will thrive again.'

'Is that all?' Françoise said, making a note in a small leather book with a gold-tipped pencil. 'You need furniture . . .'

'There is no hurry,' Bel said. 'I just need a bed, a chair, a table to work on.' She pushed open the kitchen door and paused. On the counter a large gold-tooled red leather box stood waiting for her. 'Cartier?' Bel opened the box, and Françoise peered over her shoulder, gasping. A note from Pierre was folded over the jewels. *Forgive me?* Bel screwed up the paper, and snapped the red box shut, passing it to Françoise.

'Sell them. We can put the downpayment on the apartment upstairs. You can move in, and we will use the other rooms as our workrooms. The main salon will be down here – I have no need for such a large room.' Already she imagined the rustle of silk and satin, the murmuring voices of the clients and her vendeuses; she could see the flattering golden light, smell the mingled fragrances of the women, their Coty L'Origan and Jacqueminot, the fresh cut flowers. *Mirrors*, she thought. *Like Liberty. That will double the sense of space.* 'Perhaps we will need a larger building eventually, but for now we begin with haute couture before confections, *prêt-à-porter*, homewares. We need to establish a new identity.'

'Are you sure?' Françoise slipped open the box and turned it to the light, the stones flashing. 'It's a magnificent memento . . .'

'Yes,' Bel said firmly. 'No nostalgia. Only now.'

Lot 64

SAINT-TROPEZ, AUGUST 1913

Bel pulled in to the driveway of the Lamberts' farm, chickens scattering, and honked the horn. The children ran out to greet her first, followed by the whole family. 'Welcome home,' Françoise said, kissing her cheeks, Angêle nestled on her hip. Her mother embraced Bel, fussing over how thin she had become, the dark circles beneath her eyes.

'You girls work too hard,' Madame Lambert chided her. 'When I was your age I had been married for thirty years and had four children. Why can you not find a good man?'

'Girls?' Bel said, laughing, running her hand through her bobbed hair. She turned to Françoise's father, to find a young fair-haired man beside him. His blue eyes were bright in his tanned face, and his indigo workshirt hung loose at his throat. Bel guessed he was in his early thirties, still with the unlined skin of a boy, in spite of the shade of stubble on his cheeks. His hair, too, was soft and golden. She thought of Botticelli angels. He walked towards her, and held out his hand.

'Madame,' he said. His hands were strong and rough from manual work. He seemed like a different species to her, hewn straight out of the land.

'Bel,' Françoise said. 'This is Sacha Dubois, the builder my father hired for you.'

'Sacha,' Bel said. She recovered herself. 'I have been hearing great things about how the project is going. Thank you.'

'Merci, madame,' he said.

'I can't wait to see it,' Bel said.

~

After supper, Bel carried her backpack from the Bugatti, and swung it over her shoulder. 'Are you sure you won't come?' she said to Françoise, as Sacha shook hands with her father.

'No, you go. I took a walk up there today with the children. Sacha will take care of you.' A mischievous smile played across her lips, and Bel nudged her.

'Behave.' Bel patted her backpack and bedroll. 'I'm going to camp up there tonight. All year I have dreamed of waking to that view.'

'Very well,' Françoise said. 'Take a lantern?' She passed Sacha a paraffin lamp from the porch. 'You know Sacha is living on site. If you need anything, I'm sure he'll oblige—'

'Please, allow me, madame.' He took the backpack from Bel, letting her walk ahead with Vero.

They chatted easily as they strolled up the hill in the golden evening light. 'You've lived here a long time?' she said.

'I travelled after university, but when I arrived in Saint-Tropez I couldn't bear the thought of leaving,' Sacha said.

'What did you study?'

'Engineering,' he said. 'I grew up in Normandy, near the sea. I was always practical, as a child. Always fixing things, building things. I dreamed of building bridges, huge wonderful bridges,' he said, gesturing to the water. 'But I am not so good with sitting still, and studying it seems.' He frowned. 'Words, books don't make much sense to me. I failed my exams, so I travelled.' He swung Bel's bag to his other shoulder. 'Still, look at this. What more could I wish for?'

'Indeed.' Bel gazed back across the sea. 'I don't believe in failure. A friend of mine . . .' An image of Hiro turning to her, smiling, came unbidden. 'They always said: fall down seven times, stand up eight.'

'I like that.'

'To fail at something just means you are trying.' Bel exhaled. 'Anything worth doing is worth failing at.' She glanced at him. 'Do you miss your family?'

'I am never lonely. There's always somewhere to stay. People are kind.'

'You've been living on site?'

'Yes, you do not mind?'

'Of course not,' Bel said, walking backwards for a while to look at the view.

'It means I start early and finish late.'

'I have heard how hard you are working,' she said. 'I have my spies.'

'The Lamberts are good people.' Sacha shrugged. 'Apart from their eldest, Gabriel, but then every family has a black sheep.'

'Gabriel?'

'An artist. He has taken himself off to the Languedoc—' Still he looked at her. 'They tell me you are a great designer?'

'Do they?' She tilted her head, smiling.

'I could see that from the plans for the house.'

'I'm no architect,' Bel said. 'I worked with one, once, and I learnt enough.'

'Does your work make you happy?'

'Does it bring me joy?' Bel thought for a moment. 'I have always followed that instinct. Creation should not be torture. Look at the mimosa,' she said, picking a leaf. 'You can see God was having a good day when she designed that. What could be more joyous.'

'She?'

'I have always thought of the creative Spirit as "she".' Bel shot him a mischievous smile. 'I follow joy. I listen to those little internal sparks. How do you know when you love something? How do you feel when you are truly expressing yourself?' She tapped his chest with the leaf. 'Learn to recognise that feeling, and start looking for it, rather than chasing after things or people. Life is always speaking to you, if you listen.'

'You know what you want,' Sacha said, looking down at her. 'Many people don't.' He gestured at the fork in the path. 'Are you ready? You'll see the house from just around that corner. I hope you won't be disappointed.'

By you? she thought. *Never.*

Lot 65

SAINT-TROPEZ, AUGUST 1913

Bel held the memory of seeing Miramar for the first time in her heart like a jewel. In the long years to come, she treasured the image of the low white house above the sea. She designed two bedrooms – one for her, one for guests, both with generous bathrooms. A large open living room, with a welcoming hearth for the winter evenings she planned to spend here by the fire when she retired. Two long tables – one in the kitchen, one on the terrace, with benches and chairs to seat sixteen. Miramar was to be her escape, but she wanted it to be a convivial house, full of friends and love. She laid out a walled kitchen vegetable garden, and a perfumed garden with roses, jasmine, night-scented flowers, and a salt-water pool to bathe in below the terrace, overlooking the sea. She had drawn plans for a staff flat for a caretaker above the garage, and this was where Sacha was staying.

Bel stood on the dust track looking up at her home in silence, with Sacha standing behind her. The cicadas hummed in the long grass, and the warm night wind blew against her pale linen skirt.

'Madame?' he said at last, uncertain. 'You are not disappointed?'

'No,' she said, turning to him, with tears running down her cheeks. Bel broke into a grin. 'Sacha, it's marvellous. Exactly how I dreamed it would be.'

'Thank god,' he said, and placed his hand flat on his heart.

'Come on!' Bel said, running up the last of the track. She stood by the excavated hole where her pool would one day be, and looked up at the house. The terracotta roof was mostly tiled, and the holes where the windows would go were open to the night.

'I am sorry it is not finished. We are delayed by the window supplier—'

'I don't care,' Bel said. She wanted to laugh, she wanted to hug the house to her. *My home*, she thought. *Mine*. 'I am so happy with what you have done so far, Sacha.' She turned to him. 'First, show me the studio, please?' They walked high above the house along an old sheep track, to the edge of Bel's land. There, sheltered in the bluff of the hillside near a copse of windblown cypresses, stood a small wooden shack. 'Perfect, perfect,' Bel said, running towards it. 'Oh, it looks just like a shepherd's hut, like it's always been here.'

'I used old timber, and skylights, as you asked?' Sacha jogged to keep up with her. 'I was worried it might be a little . . . rustic, for your taste?'

'No, it's exactly like the sketch I sent you.' Bel flung open the door with its faded blue paint, and stepped inside. The skylights were open, and there was no need for a wood-burning stove, but Bel could imagine how cosy it would be in the winter when she worked late into the night. No disturbance, just her and her designs in perfect flow. *In winter, the early mornings* . . . she thought, imagining the sun rise over the coast. Just as she had asked, the walls and floor had been painted white, and a long work table built beneath the north-facing windows.

Sacha gestured at the comfortable old linen-covered arm-chair by the stove. 'I found this when I was searching the markets for timber. I hope you do not mind?'

'It's perfect. How thoughtful,' Bel said, sprawling in it and gazing down at the view of her house, the sea and sky shim-mering beyond. 'I love it,' she said, resting her arm behind her head. She smiled up at Sacha. 'I love it all. Thank you.'

Sacha walked Bel back down hill, through the house's garden door. From the living room, an elegant wooden staircase swept up to her bedroom and bathroom on the top floor, where a bay window like a lighthouse would one day look out over the sea. Now the wooden frame was open to the night, and Bel could smell the sea, hear its rush in the distance. She mimed opening French windows onto the small terrace, and stepped out onto the roof.

'Watch your step,' Sacha said, holding the lantern up.

Bel laid her hands on the rail and looked out at the waves. 'Sacha, it's wonderful.' She turned to him. The gold light of the lantern held them. 'Thank you so much.'

'Are you sure you wish to sleep here tonight?' he said.

'Quite sure.' She took the backpack from him, and untied her bed roll.

'I hope you both sleep well,' he said, bending to scratch Vero's head.

'For once, I think I might,' Bel said, brushing back her hair.

Sacha paused. 'You are not what I expected at all.'

'Really?' Bel shook out the sleeping mat and threw down her pillow.

'When they said a great designer from Paris was building a house, I thought . . .'

'I hope,' she said, 'that *you* are not disappointed?'

Lot 66

SAINT-TROPEZ, AUGUST 1913

Over the days of summer, Bel worked beside Sacha, whitewashing the rooms as they came ready, and painting the new window frames and shutters sky blue. As she worked, she gathered glimpses of him like treasure. Sacha scaling a ladder, shirtless, his strong tanned back and elegant calves. Sacha walking across roof beams with the catlike grace of a tightrope walker. *Sacha*. In the evening, they walked downhill to join the Lamberts for supper, sitting up late into the night on the candlelit terrace, laughing and talking with Françoise and her family as the children dozed in their mother's arms. Each night they returned home, Sacha escorting Bel to her door, and passing her the hurricane lantern. Each night she hoped he might stay. Night after night, she lay awake on the simple cot in her bedroom, staring at the slanted ceiling, thinking of him asleep across the garden. Her body ached from painting, from gardening, and she hummed with desire like the bees in the long grass.

Bel rose early, and washed in the basin in her room. Standing naked before the cheval mirror, she turned this way and that, lifting her hair. *Mirror, mirror . . . who is the fairest of them all.* From a distance, she still had the figure of a young woman, but close to she studied the fine lines around her eyes, the fall of her breasts, the loosening skin on her knees, the backs of her hands. Bel groaned and laid her forehead against the cool looking glass. *I feel like a lovestruck schoolgirl.*

~

'Am I an old fool?' Bel said to Françoise as they shopped in the market.

'You are not old.' Their baskets were filled with fresh strawberries and peaches, soft cheeses and warm bread, spilling over their arms like cornucopias. Bel stopped to sniff a melon, inhaling its heady sweet scent, and nodded, paying the vendor.

'Oh . . . it's ridiculous.'

'What's ridiculous? Why your handsome builder has not taken you to bed?' Françoise said, laughing. 'Have you made a pass at him?'

'Of course not! He's young enough to be my son.'

'He is not.'

'Almost.' Bel wandered on, and stopped at the fishmonger to choose rascasse to grill that night. She tucked the paper-wrapped parcel into her basket beside the bottles of rosé.

'I see him watching you, when you are not looking.'

'Nonsense?' The heat rose in Bel's cheeks. 'He doesn't notice me.'

'Every man notices you, trust me. You always have your head in the clouds, designing and working, so you don't see them,' Françoise said, laughing. 'Next time you are with him, really look at Sacha.'

'That is all I do.' Bel pressed her hand to her cheek. 'Night after night I wash my lingerie by hand, and oil my skin, all for nothing.'

'Not for nothing – *souci de soi*! A woman takes care of herself, for herself.'

'I'm mad.'

'*C'est un coup de foudre.*' Françoise clutched her heart, grinning.

'What about you? Is there no one? Angêle's father?'

'Was an old friend,' Françoise said easily. 'I wanted a child.' She glanced at Bel, unsure. 'Yes, there is someone.'

'Why have I not met them?'

'You have,' Françoise said, looking down for a moment. 'She is in Paris.' *Oh?*

'I'm happy for you,' Bel said, squeezing her friend's hand.

'I know – why don't you have a little house-warming party tonight? Invite some of the neighbours? You are so good at parties, you mix people like cocktails. Ply him with eau de vie . . .' Françoise nudged her. 'I'll call an old school friend, a caterer. Meanwhile go, it's time for your appointment.' She shooed her towards the beauty salon. 'Go, spoil yourself. Life is short, Bel, have some fun while the summer lasts.'

~

That evening, Bel swung the Bugatti into her newly gravelled driveway. She could see golden lights around the pool terrace glowing like fireflies against the sunset, and a long white table set with sunflowers and lustre goblets. *Good*, she thought, smelling the saffron-scented bouillabaisse being prepared by the maid in the new kitchen. Bel checked her reflection in the mirror by the entrance door, and threw down her keys, taking off her headscarf and sunglasses. The hairdresser had swept her hair up, pinning it with fresh jasmine. Bel's body felt lean and strong from the summer, tanned from days swimming at the beach. The masseur had unknotted the last painful tension in her neck and shoulders, and she felt at ease in her skin, looking forward to the night.

After changing into one of her new designs, a fluid shift of white silk, Bel found Françoise on the terrace, directing the boys behind the bar. She raised her hand to Bel and offered her a glass of champagne.

'Thank you,' Bel said, kissing her cheek. 'I feel like a new woman.'

'Or a new man,' Françoise said, raising her chin to Sacha, who was striding across the garden towards the house. He wore a deep-blue suit and a loose tie, and his hair was still dark and damp from the bath. 'Come, join us,' she called.

The party grew, friends arriving from all over Saint-Tropez, music drifting out from the house. After dinner, Bel glanced down the table to where Sacha sat with Monsieur Lambert, talking and smoking. He wasn't looking at her, and she turned away. Sacha looked over longingly at Bel, but she now sat gazing at Gabrielle and Colette dancing by the pool, and he looked down at his hands.

'For heaven's sake,' Françoise murmured under her breath, watching them. 'Come on everyone,' she said, rising and clapping her hands. 'Tonight, we all dance.' She shooed the group from the table, making sure that Sacha ended up next to Bel.

'May I?' he said, bowing to her.

'I thought you'd never ask,' Bel said, placing her hand in his.

Lot 67

SAINT-TROPEZ, AUGUST 1913

The next morning, Bel woke in a tangle of white sheets, and rolled over to see a square of cobalt blue above her. It took her a moment to realise where she was. *Sacha*, she thought, a kaleidoscope of memories spilling free. His touch, the feel of him, the scent of his skin. She reached out with her toe to locate him, and Sacha slid his hand across her stomach, pulling her to him again.

'Good morning,' he said, grinning sleepily.

'Good morning.' She kissed him, and he turned, pressing the hard length of his body against hers, pulling the sheet over their heads.

I wanted you from the first moment, he said to her in the night. *I can't believe that you wanted me, too . . .*

I was afraid, she said.

Bel looked at him now, close to, his dark lashes framing his sea-glass eyes. *I'm not afraid anymore.* She kissed him, her eyes closing, giving in to the desire rising warm through her like the turquoise sea on the shore.

~

The hours drifted on around them. The rectangle of light above the bed changed from cobalt to apricot to rose, to midnight blue again. When they stumbled from the bed, and ran hand in hand to the pool, diving in, laughing and joyful, somewhere down the hill a church bell chimed eleven. Bel surfaced and floated on her back. *I'm alive,* she thought. *I feel alive, again.* Sacha floated beside her, reached out his hand to hers.

'I didn't know it was possible to feel this happy,' she said. As she gazed up at the star-filled sky, her perception of the world seemed to expand. Bel's mind drifted back to the young girl who swam at the waterfall with Tom, who learnt what it was to be with a man for the first time. She thought of all the women she had been since then – wife, mother, designer, businesswoman, friend. Now lover. *We are all like Russian dolls. So many different selves hidden away beneath the surface.* Bel closed her eyes, losing herself in the moment, losing all sense of where her body ended and the warm water, the liquid night air, began. *Pay attention*, she thought, *remember this*, already picturing the unstoppable days drifting away like the sand in an hourglass.

~

These were the days she would return to again and again on the silver winter nights in Paris. Days of sunshine, and brown feet, of sand in the sheets at night time, and woodsmoke in her hair. Of crisp glasses of rosé at lunch, and fresh grilled fish from the boats in the harbour. Of reading in her shady hammock. White cotton dresses, and Sacha's shirts on the line, arms entwined with her blouses. These were simple days of friends, of home, of love.

For the first time, Bel felt secure. She had a safe haven that no one would ever take away from her. Each morning when she woke beside Sacha, Bel told herself: *Remember this. Remember all of it.* She wore no watch, her diary went unwritten. They lived by the rise and fall of the sun. Only when she needed to reach for a shawl while they were playing backgammon one evening did she realise that the summer was ending, and soon she must leave for Paris.

~

Bel sat at the dining table in the main house, surrounded by the mail Françoise had kept from her at the Post Office box. *You are here for a break. There is nothing that couldn't wait until September. The whole of Paris is en vacances – why shouldn't you be?*

Among the letters she found one from Hiro, his familiar clear script marking out 'Isobel Bright', and a small butterfly. He had always kept her name, never honouring the pretence of 'Madame Kurosaki', or her married 'Madame de la Roche'. Bel opened it and tipped a small origami crane folded from blue and white paper printed with chrysanthemums onto her palm. She lifted it up and smiled, tucking it into the pocket of her skirt for safety.

My Dear Bel, he wrote.

Tell me about Saint-Tropez in summer. I picture you and your white house on the hill. Are you working? Are you drawing, still?

Of course you are. In that we are alike. I returned to my house today after seeing my mother's family in Nagano. I drew the monkeys at the hot spring for you. They look like little old men, soaking up to their necks in warm water.

We have sent the shipment of silk to your new studio in Paris, ready for your return. I hope they are everything you wished. My uncle always said: hope for the best, prepare for the worst. I hope, for you—

'You are working?' Sacha interrupted, leaning in the terrace doorway. He wore a blue-and-white-striped jersey, and high-waisted pale Oxford bags, his tanned bare feet crossed at the ankle. Bel wished she had a camera to capture the moment.

'Just catching up,' she said. She tucked Hiro's letter beneath a stack of bills. 'There's so much to do . . .'

'I've collected the limestone tiles for your bedroom terrace, if you would like to see them?' he said. 'I chose ones with tiny shells and fossils, little ferns. You might want to choose your favourites?'

'I'm sure whichever you choose will be perfect,' she said, her eye drawn to a letter from Mademoiselle Chanel's house.

'As you wish,' he said. She heard the disappointment in his voice, and looked up.

'Sacha, I'm so grateful. You do know that, don't you?

Please allow me to give you a bonus for all you have done,' Bel said, picking up her cheque book. 'I've been through all your receipts and everything is in order, but it feels the sum we agreed for your labour is too little.' She glanced up, and smiled. 'Who should I make the cheque to? It's madness, but I realise I don't know your real name.'

'A bonus?' Sacha folded his arms. 'For services rendered?'

'No!' she said, aghast. Bel set down her pen and went to him. 'No. This is business. It has nothing to do with us.' He took her face in his hands and kissed her, tenderly.

'Stay,' he said. 'Stay with me.'

'I can't.' Bel leant her forehead against his. 'Work calls.'

'I can't bear this.' His voice caught. 'You can't just *leave*.'

'Sacha, we had a wonderful summer, but it is not real life.' She took a deep breath. 'Our worlds are different. You could not bear Paris, and I could not be here all year—'

'Why?'

'Sacha, you are young still. You can have a family, a home, a life—'

'No, I only want you.' He pressed her hand to his lips, kissed the palm.

'Be happy, for both of us.' She forced a smile. 'This has been a beautiful summer.'

'You will come back?'

'Not until next August.' She saw his frustration. 'By then I wager you will be an old married man, with a baby on the way.'

'I won't. I want no one but you.' The note of petulance

in his voice snagged on her like a bramble. Bel felt a familiar sense of constriction, of being tied down. Sometimes, dealing with Sacha she felt like she was talking to Genji in one of his moods. Sacha looked down at her and shook his head. 'I can't bear it.'

'The heart is resilient,' she said, firmly. 'You can, and you will.'

'How can you be so hard? Bel, I love you—'

'Sacha, I care deeply about you—'

'Say it.' He frowned. 'You love me. I know you do.'

'Sacha . . .' She turned to the desk. 'I want you to stay above the garage for as long as you wish.' *Stay forever*, she thought. *I wish you, I wish this summer, would last forever. I wish you wouldn't ask for things I cannot give you.* She took up her pen. 'Now, who should I make the cheque to?'

'Alexandre Dubois,' he said. Bel raised her head slowly.

'My father was called Alexander,' she said. 'I should have realised – Sacha.'

'My family name, since I was small.' He dug his hands in his pockets and shrugged. 'I have never felt grown up enough to be "Alexandre".'

Bel blotted the cheque and gave it to him, standing on tiptoe to kiss him. 'To me, you will always be my Sacha,' she said. She untied the bow at the nape of her neck, and the lawn cotton dress hung loose at her waist. 'Business over,' she said. 'One last swim?'

Lot 68

PARIS, 11 NOVEMBER 1918

Five years. Five years since Miramar. In Saint-Germain-des-Prés, Bel sat beneath the crisp white marquee awning, at a terrace table in the Café de Flore to watch the people thronging the streets. 'How I miss it . . .'

'Madame?' the waiter said.

'*Un petit coup de vin blanc, s'il vous plaît.*' She looked down and rubbed Vero's ears.

In a far corner on the crimson couches, a group of artists were celebrating by arguing, noisily. *Those surrealists,* Bel thought, *always fighting.* 'Beware,' Breton cried out. 'Everything will fade, everything will vanish . . .'

Even us? Bel thought, watching a lithe couple tangoing to a Latin tune. *We are still here, we survived the years of war.* She frowned. *Has Maison BB vanished, though? Will anyone remember my work? Will they remember me?* She settled back on the cane chair, taking her mail out of her suede bag to read.

Every generation must learn anew, Hiro wrote. *By middle age you feel that life is ridiculous, history repeating itself again and again. That will continue unless we learn. With age we must get quicker at correcting ourselves when we veer off course.*

There will always be war in the world because some men – and in history it has been almost exclusively men – will always want more, will always hate a part of themselves so deeply they will destroy all they perceive as other than them, or better than them. Men like that will always appeal to the basest, most craven parts of people. Good men and women must defend against them. Such is life. War, violence, destruction. It is all so pointless.

I am an old man. Give me peace. Give me a fine morning with the promise of heat. Give me the birds in the pines welcoming the day. Give me a simple lunch and a cold beer in the shade of a tree, and a nap on the grass with the people I love. Give me the space to think, to feel, to create, to love.

Our last freedom is to choose our attitude.

Every hour, every moment is a chance to choose.

What do you want, Bel?

Always (choose) love.

Hiro

My dear Hiro, Bel wrote.

The bells call to one another across Paris. You would not recognise me. My hair has a streak of pure white. What times we have lived through, you and I. They say a million British souls are lost, and twice that wounded, more in France. Our men fell like pennies in an arcade, more piling up behind, pushing towards the abyss. How many broken hearts, and broken generations, are there, the aftermath rippling through time?

When I left Miramar in August 1913, I did not know we would be at war by the next summer. Some left Paris, but Françoise and I stayed. The Paris Guns laid siege to the city, shelling, destroying. Our windows rattled nightly. I saw Monsieur Proust one day – he walked home the night before, the sky lit up by shell bursts and searchlights. When he arrived at the Boulevard Haussmann, his hat brim was full of shrapnel.

Last night was too cold to sleep, and so I warmed myself reading your old letters.

I had a letter from London – Miss Browning, now Mrs Scott, filled me in on the Liberty news. The women had to do all the men's jobs. Her eldest went to war – as she put it: 'I said to my Jack, if you're not in khaki by the end of the month, I shall cut you dead.' And they say women are the weaker sex.

Here, many of the artists were neutral and non-combatant, painting camouflage, or nursing like Cocteau (in a uniform designed by Poiret, mind). Paris was sad and dark, blacked out at night, the cinemas and shops closed. Cattle graze in the Bois de Boulogne. What was fashionable Paris to do? Some, like Isadora Duncan, escaped the war zone to Deauville. Paris on sea. I cannot blame her after all she suffered with the loss of her children. I will never forget those tiny white coffins, the sea of white flowers.

I was content to stay. I help Vasilieff in the canteen, feeding some forty artists on two little burners. The walls may be decorated with paintings by Picasso, Chagall and Modigliani, but the meals are simple – soup, meat, vegetables. It keeps starvation from the door, and the company cheers them. We have all done our bit. Picasso and Cocteau staged Parade *with the Ballets Russes and Satie for the war charities. Gertrude Stein delivered hospital supplies in her little car, 'Auntie'. Edith Wharton opened a workroom for unemployed seamstresses. Some sixty women have support for their families. I turned my workrooms over to making uniforms.*

We have women delivering the post, conducting the trams, watering the public gardens in chic black overalls and hats. I heard the Red Cross girls arrived in Calais with skirts down to their ankles. What use is that when the world has turned to liquid mud? They cut them nine inches from the ground – some, nine inches from the waist. The steel bones of their corsets get nasty with the work they have to do – one girl said she hid hers in the lavatory and hasn't worn one since. They wear army greatcoats and Canadian flying jackets, these rebels and Suffragettes, with bobbed hair and flowers tucked into their belts. My next collection is inspired by them.

I so admire these young girls. They are thankful for small things. On Friday the Lamberts send up a basket of fish on the train from St Tropez, and I make bouillabaisse for as many friends as we can seat around the work tables in Avenue Junot.

They talk of terrible battlefields, the stunned earth. Trees destroyed and debris strewn about. Verdun was an inferno, they say.

Thank god Genji is safe. Thank god for Monet, who works at last on his 'grands decorations', his paintings of his water gardens. 'The Work', he says, done to the distant sound of guns.

So, this is victory. Chō said many years ago: grief is the dark earth from which life grows. It is the necessary counter to the light. For so many years women have asked: what can we do for our soldiers? Vogue *told us to slim down so that we use less fabric! 'Dress up so that he carries away a vision of loveliness to war.' Now, many of my staff are widowed. Many young women will have little hope of marriage. The survivors were promised a life fit for heroes, but they find themselves selling matches, or singing on street corners and peddling sheet music. What of our heroines? Women give and give. Even in the brothels of Pigalle, war veterans go free on Thursdays.*

We must remember them. I just overheard Breton saying that everything vanishes and fades. But what remains? Will anyone remember us, our work? I am no heroine, but I did my bit, and sewed uniforms, and made simple patterns for adaptable blouses and skirts that women could sew at home.

I must stand up – again – and resurrect my maison, *but is it wrong I feel a violent longing for adventure? I dance two hours a day for exercise, and do my callisthenics. In our sixties, we must keep moving. I want the agility of May Sutton winning Wimbledon! Give me glamour, give me escape! I want*

Gina Palermo's fur capes and riding britches. I want to be Sarah Bernhardt on a polar bear rug beneath a tasselled canopy. I hunger for beauty after this damnable war. This summer I will return to my beloved Miramar. When will you come?

We are all changed. Necessity has shown women can do men's jobs. No longer must we choose marriage or the convent. What now? Hiro-san, you told me many years ago that we must each find our ikigai, *our purpose in life.*

I have lived a long time now, and feel I have something to say. What have I learnt? That life breaks us, but we are stronger for it. That there is beauty in this strength.

I've learnt that we should use life up. What we love, what we use becomes beautiful with wear.

Do not save your heart for best.

Do not save living for that perfect moment which will never come. Live now.

What do I want? A simple enough question, isn't it. But then, to do something simple is incredibly hard. Simplicity is not the same as simplistic. Instead perhaps I should ask – what's my purpose? What brings me joy?

No one knows the meaning of life, but one can learn what brings meaning to life.

Tonight the bells ring. Tonight the lights go up across the city for the first time in four years. Tonight, I think of you.

I miss you.

Your Bel

~

Kate Lord Brown

Postcard of a gingko tree:

What survives us tells the tale

What remains is love

Hiro

Lot 69

PARIS, 31 JULY 1985

'To us, Hutch,' Ned said, raising his glass to her. They sat in Le Train Bleu restaurant, waiting for the evening train. 'We did it. What a week.'

'Don't speak too soon – God knows what Bel has squirrelled away in Saint-Tropez.' Mira looked around the lavish restaurant. This was Bel's Paris to her. This was the *Belle Epoque.* Gleaming tiles, gold mirrors, twinkling chandeliers, a phalanx of waiters in immaculate white aprons. Starched linen, a coupe of champagne, oysters on crushed ice. *Ned.*

'Serge is crating everything tomorrow for Tokyo,' he said.

'And we'll meet him at the apartment on Friday to sign off the last art and mirrors?'

'Exactly. Whatever is at Miramar belongs to the Lamberts.'

'I'm just curious to find out more about her.' Mira checked her watch. '*Allons-y.*'

~

High above Saint-Tropez the next morning, Ned parked the rented red Renault 5 at the side of the road beside a sweeping stone wall and metal gate. The name 'Miramar' on a discreet blue and white enamelled sign was the only clue to what lay behind the tall wall. Ned placed his hand over 'mar' and laughed softly. 'Look at that: *Mira*,' he said.

'Look? Like the Spanish?'

'I mean, Mira, like Miranda.' The intercom buzzed.

'*Allô?*' an elderly voice answered.

'Madame? It's Edward Brookes – we spoke earlier.' They listened as she muttered something and the gate creaked open.

A wide pale gravel drive swept down to a low white villa, the sea sparkling beyond. An avenue of cypresses framed the house, green against the cobalt sky. 'The Lamberts have done well for themselves,' Mira said quietly.

'Farmers generally do,' Ned said, his footsteps crunching on the gravel.

'It helps if someone like Bel leaves you a house in the hills above Saint-Tropez.'

'No kindly millionaires in your family, then?' Ned smiled.

The heavy wood front door swung open, and a frail figure in a white beekeeper suit and hat stepped out of the shadows, lifting the veil from her face. 'She looks just like Natasha,' Mira said, and raised her hand.

'Bonjour, Madame Dubois?' Ned offered his hand. 'Ned Brookes, and Mira Hutchinson.'

'I just warned the bees of your arrival,' she said, beckoning for them to follow her. Ned widened his eyes at Mira.

'I know it sounds crazy,' she said in English. 'But the head of the household must always tell the bees of events. My husband was always the one to tell them of births, marriages and deaths. You must tell the bees all the news. Now it is my responsibility.' She threw the hat down among the photographs on the console table. Mira spotted a wedding party, 1930s she guessed. *They look so happy*, she thought. *Angêle's perhaps? Is Bel among them*?

'Thank you for seeing us,' Ned said.

'I hope you have not had a wasted journey. If the Kurosakis are sniffing around for more things to sell, tell them Isobel Bright left Miramar to Françoise Lambert, and the house passed down through the family since then.' Her eyes glinted. 'The Kurosakis own the apartments – there is nothing we can do about my cousin being thrown out on the street at her age.' *After living rent-free her whole life*, Mira thought. 'But they will not have this house.'

'I assure you, Madame, we are not here to take anything from you,' she said. 'I just want to know all there is about Bel.'

'Saint-Tropez has changed since Isobel's time.' She beckoned for them to follow her. 'It was just a little fishing village then.' The house was a cluttered sixties time capsule of mid-century furniture and raffia lampshades. Mira frowned.

'It's not what I was expecting, from Bel's diary?' she said to Ned.

'Look past the decoration,' Madame Dubois said. 'Look at the bones of the house. She is everywhere.' She showed them onto the terrace. 'See? Isobel chose this view.' Mira remembered Bel's description of leaping into the pool with Sacha, a starry sky above. *Imagine*. She glanced at Ned, touching her throat.

'Did Bel leave anything here? A portrait . . .' Ned said carefully.

'If you are looking for heirlooms, there are none,' she snapped. 'There is a lithograph of Sarah Bernhardt signed "To Bel, with love, Sarah." That is all. It hung above her bed and we have not moved it.'

'Were they friends?' Mira said.

'Sarah was ten, fifteen years older than her, they were close. She came here. Now you want it, the print?' The old woman's voice shook, angered.

'That won't be necessary,' Ned said, placating. 'It belongs here.'

'Look – Natasha has taken care of *everything* in Paris for the Kurosakis, and how do they repay her? What fine jewellery there was Bel sold to support the family through wars and hard times. She was never sentimental. She sold that famous Cartier piece to pay for the apartment my cousin lives in. Now the Kurosakis are giving up both.' She shook her head. 'The younger generation cares nothing for tradition.' She pushed a battered photograph album towards Mira. 'This is all we have left of Isobel here. You are welcome to see it.'

'I said to Ned, what's the first thing you'd save in a fire?'

'Family?' Madame Dubois shrugged. 'Animals.'

'And photo albums. I couldn't understand why there

wasn't at least one album in Paris. And here it is.' Mira turned the first page. A young girl in a Victorian white pinafore with a black mourning sash stood beside a proud-looking man with luxurious moustaches and a flamboyant loose tie. 'Bel?' she said, and the woman nodded. 'That must be her father?'

'Can I photograph these, as we look through?' Ned, said, taking out his camera.

'Take it. No one here remembers Bel other than me, and I am seventy, my memory is fading. If you are selling her life, perhaps someone will want these too.'

'We're not quite selling her life,' Ned said, frowning.

'Of course you are. Everyone is picking over the carcass of her existence.' She snapped her fingertips like beaks. 'It will be the same with me the moment I stop breathing – the family will sell the land before my body is cold—'

'Look!' Mira interrupted. 'Here's Bel outside Liberty. That must be Hiro and Chō,' she said, 'and look! Her little dog, Sally.'

'Do you think that chap beside her is Tom Fraser?' Ned said, pointing at a photograph of Bel in a loose white blouse and skirt. He wore a three-piece cream flannel suit, a straw boater tipped at a rakish angle, white buckskin shoes. They had paused on a summer path, dappled light falling around them. The man turned towards her, his high white collar and pocket square catching the light. It was as if the photographer had intruded.

I remember feeling like that with Luke, Mira thought. *Bel looks radiant.* She frowned, and turned the photo over, hoping for a note in pencil. *I miss that*, she realised. *I miss feeling like that.* She pictured them strolling on after the photo was taken, not caring where they were, only that they were together. She imagined their laughter, their easy conversation. The jokes and confidences offered up like children sharing their treasures: *I've never told anyone this . . . Me too!*

'I'd put money on it being Tom,' she said, looking at his proud, handsome face. 'They look so happy,' she said quietly, slipping it back into its mounts and turning the page. 'Genji,' she said, smiling at the baby on Bel's lap. These photographs were less staged, taken in a summer garden. Bel in a white dress, Genji in a white smock. Apple blossom on the trees in the orchard.

'When did they come to France? 1890 or so?' Ned looked closer. 'I swear that's Claude Monet?'

On the next page, there was a formal wedding portrait of Bel in a simple white silk bias-cut dress, the photo torn in two.

'Pierre de la Roche,' Madame Dubois said quietly.

Mira turned the page. Several photographs had been torn out, and she flicked on. She picked up a hazy photograph of the view down to Saint-Tropez, with thumb tack holes where it had been pinned to a wall.

'That is where we are sitting now,' Madame Dubois said, tapping the page. 'Bel stayed with my family in the farm where my great-grandchildren still live and work now.' Mira turned on. 'See? Miramar, as it was when Bel first lived here.' The house was considerably smaller – modest, even. *A good house*, Mira thought, smiling. She turned the page – a party, a group of friends on the pool terrace, raising their glasses in a toast. Bel standing beside a tall young man with golden hair. *She's radiant. She looks so modern, so . . . alive.*

'Who's that, with Bel?'

'Sacha?' she laughed. 'What on earth do you want to know about him for? That old roué. He fathered half the children in Saint-Tropez by all accounts.' The old woman paused, a curious expression on her face. 'One of his sons, Alain, was working at Miramar in the late fifties, I do know that. He was a builder like his father, and he carried out the extension to the house.' She tilted her head. 'Spitting image of his papa, when he was young. Like a young Adonis. All the girls in the village were mad for him. Including me.'

'Was?' Ned said.

'My husband passed away recently.'

'Oh?' Mira said, picking up on the catch in her voice. 'I'm sorry.'

'You remind me of someone,' she said to Mira.

'Apparently, my mum visited, when my godmother worked here.' Mira looked her in the eye. 'Maybe you met her.'

'You're kidding?' Ned said.

'I mentioned to Kim we were coming down here and she said she knew the house. I told you she worked with the Kurosakis after graduating? They recommended staying with the Lamberts when she wanted to paint in the South of France.'

'Yes, Kim lived here for a few months one summer, looking after the children. A – how you say – Girl Friday, in exchange for her board at Miramar.' Madame Dubois pulled down another photo album, and pointed.

'I don't believe it,' Mira said, peering closer. 'That's Mum? And Kim?'

Lot 70

LONDON, DECEMBER 1922

My dear Hiro –

Guess where I write from? The Handley Page Pullman flight, taking me home to Paris from London. From Croydon it is only two and a half hours. I cannot believe I am sitting here, weightless above the Channel. Imagine! There are two rows of plush seats, a carpeted aisle, brocade curtains and a candelabra.

I know you do not celebrate Christmas, but I think of you, all the same. I walked along Regent Street, and the air was scented with roasting chestnuts. It is the first time I have seen Lady Liberty since we lost Sir Arthur in 1917. She told me five hundred mourners lined the lanes, with William Judd leading the store contingent, and many people from the Japan Society. They were both so kind to me, I feel his loss keenly, and she is not well.

I bought a bag of satsumas from the old stall around the

corner from Liberty – do you remember, where we would buy fruit for our lunch? There must be a nursery nearby somewhere, for I heard children singing: oranges and lemons. Yes, I walked down Regent Street with the ghosts of three young friends from long ago. I send you my love and good wishes for the new year.

I hope you like the shawl collar kimono jacket? I designed it thinking of you. They are for him or her. The secret is a fine chain in the hem so that they hang perfectly. I like to think of you wearing it. I imagine you look most elegant.

You should see the plans for Liberty! Sir Arthur would be so proud. It will be a Tudor building, made from old ship's timbers, like a vessel docked on Regent Street, full of treasures. In Paris, Paul St George Perrott is moving Maison Liberty from the Avenue de l'Opera to the Boulevard des Capucines, with some hundred employees in five workrooms, just as predicted.

Here, the new jazz women are tall and graceful, short-haired and short-skirted, independent and dashing. This is who inspires me now, women like Colette's Claudine. I am sketching pleated dresses with dropped waists.

Last night I listened to the Monte Carlo Bandits in a dive bar near the Thames. I will design for the garçonnes and flappers. We shall have colour photographs and sunbathing, scarlet nail polish and Cadillacs, kohl and bangles.

Give me youth! Give me dinner dances and cocktails, sunken baths and private bars.

I have the Millicent Sowerby and Kate Greenway books from Foyles for your nieces as you asked.

All love

Bel xx

PS pyjama suits! I am obsessed with wide-leg suits, and playsuits. Please send lots more of the oyster silk.

Lot 71

PARIS, JUNE 1923

'Goodnight, my darlings.' Françoise said to the vendeuses, and the elegant women in grey crêpe de chine dresses filed out of the Avenue Junot apartment like the ex-models they were. She wore the same charcoal-grey dress as them, but with a silver lamé bolero and ropes of pearls.

The gunmetal-grey walls of the salon were silent, where they had been alive with jazz music and the murmur of clients just hours before. Bel's new collection of flattering dresses in rich shades of Japanese purple and Persian pinks had triumphed. Even Cristóbal Balenciaga said in his low voice: *Magnifique*.

'We must change the displays tomorrow,' Bel said, looking at the mannequin beside the Picasso in the hall.

'Again? They look good.'

'It's not enough to be *good*. I want them changed every day during the shows. We have to hold people's attention. Young designers are coming through. We must be constantly surprising.' Bel thought of the first window she dressed with Hiro, the lanterns and cherry blossom. She remembered Pierre talking of the butterfly trick. *The illusion of life.* 'I want trees in flower, here. Butterflies dancing in the breeze from every window.'

'I can't believe someone of your stature is worried about competition?'

'Worried? No. But if you are in the race you must be aware of where your rivals are, and hold your course.'

'All designers are magpies.'

'We reuse and repurpose. Art is a relay. We pass the torch on and on to the future. Look at Doucet, who trained Poiret—'

'Yesterday's news. He is living with his sister now.'

'Every designer has a lineage. Lanvin looks to stained glass and Botticelli. Vionnet cut deliciously on the bias, but her influence is classical.' Bel swept her hand through the air. 'Those divine sheer dresses over Chinese silk – you can see the influence of the Callot *soeurs*. These days art and commerce and music dance with one another.' Bel did a little turn across the workroom. 'All of fashion is a conversation.' Bel stretched out her back. 'Fashion is a monster. Always hungry . . .'

'And Chanel?'

'Ah, Gabrielle has three thousand employees now. She is an original with her trousers and costume jewellery.'

'I always think it's your fabrics that set you apart.'

'We have Hiro to thank for our success. His silks have spirit.'

'Balenciaga is a genius. I like what he is doing in San Sebastián.'

'Indeed. A true couturier. The rest of us are mere doodlers in comparison. But not everyone can afford three fittings for a night gown,' Bel said. 'Sir Arthur always said he would bring art into the homes of the masses. Now Harrods are selling kimonos for eight guineas.' Bel rubbed her hands. 'We will find a price for the *jeune fille.* It's time for a *prêt-a-porter* line.'

'Can we afford it?'

'Can we afford not to? I want to draw in the girl who would buy a suit at Galeries Lafayette.' Bel kicked off her high heels. 'Come, let's get some air.'

~

Bel and Françoise took their evening promenade in the Bois de Boulogne, their chauffeur parked at a discreet distance, leaning against the bonnet of the Rolls, smoking.

'There, see her?' Bel said, pointing with the ferrule of her umbrella. 'Every accessory is perfect. What more does a young woman need? The ease of dressing in a simple knitted jacket and a pleated skirt, a little hat . . .'

'What about her?' Françoise said.

'No, feathers? Our girls need turbans for driving. They want skirts with a little fringing, for dancing . . . If they have a little *avoirdupois*, it must be comfortably supported.'

'I see Chanel is doing black crêpe de chine dresses—'

'Really?' Bel inhaled a soft laugh. 'I remember distinctly our conversation over tea at Fleurs on rue St Honoré—'

'With Balkan embroidery?'

'Hm. Interesting. Mark my words, this year will be all about Egyptomania. After the discovery of Tutankhamun, I am putting my money on Luxor blues and Papyrus golds. There—' she said, pointing at a young woman walking arm in arm with her beau up ahead. 'See, that fine turquoise trim?' Bel whistled for her dog. 'Come, Vero, we must get back to work.'

'Do you ever rest?'

'Oh, we are slowing down a little, aren't we?' She rubbed Vero's ears and clipped the chain link and velvet lead. *We are both getting older.* She thought of Sally, a bittersweet sadness sweeping over her. *Not yet, Vero.* The little dog looked up at her quizzically. *We have years yet.* 'What do you think about jewellery for men? I hear Mrs Valentino gave Rudolf a slave bracelet.'

'Rudolf is Rudolf, darling.'

'You're right.' Bel studied a young woman walking ahead. 'I think Paris will agree to disagree with London about skirts this season. We will go shorter.'

'Supper?' Françoise settled back in the car.

'Let's stop off at that darling little café on rue Mouffetard. I so enjoy eavesdropping on the young Americans.'

'I need to pop in to Sylvia Beach's library, too. She has the books I want to take to Miramar.' Bel gazed out of the window. 'I do like that part of town. Perhaps I shall retire to the Île Saint-Louis and have a little apartment with dogs and books, and be perfectly happy.'

'Retire? Leave Montmartre – you?' Françoise laughed in disbelief. 'Never.'

~

11th June 1923

I took the new Blue Train to Miramar last night. I find myself escaping here at all seasons. I love the tender spring, scented with lilacs, iris, stocks. I love the summer when it is too hot to walk on the beach. I love the melancholy autumn. I love the crisp winter months. I can think and feel clearly here.

I had a card from Genji. Our boy. He asked me to visit him at Monet's. A reconciliation, at last.

I can hardly believe it. After all these years, the unanswered letters and cards. Last night as I lay sketching in my bed at four o'clock, with Vero tucked by my feet as usual, it struck me that perhaps it is a parent's lot to love more than they are loved. My heart is overjoyed, and yet I am wary, too.

It is too much to expect everything from one person.

My life, my romantic loves, can be divided thus:

Mind – Tom

Body – Sacha

Spirit – Hiro

Hiro told me: 'In Japan we say that every person has three hearts. The first, everyone sees. The second you only show privately to loved ones. The third, your deepest, greatest, secret heart, burns with who and what we really are. This we share with no one, ever.'

Tom, my first love, was all about ideas. The idea of love. It was all new. I was idealistic, and romantic, and trusting, and swept away by him. But Tom opened my eyes to so much. It is thanks to him that I can even design a house now. For that, I will always be grateful. He had my first heart – the girl on the outside.

Sacha – oh, Sacha. The memory of that summer. Even now my old bones quicken and grow molten, remembering. I saw him last summer. He has grown stocky with age, his skin thickened. But as we passed in the market and I conversed with him and his wife, who had two small children hanging from her skirts – I saw a glimmer of the old Sacha in his sea-glass eyes. He taught me to enjoy and trust my own body. For that I am grateful. To him I gave my second heart, the secret, passionate woman in me.

And Hiro. Whose constant love has been the strength of my life. He has taught me about devotion. He has taught me about quiet attention. He has taught me that all we have to do in this life is be still and be thankful. I know Genji kept in touch with him. I am grateful for that. Perhaps it is Hiro who persuaded Genji to relent at last.

Few people are like Hiro – fully formed, constant and true. Most are like me – broken, evolving, in metamorphosis.

I was not ready for Hiro, when we met. I am now.

Hiro has my third heart, my essential self. He always has.

When I am on the Avenue Junot, I look out at Paris

through the screen of cranes he sent over the years, as they dance and spin in the wind, all the colours of the rainbow. They carry his love to me on their wings. Something has changed this year. I feel myself drawn home to him.

Hiro never tried to tie me down. He allowed me to grow and become everything I am.

Hiro has waited for me all this time.

Is it time to go to him, and to Japan?

Is it time to try? Or is it too late?

Life takes what it will from us.

All that can save us is love. Love one another. Love our work. Love our art.

Trust your burning heart when the stars are falling.

I am going to see my son!

BB

Lot 72

GIVERNY, JULY 1923

Bel's carriage trundled along the lane from Vernon to Monet's house at Giverny beneath a lavender-blue sky. She rode out through valleys of cornfields, the undulating hills dotted with red poppies. The river was lined with poplars, and cattle grazed in meadows which smelled sweetly of wild mint.

Calm down. Bel forced herself to breathe deep and slow, her stomach fluttering with nerves at the thought of seeing Genji again.

At the end of a lane bordered with pines, the carriage drew up beside a low rose-pink house with green shutters. *Just like the house Monet loved so much in Argenteuil,* Bel thought, clambering down.

'Blanche?' she called out, waving to a woman in a striped dress.

'Bel?' she said, running over and embracing her. 'It has been too long, my dear.'

'Are you well?'

'Quite well,' she said, taking her arm. 'I manage the house, and he is busy in his garden, painting, and so we rub along.'

'Look at this place,' Bel said, pausing to take in the joyous riot of colour, the borders fizzing with flowers. 'You know, an old priest told me once: "beauty is a name for God". If so, I swear the Holy Spirit resides here, she has created something truly beautiful.'

'Come,' Blanche said, laughing. 'He has not changed. Monet must paint in peace and he does not like to be disturbed when he is working, so you shall have to wait in the garden.'

'I will be perfectly content, and will not breathe a word.'

'Go, explore the meadow and the water garden?' Blanche said. 'I shall bring a tisane for you.' Bel walked on among a forest of flowers, watching Monet shambling around the far bank in his straw hat and tweeds. In the distance, a steam train chugged along the valley.

Bel guessed Genji was working too, so she sat on a divan in the shade of a striped umbrella by the lily pond with her tea, and watched Monet paint for a time, the cigarette glowing in his great beard. *How does he not set himself alight?* He had a row of small canvases set along the edge of the glass water, to catch the changing nacreous light. *This floating world*, Bel thought, watching a bright dragonfly dart among the pink flowers, settling on a nearby waterlily. All was silence and calm.

'Would you like more tea?' Blanche said quietly.

'Thank you, that was perfect,' Bel said, handing her the empty cup.

'The series he is creating for the Orangerie has something of this,' Blanche said, gesturing towards Monet with her chin. 'But those canvases are six foot tall and twelve feet across.'

'Good heavens.'

'He paints on rolling easels,' Blanche said, walking away. 'I'm sure he'll show you, later.'

Bel watched Monet studying the rafts of waterlilies, and gazed out across the pond, letting the scene permeate her senses. She saw him mark a fresh canvas with charcoal, then painting directly with six colours only. *Flame white,* she thought, *cadmium yellow, vermillion, deep madder, cobalt blue and emerald green. Six colours, an infinite palette. He paints forever now, with light.*

At last, Monet threw down his brush, satisfied. 'Is that you, Bel?' he called.

'Monsieur Monet,' she said, smiling warmly and walking over.

'My eyesight is not what it was – you could be the Queen of Sheba for all I know.' Monet embraced her, kissing both cheeks. The scent of oil paints and smoke, of tweed and pomade, reminded Bel of her father. 'See, I told you your boy would come round, given time.'

'Such time, years and years,' Bel said, taking his arm as they strolled along the gravel paths, Monet's greyhound Laertes at their side. 'Patience is not my strongest suit.'

'Then you have learnt a good lesson.' Halfway across the green Japanese bridge, he pointed into the distance. Bel saw a group of young men, bronzed from the sun, working stripped to the waist in the water, lean and lithe as rope, clearing leaves from the mirror surface. One had his dark hair tied in a ponytail. He worked with his back to her, and she stood watching. *My child. My boy.* 'My inspiration,' Monet said, gesturing across the water garden to him. 'I saw that extraordinary waterlily kimono of his.' He patted Bel's shoulder. 'He has found someone to share his life, and now they wish to go to Japan.'

'They do?'

'It is time for a new beginning for all of you.'

'Thank you. I am so grateful you took him in.'

'Your father was my dear friend,' Monet said, leaning down to scratch the head of his dog. 'The world is not an easy place for people like Genji. In this life, people like to put you in boxes, to tie you up with labels. Why can we not just be?'

'I knew you would understand him.'

'Understand? No. But difference does not bother me. My own domestic life has been somewhat complicated, so I do not judge.' Monet sighed. 'I did not get where I am without determination. I have made a good life here. I have struggled for my art, and now I am old and my sight is failing, but I have had friends and good women who supported me. I am a lucky man.' He gestured at Genji. Bel gazed across the pond, the wind on the water. 'Your boy has done good work here. I shall miss him.' The bell rang out across the gardens for lunch. 'Join us on the terrace, when you are ready.'

Bel walked on alone towards Genji along a path lined with tall blue agapanthus. *Child of my dearest friend. My son*. Bel's eyes pricked with tears. She remembered him cocooned in his swaddling cloth in Chō's arms. She remembered him running home from school, socks at half mast, cap askew on his glossy black hair. She remembered him dancing in the waterlily kimono, and turning, the horror on his face. *All this time. This lost time.* Hearing her footsteps, he turned now, shielding his eyes from the sun.

'Maman?' he said uncertainly. 'Is it you?' He clambered out of the pond, barefoot, and paced towards her, gathering speed, pulling on his loose white shirt.

'Genji.' It felt good to say his name. Bel laughed as he swept her into his arms.

'You've shrunk.' Tenderly he touched the grey streak in her hair.

'You've grown! Look at you.' She cupped his face in her hands. A tear spilled from her eye, and he wiped it away with his thumb. 'I've missed you,' she said, pressing her lips together, blinking quickly. 'I've missed you so much.' Bel held his hands, looking him up and down. 'You're a *man*.' *You were only a boy*, she thought. *You were so young* . . .

'I am strong, like a farmer now,' he said, flexing his muscles and laughing.

'Oh, Genji, it is so good to see you.' Bel hugged him tightly.

'Maman, I am sorry,' he said, his voice muffled. Bel tried to hush him, but he stepped back to look at her. 'How can you ever forgive me?'

'Of course I forgive you. I should have protected you—'

'It wasn't your fault,' he said.

'For years I have lain awake in the early hours of the morning, the past running through my mind. What could I have done differently?'

'Nothing,' he said, and gestured to the path by the water. 'Nothing at all.'

'I hear you have done wonderful work here?' she said after a time as they walked on.

'Monsieur Monet is hopeless with reality—' Genji said, laughing, 'always ordering more lilies from Latour-Marliac when he should be paying bills. But we get by, and work for love.'

'It's a magical place.' They sat on a bench at the end of the garden and looked back at the water through banks of iris and agapanthus. 'But so much work?'

'It's endless. Every day we clear the ponds so he has a perfect mirror of the sky to paint. Monet has had six gardeners working here for over twenty years. Last year Madame Kuroki, the wife of the Japanese collector, visited.' Genji smiled. 'The wisteria on the bridge was in bloom, and we talked a little. It felt good to hear the language.'

'You wish to go to Japan?'

'I want to know my roots. Inès is happy to live there for a time.'

'Inès?' Bel looked at him in surprise. 'I thought—'

'I told you.' A mischievous smiled played on his lips. 'I love all.'

'Well.' Bel breathed a laugh, shaking her head. 'Tell me about her?' Genji looked like a shy boy suddenly.

'She is the daughter of the hotel owner, where I first stayed. She has the same golden hair as you, and she takes no nonsense from me, like you—'

'Good!' she said.

'I have tried for years to convince her to marry me,' Genji said, flopping back on the bench and grinning. 'My uncle—'

'Hiro?'

'Yes. We've had a correspondence for some time. He is a wise man.' Genji looked at Bel. 'It was he who told me I should write and seek your forgiveness—'

Hiro.

'Forgiveness? You always had that. You were so young.' *We have all changed.*

'Perhaps people have a metamorphosis, too, like a butterfly,' he said, as if he were reading Bel's mind. 'Perhaps in a lifetime we are many people.'

'Then let us begin again, as friends.'

'As friends,' he said. 'Maman, Inès and I plan to marry this autumn, in Japan.'

'You do?'

'Will you come?'

~

They ate lunch on the terrace with Monet and his family. The dappled light of the lime trees fell across the white-clothed table. Lace-trimmed curtains billowed from the open windows of the pink house. Genji sat beside Inès. *They make a handsome couple*, Bel thought, watching their hands dance around one another like butterflies. *They are so in love.*

'I'd like to make a toast,' Bel said, standing. 'Monsieur Monet, thank you for the friendship and kindness you have shown my family over the years.'

'Too many years,' Monet said, raising his glass to her.

'The future is yours,' Bel said, turning to Genji. *The years ahead are theirs.* She looked up at the sound of a carriage clopping along the lane.

'Is it that time already?' Blanche said.

'My train,' Bel said, taking a last sip of wine. 'Thank you all. I shall never forget this afternoon.'

'I'll meet you at the carriage,' Genji said, pushing back his chair. 'I have something for you.'

As Bel settled herself in the seat, Genji leant into the cab and handed her a suitcase. 'Take care of this in Paris while I'm away?'

'But what is it?' Bel said.

'The waterlily kimono,' he said. 'I want you to enjoy it for a while. One day when Inès and I have settled down and built a fine house, and you have a brood of grandchildren, you can return it to me.' He leant closer and whispered in her ear. 'There is something else in there I would like you to take care of, too.'

'What is it?'

'A secret.' Genji stepped away and pressed his finger to his lips, warning her as Monet and Blanche approached to say goodbye.

'Genji, what have you done?'

'Come to Japan soon?' he called. 'Hiro longs to see you.'

Bel watched the case warily. What secrets could it hold? She glanced back at Genji, sick with nerves as the carriage lurched away. *Can I trust him? This man, my son, who betrayed me once already?*

Lot 73

PARIS, 2 AUGUST 1985

'Ned,' Mira called. 'Ned!' She found him in the drawing room talking to Serge. 'You're not going to believe this.' She held up Bel's pillow book and pointed at a passage in sepia ink.

'She had a Monet?' He took the book from her. 'Can you translate this?'

'Not just any Monet,' she said. 'A waterlily painting, one of the *Nymphéas*. Bel says it was on a round canvas – that's really unusual. The only other one I can think of is a 1907.'

'But what happened to it?' Ned looked around the empty drawing room. Serge's men were crating up the last of the paintings. 'Do you think there are more sliding screens, like the kimono?'

'Alexander Bright was a friend of Monet's. I know from the *catalogue raisonée* he owned several works by him that were lost to creditors after his death.' She glanced at Ned. 'Bel was a self-made woman. She could have bought a painting if she wished. So why did Genji send this canvas with her? Why did she hide it?'

'Do you think it's still here?'

'There's only one way to find out.' Mira looked around the room. 'All the furniture has been thoroughly checked and searched. All we're left with is the kimono and her collection of mirrors and paintings.' Mira chewed her lip. 'This place was like a—'

'Museum?' Ned said. Mira looked at him.

'It's like a shrine.' Mira gestured to the gilded wall, the waterlily kimono still hanging on its frame. Two men climbed stepladders to bring it down to the waiting crate.

'*Bonjour, ça va?*' Natasha said, poking her head through the open door. 'You are almost finished?'

'Natasha, did you ever see a painting by Monet here?'

'So many questions! A portrait? A Monet? *No!*' Her gaze hardened. 'Are the Kurosakis accusing us—'

'No one is accusing you of anything,' Ned said, evenly.

'It is impossible. *Impossible,*' Natasha said, tossing her hair. 'If Bel had a Monet the world would have seen it. She kept open house once a week, like Picasso, like Gertrude Stein. Someone would have known.' Natasha slammed the door behind her.

'Bel mentioned visiting Gertrude Stein's salons in her journal,' Mira said. 'She wrote about drinking *eau de vie*, going out driving in her Model-T with Scott Fitzgerald.' She smiled sadly. 'What a life. She saw, and knew, everyone. She was so . . . so alive. How did it all just stop?'

'Whoever kept this apartment all these years loved her an awful lot,' Ned said.

'This is the heart of the sale,' Mira said, tapping the book. 'What makes this unique is Bel, and her story.' She looked at Ned. 'That's what matters.'

'But no one knows her name,' Ned said. 'If we can find an unrecorded Monet, though . . . That would grab some headlines.'

'If it's here, we'll find it,' Mira said.

~

Later that day, Mira stood gazing out at Paris from the empty salon, with the windows open, a warm breeze blowing the chiffon curtains. From the radio in the kitchen, a pop song drifted: 'Waiting for a Girl Like You'. Ned strode through the apartment, and stopped, seeing her.

'A beauty, *non*?' Serge murmured on the way past, nudging him. 'Go on . . .' Mira turned, hearing him.

'Have you checked every square inch?' Ned said, clearing his throat. 'The lawyer will be here in half an hour for the keys and shipping inventory.'

'Yes, boss.' Serge and his men carried out the last boxes. 'Just the final mirrors to go.'

'Nothing,' Mira said, sitting back on her haunches in the salon. She looked up as Serge and his assistant carried through a large bevelled mirror. 'Check every last frame before you pack them? We are looking for a round canvas, probably 80cm diameter.'

'Of course,' Serge said. The men were exhausted. Mira had noticed how each day they began full of swagger and jokes, and by the end they grew gruff and silent.

'Where are you?' Mira said to herself, flicking through Bel's pillow book hoping for a clue. *The Monet is like looking through the lens of a telescope at pure light – mauve, eau de nil, pink.* Mira gazed across the room.

You must learn to look, she remembered Bel writing. *Just look.*

Mira closed her eyes and pinched the bridge of her nose, thinking.

Pay attention.

A kaleidoscope of images flickered back through time in Mira's mind as she thought of all she had read in the book. Bel, and Genji, playing on the floor of her cramped apartment in Montmartre. Bel, cradling a baby in her bedsit in London. Bel, alone, in a box room in the Harrises' mews house. *What's the constant?* she thought, trying to bring the picture into focus. She imagined Bel, in the country at the Red House, field glasses raised. Bel, dressed for the evening in London. A box, the glint of her opera glasses, watching.

Look. Regarder. Mira . . . Miramar . . . Mira.

She remembered walking into the apartment on the first day, her reflection multiplied in the hall mirrors. *The mirrors.* She watched Serge and his assistant climbing stepladders to unhook the silver mirror over the mantelpiece.

'A similar one sold recently for $2,000,' Ned said, checking his notes. 'That one was a bit smaller, 69cm—'

'Wait!' Mira leapt up. She reached high, running her fingers along the sides.

'Do you think . . . ?' Ned said.

Mira checked the fixings. 'Can you help me lift it off?' She braced herself, trying to ease it away from the wall. 'Damn,' she said. 'It's got theft-proof fixings. Serge,' she called, and mimed for the tool.

'That's strange. None of the other pieces, even the Picasso . . .' Serge took the wrench out of his tool belt with a flourish. He whistled for a second assistant to hold the bottom of the mirror safely. Mira and Ned stepped back, watching him slide the wrench behind the mirror and hook out the catches. Mira cried out as it slipped in Serge's hands.

'*Merde, c'est lourde*,' his assistant said, bracing himself.

'The frame's silver, and it's an old mirror, but it shouldn't be that heavy,' Mira said. 'Put it on the counter, please,' she said. Serge's men laid out a packing cloth in the kitchen, and they gently put the mirror face-down. Mira ran her fingers around the circular backing. 'It's too deep,' she said, her voice tight with excitement.

'This belonged to Bel's mother,' Ned said, checking his notes. 'It's eighteenth century.'

'It was all she inherited.' Mira reached for a packing knife. 'If you were going to hide something precious, who would you trust with it but your mother?'

'Be careful – if there's a canvas, don't cut too deep.'

'I know, I know . . .' Mira swept the knife round just enough to cut the tape and expose the tacks holding the backing in place. 'Serge, do you have pliers?' The room fell silent as she extracted the pins one by one. Outside, the afternoon swept on, but in the apartment everything stilled. She dropped the last pin onto the side, and exhaled. 'Right, let's find out . . .' She lifted the circular wooden back free, and passed it to Serge.

A disk of archive paper covered the mirror. She tapped it with her fingertip. There was a void. 'You'd expect the mirror surface to be there, wouldn't you?' Ned said, passing her a pair of tweezers. Mira found the edge of the paper, and lifted it free.

'Ned, there's a wooden stretcher,' she said, her hand shaking with excitement.

'A painting,' Serge said, the men crowding closer to see. 'But look – it has been burned, the wood.' Mira reached for a pair of white cotton gloves. 'You're right. It's charred here, but the canvas doesn't seem to have been touched. Her lips parted. 'Look, Monet's stamp.' She pointed to a mark at the bottom of the stretcher.

'This is killing me,' Ned said. 'Come on. Serge, take that side?' Between them, they lifted the circular canvas out and turned it over. Mira inhaled softly.

'*Mon dieu*,' Serge breathed.

'No, Monet,' Ned murmured, laughing.

'The waterlilies,' Mira said. 'I can't believe it.' The painting seemed to shimmer in the golden light, aquatic blues and greens sparkling on the canvas. A single group of three flowers floated at the right of the painting, rose and pink.

'Look . . .' Ned gestured from the canvas to a photo of the waterlily kimono. 'It's like a conversation.'

'Or inspiration?' Mira ran her fingers over her lips, thinking. 'Why was this hidden? If you had a Monet, wouldn't you want to look at it every day? You'd only hide it if it was—'

'Stolen?' Serge said.

'Let's get some photographs.' Ned took out his camera. 'Then we need to get everything securely at the storage tonight ready to ship to Tokyo,' he said to Serge.

'But what if it *is* stolen?' Mira said quietly. 'Why else would it have been hidden?'

'Keep reading,' Ned said, pointing at the pillow book. 'Let's hope for the sake of our client Bel has an explanation.'

Lot 74

PARIS, 2 AUGUST 1985

Mira flicked the radio on in Kim's apartment, and Sade's soulful voice filled the room. She dried her hair with a white towel, and padded across the room in a silk slip. Filling a glass with water, she paused as the buzzer sounded.

'*Allô?*' she said, hooking the receiver under her chin.

'Delivery, madame,' the concierge said. She buzzed them in, and put the door on the latch. When she heard the sound of shoes thumping up the stairs, she poked her head out and took a large white box from them. Mira kicked the door closed behind her and placed the box on the table. She shook the lid off, and picked up the card. *Couldn't have done it without you, Hutch. Meet me downstairs?* Peeling back the layers of tissue paper, her lips parted in a smile as she held up the red dress.

~

A quarter of an hour later, Mira strode along the Quai de Béthune. She had slicked her dark hair back and painted her lips red. Every head turned as she walked past. Ned stood waiting, leaning against the taxi, and she kissed him on both cheeks. 'I don't know what to say,' she said.

'Consider it a thank you, from the client,' he said, opening the door for her.

'For what?'

'For proving me wrong.' He sat back as the taxi pulled out. 'I like surprises.'

'I was just doing my job,' Mira said.

'If it wasn't for you, we might never have found the Monet,' he said. 'The Kurosakis have papers proving provenance. No one knew what had happened to it.'

'Do you ever wonder about that?' she said. 'All those sleeping artworks that just disappear from public life, tucked away in storage or miscatalogued.'

'There are treasures out there still to be found.' He smiled at her. 'You could spend a lifetime looking for something, when it's right under your nose.'

~

'We're here,' Ned said as the taxi pulled up by a set of stone steps on Place de la Concorde. The rumble of evening traffic and the hiss of fountains filled the warm air as they walked along the pale sand paths of the Tuileries to the Musée de l'Orangerie. Avenues of lime trees cast dappled shade on the people relaxing after work on the green benches. At the staff entrance, a security guard let them in. 'A curator friend owes me a favour,' he said, taking Mira's hand, leading her through the silent corridors. In the distance she heard the last visitors leaving for the day. 'Trust me?' Ned said, and covered her eyes, walking her forward into the gallery.

'Where are we going?' Mira said, laughing.

'Giverny,' he said, releasing her. Mira gasped, and turned slowly. She stood at the heart of an elliptical room. The walls were pure light and water.

'Monet's waterlilies,' she said, and they walked to the second gallery.

They sat side by side on the bench at the heart of the room, and in the silence, time seemed to slow. As she looked at the great arc of the canvases, peace settled in her as deep as the blues of the paintings. 'I'll never forget this,' she said quietly after a time, wiping away a tear. Seeing how moved she was, Ned took her hand and squeezed it.

'Are you okay?'

Mira nodded, unable to speak for a moment. *Ned.* She longed to invite him back for a nightcap. For more. *I can't*, she thought. *That concierge tells Kim everything.* She looked up at Ned's kind, handsome face. So close. It would be so easy to kiss him.

I can't, Luke . . .

The moment lingered, and passed, and Ned glanced at his watch.

'I should get going. Early flight to Tokyo.' Ned leant down and kissed her cheek. 'Take all the time you need, Hutch. The guard will let you out.'

'Thank you,' she said. *I wish. I wish I could just—* 'Thank you, for everything.' Mira raised her face to his. 'Ned—'

'It's okay, you don't have to say a thing.' His eyes creased as he smiled down at her.

'We'll always have Paris?' Mira laughed softly.

'Always.' Ned hung his jacket over his shoulder, and walked away.

What if I want more than that? she thought, watching him leave. At the doorway he looked back, just for a moment, and raised his hand in farewell.

What if I want it all? London, Paris— Tokyo?

PART THREE

TOKYO

LOT 75

TOKYO, 31 DECEMBER 1985

'Knew you'd miss me, Hutch,' Ned said, striding over Shibuya crossing at dusk with Mira. All around them, millions of lights shone across the city, neon pinks and blues glimmering, ready for the night.

'Thought I'd surprise you,' she said.

'I like surprises.' He flashed her a smile. 'Well, nice ones.'

'This was a good one, I hope?' She pulled the collar of her jacket up against the cold.

'The best.' He nudged her. 'Sorry the airline lost your luggage.'

'I'll manage.'

'You sure?' Ned glanced uncertainly at her high-heeled boots.

Mira's head reeled with jet lag. The electronic crossing clattered, and crowds streamed towards her from every direction. The high buildings soared above, neon signs fizzing in the falling light. She looked up at an image of Kōrin's *Irises*, advertising the Nezu Museum.

'I love that screen,' she said. 'Can we go?'

'You'll have to come back in the spring,' he said. 'They only display it in iris season.'

'Come back? I've only just got here.'

'Why *are* you here?' He grinned. 'Go on . . . you did miss me.'

'It was Kim's idea.' Mira hurried to keep pace with him, crowds of dark-suited figures pouring around them like ink. 'She insisted I take the waterlily kimono to Kyoto, after the sale. Something about a job?'

'And I thought you'd come to see me?' Ned noticed Mira shivering and swung his coat off, tucking it around her. A group of schoolgirls squeezed by, giggling and pointing.

'*Kawaii*,' they chorused.

'They're saying we're adorable,' Ned said.

'Hello Kitty is *kawaii*,' Mira said, bristling. 'I am not remotely *kawaii*.'

'Someone didn't get any sleep on the flight.'

'Of course I want to be there for your sale, too. Where are you holding it?'

'The New Otani,' Ned said. 'The VIP private views have gone well. The Palazzo function room overlooks the gardens, with this lovely red bridge. It's the perfect setting for our Monet.' Ned patted his waistline. 'All the dinners and schmoozing over the last couple of months have been worth it. Gold-wrapped sushi is the latest thing.'

'You're kidding.'

'There's quite a buzz. Collectors have been flying in from all over Asia. Of course everyone's gone nuts for the Monet, but you did it, Hutch. The design world certainly knows who Isobel Bright is now.'

'Kim said the Kurosakis and Lamberts have agreed to build a permanent display and archive of Bel's work in Kyoto with some of the proceeds from the sale, alongside the waterlily kimono. They're keeping the best of the drawings we picked out, and some of the dresses. They're talking about funding a scholarship for design students, too – like an East/West cultural exchange.'

'It's all thanks to you.' Ned hugged her shoulder. 'Well done. Bel would be proud of everything you've done over the last few months.'

'Thanks.' Mira leant in. 'Do you think the sale will make enough to fund all that?'

'Hope so.' His brow furrowed. 'It's hard to gauge – Tokyo's tycoons keep a low profile. No conspicuous consumption. They don't display their wealth – you have to look closely at the size of a garden, or the age of a bonsai. Our clients are all very charming, and polite – silk on the outside and pre-stressed steel inside. I can't tell what they're thinking, half the time.'

'Are you nervous?'

'If I wasn't, I wouldn't be doing my job properly.' He guided her to a side street, where red lanterns gleamed in the dim light. The road was slick with black rain, neon reflecting on the pavement, the night pulsing with music from the bars, the machine-gun racket of the pachinko halls. Ned paused beside a doorway decked out with pine and bamboo, festive rope coiling the branches. 'It's like performing. You have to be a hundred per cent on your game. The Gould sale in April set a new record for Impressionist paintings for Sotheby's. $9.9 million for Van Gogh's *Landscape with Rising Sun*. Their Monet sold for $1,375,000.' Mira whistled.

'Do you think you'll achieve that?'

'The market is hot. That collection was valued at $25 million ahead of the sale, and realised $32.6.' He smiled at her. 'You were right. The story we've told about Bel's collection has caught people's imagination. It's the story of a life. The Monet, the kimono, a forgotten designer – one woman's exacting and precise taste.'

'I still don't get why Kim insists I take the waterlily kimono to the Kurosakis with her.' Mira ducked in as Ned pushed aside a discreet indigo noren curtain to let her into the busy restaurant. 'Have you met them?'

'Your godmother enjoys mysteries I think.' He took her coat. 'Lovely dress.'

'Issey Miyake.' She smoothed the fine navy pleats. 'Seemed appropriate.' Mira waited for him to go on. 'Ned?'

'Sorry, you're rather distracting.' Mira punched his arm, and he laughed. 'No, no idea. Bonhams is dealing with their lawyers. The family is keeping a low profile.'

'I wonder why,' Mira said.

'*Irashaimase!*' the kitchen staff called in welcome. Ned

held up two fingers, and a waitress bowed. '*Hai, douzo*,' she said, and gestured to a couple of stools free at the end of the counter.

'That smells amazing,' Mira said, squeezing through. 'What on earth—?' On a small stage at the end of the room, a salaryman sang 'Like a Virgin' at the top of his lungs, the lyrics glowing on a small screen.

'*Oshibori*.' The waitress gave them warm towels to freshen up.

'I love this place. Karaoke Ramen,' Ned said, nodding to the Mama-san by the register who flicked out a gilded *sensu* fan. 'You said you were hungry?' He spoke to the waitress in Japanese. A man at the counter slurped his noodles with an audible *'ahh'* of appreciation. 'I've ordered some *saké*, hope that's okay?'

'Perfect.' Mira leant her chin on her hand. 'It's good to see you, Edward,' she said.

'See, knew you'd miss me.' Ned grinned and reached into his brown leather messenger bag. 'I have something for you.' He slid a glossy catalogue across the bar to her. Bel's gold gingko leaves and 'Bonhams' picked out in silver gleamed on the cover, along with 'Property from the Private Collection of Isobel Bright. Important art, fashion, furniture, books and artefacts'. Mira flicked through the pages, seeing the paintings and furniture she had selected with Ned, and on day two, Bel's wardrobe, each outfit posed on a mannequin. There, at the front, was the Monet. *Nymphéas, Giverny. Estimate $1–$1.5 million*.

'It's beautiful,' she said. 'You've done a great job.'

'*We* have. You were right, to put Bel on the cover, not the Monet.'

'Is the client pleased?'

'Ecstatic, according to the lawyer.'

'Funny, isn't it,' Mira said, flicking through the pages. 'A whole life – that extraordinary life – distilled down to this. What happened to her, Ned? The pillow book just stops, as she's about to go to Japan. I have so many questions still.'

He leant towards her, and took her hand, rolling the gold band between his thumb and forefinger. 'Hutch, can I ask *you* something?'

'Sure?' The fine hairs at the nape of her neck rose at his touch. She sat back as the waitress set down a hot flask and two square wooden cups between them. Ned poured Mira a cup, and passed her the flask.

'Bad luck to pour your own *saké*.'

'What do you want to know?' She filled a cup for him.

'You never talk about your husband, or your family.'

'My family's complicated,' she said, taking a sip. 'I never knew my dad, and Mum was always tied up with her work.'

'Afraid I'm boring: 2.4 kids, happy childhood, loving parents.'

'It shows.' Mira smiled wistfully. 'I guess I always felt like a mistake. I spent a lot of time with Kim, my godmother.' She sipped her drink. 'She's everything Mum wasn't. Present, kind, the "every day is an adventure" sort.'

Ned snapped open a pair of bamboo chopsticks and waited for her to go on. 'And your husband?'

'He . . .' Mira paused, her throat tightening. If she didn't have to say it out loud, it wasn't real.

'I don't mean to pry—'

'No, it's okay.' She took another sip, swallowing down the knot of emotion.

'I'm sorry.'

'Luke . . . he died,' she said. Ned inhaled in surprise.

'Mira, I'm so sorry.'

'It was . . . It was a couple of years ago now.' She smiled, frowning. 'I can't believe it still, sometimes, you know. I read something, or I see something, and I think: "Luke would love that, I must tell him."' She paused. 'And I can't.' Her voice broke, a little. 'It doesn't feel real, you know? I still live in the house we did up. I still drive the same old VW I've had since we met. It's falling to pieces but I just can't bear to get rid of it.'

'I get that,' Ned said. He waited for her to go on.

'The way he went,' she said, shaking her head. 'It was so sudden. One day he was there, the next . . .' Her brow furrowed. 'We didn't get a chance to say goodbye. There was . . . oh, there was so much we still wanted to do. But overnight it was like the world turned grey. I mean, I had to get up and go to work, and carry on . . .' Her fingers traced the fall of a firework in the air. 'But the light went out of everything.'

'I'm so sorry.' He hesitated. 'Do you mind talking about it—'

'No, I love talking about Luke. It's mad, I still talk *to* Luke. I call the answer machine just to hear his voice. I even sent him a postcard from Paris.' She breathed a laugh, and glanced at Ned. 'You mean how he died? It was a stupid accident.' Mira looked down at her hands. 'Kim said she always thought he'd go on a black run, or surfing the Banzai Pipeline.' She took a deep breath. 'But he was walking to the corner shop on a wet Tuesday afternoon between Christmas and New Year for dog food, and a drunk driver . . .' Her voice trailed off.

'I'm so sorry.' Ned squeezed her hand.

'He died instantly, they said.' Mira looked down. 'I guess that's some comfort.'

'How long were you married?'

'Only a year. We lived together for a while, but we were only just settling down, you know? Bought our first house, a dog—'

'You have a dog?'

'Battersea's finest.' Mira smiled. 'He's old, and mangy, and smells like a wet carpet, but I love him.' She pictured him sitting in the window of their cottage on Kynance Mews, watching the pigeons and pedestrians go by, the view of the observatory opposite. She felt homesick, suddenly. She wanted to be riding home on her bicycle through the evening traffic on Gloucester Road, and sweeping in through the stone arch, bumping over the cobbles, and unlocking the front door. Calling out: *Where are my boys?* just as she had a hundred times before. Mira glanced at Ned with tears in her eyes.

Where are my boys?

'Luckily the old lady next door adores him,' she said, 'so he's staying with her again while I'm away.'

'Name?'

'Miss Harris. Oh – the dog?' Mira laughed. 'Rod. As in Stewart.' Mira flipped open her wallet and passed him a photo of a small dog with a lopsided toothy grin.

'I get it, the hair.' Mira slid another photo out from behind, and smiled, passing it to Ned. 'Luke?' he said, and she nodded. A tall, broad-shouldered man with fair cropped hair grinned out of the photo, his arm slung loosely over Mira's shoulder. She looked younger, less guarded, her face a picture of open happiness. They stood in front of the red door of an old mews house.

'Cute house,' Ned said, handing the photos back. 'Kensington?'

'Yes. Kim grew up there. She helped me buy it. Kynance Mews. Do you know it?'

'Near the church? Mum and Dad live nearby. It's funny we've never bumped into one another before.'

'Perhaps we have.' Mira thought of the strange familiar sense of *déjà vu* she felt when she first saw him.

'I would have remembered you.' He sipped his drink. 'I'd love a dog, but Tokyo's not the ideal place. You know we have cat cafés here? People live in such tiny spaces there's not room to—'

'Swing a cat?' Mira laughed. 'So you go to a café instead? That's mad?' She was so tired she thought she might be hysterical.

'Homes are modest.' Ned gestured at the businessman. 'Your average salaryman is loyal to the company, he goes day after day to his steady job, gets his 120 yen ticket for the JNR, squeezes in, comes to a place like this to let off steam, or goes shopping in Akihabara for another gadget he doesn't need, then goes back home and does it all again the next day. Is that life?'

'It's *a* life.' Mira pushed aside her bowl of noodles.

'Not hungry?'

'I'm not sure what I am. I don't know what day it is, what I'm doing here—'

'Right now, you are having a drink with me. Here's to you, Hutch.' They chinked their cups and he gestured to the karaoke. 'Tempted?' Mira shook her head. 'All work no play?'

'You know me. I was transcribing the last of Bel's pillow book on the flight. Kim wants the original to stay with the kimono, on display in the collection she's curating.'

'I think it's the most interesting thing to come out of the apartment.'

'More than the Monet? Or the kimono?'

'I'm not allowed to sell the kimono.'

'Bel's book is amazing.' She twisted the ring on her finger. 'We only had five days, but that little book contains a lifetime.' Mira looked at the solitaire diamond glinting in the lamplight. 'All we have are moments.' She shook her head. 'Fifty years of moments, threaded together – hopes and dreams, love and hate. Everything Bel survived.'

'We all need that resilience.'

'You're right. I mean, look at me – I'm a widow at twenty-five. People say dumb things like: *At least you didn't have children*. Like that makes it easier? I really, really wanted children.' She blinked quickly. 'I would love to have a little boy, or a girl, and glimpse their Dad's face in theirs, or the ghost of his smile, or his hands.' Mira turned hers in front of her face. 'I don't know why I still wear this. I guess it keeps people at arm's length—'

'But not me,' Ned said.

'Not you.'

'I get it, I wore a ring for years, after.'

'You were married?' Mira said, surprised.

'What's that Japanese saying? It is better to leave many things unsaid.'

Mira widened her eyes, waiting. 'Edward?'

'We were college sweethearts, don't you know?' He swirled his drink. 'Shagged my best friend. You know the drill.' His tone was offhand, but when Ned looked at her she saw how much it hurt, still. He leant towards her, confiding. 'Put it this way, I don't keep a photo of her in my wallet. Or him.'

'We make a fine pair,' she said. 'A broken-hearted widow and a—'

'Cuckold? Isn't that the term?' Ned mimed antlers. 'Gullible fool?'

'A kind and decent man,' she said. 'There's nothing wrong with trusting people—'

'Just trusting the wrong person?'

'Exactly.' She smiled. 'Bit of a cliché, isn't it? The whole *Madama Butterfly* thing.'

'Am I Cio-Cio-San?' Ned laughed. 'Caroline was as English as they come. She had the exact look of her father chasing a fox when she ran me to ground.'

'Does that make you the unspeakable or the uneatable?' Mira pondered.

'Ha. Oscar Wilde? Very good.'

'I visited his tomb when we were in Paris, in Père Lachaise,' she said. 'The whole thing was covered in red lipstick marks.' Mira looked up as the businessman finished singing, and flopped down on a stool nearby. 'Crazy to think Bel knew him.'

'*Konnichiwa!*' He raised his beer to them. '*Kampai!* English?'

'Yes, English,' she said.

'Long life and health! You stay Tokyo? You like Japan? Harajuku, manga—'

'We're going to Kyoto,' Mira said.

'Ah! Kyoto!' he said, nodding blearily. 'If I have car, I drive you. But Tokyo expensive. So expensive,' he said, flicking imaginary money. 'You choose, beer or car.' He threw his head back, laughing. 'I choose beer. I have cooler, I have colour TV, all I need.' He gulped down his drink, and pointed at Ned's shoes. 'Your feet so big! So big!'

'You know what they say?' Ned said.

'Big feet, big shoes?' Mira murmured.

'You sing, yes?' the man said.

'Why not?' Mira jumped down from her stool and spoke

to the host. 'What's it called – sometimes it's hard – you know the one – to be a woman?' She walked over to the microphone. At the chorus, Mira waved her arms. Soon the whole bar was singing along: *Stand by your man . . .*

'How can I possibly top that?' Ned said, applauding. He ordered more drinks and they sat back to watch a group of young girls giggle their way through 'Relax'.

'Your turn,' Mira said. She signalled to the host and pointed at Ned.

'I can't, I have an awful voice – truly dreadful.' He grimaced.

'You can't possibly be worse than me.'

'Nails down the blackboard bad.'

'I don't believe you.' She took his hand. 'How about a duet?'

LOT 76

TOKYO, JANUARY 1986

On New Year's Day they joined the crowds thronging the streets, and Mira browsed the shops of Nakamise and Kappabashi, the stalls of plastic sushi and curios sold around the shrine of Asakusa. It felt more like a carnival compared to Meiji's peaceful Shinto shrine. Mira stepped aside to let a delivery man cycle past with boxes of noodles balanced high. Acrobats, fortune tellers and beggars thronged the street just as they had for centuries, but against posters of anime characters in shop windows and gleaming neon signs. Girls in fur-collared jackets and kimonos mingled with punks and elderly couples in dark indigo robes. Beneath the huge temple bell of Senso-ji, joss sticks perfumed the air, and gingko leaves drifted across the pavement like confetti.

'How does this ever feel like home?' she said to Ned, stopping to look at a stall selling bamboo stem parasols, folded like the gills of pale mushrooms. 'I don't think I've ever felt so alien anywhere on the planet.' She looked around the heaving pavements and spotted a wooden stall near a bare tree tied with pieces of paper like a flock of white birds. 'Is that a fortune teller?' she said.

'It's nonsense,' Ned said.

'Come on!' Mira took his hand and dragged him over. She shook a bamboo vase of sticks and cast them on the counter. The old man selected a wooden drawer from the shelves at his back, and passed her a slip of paper:

'I'm going to take that as a Very Good Sign,' she said, tying it to the tree.

Later, they walked past the shabby, elegant white houses of the British Embassy, with pale blue shutters and tired winter gardens, where faded lanterns lingered long after the party had gone.

'Number one of number one town,' Ned said. 'What an address.' Following the crowds carrying Japanese flags and chanting *banzai*, they wound their way through the grounds of the Imperial Palace. The palace was almost invisible from the city, hidden behind tall trees and banks of pine and willow. Not until the final turn of the path did she see the buildings. 'They say that Edo castle was built with human pillars, people buried alive in the foundations,' he said, and Mira grimaced. She stopped to look at the families taking photos by the willow bridge watchtower. The sight of the couples with their tiny children touched her. She felt their warmth, their zest for life.

'Imagine,' Mira said, straining to see the Imperial family,

'when Genji worked in these gardens they believed the Emperor was a god. That his people were the chosen ones . . .'

'They're not the only ones to have believed that through history, and it rarely ends well.' Ned raised his voice above the cries of '*Banzai*'. He looked at his watch and pointed towards the exit. 'I have work to do, I'm afraid.'

'And I have a pillow book to finish copying.' She stood on tiptoe and kissed his cheek.

'Walk you back to the Imperial Hotel?'

'That's okay, you're busy. I'll find my own way.'

'Happy New Year, Hutch,' he said, and walked away.

LOT 77

TOKYO, JANUARY 1986

A few days later, Mira followed a group of people dressed in black tie and evening gowns along the marble corridor to the Palazzo Otani suite. Her Manolo Blahnik pumps clicked on the tiled floor, and she caught her reflection in one of the floor-length mirrors panelling the hall. Soft gold light haloed the mirror, and the woman looking back at her seemed younger, more confident than she had felt in a long time. Mira had scoured the chic boutiques in Omotesandō, but found nothing quite right for tonight. Finally, she headed to Harajuki, strolling among the pink-haired punks and kids with ghetto blasters, looking for something that would make her feel herself, but better. She smoothed down the Yamamoto gown she had bought from a vintage store that morning, and stepped forward, smiling at the young woman with the clipboard, who waved her through to the reception.

Mira searched the crowd for Kim, and found her standing

near the full-length windows, looking out at the red bridge spanning the water garden.

'Look at you,' Kim said, embracing her. She wore a Vivienne Westwood mini-crini, and yellow platform sandals. Her dyed black hair was swept up into a pointed chignon, and her vivid lips were pressed together in an amused smile. Growing up, Kim always reminded Mira of imaginative, carefree Mymble in the Moomin books. 'Yamamoto? Love it.'

'Harajuku thrift shop,' Mira said, giving her a twirl.

'I taught you well.'

'*Bon*,' Madame Lambert said, walking over.

'Natasha taught you something in Paris, too,' Kim said.

'Natasha?' Mira said in surprise. 'Thank you – I think.' She took a glass of champagne from the tray, and smiled at the young man serving. '*Arigato*.' She looked at the women. 'You two know one another?'

'We go back a long way, to Miramar . . .' Kim said.

The lights dimmed in the room, and only the spotlit podium remained brightly lit, 'Bonhams' picked out in silver lettering. People started shuffling into the rows, and Mira guided Kim to the reserved seats. 'Check out the front rows,' she whispered. 'Ned's got his best buyers right in the line of fire.'

Ned strode across the room and picked up his notes.

'He's a fine-looking man, honey,' Kim whispered to Mira. Ned's dark hair shone in the spotlight, brushing the broad shoulders of his evening jacket. A hum of anticipation murmured around the rows. Ned looked across to the bank of telephone operators, and the young man closest to him gave the thumbs up.

'Good evening, ladies and gentlemen,' Ned said. 'Bonhams is delighted to welcome you to a very special sale this evening.'

Across from him, a projected image of Chō's kimono dominated the room, and the title of the sale, *The Private Collection of Isobel Bright*, appeared across it in English and Japanese. The hum of voices stilled as two porters with white gloves carried the Monet canvas onstage. Mira had arranged for it to be framed in elegant silver leaf, and the canvas shone with light.

'Let's begin.' Ned looked at Mira, who smiled encouragingly. She took Kim's hand in hers. 'This evening's sale commences with Lot number one, a spectacular find. '*Nymphéas*. A circular canvas by Claude Monet, dated c1907.' Ned looked slowly around the room, reeling the tension in. 'Who will give me $1 million?'

'Look at the front row, they're just squirming,' Kim whispered. A woman in a purple taffeta gown raised her paddle.

'$1 million,' Ned said calmly. A telephone operator raised their hand, and the bids streamed in.

'Come on, come on . . .' Kim said under her breath.

'Do I hear $1.5 million?' Ned said. 'Thank you, sir.'

Mira's grip on Kim's hand tightened as the figures climbed. Frantic signals from the phone operators raised the bids for overseas buyers, and paddles in the room raised time and again. 'Are we all done at $1.75 million?' Ned said. 'I have a bidder on the phones at $1.8 . . .' He looked around and pointed. 'We have a new bidder in the room. $1.85 million.' The crowd gasped.

'I can't look,' Mira said, her heart pounding.

'Look at him go, honey,' Kim murmured. 'This is everyone's futures being made tonight.'

'All done at one million, eight hundred and fifty thousand dollars. Sold, to the gentleman in the front row,' Ned said, banging down his gavel triumphantly. The room erupted with applause, and people gave a standing ovation. Ned looked for Mira, and she raised her hands, applauding him. He winked as the porters replaced the Monet with the drawing of a mother and child. 'Moving on. Lot two, a Picasso pen and ink sketch . . .'

~

'I can't believe it,' Mira said to Kim and Natasha after the sale.

'Believe it. Isobel had amazing taste,' Natasha said. 'She would be proud of you.'

Mira looked at her in wonder, trying to reconcile the elegant silver-haired woman before her with the anonymous cleaner she had met on the first day in the apartment. Kim saw her look, and laughed. 'I know what you are thinking.'

'I am thinking that my Godma is a wicked woman for deceiving me so cruelly.' Mira frowned. 'Did you both hide Bel's pillow book, too?'

'Maybe.' Kim pursed her lips. 'Oh, alright, yes, we did. When the Kurosakis told me about the apartment, I came straight over and bumped into Natasha. I just remembered how much fun you had when you were little on our magical mystery tours. I wanted you to have an adventure, sweetie. To let Bel's story bring you back to yourself.'

'What if I hadn't found it?' Mira said.

'We'd have given you a hint,' Natasha said. 'Hiro Kurosaki kept it on the desk in her study, like a memorial. So formal.' Natasha shook her head.

'I understand why he wanted to edit her life. He wanted her to have a perfect legacy, in time to stand alongside Chanel or Dior.'

'Hiro? No, no …' Natasha shook her head. 'It was all Isobel. She edited her diaries into that pillow book. She cleared her apartment, ready for the next chapter in her life.'

'Wait? Why?' Mira said.

'To make space for him. A clean page.'

'I don't understand.'

'She loved Hiro Kurosaki,' Kim said gently.

'Françoise wanted to continue with Maison BB,' Natasha said, 'but Bel had done all she wanted with her designs. She had worked so hard, for so long. She just wanted to retire, to *live*. She wanted the archive, the Foundation we are making now. Bel wanted to inspire the next generation.'

'Why was she forgotten?'

'Fashion never stands still,' Kim said. 'A market matures, a brand name weakens.'

'Bel had no wish to be as big as Chanel. When she left, everyone lost heart. They sold a few designs to madam shops in London to make up models in Great Portland Street "based on Paris", sent a few skips – wicker baskets – with gowns for fashion parades. Then there was the Wall Street Crash in 1929 when the luxury trade imploded.' Natasha's fingers swept the air. 'Françoise kept the *maison* workrooms going in our apartment through the war as a cover for their work with the Resistance—'

'Wait, the Resistance?' Mira interrupted.

'That is another story.' Natasha draped her scarf. 'After she lost my mother, Angêle, Françoise gave up. It all ended. Like a fairy tale, Bel's apartments, her life, went to sleep.'

'People try, all the time, to edit a life, to make sense of it,' Kim said. 'But life is messy. Bel's story – the real story, is the kinship of some remarkable friends.' She took Mira and Natasha's arms. 'That's the story I want the archive to tell. Bel helped Françoise. Françoise cared for Natasha when Angêle was killed. I grew up in a little mews house Bel bought for my great-grandparents—'

'Your maiden name – Kim Harris!' Mira said, making the connection. 'Mrs Harris – the people who took Bel in when she was orphaned?'

'She was Nana the Great,' Kim said, laughing. 'She and my nana were still taking in laundry and sewing when I lived in the run-down little mews house next door—'

'That you helped me buy?'

'Bel gave the houses to my family. Everyone has secrets,

especially Bel. She never made a big thing about it, but she never forgot a kindness.'

'She was generous to the last,' Natasha said. 'She took care of everyone.'

'And it was your grandmother who introduced you to the Kurosakis and Lamberts,' Natasha said to Kim.

'Maison Harris had been on Bel's books for years, supplying embroidery,' Kim said. 'When I wanted work experience in Japan with silks after college, she put me in touch.'

'I hadn't seen Kim for thirty years, but recognised her straight away from Miramar,' Natasha said, smiling. 'I remember you, all Biba and Mary Quant, tottering off the Blue Train in white platform boots.'

'Feels like yesterday. And soon after that I became Godma to a very special young woman, who has had a terrible time.' Kim squeezed Mira's hand. 'I'm so proud of you.'

'How do you go on—' Mira said, a wave of grief catching her off guard.

'One day at a time, sweetie. You find one good moment each day, then two, then three.'

'Just like Sei Shōnagon a thousand years ago? And Bel?'

'Just like Bel. That woman knew more about the things that make life worth living than anyone,' Kim said kindly. 'Her wisdom passed down to me through Françoise, and I've passed as much as I can to you.'

'My fairy godmother?' She looked at Natasha. 'You could have told me you knew one another.'

'I thought after everything you have been through you

needed a little puzzle to solve, to hear it from Bel first hand,' Kim said. 'I never expected that you would find a Monet. She was full of surprises, to the last.'

'But what happened to her?' Mira said.

'For the answer, we will have to go to Kyoto,' Kim said. 'You know, the Kurosakis confirmed the story Bel had written down, about how the canvas came to be with her.'

'Do you really think Monet knew?' Natasha said.

'Genji told them he did.' Mira shrugged.

'I understand that, not being able to see something beautiful destroyed,' Kim said, looking over as Ned strode across the packed room towards them. 'Honey, the way he looks at you . . .' she murmured.

'I'm scared,' Mira said quietly.

'You like this man, don't you? You told him?' Mira nodded. 'Good.'

'I can't . . . I can't lose someone again. What if—'

'What if? Life is full of what ifs.' Kim hugged her, spoke close to her ear. 'What did I tell you after Luke died? The way to honour someone you've lost is to be the things you loved most about them. Luke lived life to the full. We have to risk ourselves time and time again.' She stepped back and cupped her face in her hands. 'It's broken my heart seeing what losing Luke has done to you. It's like you've been hollowed out.'

Hollow and bruised, thought Mira. *My whole body has ached with grief.*

'Do you remember that Japanese book you sent me, after Luke died?' she said.

'The Tanizaki?'

'I get it now. Without shadows, there's no beauty. We need the darkness, too.'

'There, I knew you'd figure it out.' Kim's eyes sparkled. 'Carpe diem, honey. You are *allowed* to be happy. Luke wouldn't want it any other way.'

'We did it, Mira,' Ned said to her.

'Congratulations.' Mira hugged him. *I want this. I want to feel happy again. When's the last time I really revelled in my body, or the feel of someone . . . ?* He took her hand and held it in his, strong and reassuring. *I want to feel alive again.*

'You really played us,' Ned said, pointing at Natasha. 'You were in on it all along?'

'There are some advantages to being an old woman.' Natasha shrugged. 'If you wish to be invisible, you can be.'

'There is nothing invisible about you tonight, my dear,' Kim said, seeing a couple of elegantly dressed men in dark kimonos watching them. 'Come on, Tash, let's leave these kids to their evening. We have some catching up to do.' She pecked Mira on the cheek. 'See you at the airport.' Kim shooed her away. 'Go on, take this gorgeous man out on the town before I do.'

LOT 78

KYOTO, JANUARY 1986

In Kyoto, Mira sat sipping green tea in her hotel room, watching the sun rise over Nijō Castle. The windows were sealed against the cold, the room entirely silent. She was exhausted, yet couldn't sleep, and had lain wide awake in bed watching the grey winter light leak beneath the curtains. Now she sat in a pool of gold from the lamp beside the bed. In the corner, the television silently played a soap opera with actors dressed as samurai and geisha, the screen reflecting on the window. Mira reached for the packet of 'Melting Kiss' she'd bought from the vending machine in the lobby, and unwrapped a sweet. Images from the evening before came to her – flying above the clouds, the plane drifting west. Beneath her, Mira saw the snow-capped peak of Mount Fuji. 'It's beautiful, just like the Hokusai prints Bel had framed in her apartment,' she said to Ned. 'Strange to think it's a sleeping volcano.'

'The old prints show it smoking.'

'Crikey.' Mira turned to look at him. 'Do you think you'll stay here forever.'

'Forever?' He held her gaze steadily. 'Nothing lasts forever.'

'Isn't that a Japanese concept? *Mono no aware.*'

'Now who's been doing their homework?' He shook his head. 'The culture has a deep feeling for the impermanence of life—' Mira's expression clouded. 'No, I won't stay forever,' he said. 'In fact, I'm thinking of resigning.'

'You are? Where will you go?'

'I find that there's quite a lot pulling me home to London, these days.'

Mira thumped the unforgiving bean pillow, trying to get comfortable. She stumbled through to the bathroom and tried to decipher the complicated, heated loo, leaping up in surprise as a jet of water shot out. She pulled off her soaked t-shirt, swearing under her breath, and looked back to the room as the shrill telephone cut through the silence.

'Hello?' she mumbled, brushing her hair back from her face.

'Good, you're up,' Ned said cheerily. 'Have you had breakfast? I have something to show you.'

~

'Ow.' Mira stumbled on the gravel path leading to Ryōan-ji.

'How's the jet lag?' Ned said, catching her.

'Don't.' Everything about the country confused her. After

the noise and neon of Tokyo, the narrow streets and stone walls of Kyoto, the misty paths and gently dripping trees reminded her of rural England. *Why is it your brain always looks for similarities?* she thought. *Maybe it's human nature to look for connections, for familiar things.* She glanced at Ned. *And people.* Her feet were numb with cold, and sore from the high heels of her boots. 'I wish I'd bought trainers,' she said, glancing at Ned's comfortable loafers.

'Hold on,' he said, guiding her towards the temple entrance. A row of rubber slippers on a simple wooden rack faced them. 'See? Wishes do come true.' She leant on his arm as she unzipped her boots, slipping her stockinged feet into the sandals.

'I think my toes just sighed with relief.'

'You're shorter, Hutch,' he said, kicking off his shoes.

'No, you're taller.'

'Let's not fight in front of the nice monk.' He put his arm around her shoulder, and led her towards the famous gravel garden. They joined an old couple in dark kimonos, who sat contemplating the peaceful space on a simple wooden bench.

'It's smaller than I expected,' she said.

'Music to any man's ears.' Mira nudged him. 'Give it time,' he said quietly. 'Just look. There are fifteen stones and infinite meanings, or so they say.'

They sat in silence. All Mira could hear was the muffled sound of the rain, of water dripping from the peaceful trees. Mira remembered Kim's words after Luke's accident: *Breathe. Just breathe. That's all you have to do. Forget everything else.* Mira glanced at Ned. *I'm here. Now. With you.* She looked back at the garden and let her mind grow still. Beauty, colour, had always been like breathing to her. She had an instinct for what worked. But for so long it was like someone had turned down the saturation on the world, everything had faded to grey, drowned out by grief and anger. Now, she gathered the things she had seen over the last weeks like jewels. *The first glimpse of the kimono. The waterlilies.* The gravel became as water, and the rocks like mountains. The wall seemed to recede into infinity.

'Shall we?' Ned said, and Mira stirred in surprise. At some point the old couple had left, but she hadn't noticed. They were alone, and his hand was warm as he helped her up.

Mira winced, squeezing her feet back into her torturous boots. 'I get it,' she said. 'I understand why you love this place.'

'There's something else I want to show you,' he said. 'I can give you a piggy back?'

'Ha ha,' Mira said, walking grimly on. 'Can't we go?'

'It's not far, I promise.' Somewhere a brazier burned, and the air smelt smoky, a bonfire mixing with incense. The chill wind carried rain, a fine mist that freshened her cold cheeks. Raindrops glistened on the bare branches of a tree like crystals. Ned paused in front of a carved round stone. 'This is a *tsukubai*, a stone wash basin. The inscription is something like: *I learn only to be contented*.' He looked down at Mira, and waited for her to look at him.

'I like that. Say it again.'

'*I learn only to be contented.*'

'Ned—'

'It's okay. You don't need to tell me you're hurt and broken, and not to bother.' Ned frowned, gathering his courage. 'You see, we're all broken. But broken people get to be brave.' *Like Bel.* 'We know the risks—'

'I don't want to feel broken anymore,' Mira said, her eyes pricking with hot tears.

'So trust me?' He looked at her, his face open and vulnerable. 'In time—'

She took his cold face in her hands, and kissed him.

'You were taking *too much* time,' she whispered.

'Always in a hurry. Always rushing around . . .' He brushed a strand of hair from her cheek. 'You and I have been through a lot. I know I'm not all moons in June, but I find I have fallen in love with you, Hutch.' He held her close, and laid his chin on the top of her head.

'That makes two of us,' she said, closing her eyes, giving in to the warmth of his embrace.

LOT 79

KYOTO, JANUARY 1986

'Hold on,' Ned said to the taxi driver. 'Pull over here, please.' He jumped out. 'Won't be a minute.' Mira let her head rest back, watching him stride through the crowds thronging the street outside the department store. Ned stood head and shoulders above all, his hair tinged with gold in the winter light. She felt drowsy. *Contented?* she thought. *Is this what it feels like?* Not mad, crazy first love. Something easy and peaceful. She felt safe. Like she had come home.

Crowds thronged the street ahead of the taxi, the cuckoo clock crossing just audible in the muffled silence of the car. A billboard image flickered above with young women doing aerobics in neon pink leotards and legwarmers. Mira watched a traffic policeman directing cars with balletic grace, white truncheon raised. A file of schoolchildren in quaint uniforms waited to cross, beside a couple of punks with orange bleach-blonde hair. The taxi was immaculate, with pristine antimacassars which reminded Mira of a great aunt's house in

Bournemouth. The driver sat staring ahead, his white gloves resting on the steering wheel.

'There you go.' Ned jumped in and handed a box to Mira. 'Thank you, driver.'

'Presents?' She lifted out a pair of Nikes. 'My Prince Charming,' she said, wriggling round to put her boots up on Ned's lap. He unzipped each boot, kissing the arch of her foot before sliding on the trainer.

'Do they fit, Cinders? I did have to go to the men's department . . .'

'Not so charming?' Mira laughed. 'Thank you. My feet thank you.'

'The boots are gorgeous. Wear them later if you like—' He raised an eyebrow.

'*Edward.*'

'—but first we have some walking to do.'

~

Ned and Mira checked into their ryokan, and left all but one bag there. He spoke to the owner, who led them out onto the street, pointing ahead into the hills.

'It's not far, apparently,' Ned said, taking the bag from Mira.

'I feel like we're bringing the kimono home,' she said.

'Let's see what Kim has found out.' Ned took her hand, and they walked on along the silver river into the wooded hills.

After a time, they reached the Kurosakis' estate. From the

road, there was just a finely slatted wooden fence, set below a bright bamboo forest. Slivers of morning light filtered through the fresh green stalks rising high above them. The only suggestion that it was a house came from the incense smell of cedar Mira could smell on the crisp, cold air. Ned pressed the intercom buzzer. A tailless grey cat trotted past on the verge, ignoring them as a panel of the fence swung silently open.

'I guess this is it?' Mira said, going first. They stood in silence, and the gate closed behind them. 'Ned. It's beautiful,' she said, gazing across the water garden.

'It's like a *shinden*,' Ned said, 'the mansions of noblemen and samurai. They weren't just warriors, but scholars as well.' A symmetrical modern glass house seemed to float around three sides of the garden, extending out over a stream and ponds. Gravel paths led off in all directions from the entrance. This was a garden for contemplation. All Mira could hear was the sound of running water, the wind in the bamboo forest, the call of birds.

'Whoever lives here has great taste,' Mira said, as an elderly gardener in an indigo-blue apron approached them, wheeling a barrow. He was deeply tanned, with gunmetal-grey hair drawn back in a high topknot, and a neatly trimmed beard.

'*Arigato*,' he said, and bowed. They both looked at him in surprise. 'Mr Brookes, Mrs Hutchinson?'

'How do you do,' she said, and searched her pocket for her business card. The old man waved his hand. He beckoned to them, and threw his gloves into the barrow.

'Come,' he said.

'Mira!' Kim called out brightly, appearing on the terrace. The old man bowed, and gestured for them to join her. 'Thank you, *arigato*!' She embraced them both. *Something's wrong*, Mira thought, as Kim chattered on. *Something's upset her. She's on edge.* '. . . yes, that's one of the Kurosaki sons. He was an architect, quite famous. You may have seen his work in Tokyo.' The old man shuffled away along the gravel path. 'Maybe you've heard the old Japanese saying, "Fall down seven times, stand up eight?"' Kim gestured across the garden. 'The houses are designed to be rebuilt. Like many families in Japan, the Kurosakis have stood up. Again and again.'

'Kim, is everything alright?' Mira said.

'Yes, yes.' She glanced at the case in Ned's hand. 'You have brought the kimono?'

They followed Kim to the house and took off their shoes in the lobby, putting on cotton slippers. The house was as extraordinary as the garden, seeming to merge with the landscape. The polished cedar floor gave way to glass, suspended above the pond where koi carp slid noiselessly through the water, gleaming gold and silver beneath Mira's feet.

'Please,' Kim said, gesturing to a low black table. An abstract circle, an *ensō* zen calligraphy hung on the wall behind them, the only decoration in the room. 'If you are cold, we have blankets,' she said to Mira.

'No, thank you.' The brazier under the table warmed her. Mira glanced up at the *tokonoma* alcove beside her, and a single maple branch in an old *kintsugi* vase. 'How beautiful,' she said, looking at the three urns there.

'Three elements – heaven, earth and mankind in balance. One of the granddaughters brings a fresh *ikebana* arrangement each day. The vase belonged to Genji,' she said. 'It broke, once, but he mended it, and now it is more precious than ever.'

She sounds nervous, Mira thought. 'Kim, what is it?'

'They say the son you just met was made on that day—' She broke off, and looked down at her hands. 'The day of the flowers of Edo.'

LOT 80

KYOTO, JANUARY 1986

A middle-aged woman with a deep-blue kimono knelt beside the table and handed Mira a bowl of steaming green tea in a raku bowl. The tips of her elegant bob swung as she bowed.

'*Arigato*,' Mira said.

'This is the eldest daughter,' Kim said. 'She does not speak English, but she understands everything.'

'I'm sure you speak better English than I speak Japanese.' Mira looked around her, at the bamboo forest behind them, at the tranquil water garden ahead.

'May I see the kimono?' Kim said. 'I only had a quick peek in Paris.'

Mira unclipped the case and lifted the lacquered box onto the table. The winter sun caught the silver-gilded lid as it opened, sending a shaft of light across the dark wood. She folded back the layers of tissue paper like a flower blooming, and turned the box towards Kim. The watery blue silk gleamed as fresh as the day it was woven.

She sighed as she touched the heavy fabric. 'The Kurosakis make some of the best contemporary kimonos. They are walking works of art. They sell for a million yen, and more, in the boutiques of Omotesandō. Nothing compares to this.' She looked at Mira. 'Go on, put it on?'

'I can't!'

'Go on . . . It's going to be on display here eventually. Wear it one last time?'

Mira stood and lifted out the kimono, the silk trailing behind her like water, the fabric expanding out in a long train of colour across the simple tatami mats, a river running home. Kim called to the family in Japanese. Soon a group of people gathered. Mira glanced over her shoulder at Ned, who sat watching her, his gaze constant, full of love.

'Thank you,' Kim said. Mira slipped off the gown and handed it to her. She passed it to the old man. 'It was made by his ancestors. This house will become a museum dedicated to the work of Isobel Bright and Kurosaki silk, so that many, many people will enjoy it. We've brought it home.' Two of the children slid back the shoji screens, and a kimono stand stood waiting for it. Between them they draped and arranged the kimono as the family watched. Mira sat back with Ned and took his hand. The kimono shimmered in the soft light. 'You have made an old woman very happy,' Kim said.

'I'm glad,' she said. 'But now, please tell us. What happened to Bel and Hiro, and Genji? What happened to all of them? Why did she just disappear?'

'I met Hiro-san and Genji when I worked here in the

fifties,' Kim said. 'But I had no idea he'd insisted the apartment in Paris should be kept just as Bel left it. Isobel Bright did a great thing for the Kurosakis, caring for Chō's child.' She looked out at the garden as a toddler ran along the gravel path, followed by his mother. 'Family is everything. When you are gone, who cares about prizes, or money? People remember those who cared about them. They care very much about *fureai* here – the bond between the generations. So much of life is imperfect. Hiro lived through terrible loss – his sister, and Bel, the woman he loved. He saw great wars, such destruction – earthquakes, the horrors of Nagasaki and Hiroshima.' Mira pictured him, the still centre at the flash of light, the vortex of wind and rain, the sky of fire. 'But he was the kindest man I have ever met. Hiro-san always said you only need three things for a happy life: community, nature, a sense of the sacred. He found that in his family, his work, this garden.' Kim looked at Mira. 'Only one thing was missing. No life is perfect. But he held in his heart one perfect place for Bel. Now we will bring the best of her designs here, and honour their memories together.'

'He never left Kyoto?'

'He visited Paris only once, to close the apartment with Genji-san.' Mira thought of the inscription at the end of Bel's pillow book, the gingko leaves. *Even though a river of tears flows through this body, the flame of love will not be quenched.* 'There was nothing in Paris for him, without Bel. They kept the apartment, just as Bel asked, for Genji's lifetime. Maybe it was like keeping part of her alive.'

'I brought the journal, too.' Mira slid the silver-bound book across the table.

'The pillow book.'

'Do you think she destroyed the rest of her journals?' Ned said.

'As with the apartment. It wasn't how she lived, but as she left it,' Kim said.

'I don't understand?'

'She was making space for Hiro, wasn't she? For the life they would share together.' Mira's eyes pricked with unexpected tears.

'Tell me something: was there a portrait of Bel?' Ned said.

'The infamous Schiffer? His scandals outstripped his reputation,' Kim clicked her tongue. 'He met the end he deserved. Few remember him now.' She spoke to one of the women, and beckoned for them to follow her. She slid back two silk-lined shoji screens, just like the ones in the Avenue Junot apartment. 'This was Hiro-san's room.' The woman opened a drawer lined with black velvet and lifted out a small wooden cabinet. She opened the panels to reveal a reclining nude.

'Bel?' Ned said.

'She's beautiful,' Mira said quietly.

'Not Bel.' Kim closed the panels and placed it back in the drawer. 'Hiro couldn't bear Schiffer's spiteful act. He borrowed money from the Libertys and bought it anonymously from the Academy, to save her shame. When he tried to repay them, they wouldn't hear of it.'

'He kept it, all the same?'

'He tried to destroy it, but it was her face, if not her body.' Kim sighed. 'History is written by the survivors.' Her hands wrote on the air. 'Hiro did what he felt was right for Bel's legacy. Sometimes he regretted not doing more.'

'Regret is pointless,' Ned said.

'You're right, dear boy.' Kim nodded. 'The Lamberts wanted everything to stay the same, but Bel embraced change. It's the way of life. For things to remain, they must evolve. Now, Bel's belongings have found a new home, and the Foundation here means her legacy survives. All of fashion is a conversation. Hiro's silks, Bel's designs – the things they made together, all that love goes on.'

'But what happened to Bel?' Mira said.

'I spoke to Genji's son this morning to ask permission to tell you,' Kim began, and bowed her head. 'Are you sure you want to know?'

'Yes,' Mira said, taking her hand. 'Kim? What is it?' *I've never seen you like this.*

'When she learnt that Genji was to marry, she knew it was time to come home, to Hiro. After giving so much to others, she wanted what she had always longed for. Family. She loved Genji and Hiro, she loved Françoise Lambert and her family. Perhaps when you travel over the course of a lifetime you leave a little of your heart wherever you have been happy.' Kim looked at Mira. 'She was going to marry Hiro. There is a telegram she sent him, saying that she had arrived safely in Tokyo, that they would be coming to Kyoto with Genji.' She paused. 'They never did.'

LOT 81

TOKYO, 31 AUGUST 1923

Bel clutched the train window as it lurched to a halt, and her heart gave a flutter, like a bird in a cage.

What do you think about two weddings? Hiro had written. *Marry me, Bel. Live with me. Japan or France or wherever you wish. We have worked so hard for so long. There is more to life. Let's live.*

I am lucky to have you, she wrote back. *I feel like I have been searching for something all my life, when it was right in front of me all this time. Who was it said you think you are escaping, running away, but you always run into yourself. The longest journey is the quickest way home? Something like that. You bring me peace, Hiro. I'm coming home.*

When I think of you, I think of the way the morning sun always warms a certain spot of the banister at Miramar every day.

You taught me to notice things like that.

Yes, I will marry you. Yes, yes.

'Maman!' Genji cried, waving his arm above the whirling crowds at Shimbashi Station. Bel craned her neck to see him, and spotted the bright flame of Inès's hair amid the sea of people. Genji pushed his way through and embraced her, lifting Bel off the train. A lithe dog the colour of burnished conkers trotted after him, and gave her an exploratory sniff.

'Look at you!' she said, taking Genji's face in her hands. It still surprised her to see the wrinkles around his eyes as he smiled. 'Inès,' she said, pulling her in to a hug. 'And who's this?' Bel leant down to rub the dog's ears.

'She is Maron. Like chestnuts. Come,' Genji said, talking to the red-capped porter in Japanese, and gesturing to the exit. 'We'll take a taxi to your hotel. Hiro-san has booked the new Imperial Hotel for you. He thought you would appreciate Frank Lloyd Wright's design. It's already *the* fashionable meeting place for expats and crooks.'

'I'll fit right in,' Bel said, smiling.

~

Bel went later with Genji to watch him at work in the Imperial gardens. She sat in the shade, sketching him as he watered the borders, a red hose spraying as he moved gracefully along the pebble paths. He wore a wide-brim straw hat, a dusky robe. Crickets sang in the dry grass, and nearby a white cat with blue eyes sat watching her.

Bel thought of her last conversation with Françoise. How she had looked at her with the same watchful expression.

'Are you sure?' Françoise said, frowning.

'Hiro asked me to marry him long ago.' She remembered another time: *Come with me. Be my wife. We can raise the child together* . . . 'I put my work first.'

'But you have had a wonderful life.' Françoise embraced her.

'And you have been a wonderful friend.' Her voice was muffled by the deep fur collar of Françoise's coat. 'I know I am leaving the *maison*, and Miramar, in your safe hands. And Vero.' The little dog looked up at the mention of her name. 'We are both old ladies,' she said, rubbing her ears. 'Promise you will wait for me until I am home?'

'You shouldn't be travelling alone halfway across the world—'

'I owe Hiro, and Genji, this. I left a brief letter on my desk, just in case.' She looked at Françoise clear-eyed. 'If anything happens, the apartments, my artworks, go to Genji. But Miramar is yours.'

'Oh, Bel . . .' Françoise hugged her, blinking away tears. 'You are too generous. After all you have done for me.'

'Tell Sacha to do the repairs ready for the summer?' Bel said. 'I can't wait to show Hiro the house. I can't wait for you to meet him.'

'But when will you be back?' Françoise said.

'A few weeks. We will be spending a third of the year in

Japan, a third in France, and a third travelling. That's the deal,' Bel said smiling.

'Call that retirement?'

'I call it compromise,' Bel said as she walked away. 'It's never too late . . .'

LOT 82

KYOTO, JANUARY 1986

'I wanted to show you this.' Kim stood with Mira and Ned on the banks of the mirror pond in Hiro's water pavilion. 'Hiro-san and Bel were to celebrate their wedding at Kinkaku-ji. He knew she would love the famous Golden Pavilion.' She paused and blinked quickly. 'But of course they never did.' Hiro's pavilion reflected a perfect mirror image in the still water. 'The temple inspired this garden.'

'I read a book at university,' Ned said, gazing across the water.

'Mishima?' Kim said, and he nodded. 'In 1950 a monk burned it to the ground because he loved it so much.'

'That doesn't make sense,' Mira said. 'Why destroy the thing you love?'

'*Basara* – obsession,' Kim said. 'The man wanted the rapture of seeing it consumed by fire.'

'Kim,' Mira said uneasily. 'What happened?'

'I . . . I'm trying to find the words to tell you.'

'A fire?' Mira hugged herself, looking at the altar, the photographs beyond the candle flames, the gently smoking incense. *Bel.*

'A great fire.' Kim unfolded a sheet of paper. 'Let me read you what Hiro wrote, afterwards.'

~

'Bel was in Tokyo, 1st September, 1923,' Kim read. 'The high heat of summer had passed, and I imagine her sleeping peacefully, moonlight gilding the dark room in the Imperial, her wedding dress hanging waiting, creases easing from the silk. A few streets away, Genji and Inès slept deep and quiet in their new home, the old wooden house in Hibiya cradling them like a nest – two beloved bodies, three heartbeats – Inès did not know she was pregnant with their first child, yet.

'I like to think of them, their peaceful beds coasting on a tranquil sea of fresh tatami mats smelling sweetly of pale grass and caramel. Genji had little, but what more did they need – a few clothes in the cedarwood closet, two cups, two bowls, two sets of chopsticks. Everything was still to come.

'Bel always slept with a window ajar for fresh air. Perhaps she heard the city wake – a distant cockerel, bicycle bells in the street, the conversation of a family next door. At dawn the electrical cables festooning the street outside trembled in the winds like cobwebs across the soft light of the paper *shoji* screen.

'Later, they planned to travel to Kyoto, to me, for the

weddings. The family reunited at last. Ours was the future. Ours was a gentle hope, a happiness which astonished me.

'Towards midday the mirror surface of the water in the vase rippled, slightly.

'In the little kitchen, Maron, their dog, sighed in her sleep and stretched across the doorway like a draught excluder. She was a mutt – a street dog, not one of the pampered tiny creatures women have taken to carrying in their handbags. Genji recognised something in her, a nobility, and when she followed him home he let her curl up beneath the table and stay. He bathed her, and scrubbed her 'til her fur shone like burnished chestnuts. When he worked at the Imperial gardens, the dog waited all day at the street door of the new house for him. When they slept, she watched over them. Always.

'The hands of Bel's watch wound on relentlessly towards midday. I know she would have been up at first light, busy and excited, keen to be off. Neither of us were ever ones to waste the day. We had so many plans.

'In the houses all around the city, people were lighting their braziers for lunch.

'How often the things which destroy us are close to home. It is the unremarked, the quotidian that gets us, every time. The wet road. The one-too-many. The untended fire.

'People described a sudden hush. The noise building like the rumble of an oncoming train. I imagine the dog opening one amber eye, and pricking her ears, alert.'

LOT 83

TOKYO, 1 SEPTEMBER 1923

> H – I love you. I love you. I love you!
>
> I'm coming home. B.

Bel handed the telegram to the receptionist at the desk of the Imperial. 'Please send this immediately.' She glanced at the clock – nearly noon. 'We shall be arriving in Kyoto this evening, and I wish to let Mr Kurosaki—' She broke off as she felt a tremor in the counter. 'What on earth?' Bel's eyes widened in shock as she looked at the vase of flowers on the counter, and saw the water rippling.

A momentary hush. It was as if the world's noise switched off suddenly. And then a great jolt, the creak and groan of the building, shifting.

The room seemed to sway from side to side, and Bel gripped the counter. Someone cried out – was it her? The world dropped beneath her. The air seemed alive to her, people falling and screaming. She saw the vase of flowers suspended mid-air before it smashed.

Then the sirens began.

'Get away from the windows!' someone yelled. There was an awful noise, a grinding of earth and stone.

'Madame Bright, you must shelter,' the receptionist shouted. 'We will be safe here. The building is earthquake-proof—'

'But you don't understand, my son—!' Bel cried, struggling towards the door once the shaking subsided. 'I must get them here. Their house is only a street away—'

'Madame! Please! It isn't safe—' he shouted, going after her, pushed back by the crowd of people pressing into the hotel like a leaf on the tide.

By the time he reached the street, Bel had gone.

~

Hiro unfolded Bel's letter again, and smiled:

At last I am the person I was meant to be. I have had such a marvellous life, Hiro, I just wish I had let myself enjoy it all more.

Thank you. All these years you have given me a safe harbour, a place in the world. You have given me somewhere to belong. I want to step into the future with you at my side, if you will have me?

You said to me once: people belong together as long as they believe in one another. All these years, you believed in me, and I in you.

If one only loves when one is ready for change, then I am ready.

I love you.

I am coming home.

Hiro padded across the tatami mat in white tabi socks, and slipped on *geta* at the door of the wooden house. *Are they comfortable, your shoes?* He remembered Bel asking him when they first met at Liberty. *Yes, they are good for your health.* The next day he brought her a pair to try, and Bel tottered backwards and forwards across the store, laughing.

Her laugh. Her smile.

Hiro slid the *shoji* screen closed, and turned, looking out across the water garden he had made for her. He took a sheet of origami paper from the sleeve of his kimono, and as he walked, he folded one last crane for Bel, the movement of his hands needing no thought after so many years. He remembered saying goodbye to her, at the station in London. Standing with her watching Genji sleep in the pram. 'One day,' he had said, 'you will long for this day, in all its chaos and noise.'

'Stay. Stay with me,' Bel said, her voice choked with tears. 'I can't do it without you.'

'Yes, you can.' He took hold of her shoulders. '*Naseba naru.* Take action, with willpower and discipline. You will make your dreams come true, and I will be so proud of you.' He held her close, ignoring the sharp glances of the men and women crowding along the platform. 'I will help you as much as I can. We must both follow our destinies. I have to go back to Japan, and make a good future for the family. For all of us.'

Did I make the right decision? Returning had brought wealth, and stability, but at what cost? *Now I am free. I have done my duty. It's time for the younger generations to step up. Even Genji.* This is all he worked for. Walking along the terrace, Hiro glanced into the water pavilion. The gilded *tokonoma* altar gleamed in the half-light, with offerings for Chō, the firefly coal of incense smoking blue. *Bel is coming, Chō-san, she is coming home to me.*

After his fluid tai chi exercises, Hiro stoked the brazier in the pavilion to keep himself warm, and knelt down to meditate, folding his dark kimono around him like wings. Somewhere in the garden he could hear the sounds of the maid and the gardener talking, the laughter of his cousin's children rising on the cool autumn air like bubbles.

Wait for me.

I am good at waiting, he thought. *I have waited a lifetime for you.* Hiro gazed out across the garden. *I have not wasted my time,* he thought. *Everything I have built has been for you.* Though his eyes closed gently, Hiro smiled. *I would wait forever, for you. Something left unfinished is always appealing, a gesture left open to the future. What we began has no end, Bel.*

At any moment, he expected the high wooden fence to slide back, and for Bel to walk into their home. He could imagine her face, her surprise, her beautiful laugh. He knew her golden hair was silver white now, like his. *But our hearts are young. We have many good years to come.* As he waited, he kept the crane in his hand. *One thousand cranes*, he thought, sharpening the crease with his thumbnail. *One wish.*

Come home, Bel. Come home to me.

As he waited, a silver city of two million souls was destroyed. A city of electric light and trains and trams. A city of wood, of fire, of wind. The news rippled across the globe, as the fires spread throughout the day. A dragon's breath turned the sky red. Rocks and rubble melted into glittering glass. People were lifted into the air like feathers, like burning butterflies by the updraft of the flames, and simply disappeared.

The housekeeper came rushing to tell Hiro the news, kneeling, bowing low. She told him with her eyes on the ground, afraid to look at him.

Hiro's cry sent the wild geese rising from the lake, dark calligraphy flowing over the white page of the sky.

LOT 84

KYOTO, JANUARY 1986

'When the Great Kantō earthquake struck,' Kim said, Genji and his wife made straight for the outer precincts of the Imperial Palace. That is what saved them. He knew his mother was safe at the new hotel. Or so he thought.' She looked at her hands. 'Japan lies on a fault line between the Pacific and Asian plates.' She ground her knuckles together. 'I've experienced some earthquakes, but this was different. 8.2 on the Richter scale. People at sea said they could see the land buckling and rippling. Many of the people in the parks, and places like Asakusa Temple, survived. Those in Yokoamichō Park were not so lucky. Thirty-eight thousand people perished there in the firestorms. They called them the "flowers of Edo".'

'God, how awful,' Mira said.

'I don't understand? Bel survived the earthquake?' Ned said. 'She was seen?'

'It wasn't the quake itself which killed over a hundred

thousand people – it was the fires.' Kim looked at them, her eyes glistening. 'People had just lit their grills to cook at lunchtime. The tremendous winds fanned the flames from the braziers into great fire whirls, and the old wooden buildings went up in an inferno.' She paused. 'Genji's street of old wooden houses was incinerated.'

'I can't bear it,' Mira said. *Not our Bel.*

'Hiro-san never gave up hope,' Kim went on quietly. 'Forty thousand people disappeared. He refused to believe that Bel was among them. For weeks, he searched.'

'Bel's hotel survived?' Ned said.

'Yes, it was designed to withstand even a terrible earthquake like this one. Ironically it was inaugurated on the first of September.' Kim pressed her lips together. 'The receptionist told Hiro that Bel went out to bring her son and his wife to safety.' She raised her face. 'Bel didn't return.'

'She can't – she can't have just disappeared?' Mira said, choked with tears.

'Genji-san had to live with the guilt his whole life,' Kim said.

'She was so brave,' Ned said. 'What a way to die.'

'No, you don't understand,' Kim said, blinking away tears. 'They found her. Hiro found her.'

LOT 85

SEPTEMBER 1923

'Where is she?' Hiro swept through the crowded corridors of the hospital, Genji running after him. 'Where is she, the woman with green eyes?' he cried again as a nurse ran forward. They spoke quickly and she led him to a side ward. The high white walls reverberated with the sounds of quiet voices, with weeping. The nurse pointed to a bed at the end, the pale curtains drawn against the autumn sun gleaming gold through the opaque windows. Hiro lowered his head for a moment, steeling himself, then pulled the curtain aside.

'She's so small,' Genji said. 'Is the Embassy sure? An English child—'

'It's her,' Hiro said, stepping forward, his face stricken. At the sound of his voice, Bel turned her bandaged head.

'Hiro?' she said faintly. 'Is it you?'

'I'm here,' he said, falling to his knees beside the bed. He gently touched her hand. 'Bel. My poor Bel.'

'How . . . how did you find me?'

'Maman,' Genji said, standing beside Hiro. 'We went to every hospital, every makeshift clinic. We searched for days. Everywhere . . .' His voice trailed off, choked with tears. 'You were looking for me, weren't you? It's my fault. Why did you not stay at the hotel, why—?'

'Enough,' Hiro said sharply.

'No . . . not . . . your fault. I want . . .' Bel said, gasping for air. Hiro stood, leaning closer to hear. He looked down at her emerald eyes, bright with tears.

'Yes?' He held her gaze. 'Anything, Bel. Whatever you need—'

'Marry me . . . before it is too late.' Hiro screwed his eyes closed, and nodded, unable to speak. 'I wasted so much time . . .'

'No.' Hiro gently pressed his lips to her head. 'No. Everything is as it is.' He turned to Genji. 'Fetch the priest.'

'But—'

'*Now.*' He waited for Genji to leave, then turned again to Bel. 'I am so sorry,' he said, his hands cupping the air, afraid of hurting her. 'I should have been with you.'

'No . . . no,' Bel whispered, blinking back tears. 'I tried . . . to save them. The fire—' Her glistening eyes opened wide. 'I couldn't—' Hiro soothed her, a tight knot of tears in his throat. 'Someone carried me to the gardens . . .' She blinked quickly. 'It's mad . . . I thought it was you.' A tear spilled from her eye. 'You saved me.'

'You are safe now,' he said, wiping at his cheek with the

back of his hand. The curtains pulled aside and the priest stood with Genji. 'I'm never leaving you again.'

''Til death us will part, too soon . . .' Bel said, her eyes creasing with a smile. 'I love you, Hiro. Take me home.'

~

They sat down at the edge of the water, and Mira waited for Kim to compose herself and go on. 'She lived?' Mira said, taking Ned's handkerchief. 'Oh, Bel . . .'

'Hiro kept his word,' Kim said. 'After they married, they wrapped Bel in white silk, to ease the burns. He carried her to the plane himself.' Mira pictured him, cradling Bel in his arms. 'He arranged everything – the nurses, the doctors. There was nothing anyone could do. She survived the fire, but the smoke . . .'

'She was dying?' Mira said.

'Bel saw the garden Hiro made for her.' Kim looked out at the water. 'Hiro sat with her right here, holding her in his arms to the end.' Mira touched the smooth wood, and imagined Hiro cradling Bel, the dark wings of his kimono folded over her white body. *Oh, Bel*, she thought, gazing out to where the family tended the garden, the stream flowing out to the silver river. *This was the last thing you saw?* A sob caught in her throat. *You came halfway round the world, but you found your home.*

'What happened to Hiro?' Mira said, wiping her eyes.

'He kept working.' Kim took a ragged breath. 'What else could he do? He was made a "Living National Treasure" for his work as a designer.' She pointed at a photograph on the altar.

'Is that Hiro?' Mira said, looking at the photograph of an elderly man in a beret with a long white beard. 'I bet Bel sent him the hat?'

'Yes, she did. He wore it always, and the same indigo kimonos. He said it saved time dressing in the morning.' Kim handed the photo to Ned. 'He lived to well over a hundred years old.'

'Amazing,' Ned said.

'I'm so glad I met him,' Kim said, smiling sadly. 'Hiro was a man of great devotion.' She took down the photo of Bel beside his. 'His love for her was constant. Now for him it became a question of waiting to join her.' She waved her hand through the air. 'He told me that Buddhism, Shinto believe we are all one. We are all the water, fire, earth, we all become air. Hiro-san knew that in time he would join her.' She gestured at the garden. 'Their ashes were scattered in the stream, right here.'

They're here, together, Mira thought.

Kim turned to her. 'Will you work with us to curate the archive for the new Foundation? It's what Bel wanted. There are many letters from her to Hiro which will fill in the missing parts of the pillow book.'

'I'd be honoured,' Mira said.

'For now, you might want to read this. His last letter to her.' Kim handed her a yellowed sheet of paper, and squeezed her shoulder as she walked on into the garden with Ned.

Mira unfolded the letter.

My Bel,

They say the dying regret that they have not lived with courage. That is not true of me.

My family think I should not work so hard. But like you, my work was my life. Creation was my life. My fabrics, my garden, my love for you. We are artists, Bel, both driven to create. I would not have had it any other way. Just more time, with you.

They say too that the dying wish they had expressed their feelings. I told you of my love, and I know that you loved me.

You are my wife. I love you. In the end, that is all that matters. Not how much time we had.

From the moment I saw you darting along Regent Street like a hummingbird with your coat's emerald edges flashing, I loved you.

Only you.

I always believed that you lose part of yourself when someone you love dies, but in loving you I learnt that you just emerge a new version of yourself.

I have lived all these years carrying your love inside my heart, a secret only we shared. My heart broke open when I lost you. Some bright spark of your soul found shelter there. And now I carry it home to you, lighting my way.

I said to you as you took your last breaths in my arms: we are all the moon, the sun, the stars. You will guide me home.

Wait for me, Bel. I am coming.

I love you.

Hiro

Kim waited for Mira at the curve of the mirror pond as Ned walked on to photograph the house.

'Thank you,' Mira said, hugging her as she handed back the letter. 'It's beautiful. But it's so unfair – the life that was snatched away from them.' Mira wiped at the corner of her eye. *Like me, and Luke.*

'Life has a way of blindsiding you. It doesn't get easier. You just get better at living,' Kim said kindly. 'We all die, honey, even Bel. All of this – her life in London, in France, in Japan – is in her work. Every design, every dress, every interior is still infused with life *because* of how she lived.' Kim shrugged. 'Nothing is truly lost. It's the same with people. We're all the remains of love.'

'I want everyone to know her story,' Mira said, her eyes shining.

'I will tell you *all* of the stories Hiro told me over the years.' Kim smiled. 'His love for her didn't just disappear in September 1923. Now it lives in you, I can see. Tell the world about Isobel Bright, Mira. A legend lives only as long as it is spoken about.' She squeezed her hand. 'I'll wait for you in the house.'

Mira looked up and saw Ned walking back along the water's edge. She imagined Bel's empty apartments in Paris, newly whitewashed and floors polished. The new owners throwing the high windows open to the sounds of Montmartre. New lives beginning.

She reached into her bag for her red notebook. Beside it sat her translation of Bel's pillow book. Mira turned to a new page, thinking of all she'd read there.

What makes life worth living, she wrote, and smiled. Bel's story had breathed life into her own.

As she waited for Ned, she looked across the mirror pond and pictured Bel and Genji, walking with Monet in Giverny, pausing on the green bridge, the waterlilies below. Mira thought of Hiro, waiting here day after day for Bel, as steady as a rock in a stream, the seasons flowing on around him.

Time and life race away, she wrote. *We all have clocks and calendars, marking out our lives – past, present, future. But it's not real. All we have are moments. Moments of love. Moments that pierce our hearts and go with us, to the end.*

Mira looked at Ned's face as he walked back, at the love so clearly written there. *Moments like this.* She walked towards him, gathering pace. Two cranes on the silver water unfolded their white wings, and beat forward on the air, the surface shimmering. The birds rose up above the couple kissing by the mirror pond, rose up above the pavilion built by love. In the end, that is what we all must do. We go on. Sometimes we fall. Then we learn to stand, and we go on again.

And then, at last, we rise, and rise.

Author's Note

2025 marks the start of Liberty's 150th anniversary year, and 2026 marks one hundred years since Claude Monet painted the last of the *Nymphéas.* In July 1926, just as he had before, Monet burned and destroyed some sixty canvases. He died at noon on 5 December 1926. On 17 May 1927, the paintings at the Musée de l'Orangerie were dedicated. For fifty years, the gardens at Giverny ran wild until Lila Acheson Wallace rescued them. When I visited them twenty years ago, I knew I would write a story about them one day.

A word about names – in 1875, a young Japanese boy really was working with Liberty. He is recorded as Hara Kitsui, Hari Kitsui, or Hara Kerossaki – all of which are wrong. I rechristened him Hiro Kurosaki in consultation with a Japanese friend, and invented a story for him, and a sister. Writing in English, I have used the format 'first name, family name' for Japanese names rather than the customary way. The original employees of Liberty, Miss Browning, Mr Judd and Mr Carty, existed – these are imagined versions of them.

The Great Kantō Earthquake was a tragedy that destroyed 70 per cent of Tokyo and 80 per cent of Yokohama, and claimed over 140,000 lives. Forty thousand of these people were missing, presumed dead. The next big earthquake is overdue. But Japan is a resilient country. In the devastation of Hiroshima, four ginkgo trees survived, and new growth came within days. The gingko remains a symbol of resilience and hope.

Many people helped bring this story to life. I'd like to thank my remarkable agent, Lisa Highton, and all at Jenny Brown Associates. Thank you to Clare Hey, editor extraordinaire, to Louise Davies and the brilliant team at Simon & Schuster UK. I am so lucky to be working with you all.

Thank you to Charlotte Byrne of Liberty & Co, Callum Brogan of the Imperial War Museum, and Westminster Archives for your help with my research. Thank you to several people who helped get the details right: Niamh, Shakespeare and Company; Yoshi Inada; the Japan Society, London; Vanessa Coupe, for advice on period costume. Thank you to Lucinda Bredin and Bonhams for kind permission to host Ned's auction, and to Shinichiro Kataoka, and the Hotel New Otani.

Thank you to Lady Miranda Hutchinson for bidding to have a character named after her at the Bridwell Park charity auction for Regain. Thank you also to Kim Williams, who bid on the Children In Read auction.

Finally, thank you to my family. There's a Japanese

saying, '*ichi-go ichi-e*', which reminds us to treasure every fleeting moment. I'm so glad those moments are spent with you.

August 2025

Discover more from Kate Lord Brown . . .

The Golden Hour

From decadent Cairo in the 1930s to bohemian Beirut in the 1970s, an epic yet intimate story of great love and lasting friendship . . .

As her home, Beirut, teeters on the brink of war, Polly Fitzgerald has one last story to tell – about her best friend, Juno, and their life together in Cairo. Juno was vital and brilliant – and determined to succeed in her ambition to uncover Nefertiti's tomb.

But Juno and Polly's friendship was bound by a secret, one that has never been told. Now, as Polly's daughter, Lucie, travels to Beirut to be with her dying mother, the mystery of what happened many years ago must be revealed . . .

'Exquisite' Ruth Hogan
'Evocative' *Good Housekeeping*
'Epic, sweeping and gloriously romantic' Veronica Henry
'Sumptuous and immersive' *Platinum*

Available now in paperback, ebook and audio

SIMON & SCHUSTER